the Dreamer

STORY AND ART BY LORA INNES

COLORS BY LORA INNES (CHAPTERS 7-8)
& JULIE WRIGHT (CHAPTERS 9-12)
COLLECTION EDITS BY JUSTIN EISINGER AND ALONZO SIMON
COLLECTION PRODUCTION BY CHRIS MOWRY
COVER BY LORA & MICHAEL INNES

ISBN: 978-1-61377-031-3

14 13 12 11   1 2 3 4

IDW®

Ted Adams, CEO & Publisher
Greg Goldstein, Chief Operating Officer
Robbie Robbins, EVP/Sr. Graphic Artist
Chris Ryall, Chief Creative Officer/Editor-in-Chief
Matthew Ruzicka, CPA, Chief Financial Officer
Alan Payne, VP of Sales

Become our fan on Facebook **facebook.com/idwpublishing**
Follow us on Twitter **@idwpublishing**
Check us out on YouTube **youtube.com/idwpublishing**
www.IDWPUBLISHING.com

THE DREAMER, VOLUME 2: THE KIP'S BAY AFFAIR. NOVEMBER 2011. FIRST PRINTING.

THE DREAMER IS STILL FOR MIKE,—
MY REAL-LIFE ALAN WARREN.

Name: Beatrice Whaley

Date: September 14, 1776

POP QUIZ
What Did You Learn In The Dreamer So Far?

1. Match the picture to the right description.

♡ BFF  ★ That's me! ↓

fashionista-in-training

a. **Bea Whaley:** Our star, a drama queen whose Broadway aspirations are interrupted suddenly by dreams. ★★★

b. **Yvette Howe:** Vivacious friend and devil's advocate.

c. **Ben Cato:** Quarterback who finally asks our star out during the winter play auditions after school. (I've only liked him since MIDDLE SCHOOL!)

d. **Liz Winters:** Best friend since elementary school and the voice of reason.

e. **John Mulligan:** Annoying! cousin who doesn't know when to keep his mouth shut.

a. **Major Alan Warren:** Our brave and handsome hero, an apple farmer from Boston and cousin of America's most famous patriot, Dr. Joseph Warren.

b. **Captain Nathan Hale:** School teacher who enlisted out of a patriotic sense of duty, but has spent most of the war on the sidelines.

c. **Private Frederick Knowlton:** Col. Knowlton's 16 year-old son.

d. **General William Howe:** Commander-in-Chief of the British armed forces in America.

e. **Lt. Colonel Thomas Knowlton:** Bunker Hill hero and commanding officer of Knowlton's Rangers, the Continental Army's most elite fighting force.

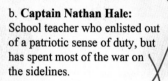

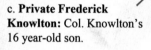

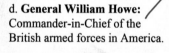

♡ ♡ BOO! → MR. GRUMPY ←

SMARTY PANTS

2. At the start of our story, Bea begins having vivid, realistic dreams about which war?
   a. the Civil War
   (b.) the American Revolution
   c. World War II

3. In a few sentences, describe what happens to Bea when she dreams.
   Every time she falls asleep, she wakes up in 1776. Each dream starts exactly where the last one left off. She can't remember any sort of life she lived in the past, even though it seems like she had one there.   (Alan seems to remember me, though!)

4. After Alan rescues Bea from General Howe's ship, he tells her he knows she is ANGRY! with him, but won't tell her why.

5. A painting upsets Bea on her date with Ben at the art museum. What is the painting about?
    a. The painting features Thomas Knowlton and General Howe.
    b. The painting shows the death of a soldier named Warren. *Oh no!*
    c. The painting is of a bloody battle at a place called Breed's Hill.
    <u>d. All of the above.</u>

6. Which does Bea have to help herself fall asleep after she leaves the museum early? *and my date! (Bad idea)*

    Camomile Tea   ~~Warm Milk and Cookies~~   (Her Mother's Sleeping Pills) *(also a bad idea)*

7. Put the following events in order.

  4   Bea and Nathan accidentally stumble across the British army marching through the woods.

  8   The Continental Army makes it back to Manhattan safely, but the British are now in possession of Long Island.

  5   Bea and Nathan return to warn the Rangers, but the Rangers get ambushed in the woods anyway.

  2   General Howe finds a secret pass and positions his army between the Americans and their forts.

  #1   Alan has already left with the Rangers so Bea convinces Nathan Hale to help her find him.

  7   In the middle of the night, General Washington orders a secret retreat of the entire army.

  6   After a bloody battle, Bea and the Rangers make it back to the forts. *(That was scary!!)*

  3   Bea and Nathan find the Rangers, only to discover that the events in the painting occurred a year before. The Warren who died there was Alan's cousin. Alan sends them away. *≡ oops! ≡*

Mrs. Alan Warren

8. True or False: After the battle, Alan and Nathan get into a fight because...

  T   Alan is angry that Nathan brought Bea onto the battlefield.

  T   Nathan accuses Alan of taking advantage of his cousin's martyrdom to rise through the ranks of the army.

  F   Nathan declares his love for Bea. *HA! HA!*

9. Yvette checks on Bea the next day because she missed school. Bea tells her about the dreams. What is Yvette's advice?
    a. It's okay to date both Ben and Alan- how will they find out?
    b. Keep taking those sleeping pills- that seems to work! *← She DEFINITELY did not say THAT!*
    c. You can't ignore your real life for these dreams- what if they stop?
    <u>d. Both a. and c.</u>

10. Does Bea take Yvette's advice? *What are you waiting for ??*

    ____ YES   ____ NO **X** **KEEP READING TO FIND OUT...** ⟶

TURN THE PAGE ALREADY!!

Final Grade: ____ *A+*

Chapter Seven

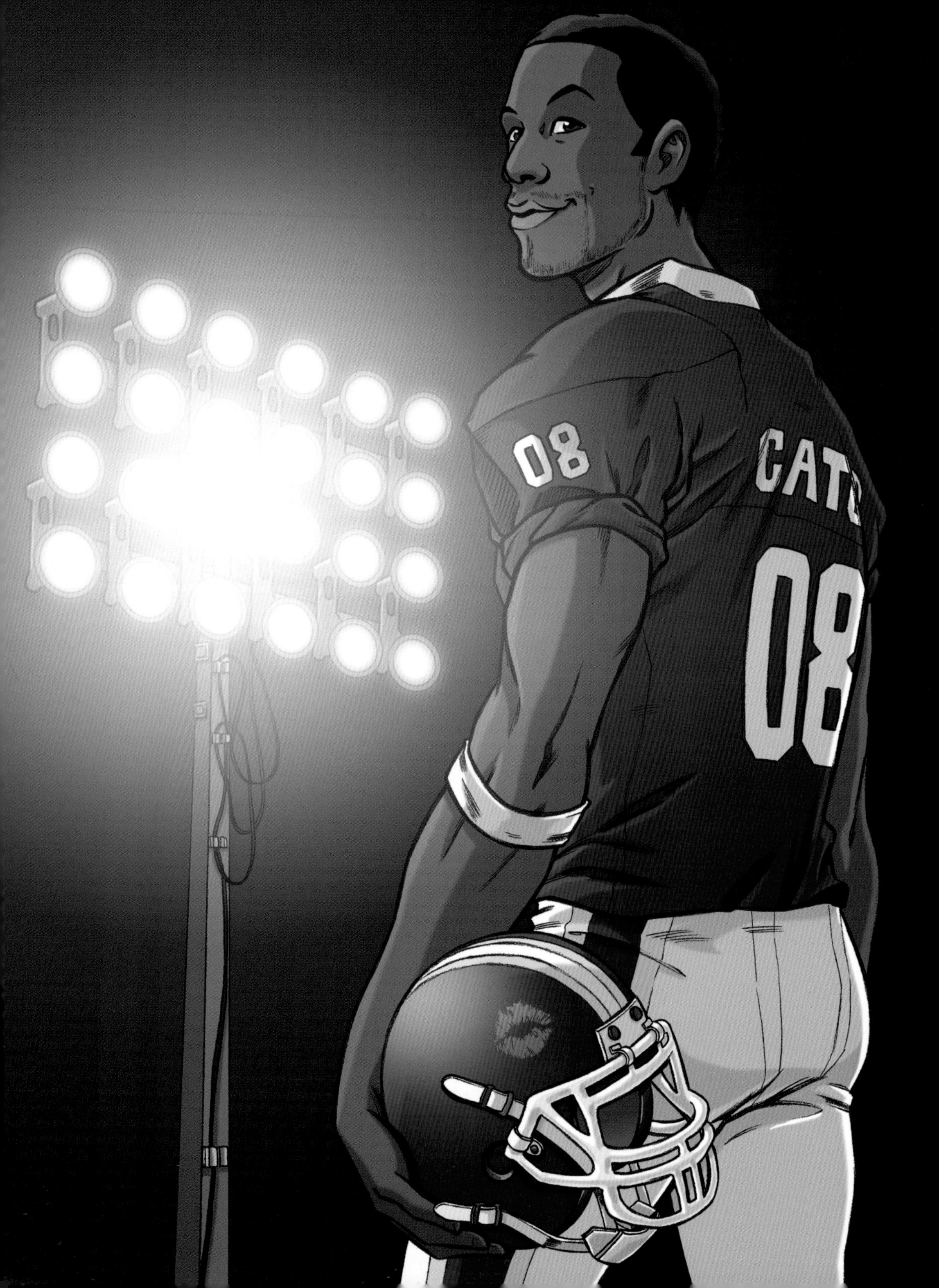
08
08

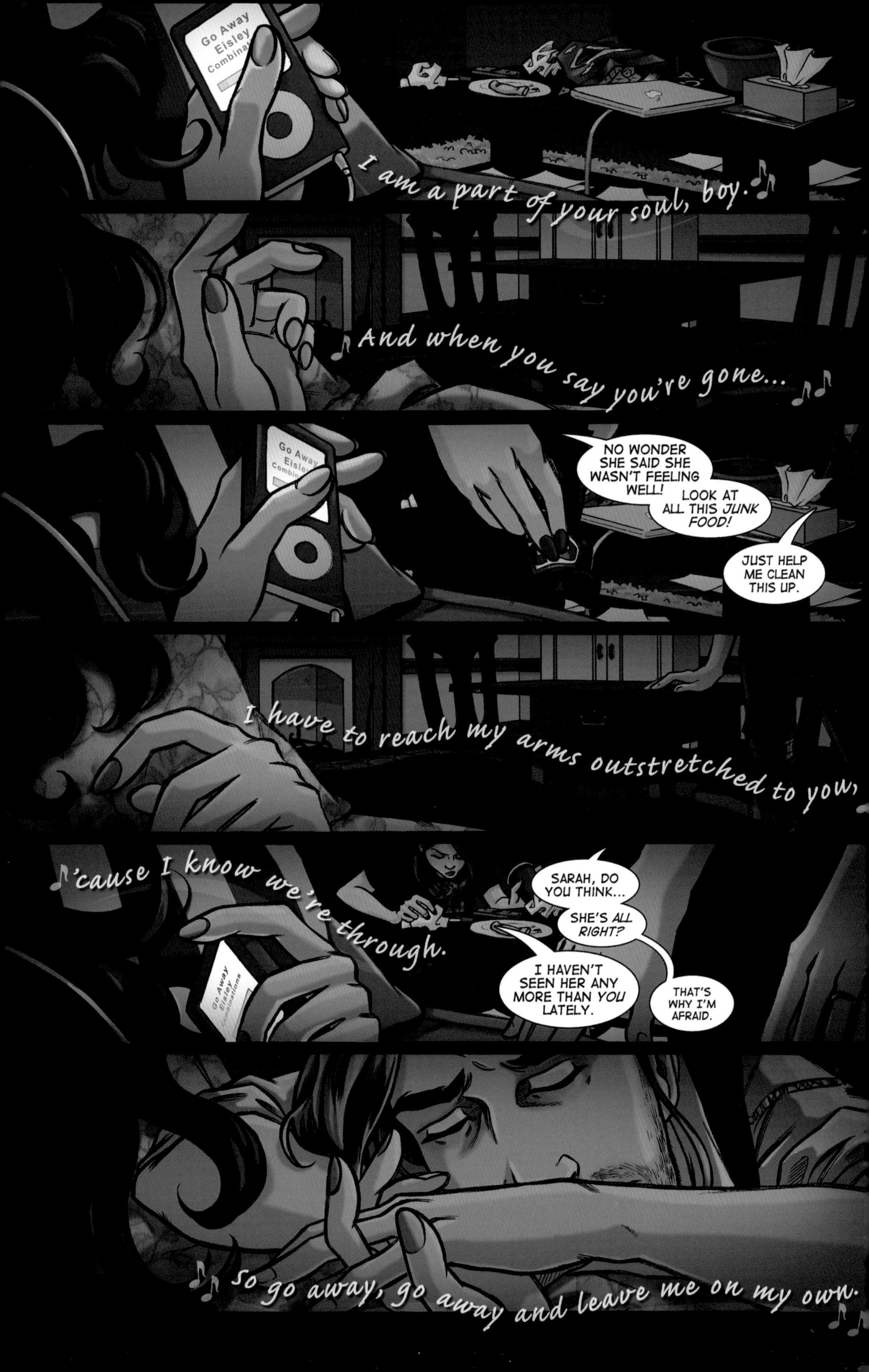
Go Away
Eisley
I am a part of your soul, boy.
And when you say you're gone...
NO WONDER SHE SAID SHE WASN'T FEELING WELL!
LOOK AT ALL THIS JUNK FOOD!
JUST HELP ME CLEAN THIS UP.
I have to reach my arms outstretched to you,
'cause I know we're through.
SARAH, DO YOU THINK...
SHE'S ALL RIGHT?
I HAVEN'T SEEN HER ANY MORE THAN YOU LATELY.
THAT'S WHY I'M AFRAID.
Go Away
Eisley
Combinations
So go away, go away and leave me on my own.

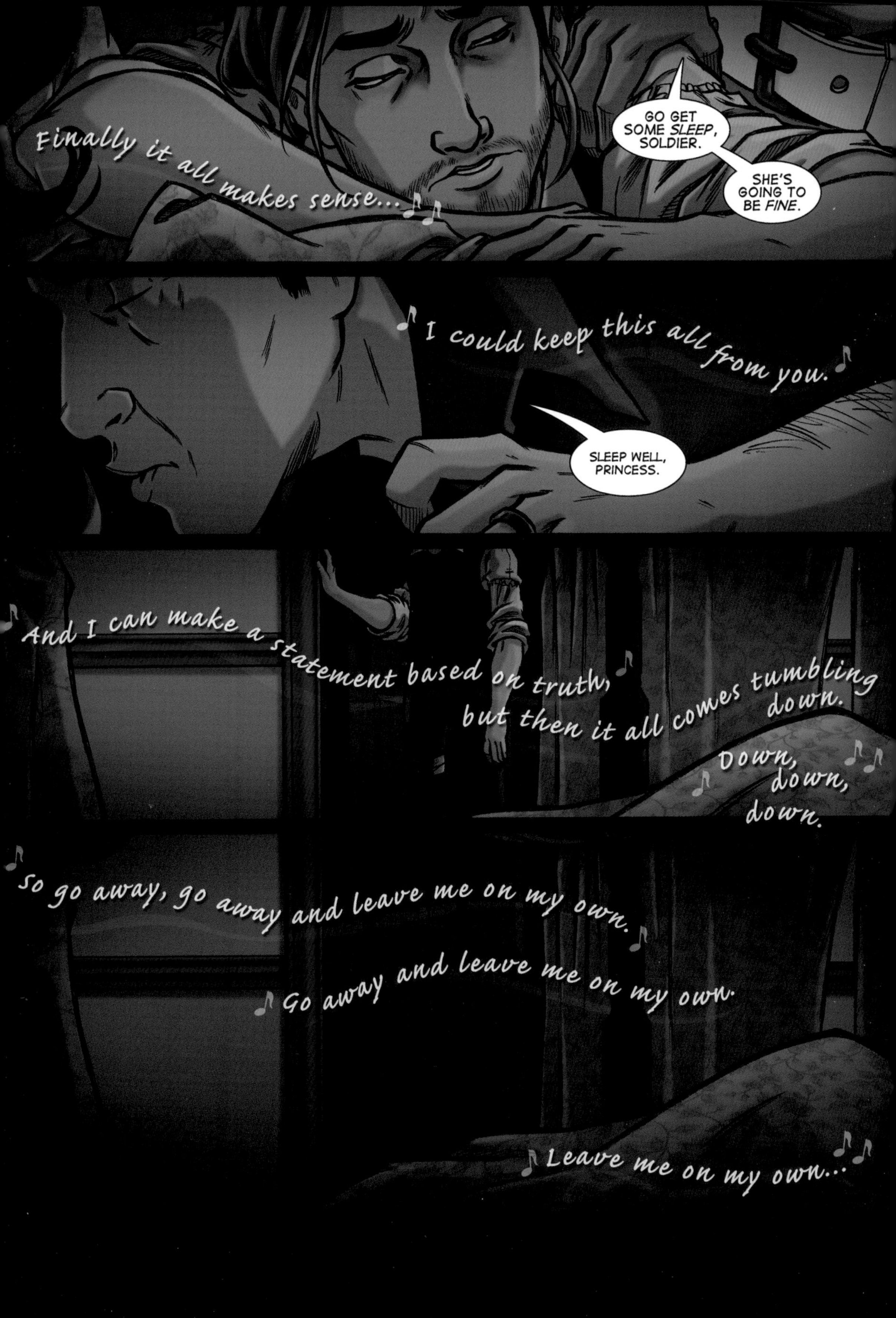

Finally it all makes sense...
GO GET SOME *SLEEP*, SOLDIER.
SHE'S GOING TO BE *FINE*.
I could keep this all from you.
SLEEP WELL, PRINCESS.
And I can make a statement based on truth,
but then it all comes tumbling down.
Down, down, down.
So go away, go away and leave me on my own.
Go away and leave me on my own.
Leave me on my own...

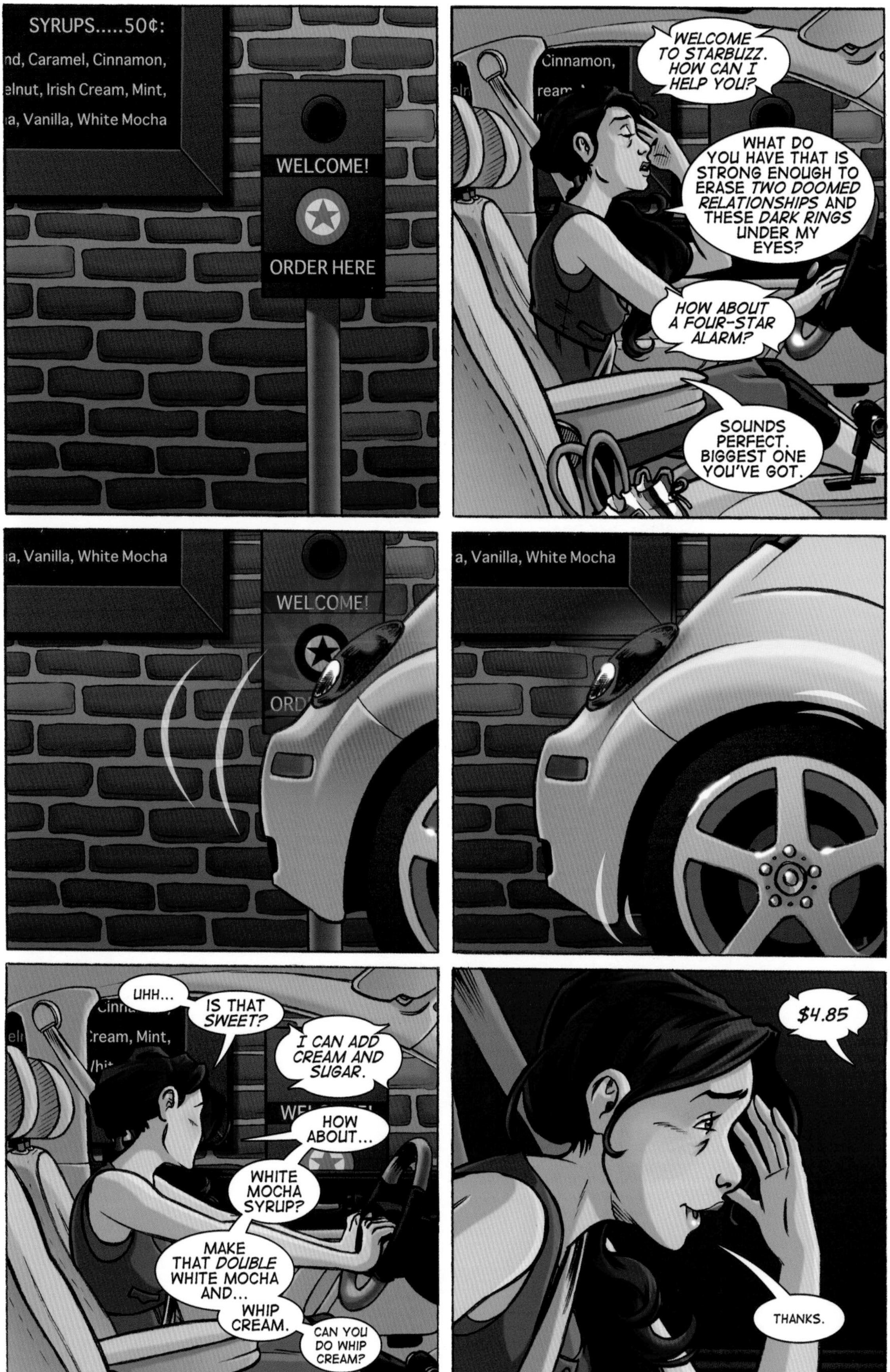
SYRUPS.....50¢:
nd, Caramel, Cinnamon,
elnut, Irish Cream, Mint,
a, Vanilla, White Mocha
WELCOME!
ORDER HERE
WELCOME TO STARBUZZ. HOW CAN I HELP YOU?
WHAT DO YOU HAVE THAT IS STRONG ENOUGH TO ERASE TWO DOOMED RELATIONSHIPS AND THESE DARK RINGS UNDER MY EYES?
HOW ABOUT A FOUR-STAR ALARM?
SOUNDS PERFECT. BIGGEST ONE YOU'VE GOT.
a, Vanilla, White Mocha
WELCOME!
a, Vanilla, White Mocha
UHH...
IS THAT SWEET?
I CAN ADD CREAM AND SUGAR.
HOW ABOUT...
WHITE MOCHA SYRUP?
MAKE THAT DOUBLE WHITE MOCHA AND...
WHIP CREAM.
CAN YOU DO WHIP CREAM?
$4.85
THANKS.

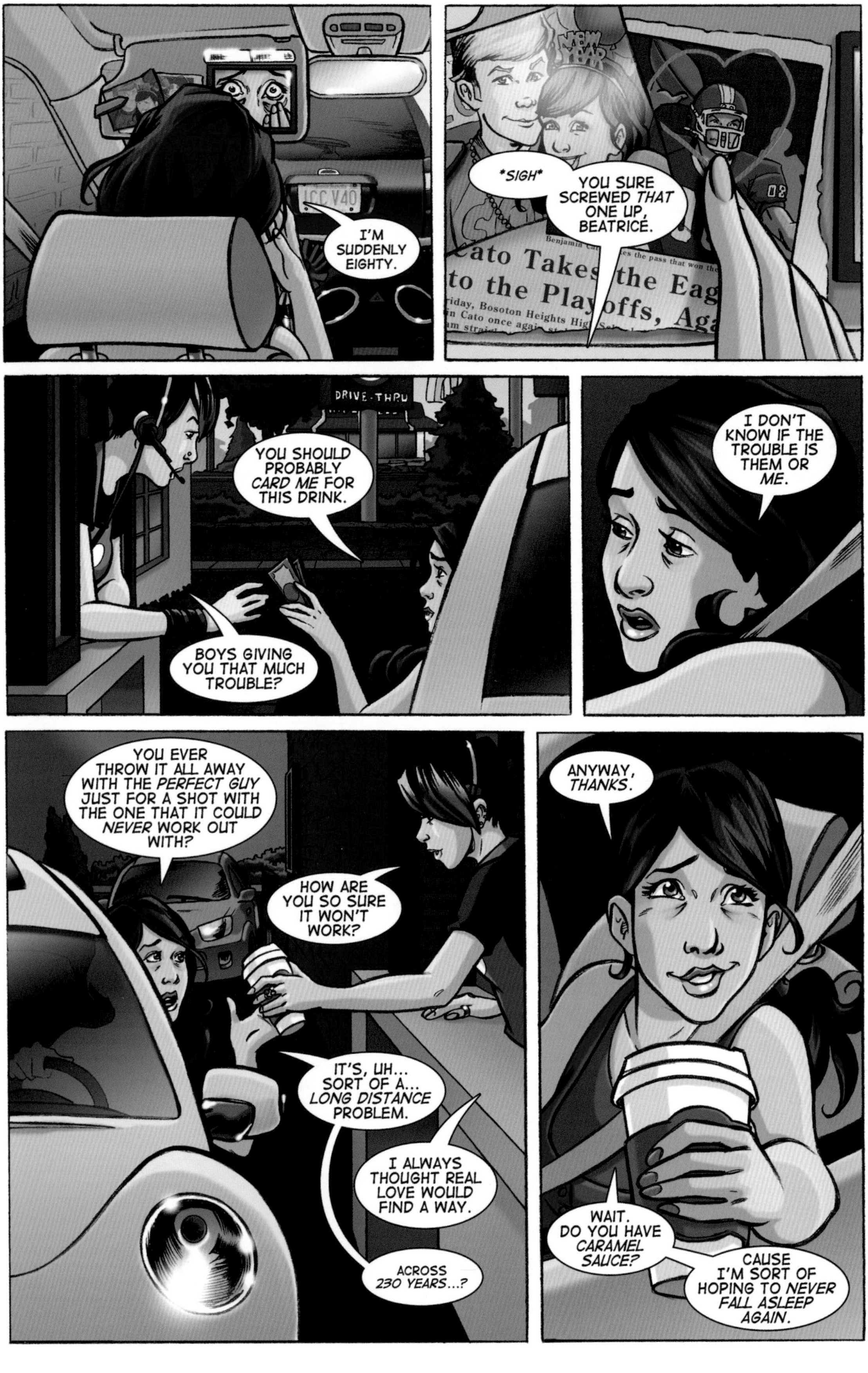
I'M SUDDENLY EIGHTY.
SIGH
YOU SURE SCREWED *THAT* ONE UP, BEATRICE.
DRIVE-THRU
YOU SHOULD PROBABLY *CARD ME* FOR THIS DRINK.
BOYS GIVING YOU THAT MUCH TROUBLE?
I DON'T KNOW IF THE TROUBLE IS THEM OR *ME*.
YOU EVER THROW IT ALL AWAY WITH THE *PERFECT GUY* JUST FOR A SHOT WITH THE ONE THAT IT COULD *NEVER* WORK OUT WITH?
HOW ARE YOU SO SURE IT WON'T WORK?
IT'S, UH... SORT OF A... *LONG DISTANCE* PROBLEM.
I ALWAYS THOUGHT REAL LOVE WOULD FIND A WAY.
ACROSS *230 YEARS*...?
ANYWAY, *THANKS*.
WAIT. DO YOU HAVE *CARAMEL SAUCE?*
CAUSE I'M SORT OF HOPING TO *NEVER FALL ASLEEP* AGAIN.

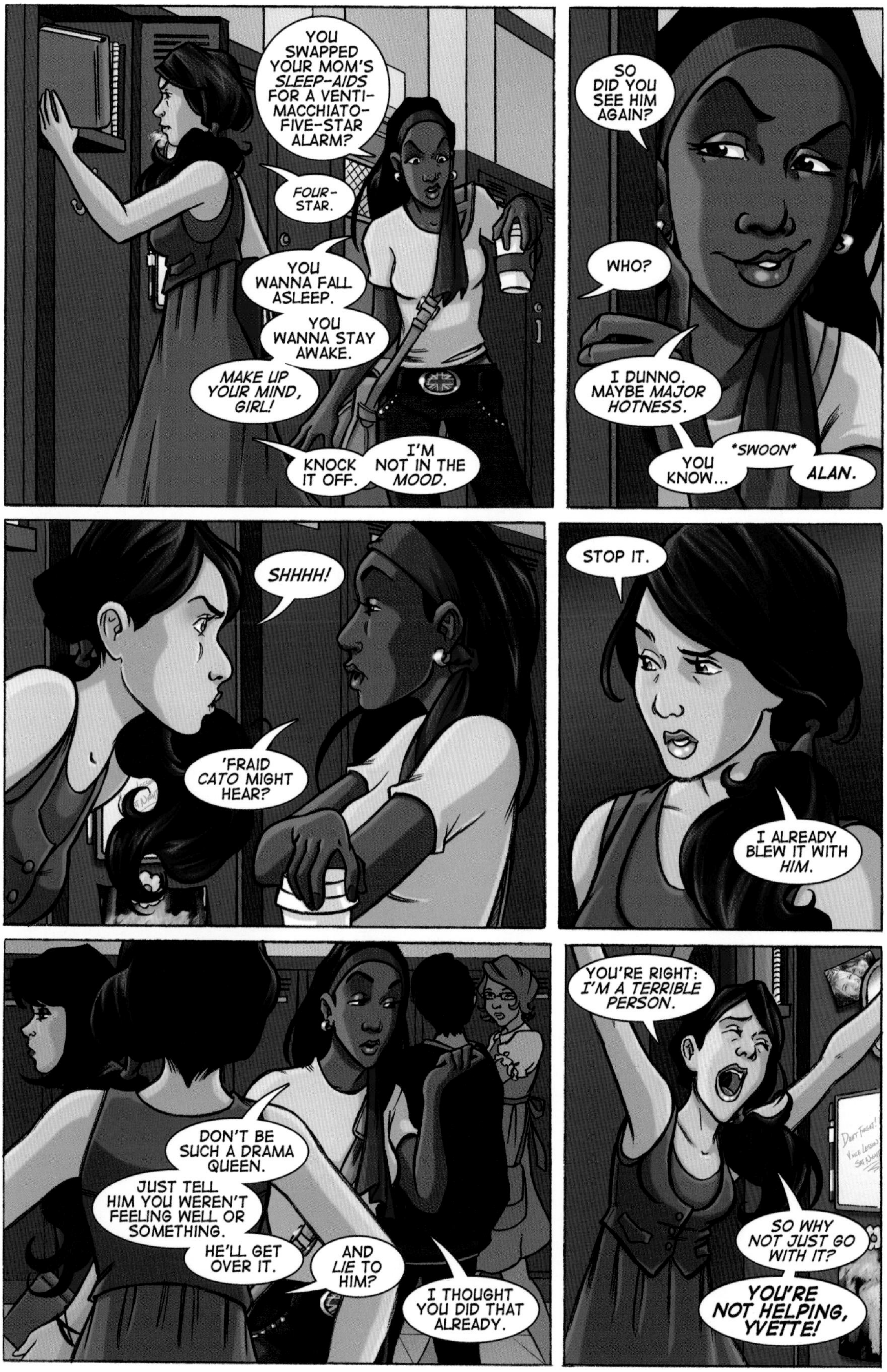
YOU SWAPPED YOUR MOM'S *SLEEP-AIDS* FOR A VENTI-MACCHIATO-FIVE-STAR ALARM?
FOUR-STAR.
YOU WANNA FALL ASLEEP.
YOU WANNA STAY AWAKE.
MAKE UP YOUR MIND, GIRL!
KNOCK IT OFF.
I'M NOT IN THE *MOOD.*
SO DID YOU SEE HIM AGAIN?
WHO?
I DUNNO. MAYBE *MAJOR HOTNESS.*
YOU KNOW...
SWOON
ALAN.
SHHHH!
'FRAID *CATO* MIGHT HEAR?
STOP IT.
I ALREADY BLEW IT WITH *HIM.*
DON'T BE SUCH A DRAMA QUEEN.
JUST TELL HIM YOU WEREN'T FEELING WELL OR SOMETHING.
HE'LL GET OVER IT.
AND *LIE* TO HIM?
I THOUGHT YOU DID THAT ALREADY.
YOU'RE RIGHT: *I'M A TERRIBLE PERSON.*
SO WHY NOT JUST GO WITH IT?
YOU'RE NOT HELPING, YVETTE!

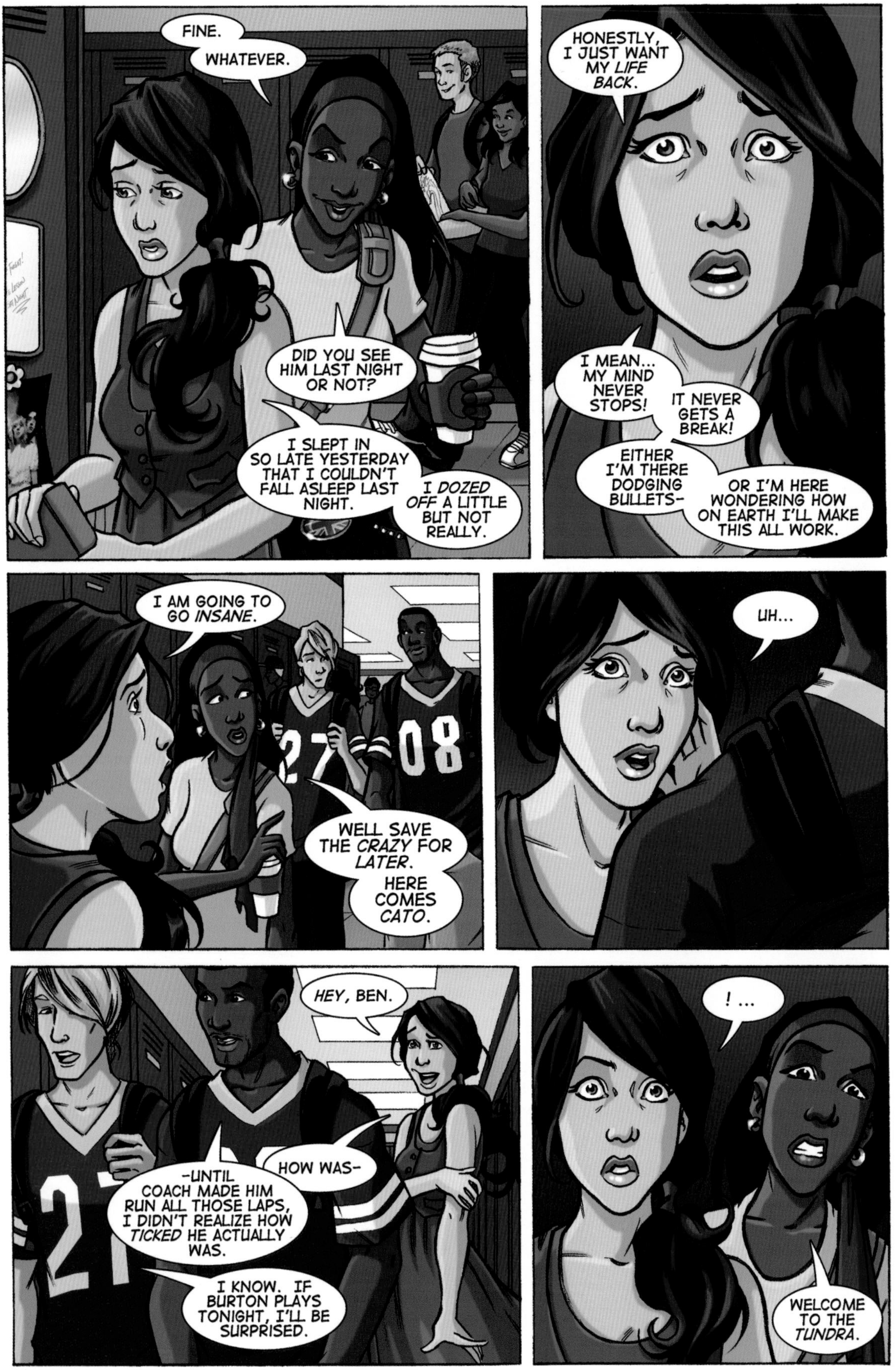
FINE.
WHATEVER.
DID YOU SEE HIM LAST NIGHT OR NOT?
I SLEPT IN SO LATE YESTERDAY THAT I COULDN'T FALL ASLEEP LAST NIGHT.
I *DOZED OFF* A LITTLE BUT NOT REALLY.
HONESTLY, I JUST WANT MY *LIFE BACK*.
I MEAN... MY MIND NEVER STOPS!
IT NEVER GETS A BREAK!
EITHER I'M THERE DODGING BULLETS-
OR I'M HERE WONDERING HOW ON EARTH I'LL MAKE THIS ALL WORK.
I AM GOING TO GO *INSANE*.
WELL SAVE THE *CRAZY* FOR *LATER*.
HERE COMES *CATO*.
UH...
HEY, BEN.
HOW WAS-
-UNTIL COACH MADE HIM RUN ALL THOSE LAPS, I DIDN'T REALIZE HOW *TICKED* HE ACTUALLY WAS.
I KNOW. IF BURTON PLAYS TONIGHT, I'LL BE SURPRISED.
! ...
WELCOME TO THE *TUNDRA*.

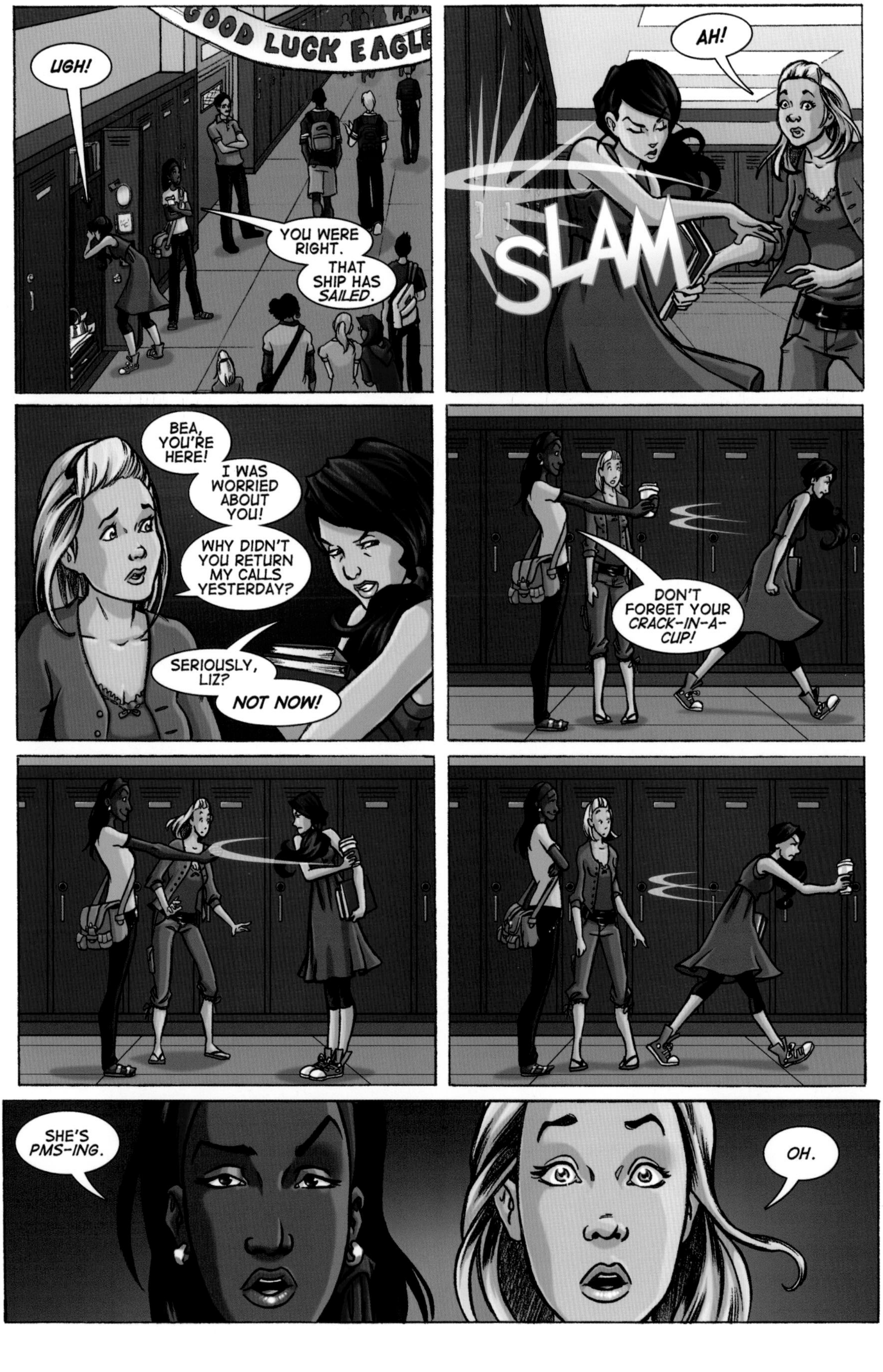
GOOD LUCK EAGLE
UGH!
YOU WERE RIGHT.
THAT SHIP HAS SAILED.
AH!
SLAM
BEA, YOU'RE HERE!
I WAS WORRIED ABOUT YOU!
WHY DIDN'T YOU RETURN MY CALLS YESTERDAY?
SERIOUSLY, LIZ?
NOT NOW!
DON'T FORGET YOUR CRACK-IN-A-CUP!
SHE'S PMS-ING.
OH.

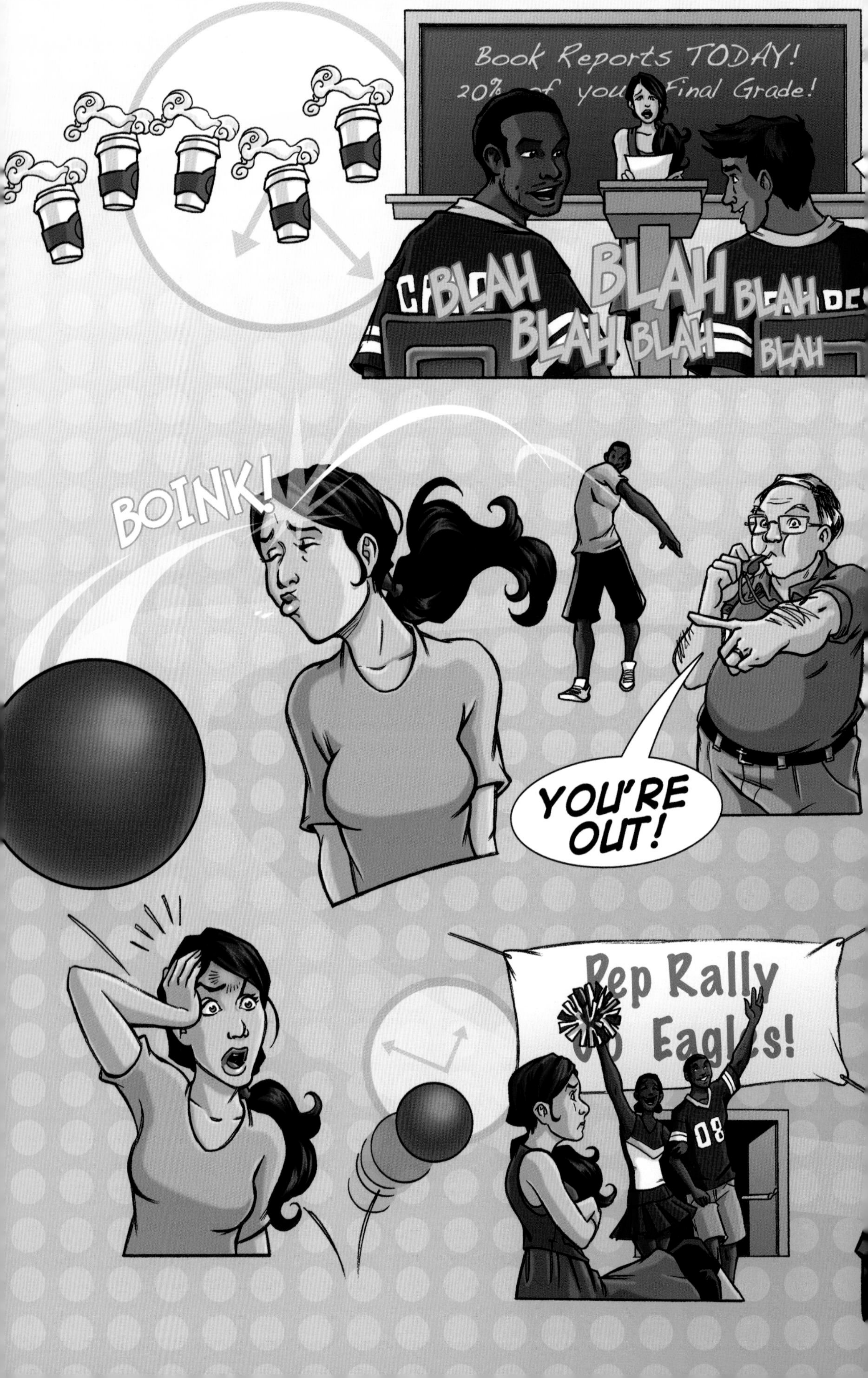
Book Reports TODAY!
20% of you Final Grade!
BLAH BLAH BLAH BLAH BLAH BLAH
BOINK!
YOU'RE OUT!
Pep Rally
Eagles!
08

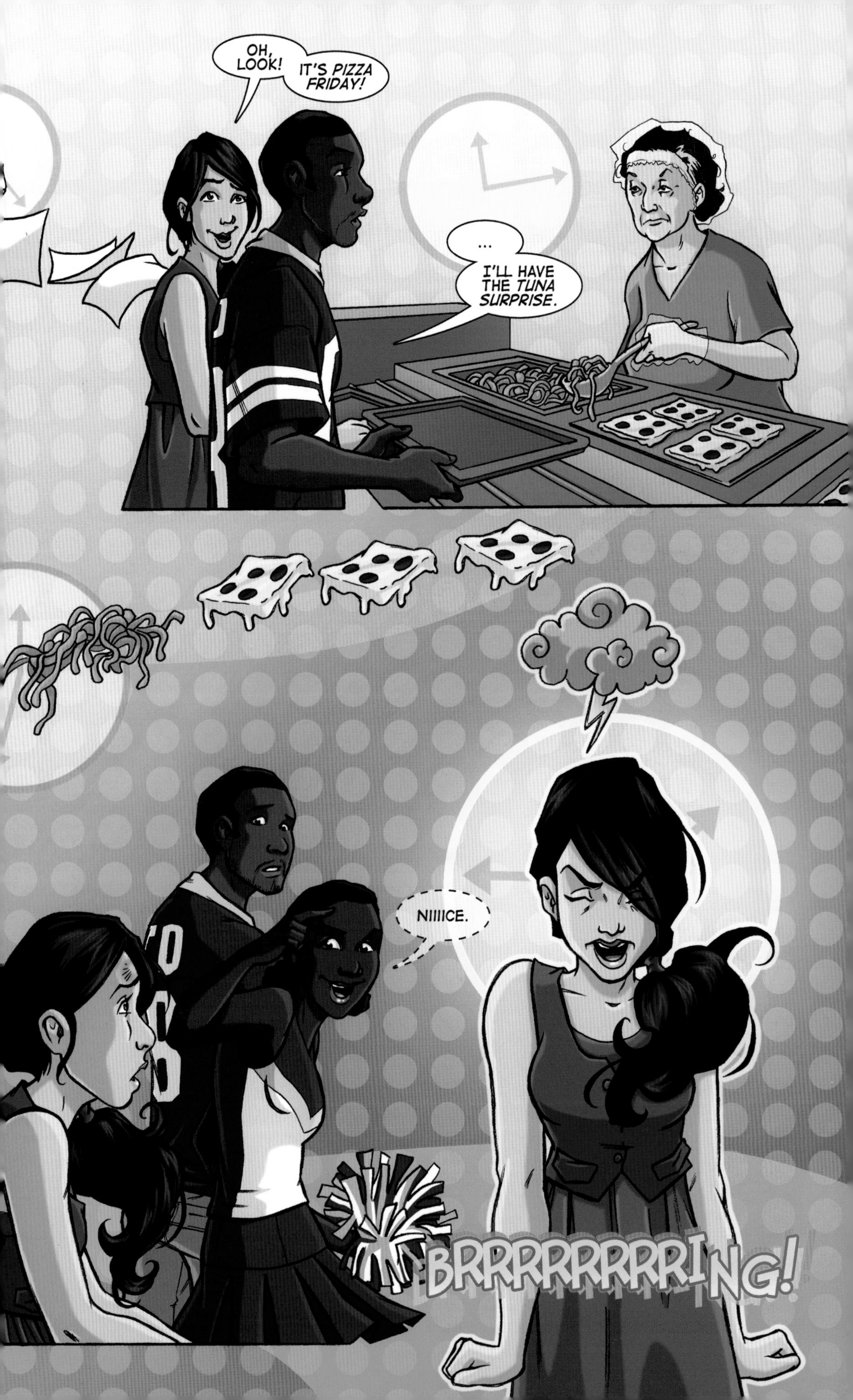
OH, LOOK!
IT'S PIZZA FRIDAY!
...
I'LL HAVE THE TUNA SURPRISE.
NIIIICE.
BRRRRRRRRRING!

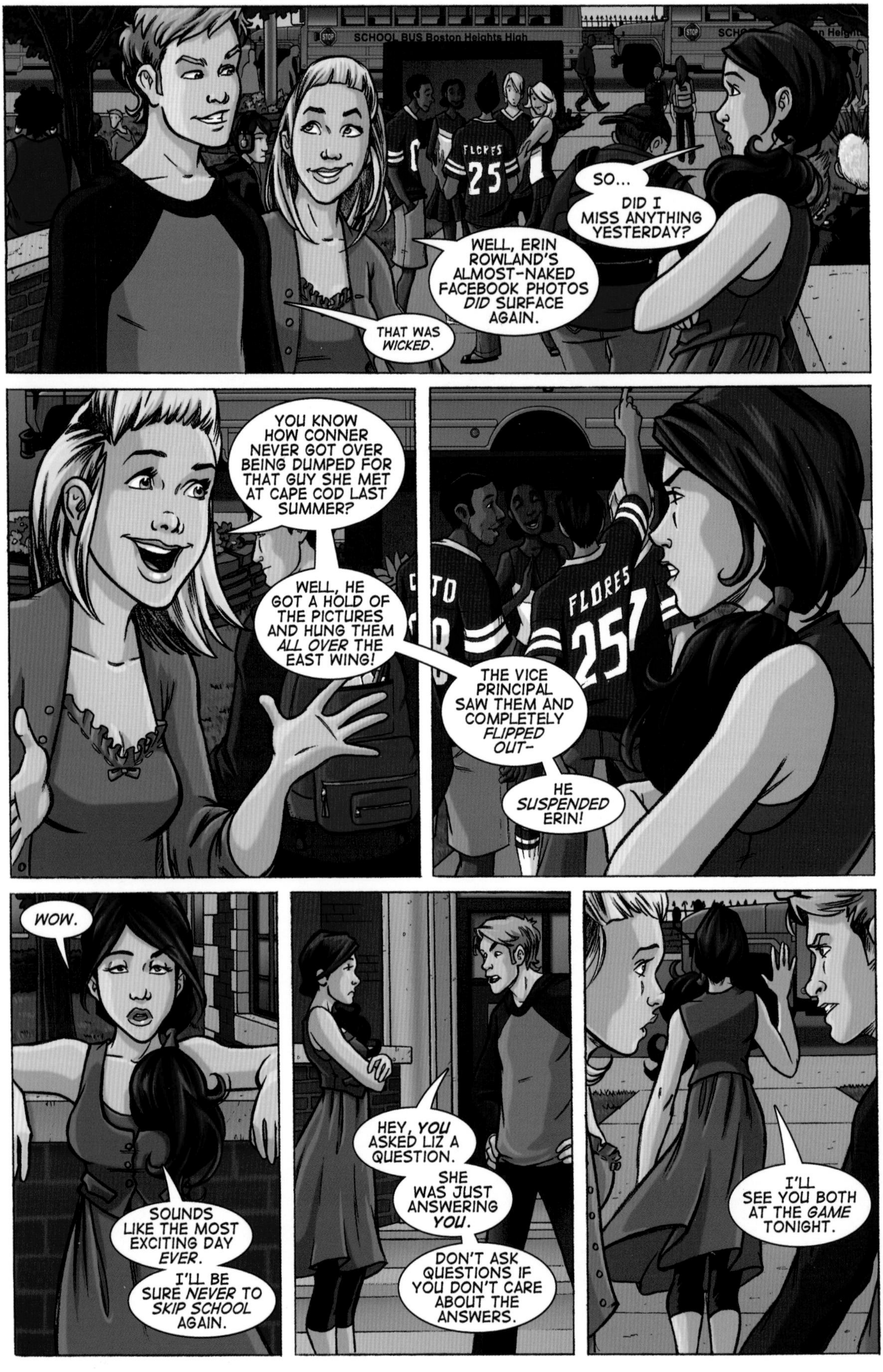
SCHOOL BUS Boston Heights High
FLORES 25
SO... DID I MISS ANYTHING YESTERDAY?
WELL, ERIN ROWLAND'S ALMOST-NAKED FACEBOOK PHOTOS *DID* SURFACE AGAIN.
THAT WAS *WICKED*.
YOU KNOW HOW CONNER NEVER GOT OVER BEING DUMPED FOR THAT GUY SHE MET AT CAPE COD LAST SUMMER?
WELL, HE GOT A HOLD OF THE PICTURES AND HUNG THEM *ALL OVER* THE EAST WING!
THE VICE PRINCIPAL SAW THEM AND COMPLETELY *FLIPPED OUT*-
HE *SUSPENDED* ERIN!
WOW.
SOUNDS LIKE THE MOST EXCITING DAY *EVER*.
I'LL BE SURE *NEVER* TO *SKIP SCHOOL* AGAIN.
HEY, *YOU* ASKED LIZ A QUESTION.
SHE WAS JUST ANSWERING *YOU*.
DON'T ASK QUESTIONS IF YOU DON'T CARE ABOUT THE ANSWERS.
I'LL SEE YOU BOTH AT THE *GAME* TONIGHT.

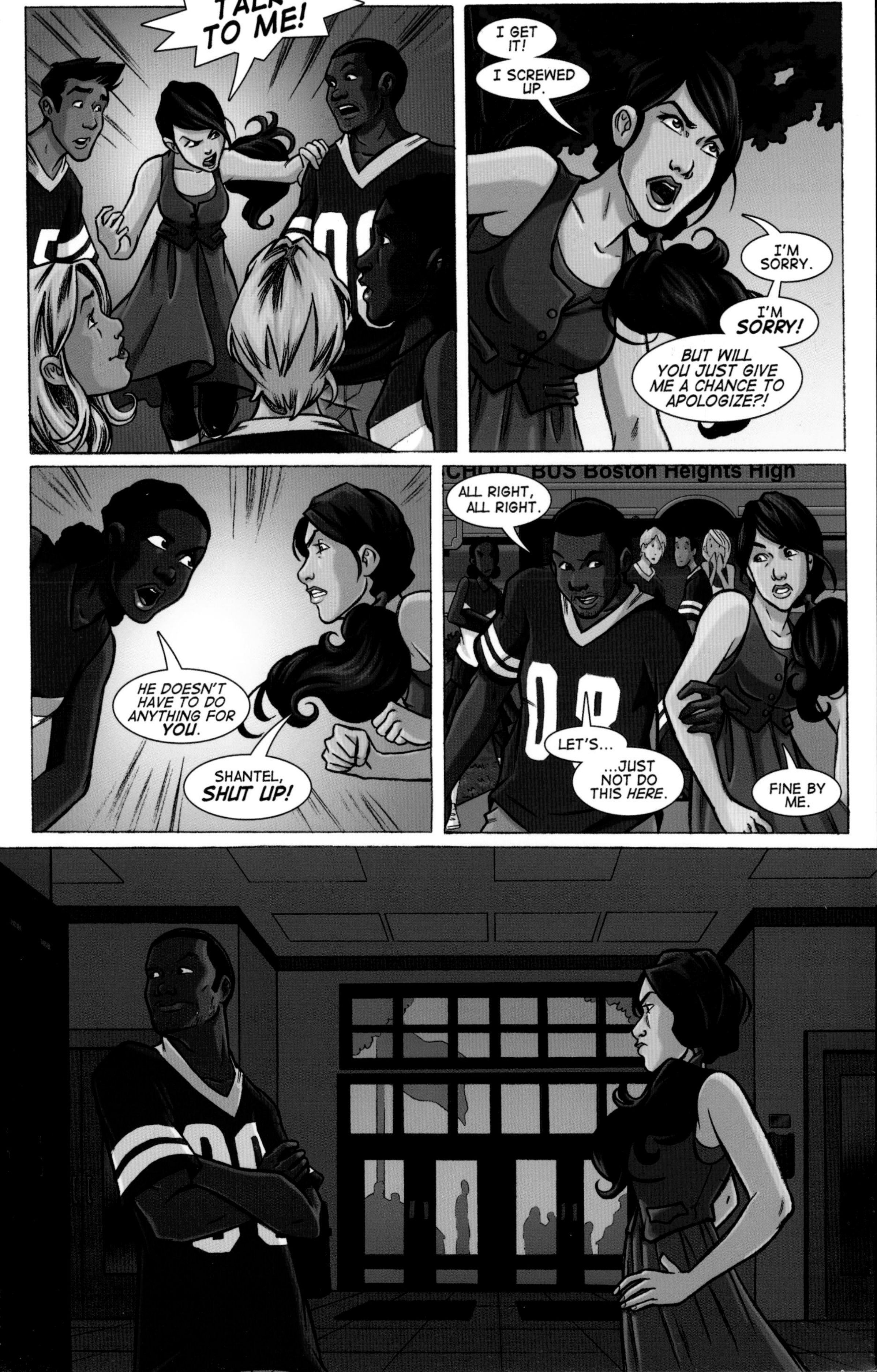
TALK TO ME!
I GET IT!
I SCREWED UP.
I'M SORRY.
I'M SORRY!
BUT WILL YOU JUST GIVE ME A CHANCE TO APOLOGIZE?!
HE DOESN'T HAVE TO DO ANYTHING FOR YOU.
SHANTEL, SHUT UP!
SCHOOL BUS Boston Heights High
ALL RIGHT, ALL RIGHT.
LET'S...
...JUST NOT DO THIS HERE.
FINE BY ME.

I'M SORRY I CUT OUT OF THE MUSEUM EARLY.

I'M SORRY I WAS RUDE TO YOU IN YOUR TRUCK.

I'M SORRY I SKIPPED SCHOOL YESTERDAY.

I JUST...

THERE'S ALL KINDS OF *CRAP* GOING ON IN MY LIFE RIGHT NOW.

AND, TO BE HONEST, I DON'T REALLY WANT TO DUMP ALL OF IT ON YOU.

BUT PLEASE BELIEVE ME— THERE IS *CRAP*.

DUMP TRUCKS *FULL* OF CRAP.

AND...

AND I LET IT GET IN THE WAY OF OUR *DATE*.

I SHOULDN'T HAVE, AND I WAS TOTALLY RUDE TO YOU...

AND I PROBABLY *DESERVE* THE FREEZE OUT...

...BUT...

CAN WE JUST, LIKE, *START OVER?*

I *LIED.*

I HATE ART.

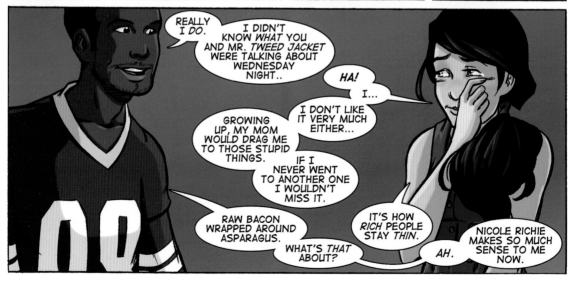

REALLY I *DO.*

I DIDN'T KNOW *WHAT* YOU AND MR. *TWEED JACKET* WERE TALKING ABOUT WEDNESDAY NIGHT..

HA!

I...

I DON'T LIKE IT VERY MUCH EITHER...

GROWING UP, MY MOM WOULD DRAG ME TO THOSE STUPID THINGS.

IF I NEVER WENT TO ANOTHER ONE I WOULDN'T MISS IT.

RAW BACON WRAPPED AROUND ASPARAGUS.

WHAT'S *THAT* ABOUT?

IT'S HOW *RICH* PEOPLE STAY *THIN.*

AH.

NICOLE RICHIE MAKES SO MUCH SENSE TO ME NOW.

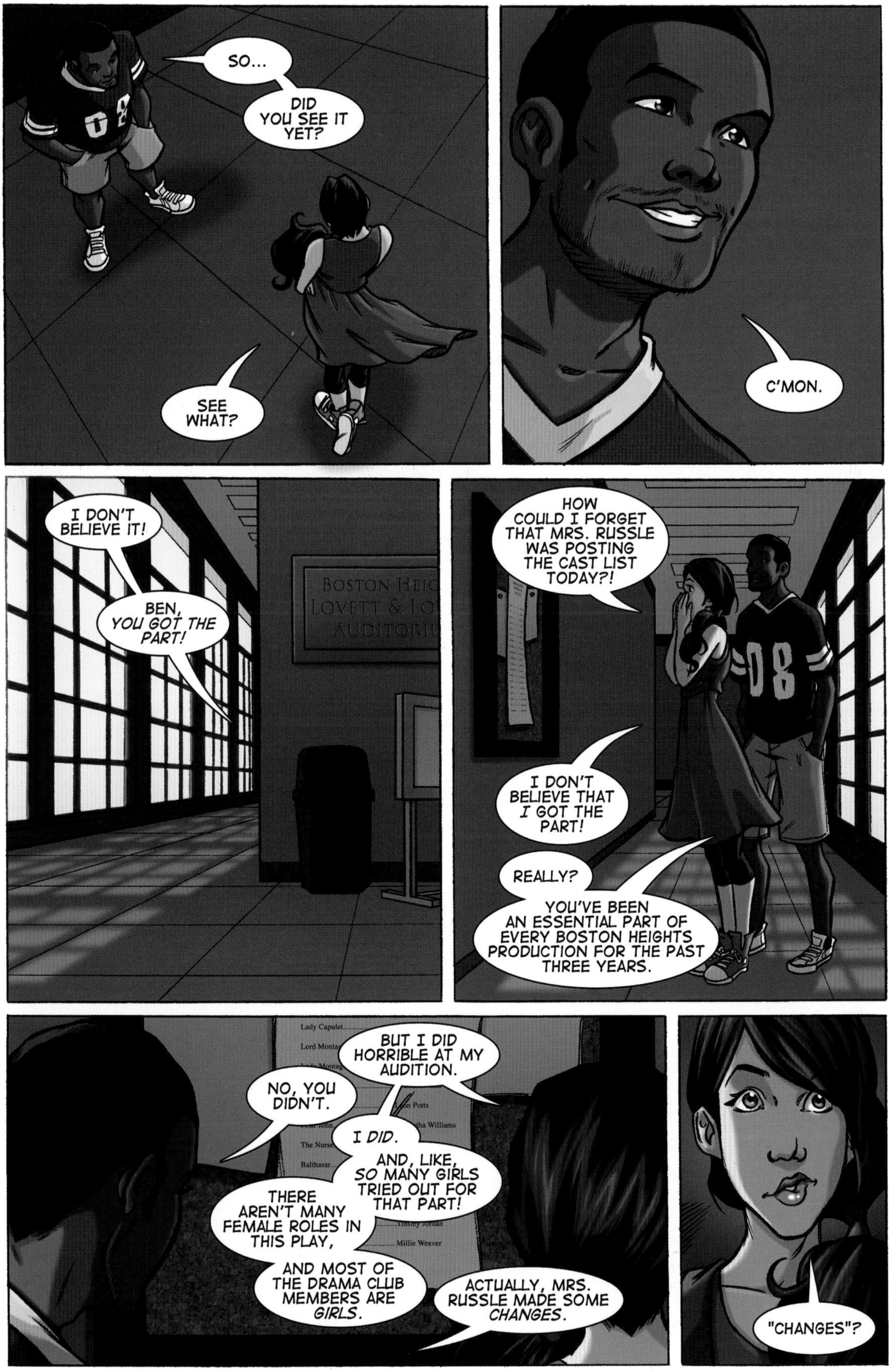

SO...
DID YOU SEE IT YET?
SEE WHAT?
C'MON.
I DON'T BELIEVE IT!
BEN, *YOU GOT THE PART!*
HOW COULD I FORGET THAT MRS. RUSSLE WAS POSTING THE CAST LIST TODAY?!
I DON'T BELIEVE THAT *I* GOT THE PART!
REALLY?
YOU'VE BEEN AN ESSENTIAL PART OF EVERY BOSTON HEIGHTS PRODUCTION FOR THE PAST THREE YEARS.
BUT I DID HORRIBLE AT MY AUDITION.
NO, YOU DIDN'T.
I *DID*.
AND, LIKE, *SO* MANY GIRLS TRIED OUT FOR THAT PART!
THERE AREN'T MANY FEMALE ROLES IN THIS PLAY,
AND MOST OF THE DRAMA CLUB MEMBERS ARE *GIRLS*.
ACTUALLY, MRS. RUSSLE MADE SOME *CHANGES*.
"CHANGES"?

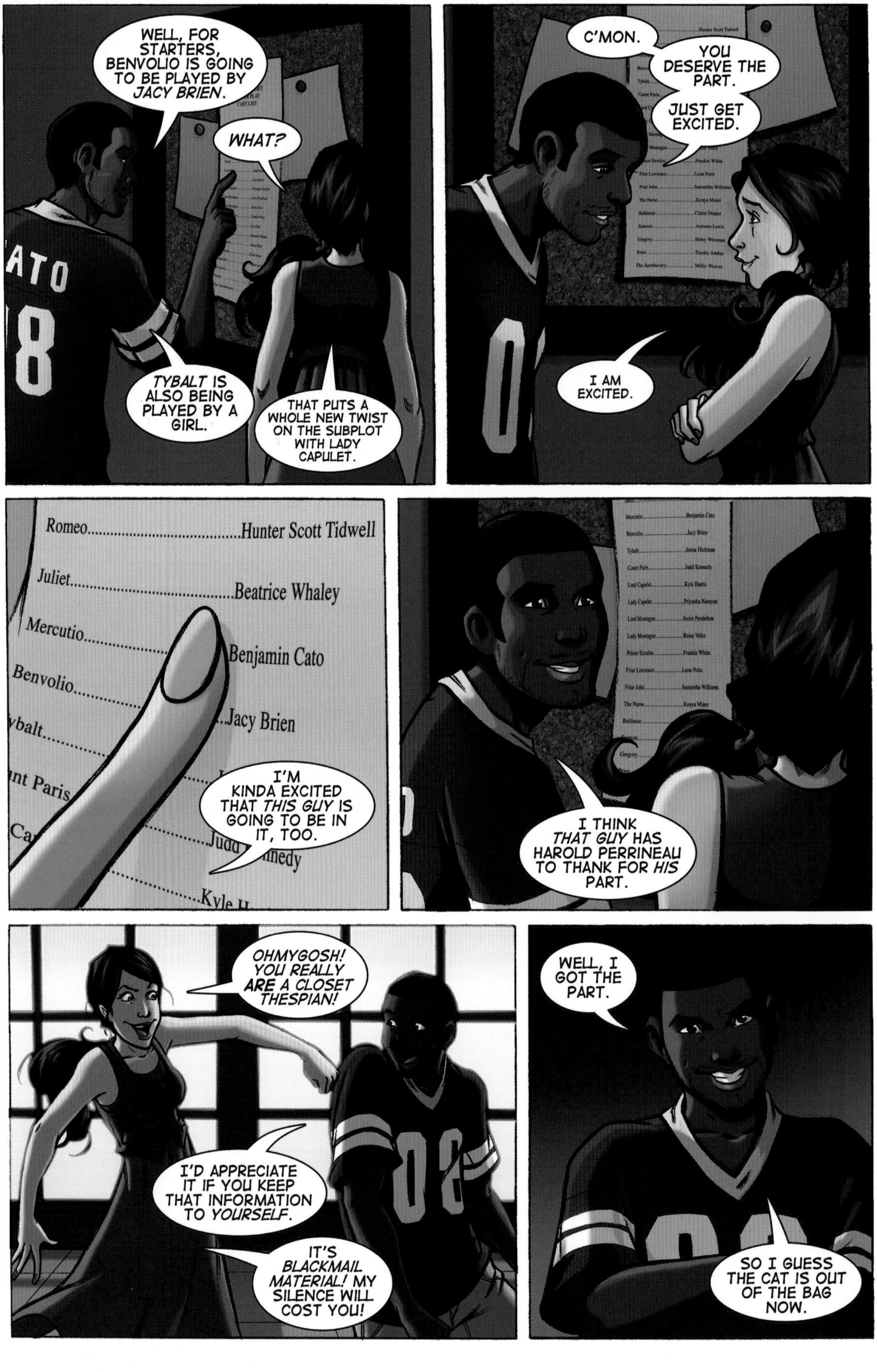
WELL, FOR STARTERS, BENVOLIO IS GOING TO BE PLAYED BY JACY BRIEN.
WHAT?
TYBALT IS ALSO BEING PLAYED BY A GIRL.
THAT PUTS A WHOLE NEW TWIST ON THE SUBPLOT WITH LADY CAPULET.
C'MON.
YOU DESERVE THE PART.
JUST GET EXCITED.
I AM EXCITED.
Romeo....Hunter Scott Tidwell
Juliet....Beatrice Whaley
Mercutio....Benjamin Cato
Benvolio....Jacy Brien
I'M KINDA EXCITED THAT THIS GUY IS GOING TO BE IN IT, TOO.
I THINK THAT GUY HAS HAROLD PERRINEAU TO THANK FOR HIS PART.
OHMYGOSH! YOU REALLY ARE A CLOSET THESPIAN!
I'D APPRECIATE IT IF YOU KEEP THAT INFORMATION TO YOURSELF.
IT'S BLACKMAIL MATERIAL! MY SILENCE WILL COST YOU!
WELL, I GOT THE PART.
SO I GUESS THE CAT IS OUT OF THE BAG NOW.

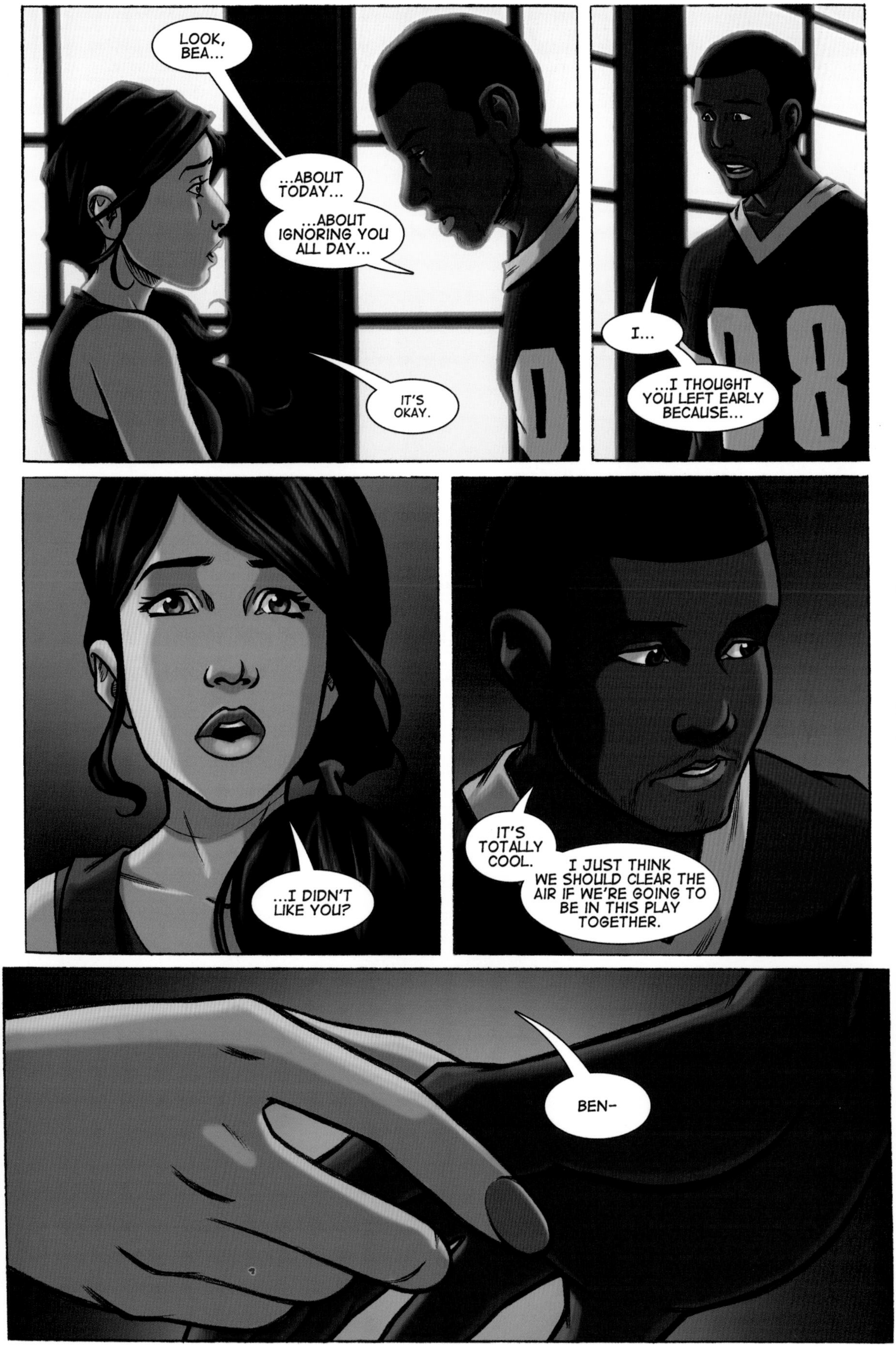
LOOK, BEA...
...ABOUT TODAY...
...ABOUT IGNORING YOU ALL DAY...
IT'S OKAY.
I...
...I THOUGHT YOU LEFT EARLY BECAUSE...
...I DIDN'T LIKE YOU?
IT'S TOTALLY COOL.
I JUST THINK WE SHOULD CLEAR THE AIR IF WE'RE GOING TO BE IN THIS PLAY TOGETHER.
BEN-

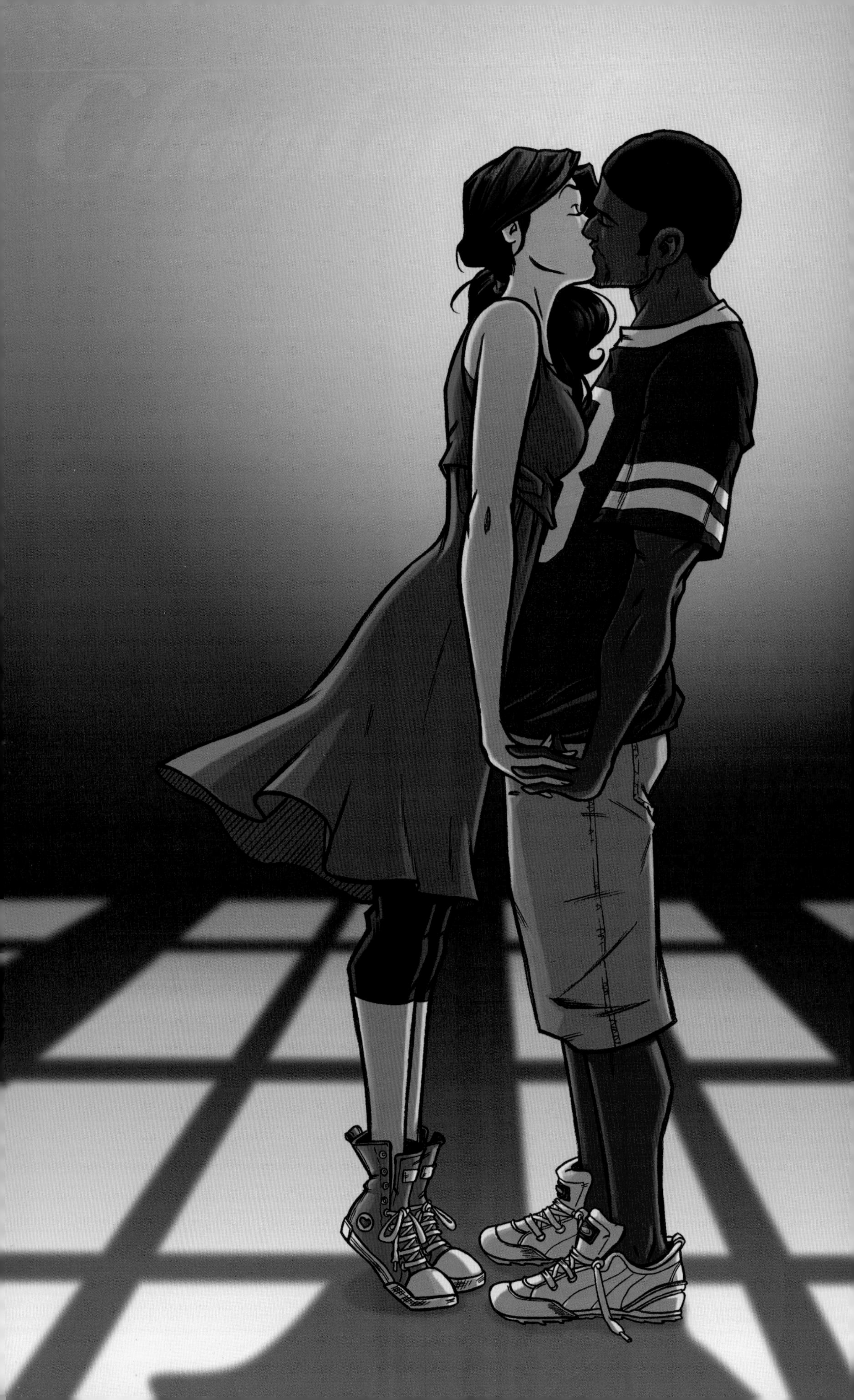

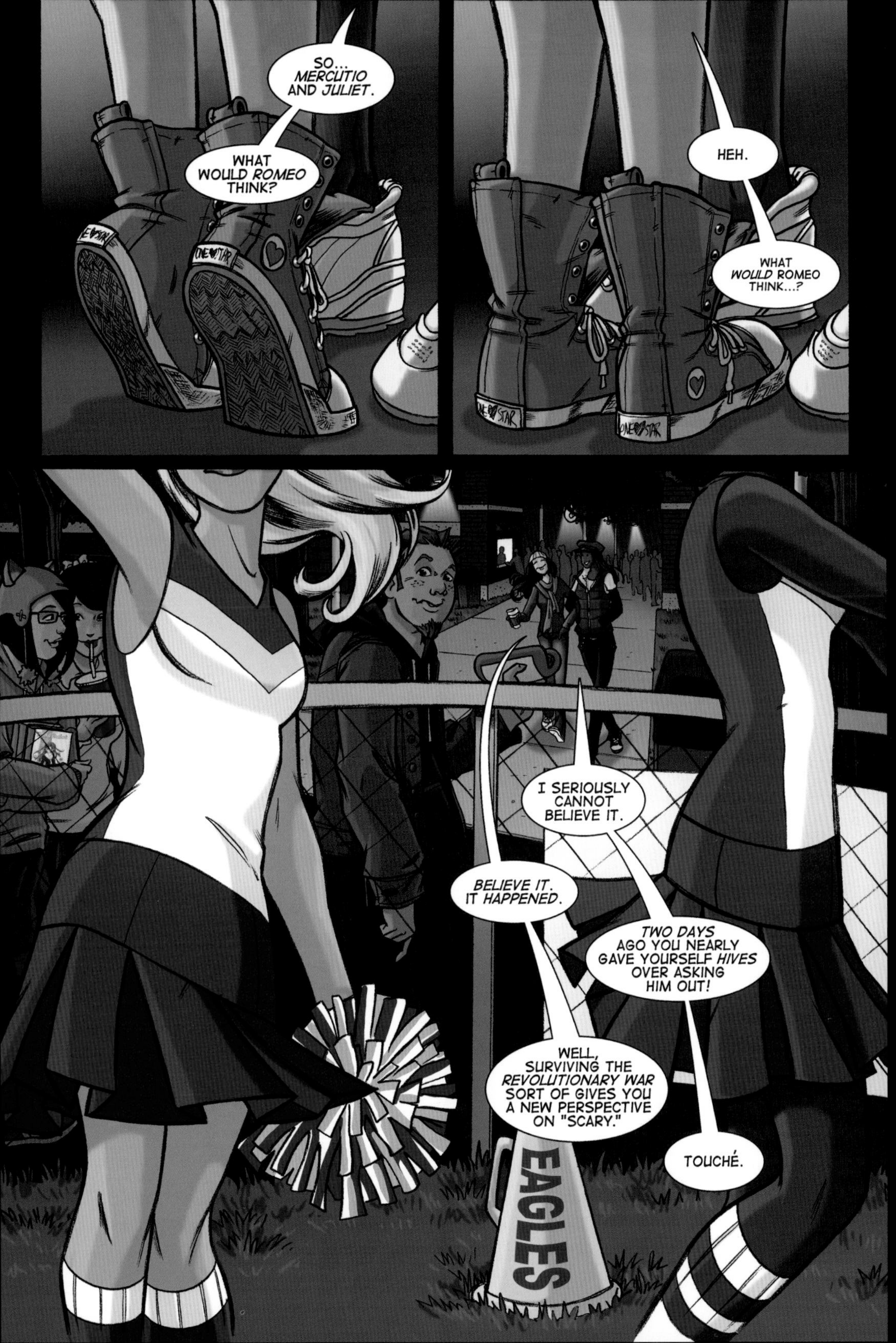
SO... MERCUTIO AND JULIET.
WHAT WOULD ROMEO THINK?
ONE♥STAR
HEH.
WHAT WOULD ROMEO THINK...?
I SERIOUSLY CANNOT BELIEVE IT.
BELIEVE IT. IT HAPPENED.
TWO DAYS AGO YOU NEARLY GAVE YOURSELF HIVES OVER ASKING HIM OUT!
WELL, SURVIVING THE REVOLUTIONARY WAR SORT OF GIVES YOU A NEW PERSPECTIVE ON "SCARY."
TOUCHÉ.
EAGLES

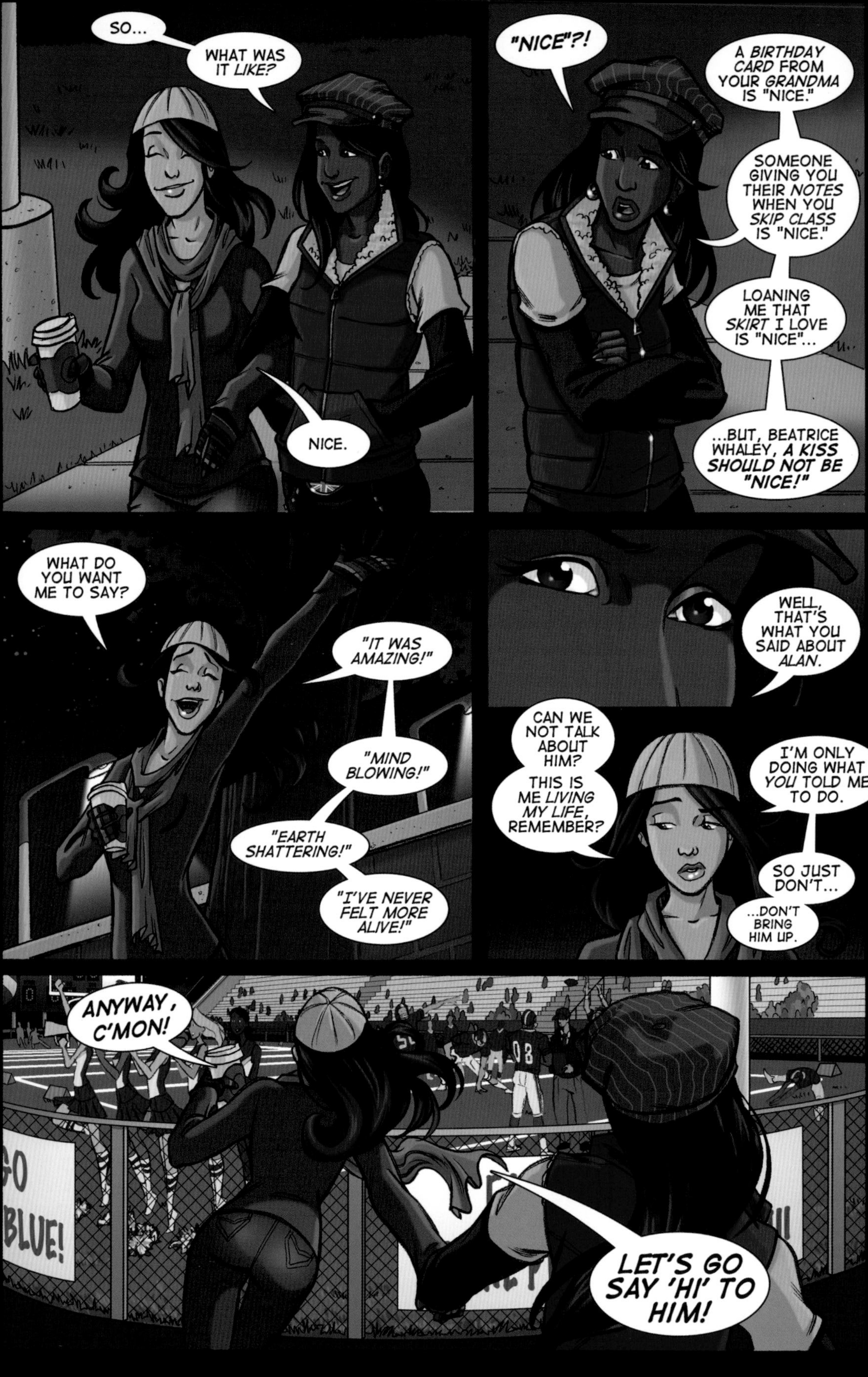
SO...
WHAT WAS IT *LIKE*?
NICE.
"NICE"?!
A *BIRTHDAY CARD* FROM YOUR *GRANDMA* IS "NICE."
SOMEONE GIVING YOU THEIR *NOTES* WHEN YOU *SKIP CLASS* IS "NICE."
LOANING ME THAT *SKIRT* I LOVE IS "NICE"...
...BUT, BEATRICE WHALEY, ***A KISS SHOULD NOT BE "NICE!"***
WHAT DO YOU WANT ME TO SAY?
"IT WAS AMAZING!"
"MIND BLOWING!"
"EARTH SHATTERING!"
"I'VE NEVER FELT MORE ALIVE!"
WELL, THAT'S WHAT YOU SAID ABOUT *ALAN*.
CAN WE NOT TALK ABOUT HIM?
THIS IS ME *LIVING MY LIFE*, REMEMBER?
I'M ONLY DOING WHAT *YOU* TOLD ME TO DO.
SO JUST DON'T...
...DON'T BRING HIM UP.
GO BLUE!
ANYWAY, C'MON!
LET'S GO SAY 'HI' TO HIM!

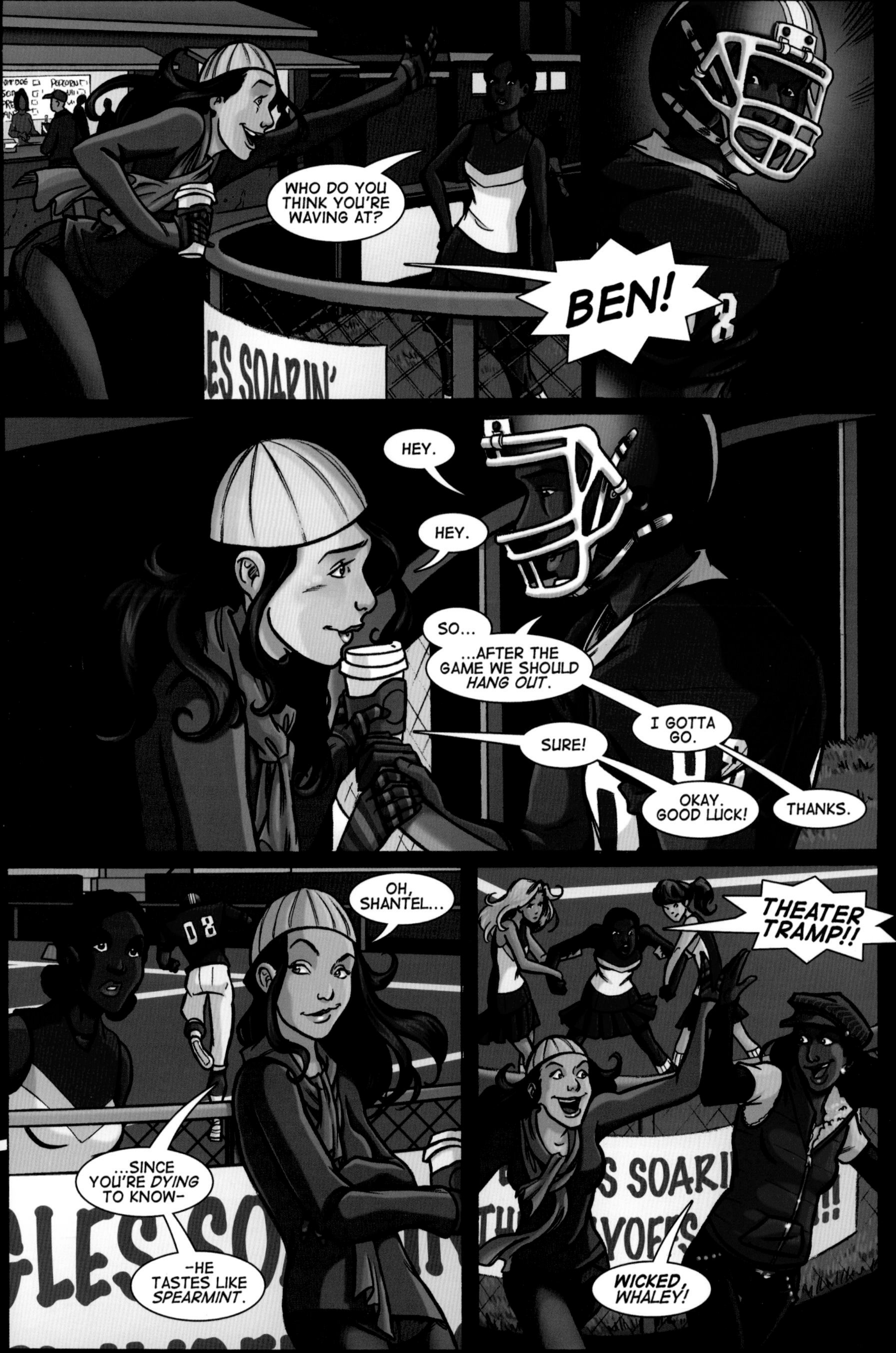
WHO DO YOU THINK YOU'RE WAVING AT?
BEN!
HEY.
HEY.
SO...
...AFTER THE GAME WE SHOULD *HANG OUT*.
I GOTTA GO.
SURE!
OKAY. GOOD LUCK!
THANKS.
OH, SHANTEL...
...SINCE YOU'RE *DYING* TO KNOW-
-HE TASTES LIKE *SPEARMINT*.
THEATER TRAMP!!
WICKED, WHALEY!

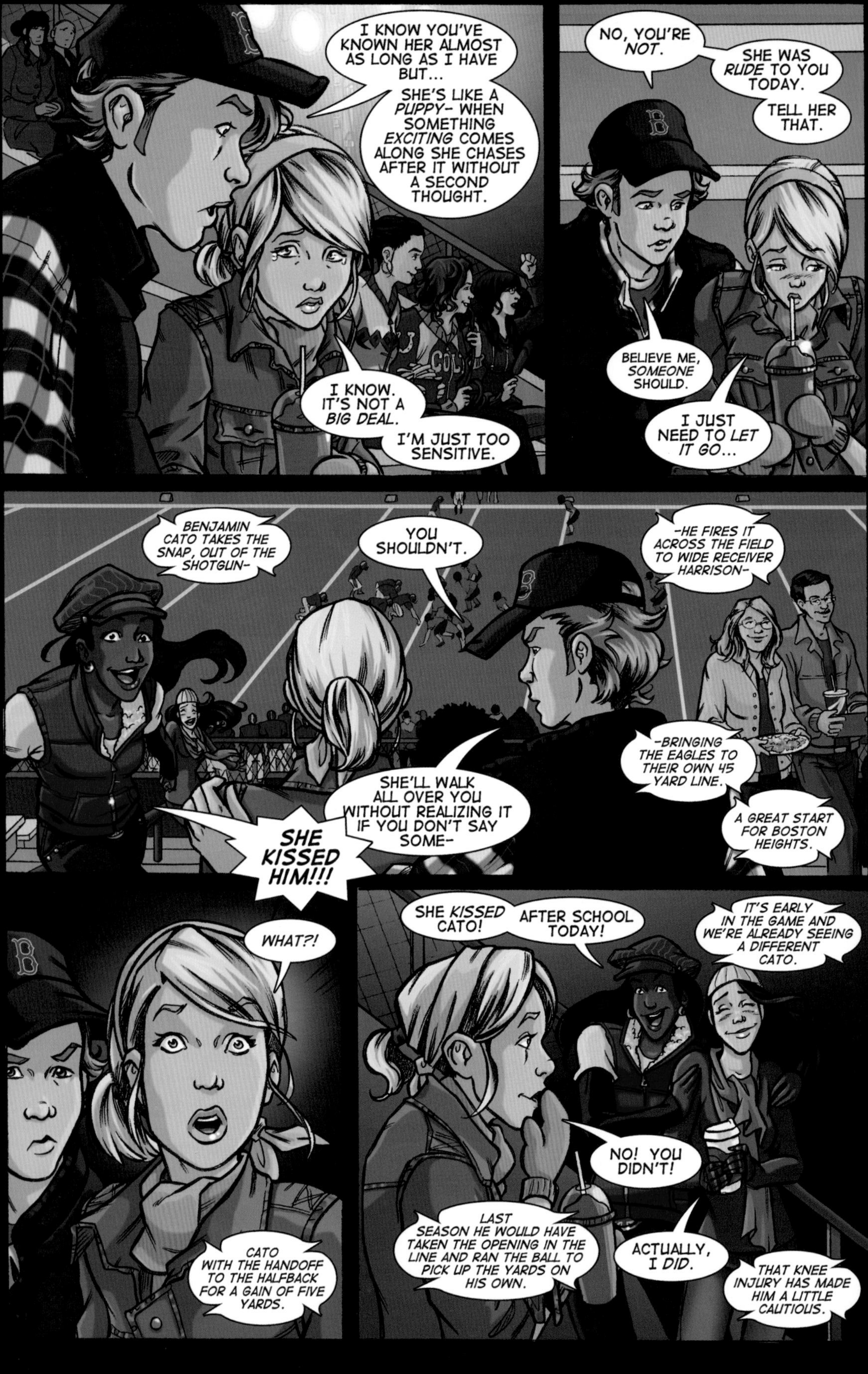
I KNOW YOU'VE KNOWN HER ALMOST AS LONG AS I HAVE BUT...
SHE'S LIKE A PUPPY- WHEN SOMETHING EXCITING COMES ALONG SHE CHASES AFTER IT WITHOUT A SECOND THOUGHT.
I KNOW. IT'S NOT A BIG DEAL.
I'M JUST TOO SENSITIVE.
NO, YOU'RE NOT.
SHE WAS RUDE TO YOU TODAY.
TELL HER THAT.
BELIEVE ME, SOMEONE SHOULD.
I JUST NEED TO LET IT GO...
BENJAMIN CATO TAKES THE SNAP, OUT OF THE SHOTGUN-
YOU SHOULDN'T.
-HE FIRES IT ACROSS THE FIELD TO WIDE RECEIVER HARRISON-
-BRINGING THE EAGLES TO THEIR OWN 45 YARD LINE.
A GREAT START FOR BOSTON HEIGHTS.
SHE'LL WALK ALL OVER YOU WITHOUT REALIZING IT IF YOU DON'T SAY SOME-
SHE KISSED HIM!!!
WHAT?!
CATO WITH THE HANDOFF TO THE HALFBACK FOR A GAIN OF FIVE YARDS.
SHE KISSED CATO!
AFTER SCHOOL TODAY!
IT'S EARLY IN THE GAME AND WE'RE ALREADY SEEING A DIFFERENT CATO.
NO! YOU DIDN'T!
LAST SEASON HE WOULD HAVE TAKEN THE OPENING IN THE LINE AND RAN THE BALL TO PICK UP THE YARDS ON HIS OWN.
ACTUALLY, I DID.
THAT KNEE INJURY HAS MADE HIM A LITTLE CAUTIOUS.

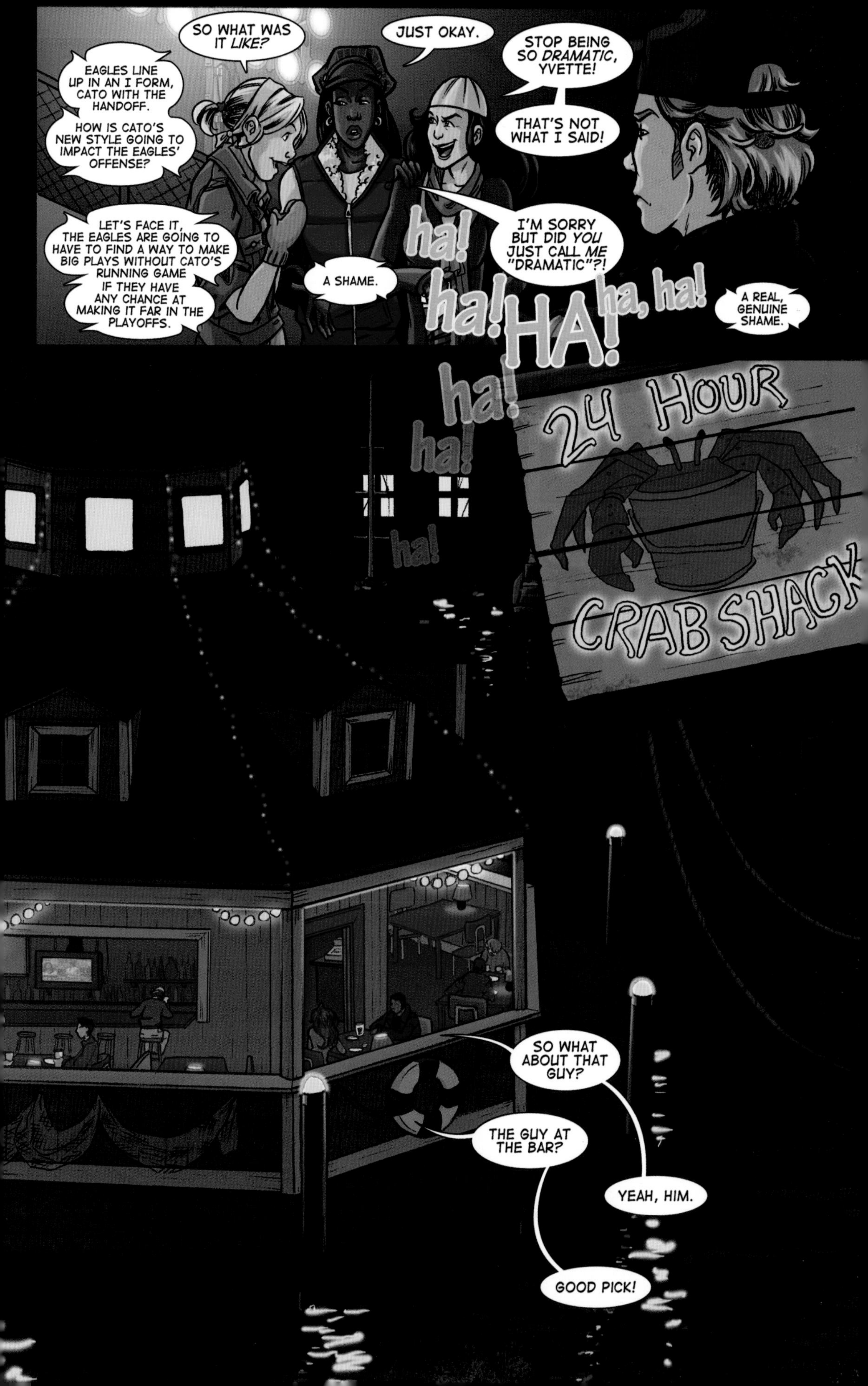
EAGLES LINE UP IN AN I FORM, CATO WITH THE HANDOFF.
HOW IS CATO'S NEW STYLE GOING TO IMPACT THE EAGLES' OFFENSE?
SO WHAT WAS IT *LIKE?*
JUST OKAY.
STOP BEING SO *DRAMATIC*, YVETTE!
THAT'S NOT WHAT I SAID!
LET'S FACE IT, THE EAGLES ARE GOING TO HAVE TO FIND A WAY TO MAKE BIG PLAYS WITHOUT CATO'S RUNNING GAME
IF THEY HAVE ANY CHANCE AT MAKING IT FAR IN THE PLAYOFFS.
A SHAME.
I'M SORRY BUT DID *YOU* JUST CALL *ME* "DRAMATIC"?!
ha! ha! HA! ha, ha!
A REAL, GENUINE SHAME.
ha! ha! ha!
24 HOUR CRAB SHACK
SO WHAT ABOUT THAT GUY?
THE GUY AT THE BAR?
YEAH, HIM.
GOOD PICK!

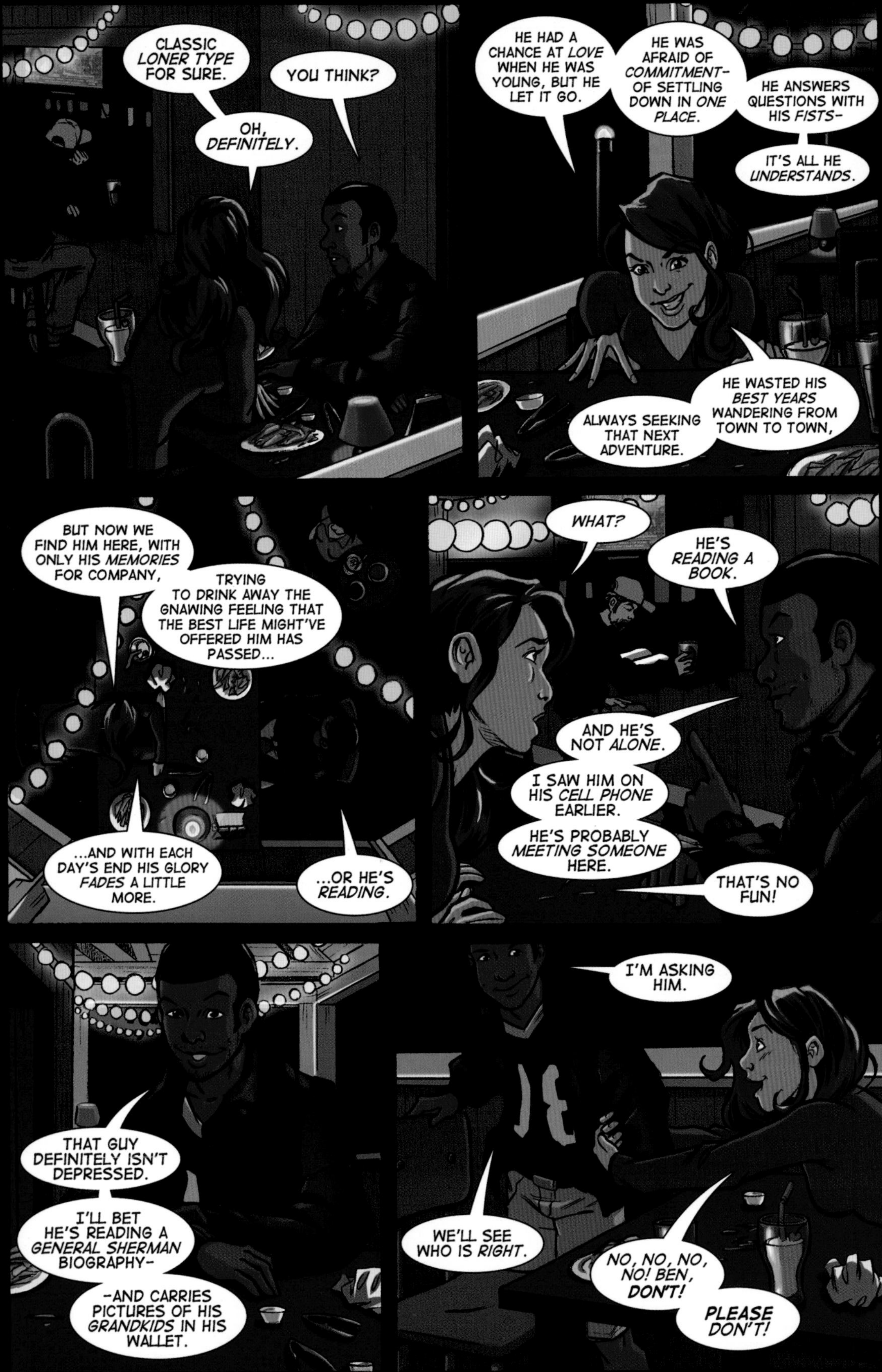

CLASSIC *LONER TYPE* FOR SURE.
YOU THINK?
OH, *DEFINITELY*.
HE HAD A CHANCE AT *LOVE* WHEN HE WAS YOUNG, BUT HE LET IT GO.
HE WAS AFRAID OF *COMMITMENT*- OF SETTLING DOWN IN *ONE PLACE*.
HE ANSWERS QUESTIONS WITH HIS *FISTS*-
IT'S ALL HE *UNDERSTANDS*.
HE WASTED HIS *BEST YEARS* WANDERING FROM TOWN TO TOWN,
ALWAYS SEEKING THAT NEXT ADVENTURE.
BUT NOW WE FIND HIM HERE, WITH ONLY HIS *MEMORIES* FOR COMPANY,
TRYING TO DRINK AWAY THE GNAWING FEELING THAT THE BEST LIFE MIGHT'VE OFFERED HIM HAS PASSED...
...AND WITH EACH DAY'S END HIS GLORY *FADES* A LITTLE MORE.
...OR HE'S *READING*.
WHAT?
HE'S *READING A BOOK*.
AND HE'S NOT *ALONE*.
I SAW HIM ON HIS *CELL PHONE* EARLIER.
HE'S PROBABLY *MEETING SOMEONE* HERE.
THAT'S NO FUN!
THAT GUY DEFINITELY ISN'T DEPRESSED.
I'LL BET HE'S READING A *GENERAL SHERMAN* BIOGRAPHY-
-AND CARRIES PICTURES OF HIS *GRANDKIDS* IN HIS WALLET.
I'M ASKING HIM.
WE'LL SEE WHO IS *RIGHT*.
NO, NO, NO, NO! BEN, ***DON'T!***
PLEASE DON'T!

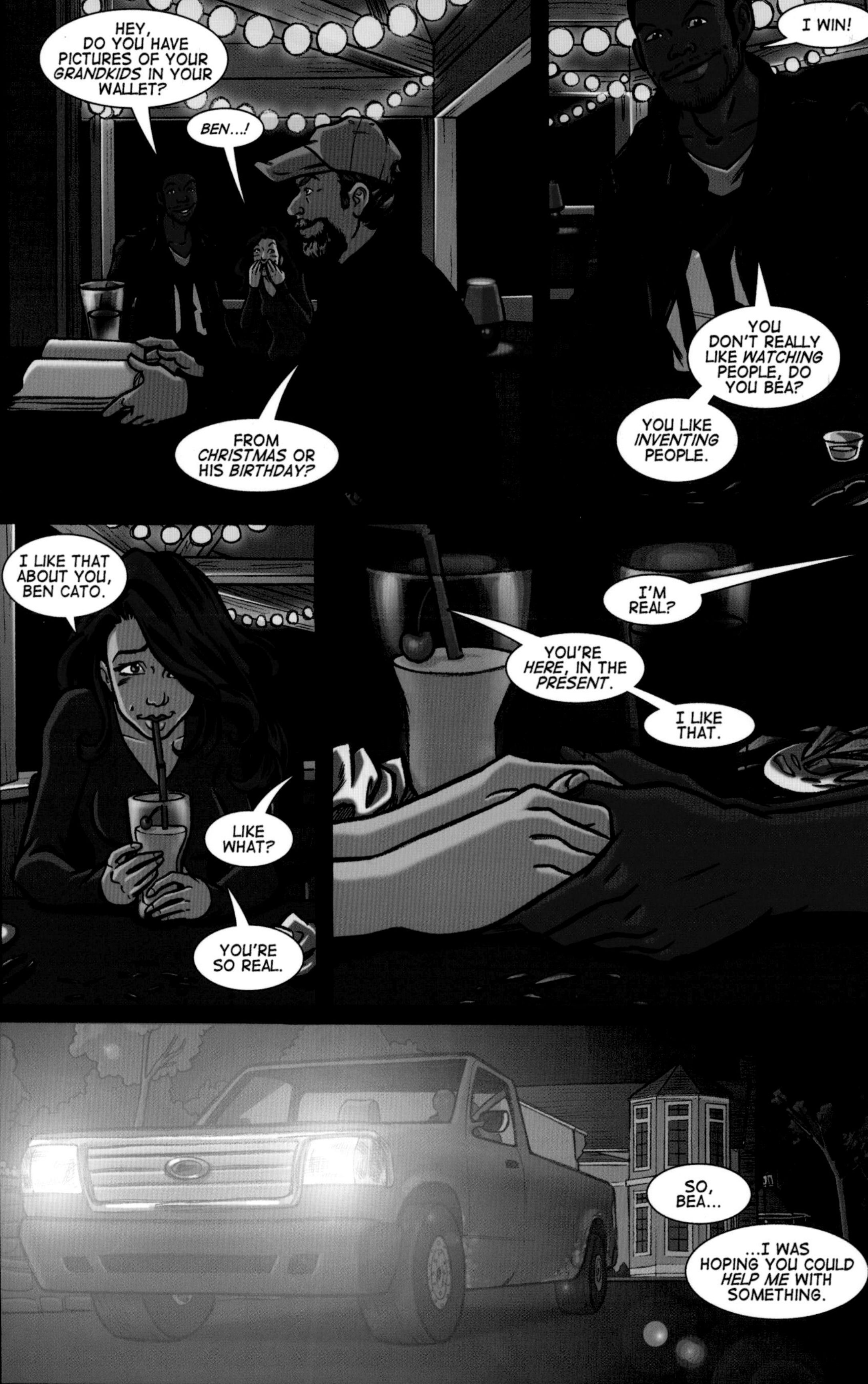
HEY, DO YOU HAVE PICTURES OF YOUR GRANDKIDS IN YOUR WALLET?
BEN...!
FROM CHRISTMAS OR HIS BIRTHDAY?
I WIN!
YOU DON'T REALLY LIKE WATCHING PEOPLE, DO YOU BEA?
YOU LIKE INVENTING PEOPLE.
I LIKE THAT ABOUT YOU, BEN CATO.
LIKE WHAT?
YOU'RE SO REAL.
I'M REAL?
YOU'RE HERE, IN THE PRESENT.
I LIKE THAT.
SO, BEA...
...I WAS HOPING YOU COULD HELP ME WITH SOMETHING.

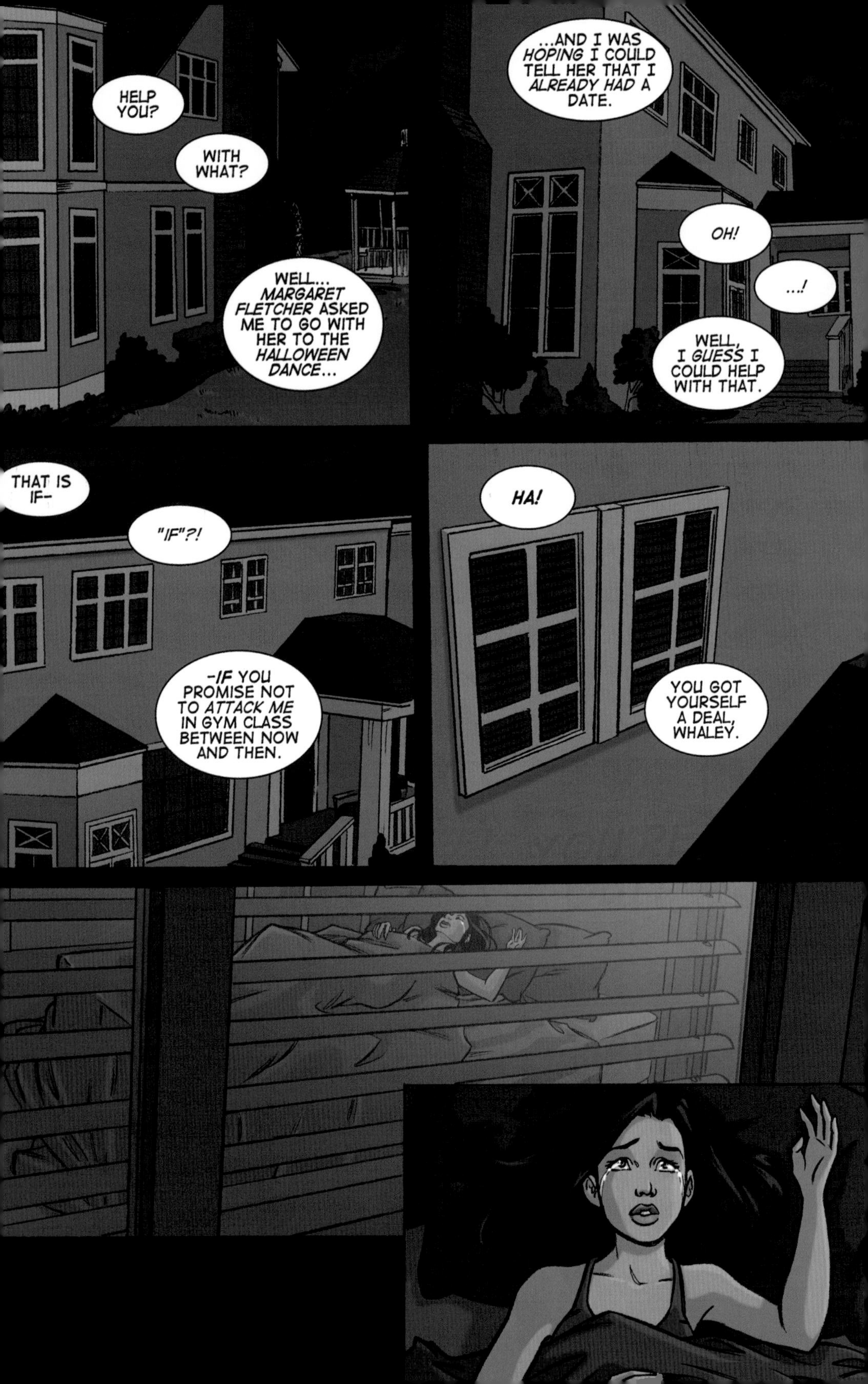
HELP YOU?
WITH WHAT?
WELL... MARGARET FLETCHER ASKED ME TO GO WITH HER TO THE HALLOWEEN DANCE...
...AND I WAS HOPING I COULD TELL HER THAT I ALREADY HAD A DATE.
OH!
...!
WELL, I GUESS I COULD HELP WITH THAT.
THAT IS IF-
"IF"?!
-IF YOU PROMISE NOT TO ATTACK ME IN GYM CLASS BETWEEN NOW AND THEN.
HA!
YOU GOT YOURSELF A DEAL, WHALEY.

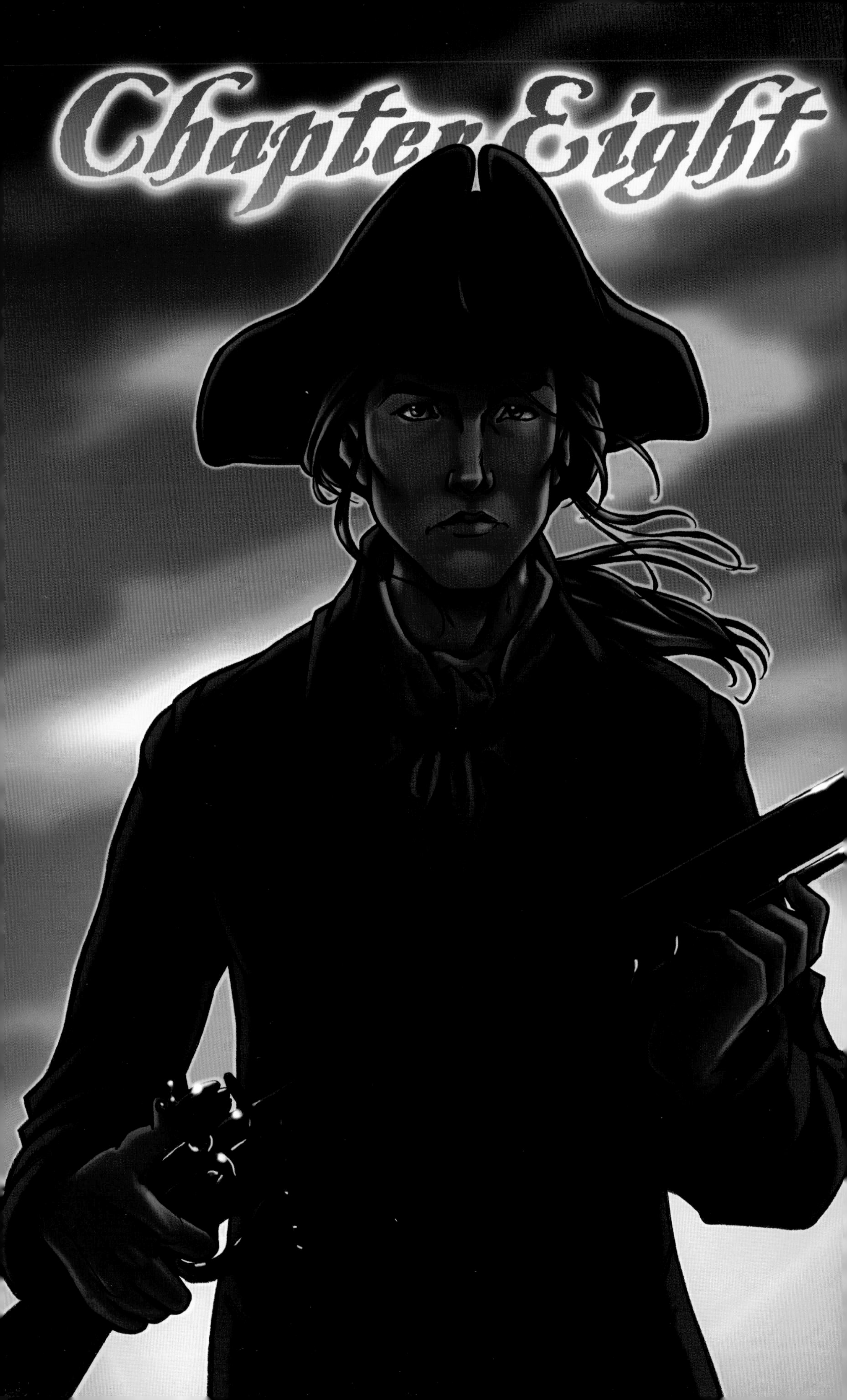
Chapter Eight

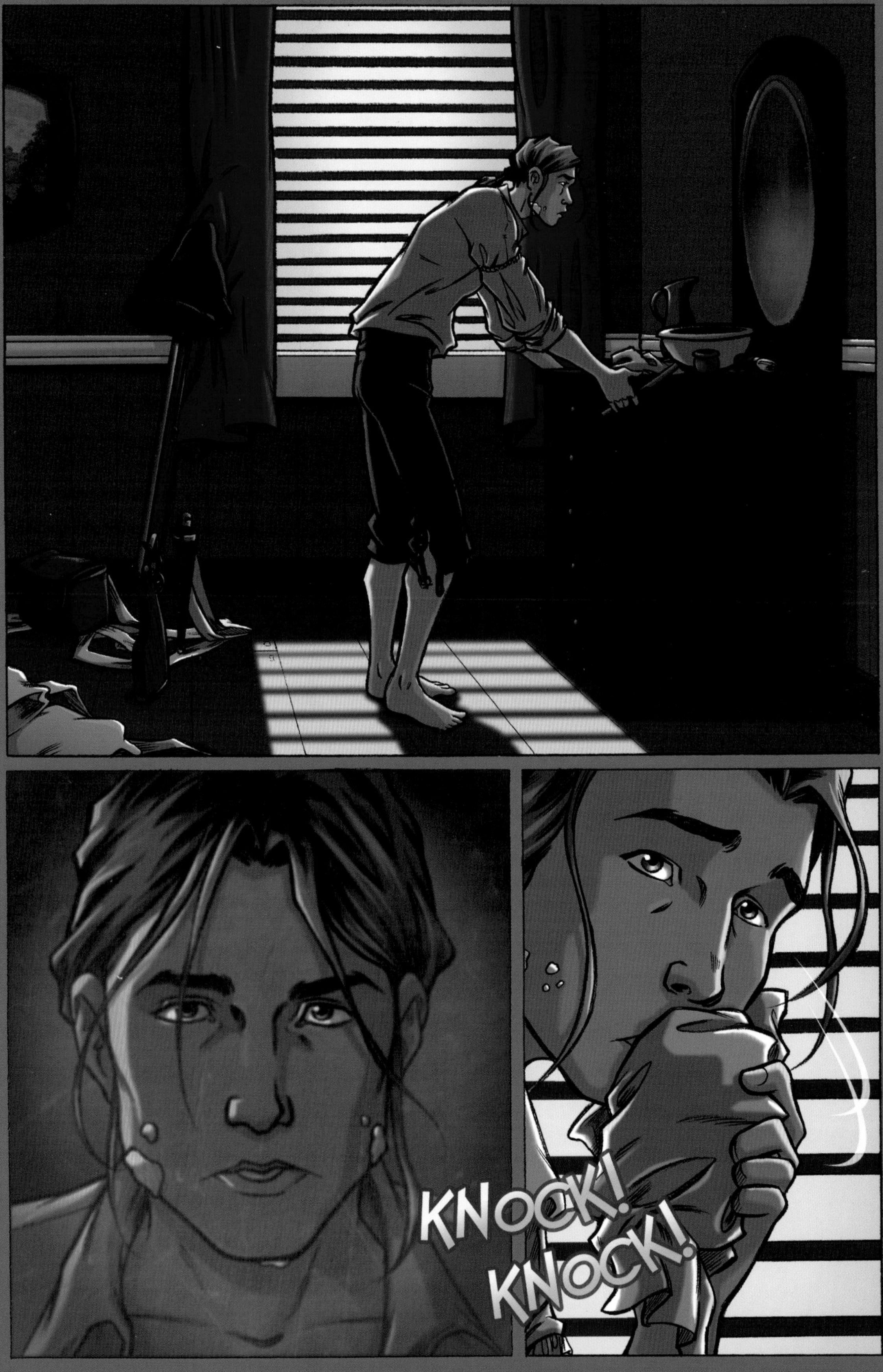
KNOCK!
KNOCK!

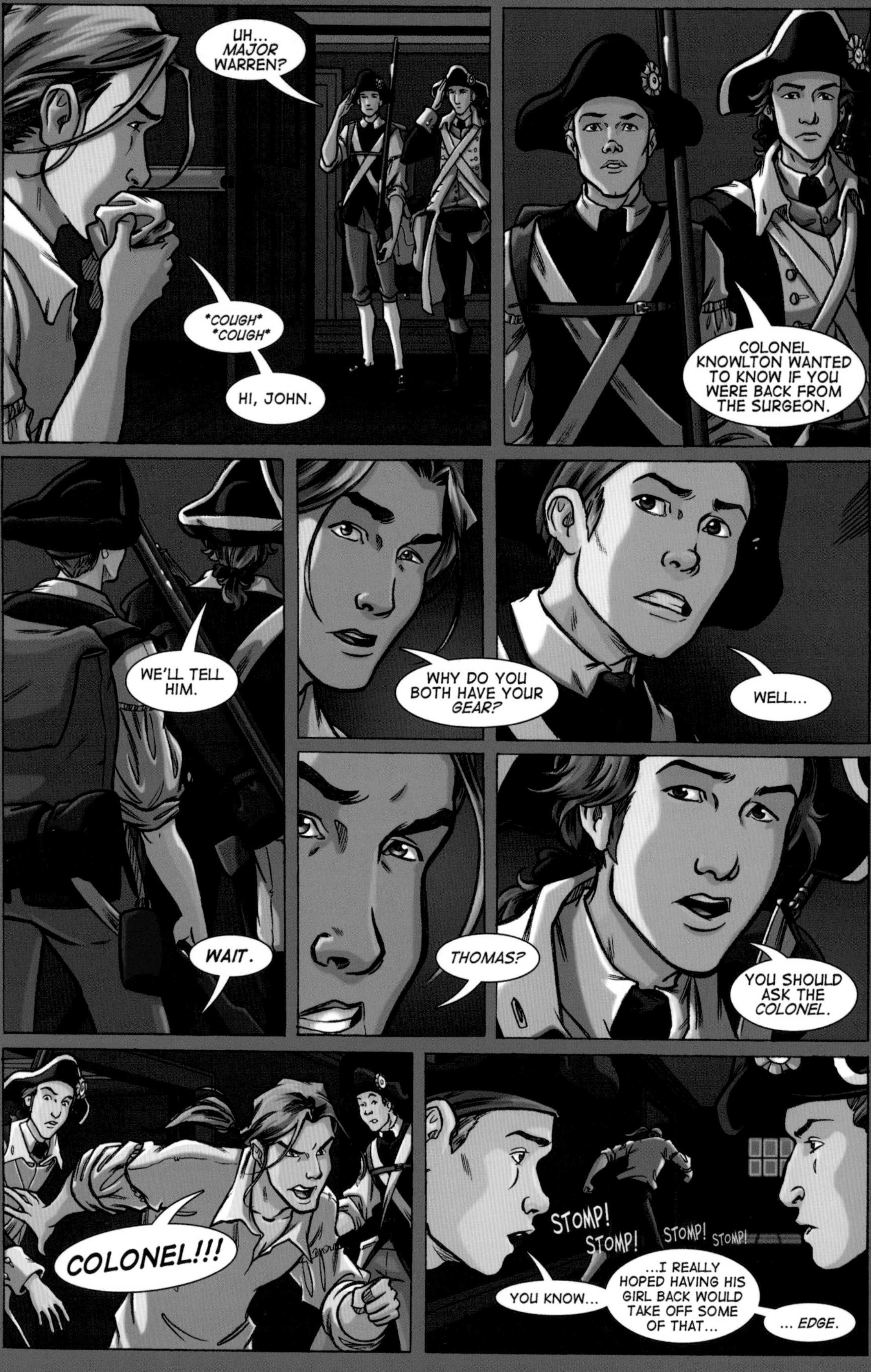
UH... MAJOR WARREN?
COUGH *COUGH*
HI, JOHN.
COLONEL KNOWLTON WANTED TO KNOW IF YOU WERE BACK FROM THE SURGEON.
WE'LL TELL HIM.
WHY DO YOU BOTH HAVE YOUR GEAR?
WELL...
WAIT.
THOMAS?
YOU SHOULD ASK THE COLONEL.
COLONEL!!!
STOMP! STOMP! STOMP! STOMP!
YOU KNOW...
...I REALLY HOPED HAVING HIS GIRL BACK WOULD TAKE OFF SOME OF THAT...
... EDGE.

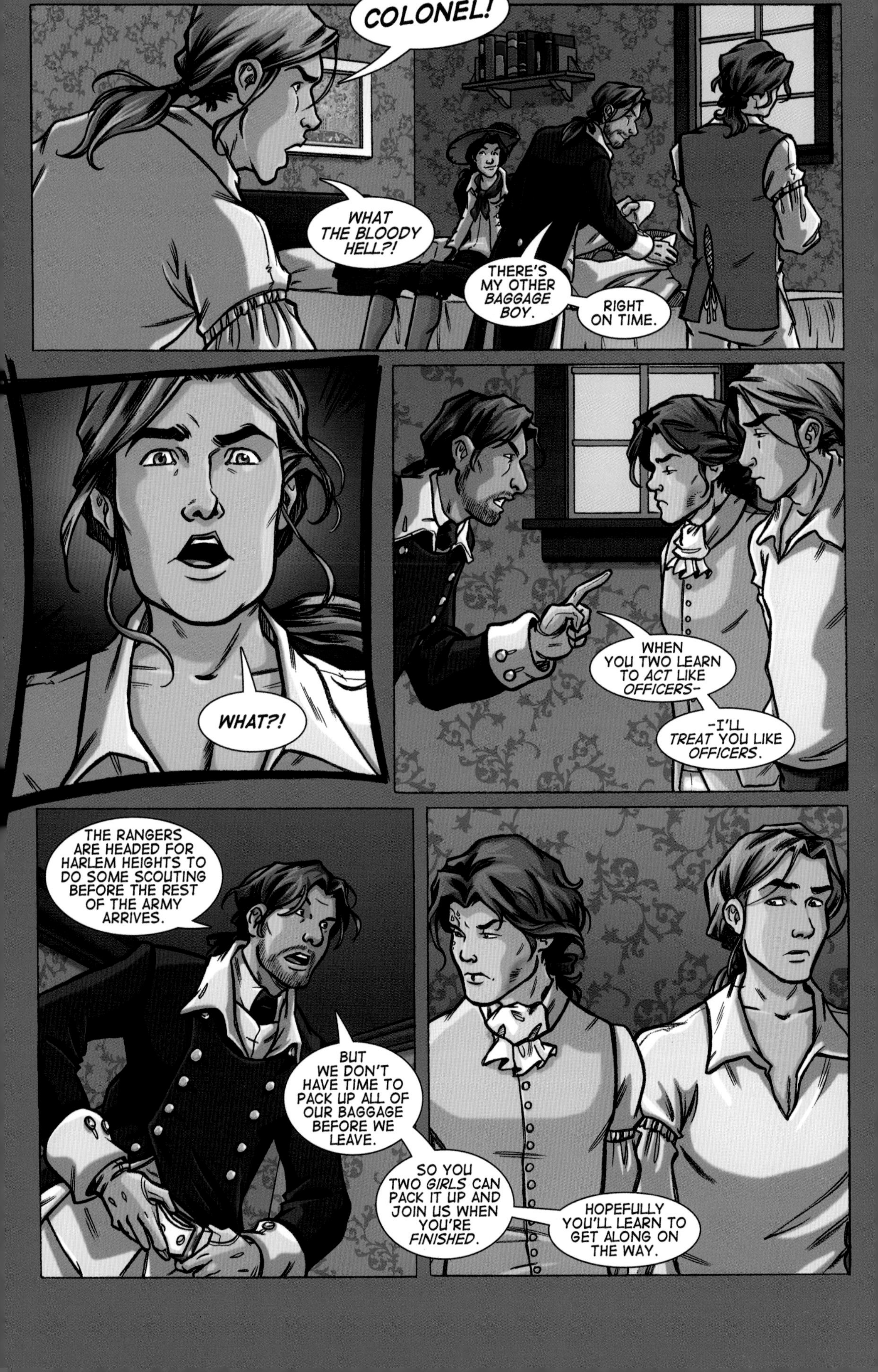
COLONEL!
WHAT THE BLOODY HELL?!
THERE'S MY OTHER BAGGAGE BOY.
RIGHT ON TIME.
WHAT?!
WHEN YOU TWO LEARN TO ACT LIKE OFFICERS-
-I'LL TREAT YOU LIKE OFFICERS.
THE RANGERS ARE HEADED FOR HARLEM HEIGHTS TO DO SOME SCOUTING BEFORE THE REST OF THE ARMY ARRIVES.
BUT WE DON'T HAVE TIME TO PACK UP ALL OF OUR BAGGAGE BEFORE WE LEAVE.
SO YOU TWO GIRLS CAN PACK IT UP AND JOIN US WHEN YOU'RE FINISHED.
HOPEFULLY YOU'LL LEARN TO GET ALONG ON THE WAY.

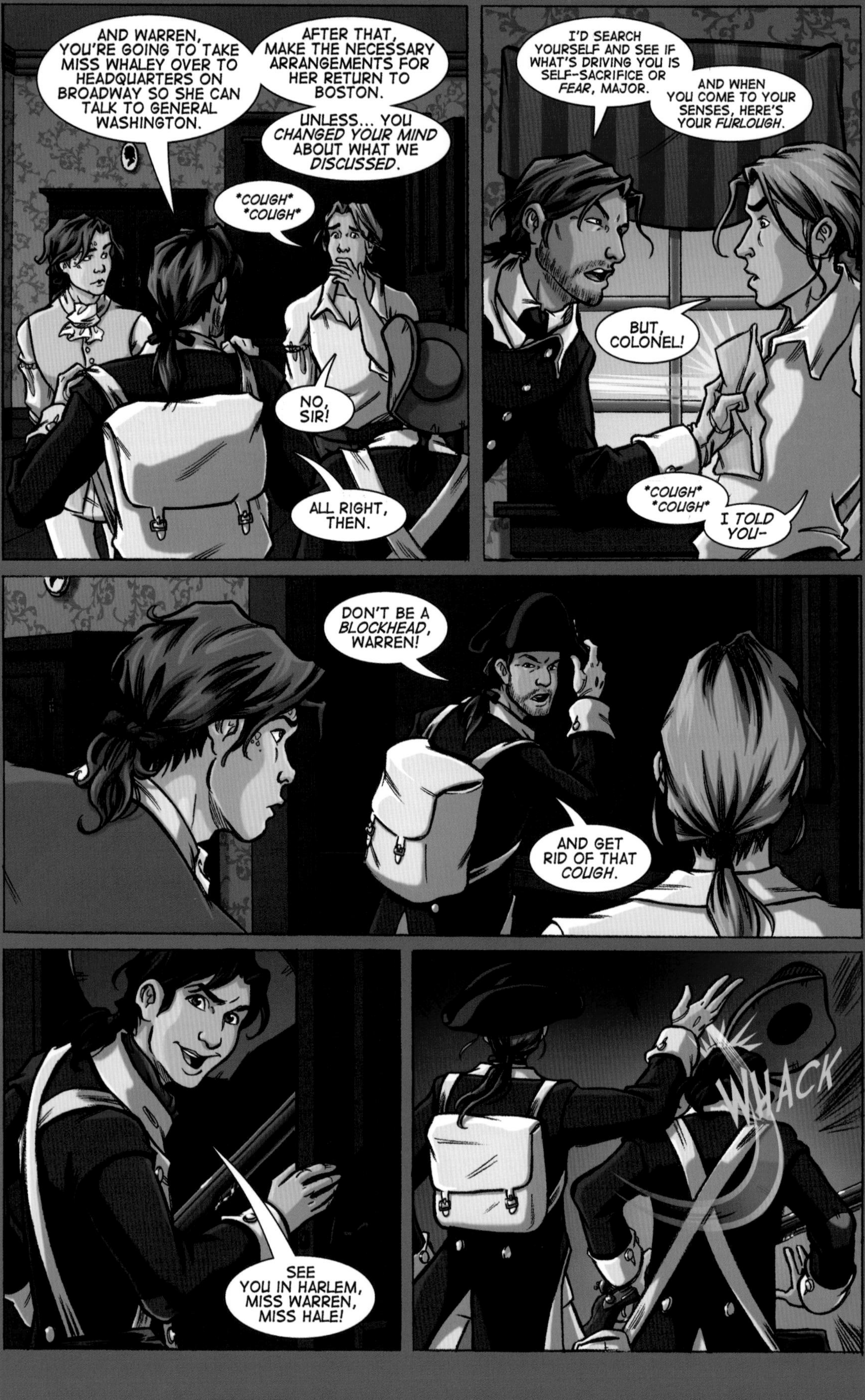
AND WARREN, YOU'RE GOING TO TAKE MISS WHALEY OVER TO HEADQUARTERS ON BROADWAY SO SHE CAN TALK TO GENERAL WASHINGTON.
AFTER THAT, MAKE THE NECESSARY ARRANGEMENTS FOR HER RETURN TO BOSTON.
UNLESS... YOU *CHANGED YOUR MIND* ABOUT WHAT WE *DISCUSSED*.
COUGH *COUGH*
NO, SIR!
ALL RIGHT, THEN.
I'D SEARCH YOURSELF AND SEE IF WHAT'S DRIVING YOU IS SELF-SACRIFICE OR *FEAR*, MAJOR.
AND WHEN YOU COME TO YOUR SENSES, HERE'S YOUR *FURLOUGH*.
BUT, COLONEL!
COUGH *COUGH*
I *TOLD* YOU-
DON'T BE A *BLOCKHEAD*, WARREN!
AND GET RID OF THAT *COUGH*.
SEE YOU IN HARLEM, MISS WARREN, MISS HALE!
WHACK

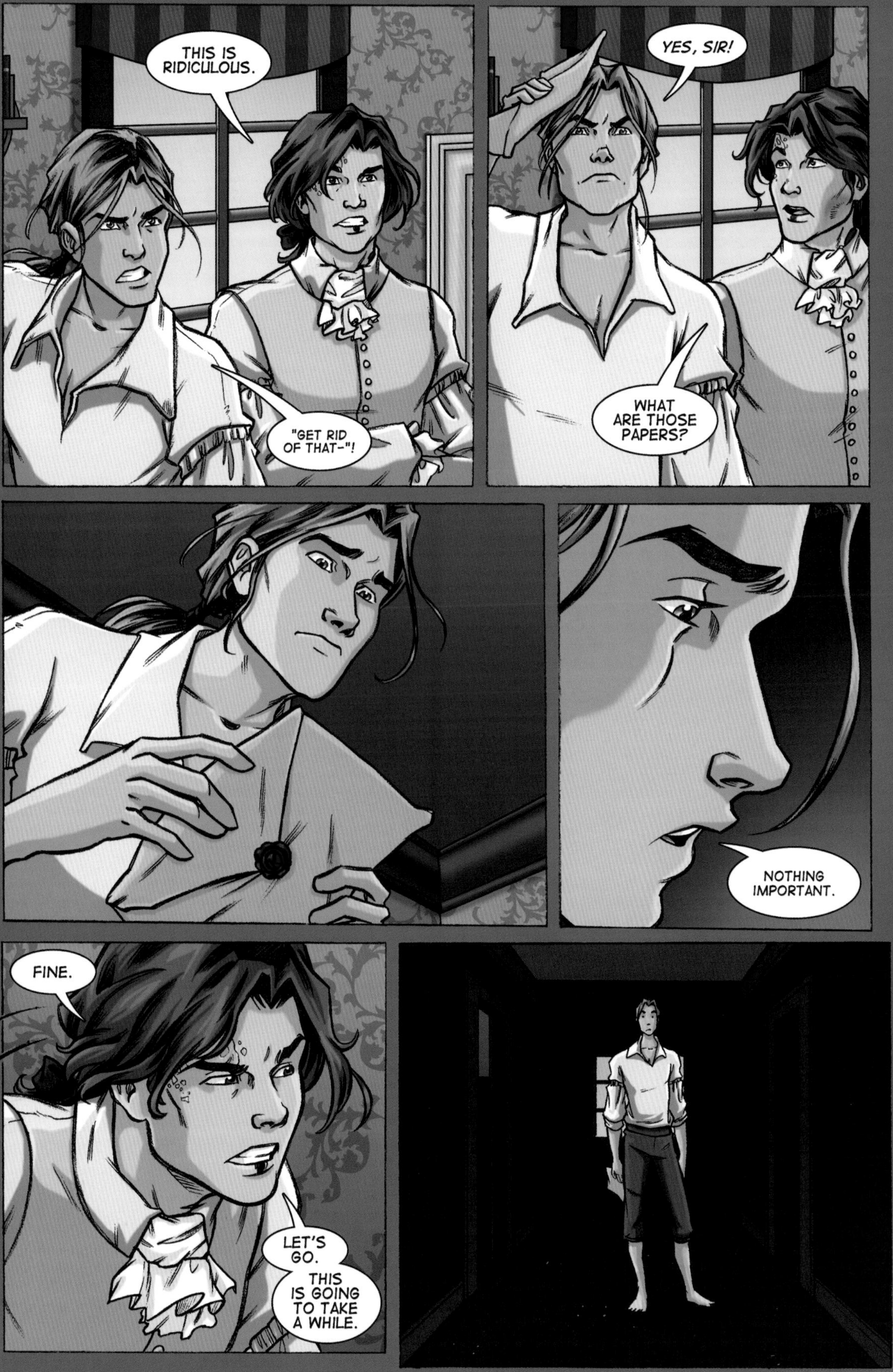
THIS IS RIDICULOUS.
"GET RID OF THAT-"!
YES, SIR!
WHAT ARE THOSE PAPERS?
NOTHING IMPORTANT.
FINE.
LET'S GO.
THIS IS GOING TO TAKE A WHILE.

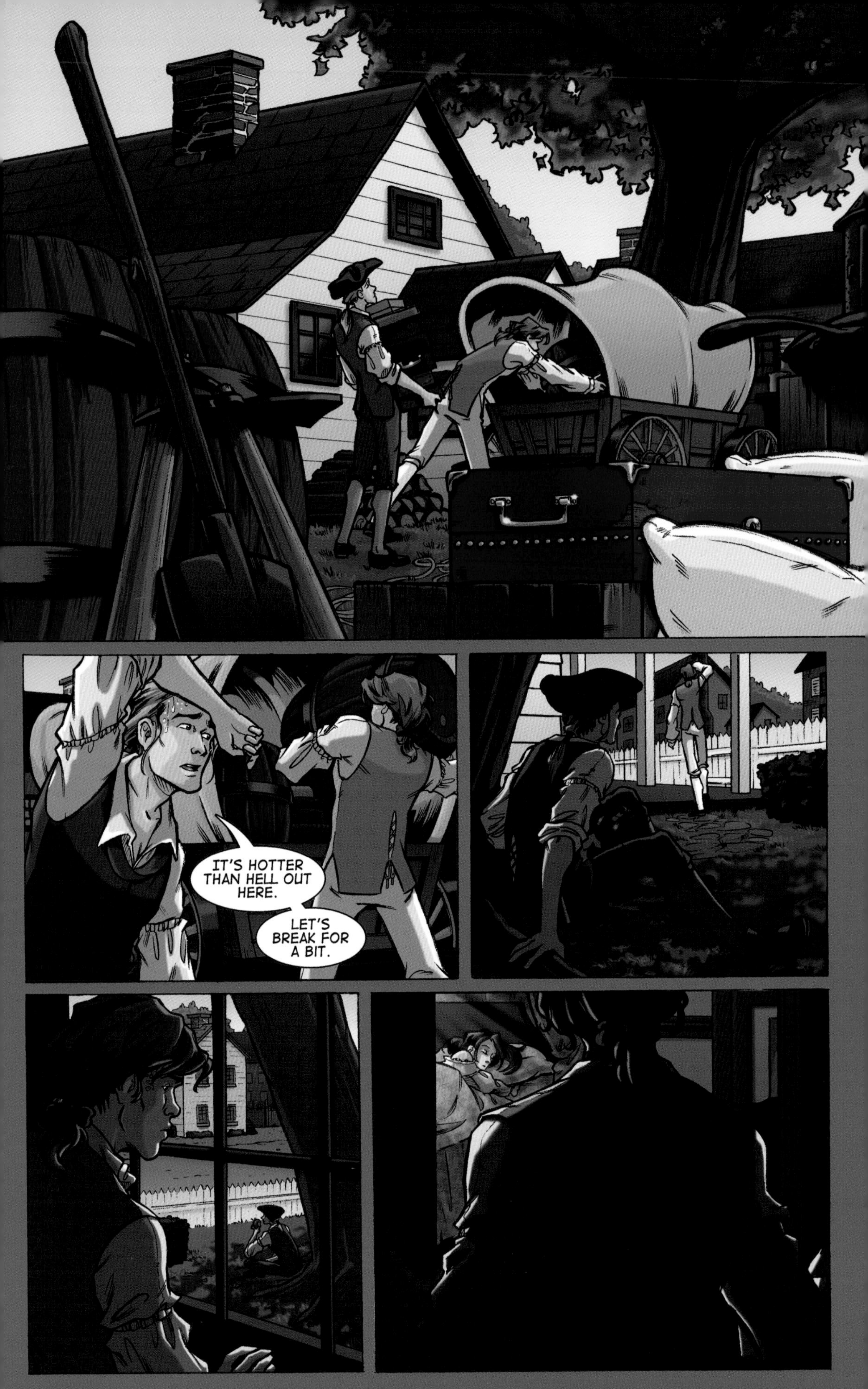
IT'S HOTTER THAN HELL OUT HERE.
LET'S BREAK FOR A BIT.

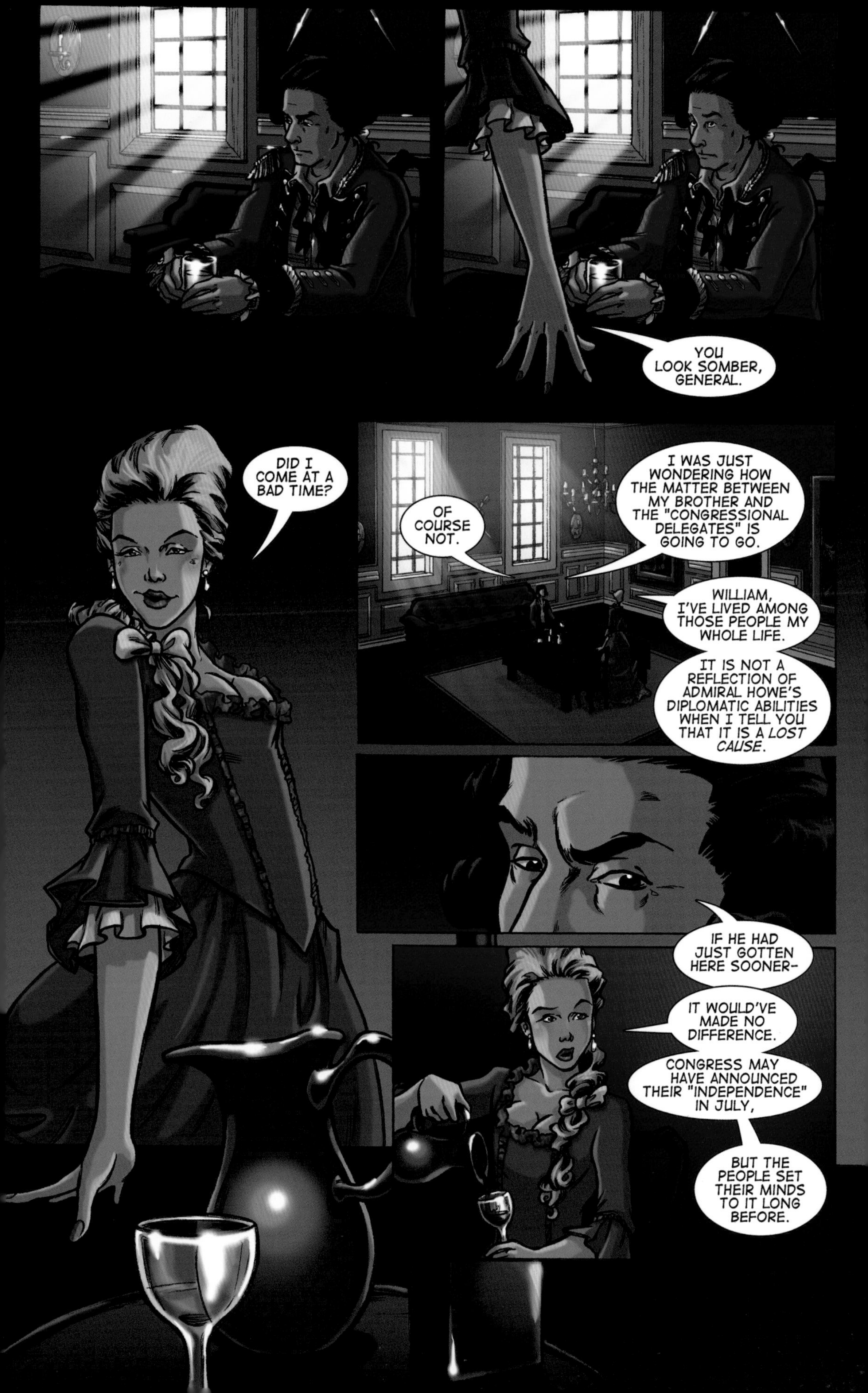
YOU LOOK SOMBER, GENERAL.
DID I COME AT A BAD TIME?
OF COURSE NOT.
I WAS JUST WONDERING HOW THE MATTER BETWEEN MY BROTHER AND THE "CONGRESSIONAL DELEGATES" IS GOING TO GO.
WILLIAM, I'VE LIVED AMONG THOSE PEOPLE MY WHOLE LIFE.
IT IS NOT A REFLECTION OF ADMIRAL HOWE'S DIPLOMATIC ABILITIES WHEN I TELL YOU THAT IT IS A *LOST CAUSE*.
IF HE HAD JUST GOTTEN HERE SOONER-
IT WOULD'VE MADE NO DIFFERENCE.
CONGRESS MAY HAVE ANNOUNCED THEIR "INDEPENDENCE" IN JULY,
BUT THE PEOPLE SET THEIR MINDS TO IT LONG BEFORE.

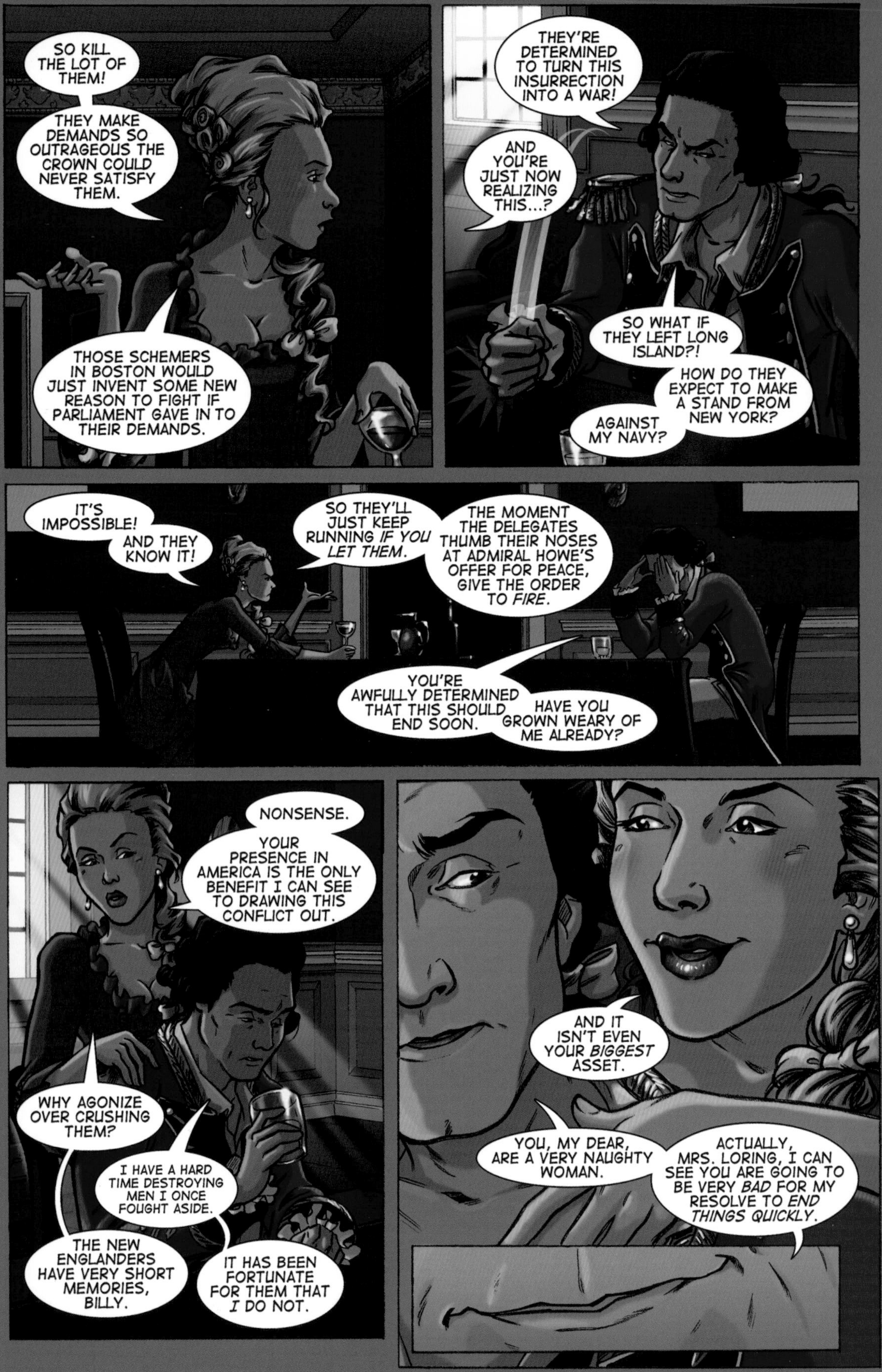
SO KILL THE LOT OF THEM!
THEY MAKE DEMANDS SO OUTRAGEOUS THE CROWN COULD NEVER SATISFY THEM.
THOSE SCHEMERS IN BOSTON WOULD JUST INVENT SOME NEW REASON TO FIGHT IF PARLIAMENT GAVE IN TO THEIR DEMANDS.
THEY'RE DETERMINED TO TURN THIS INSURRECTION INTO A WAR!
AND YOU'RE JUST NOW REALIZING THIS...?
SO WHAT IF THEY LEFT LONG ISLAND?!
HOW DO THEY EXPECT TO MAKE A STAND FROM NEW YORK?
AGAINST MY NAVY?
IT'S IMPOSSIBLE!
AND THEY KNOW IT!
SO THEY'LL JUST KEEP RUNNING *IF YOU LET THEM*.
THE MOMENT THE DELEGATES THUMB THEIR NOSES AT ADMIRAL HOWE'S OFFER FOR PEACE, GIVE THE ORDER TO *FIRE*.
YOU'RE AWFULLY DETERMINED THAT THIS SHOULD END SOON.
HAVE YOU GROWN WEARY OF ME ALREADY?
NONSENSE.
YOUR PRESENCE IN AMERICA IS THE ONLY BENEFIT I CAN SEE TO DRAWING THIS CONFLICT OUT.
WHY AGONIZE OVER CRUSHING THEM?
I HAVE A HARD TIME DESTROYING MEN I ONCE FOUGHT ASIDE.
THE NEW ENGLANDERS HAVE VERY SHORT MEMORIES, BILLY.
IT HAS BEEN FORTUNATE FOR THEM THAT *I* DO NOT.
AND IT ISN'T EVEN YOUR *BIGGEST* ASSET.
YOU, MY DEAR, ARE A VERY NAUGHTY WOMAN.
ACTUALLY, MRS. LORING, I CAN SEE YOU ARE GOING TO BE VERY *BAD* FOR MY RESOLVE TO *END THINGS QUICKLY*.

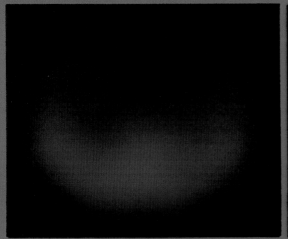

ALAN...?

NATHAN?!

I'M SORRY!

I SHOULDN'T BE HERE—

NO, WAIT.

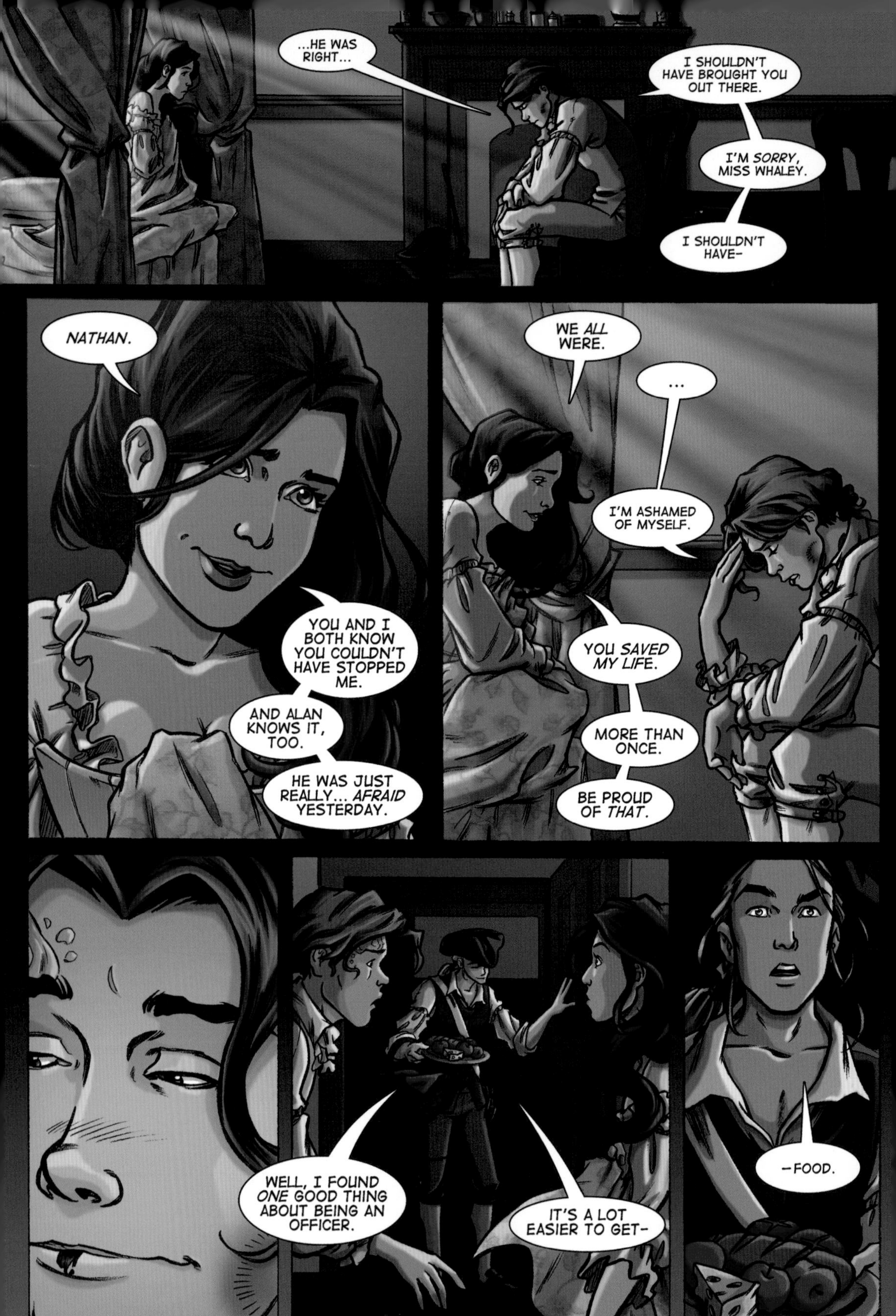
...HE WAS RIGHT...
I SHOULDN'T HAVE BROUGHT YOU OUT THERE.
I'M SORRY, MISS WHALEY.
I SHOULDN'T HAVE-
NATHAN.
YOU AND I BOTH KNOW YOU COULDN'T HAVE STOPPED ME.
AND ALAN KNOWS IT, TOO.
HE WAS JUST REALLY... AFRAID YESTERDAY.
WE ALL WERE.
...
I'M ASHAMED OF MYSELF.
YOU SAVED MY LIFE.
MORE THAN ONCE.
BE PROUD OF THAT.
WELL, I FOUND ONE GOOD THING ABOUT BEING AN OFFICER.
IT'S A LOT EASIER TO GET-
-FOOD.

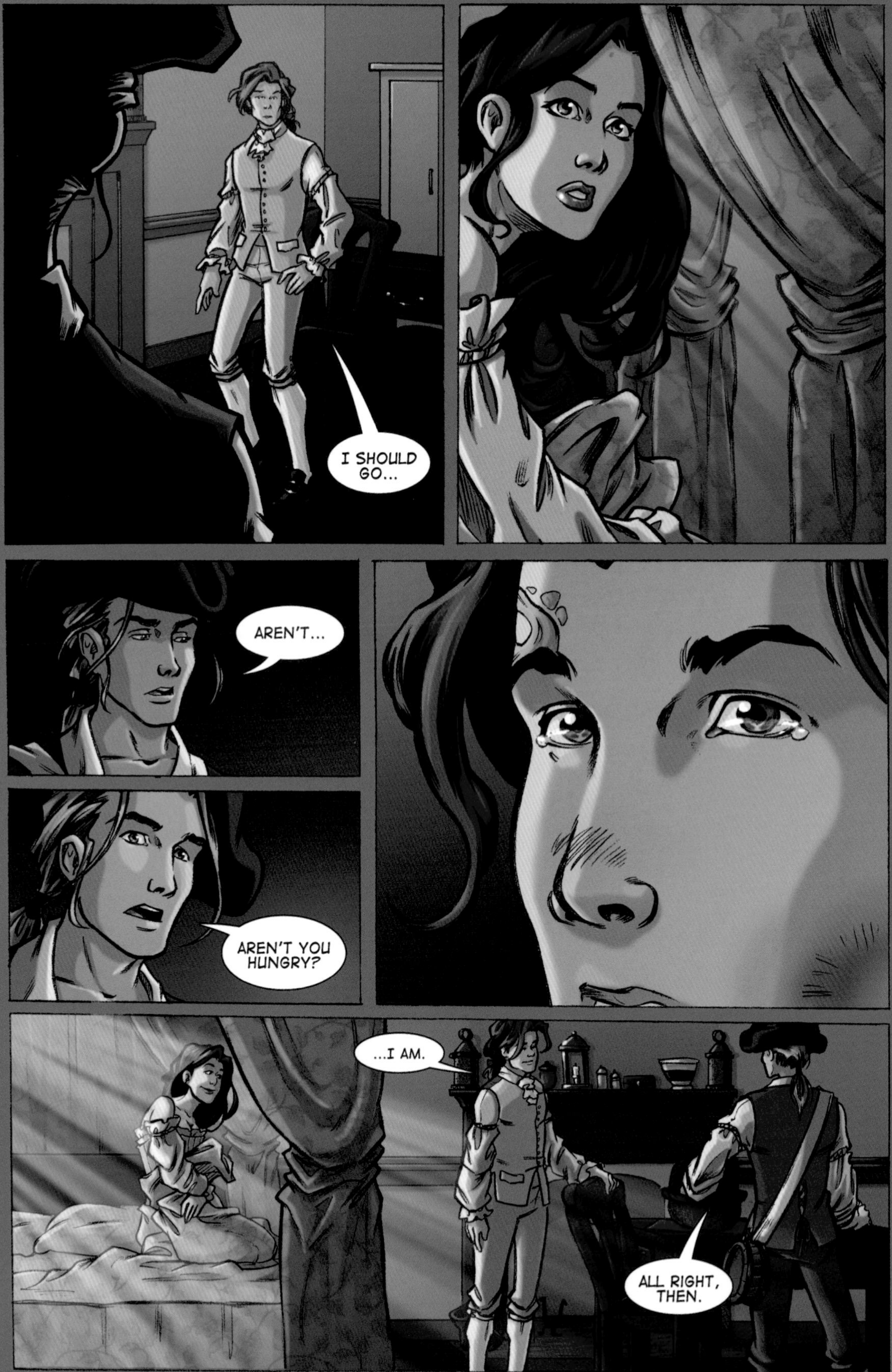
I SHOULD GO...
AREN'T...
AREN'T YOU HUNGRY?
...I AM.
ALL RIGHT, THEN.

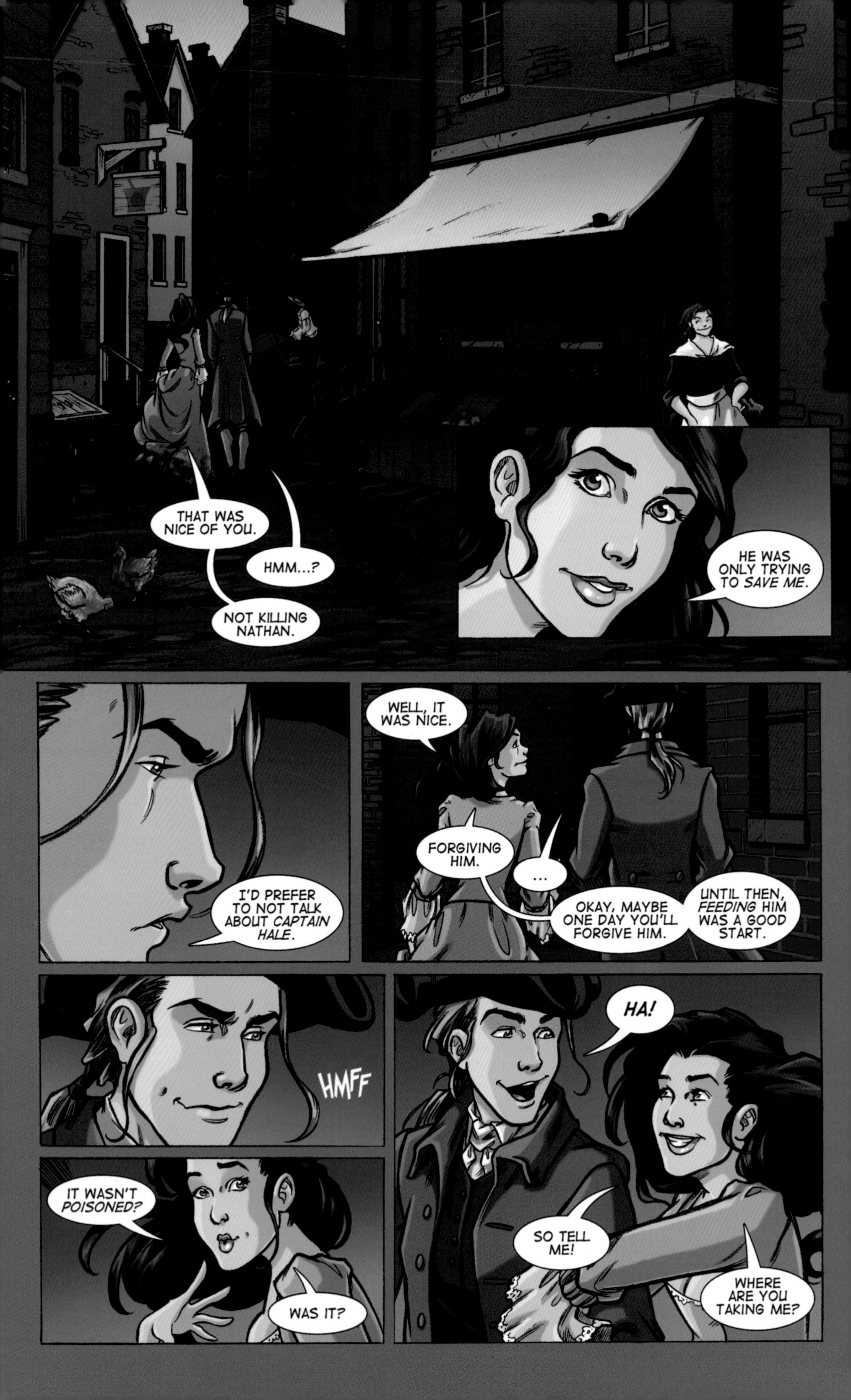
THAT WAS NICE OF YOU.
HMM...?
NOT KILLING NATHAN.
HE WAS ONLY TRYING TO *SAVE ME*.
I'D PREFER TO NOT TALK ABOUT *CAPTAIN HALE*.
WELL, IT WAS NICE.
FORGIVING HIM.
...
OKAY, MAYBE ONE DAY YOU'LL FORGIVE HIM.
UNTIL THEN, *FEEDING* HIM WAS A GOOD START.
HMFF
IT WASN'T *POISONED*?
WAS IT?
HA!
SO TELL ME!
WHERE ARE YOU TAKING ME?

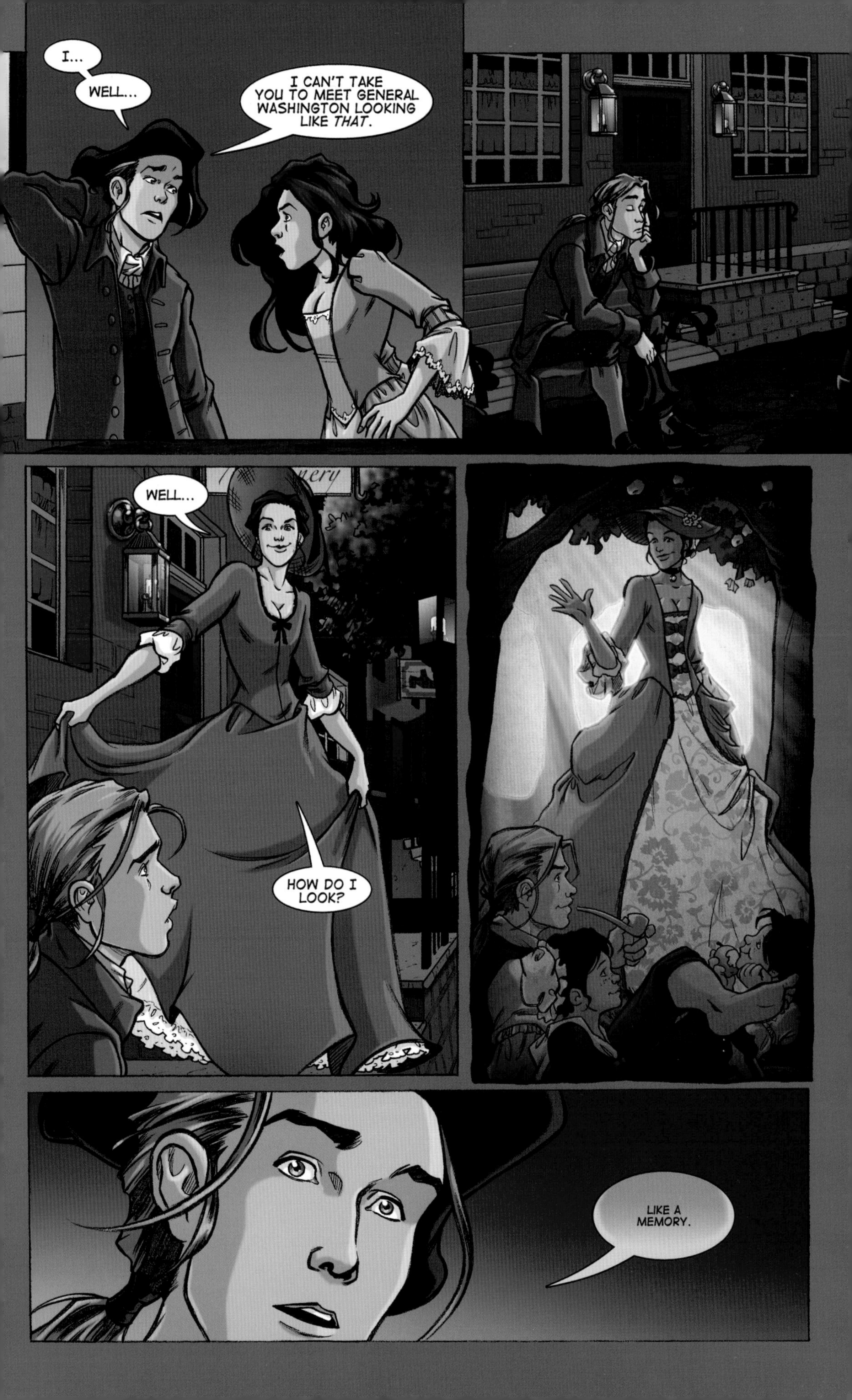
I...
WELL...
I CAN'T TAKE YOU TO MEET GENERAL WASHINGTON LOOKING LIKE *THAT*.
WELL...
HOW DO I LOOK?
LIKE A MEMORY.

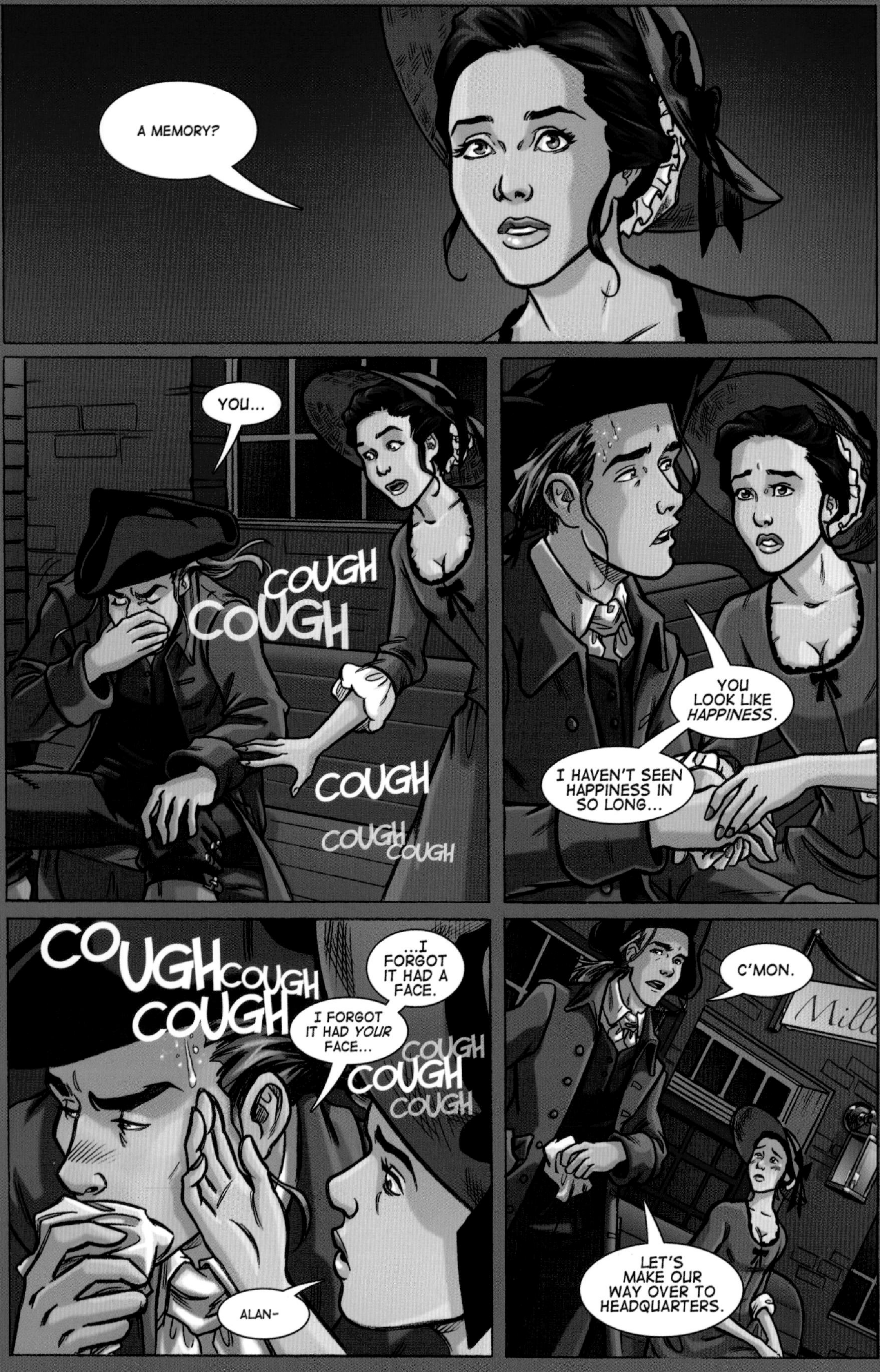
A MEMORY?
YOU...
COUGH
COUGH
COUGH
COUGH COUGH
YOU LOOK LIKE HAPPINESS.
I HAVEN'T SEEN HAPPINESS IN SO LONG...
COUGH COUGH
COUGH
...I FORGOT IT HAD A FACE.
I FORGOT IT HAD YOUR FACE...
COUGH
COUGH
COUGH
ALAN-
C'MON.
LET'S MAKE OUR WAY OVER TO HEADQUARTERS.

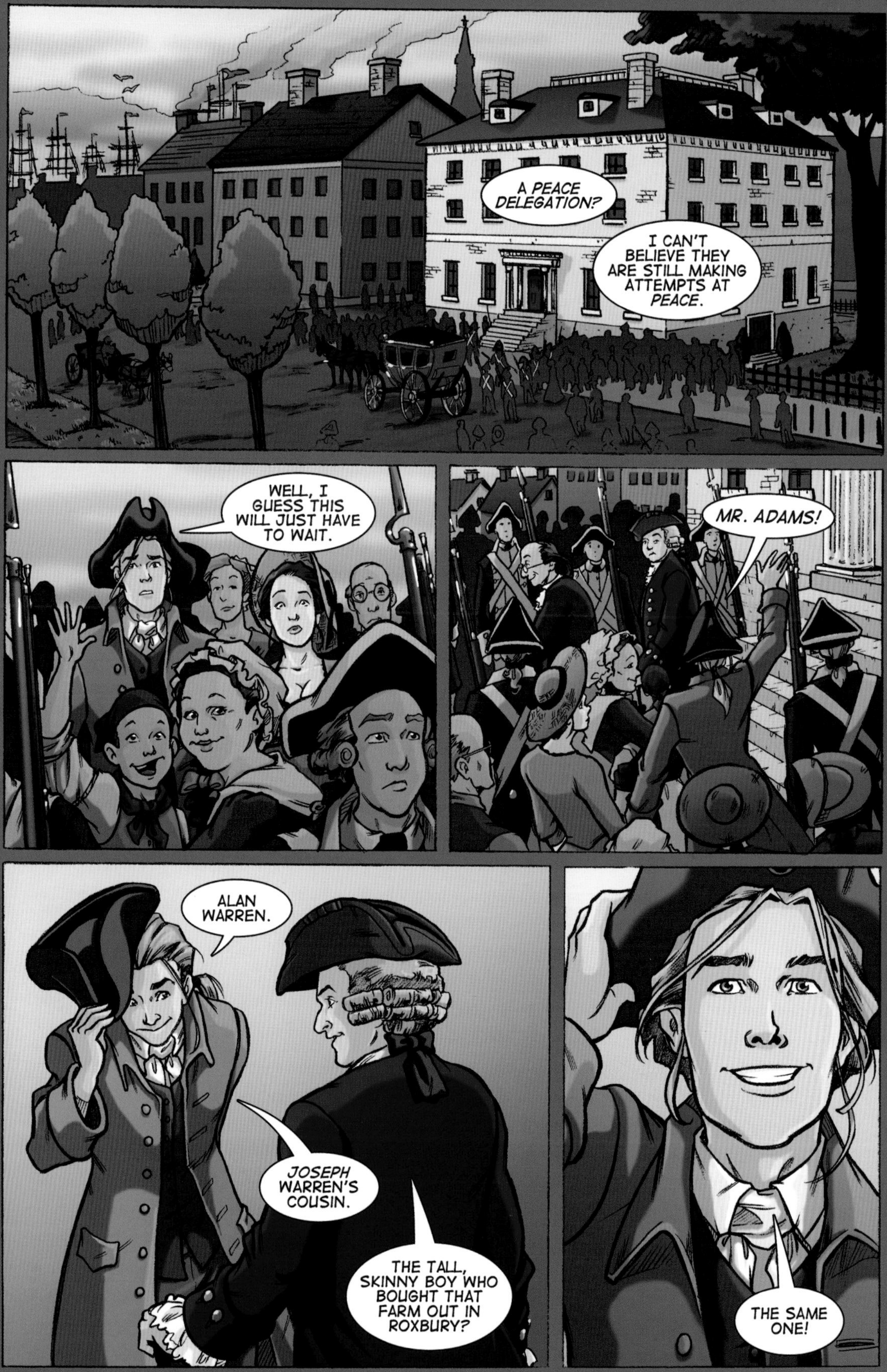

A *PEACE* DELEGATION?
I CAN'T BELIEVE THEY ARE STILL MAKING ATTEMPTS AT *PEACE*.
WELL, I GUESS THIS WILL JUST HAVE TO WAIT.
MR. ADAMS!
ALAN WARREN.
JOSEPH WARREN'S COUSIN.
THE TALL, SKINNY BOY WHO BOUGHT THAT FARM OUT IN ROXBURY?
THE SAME ONE!

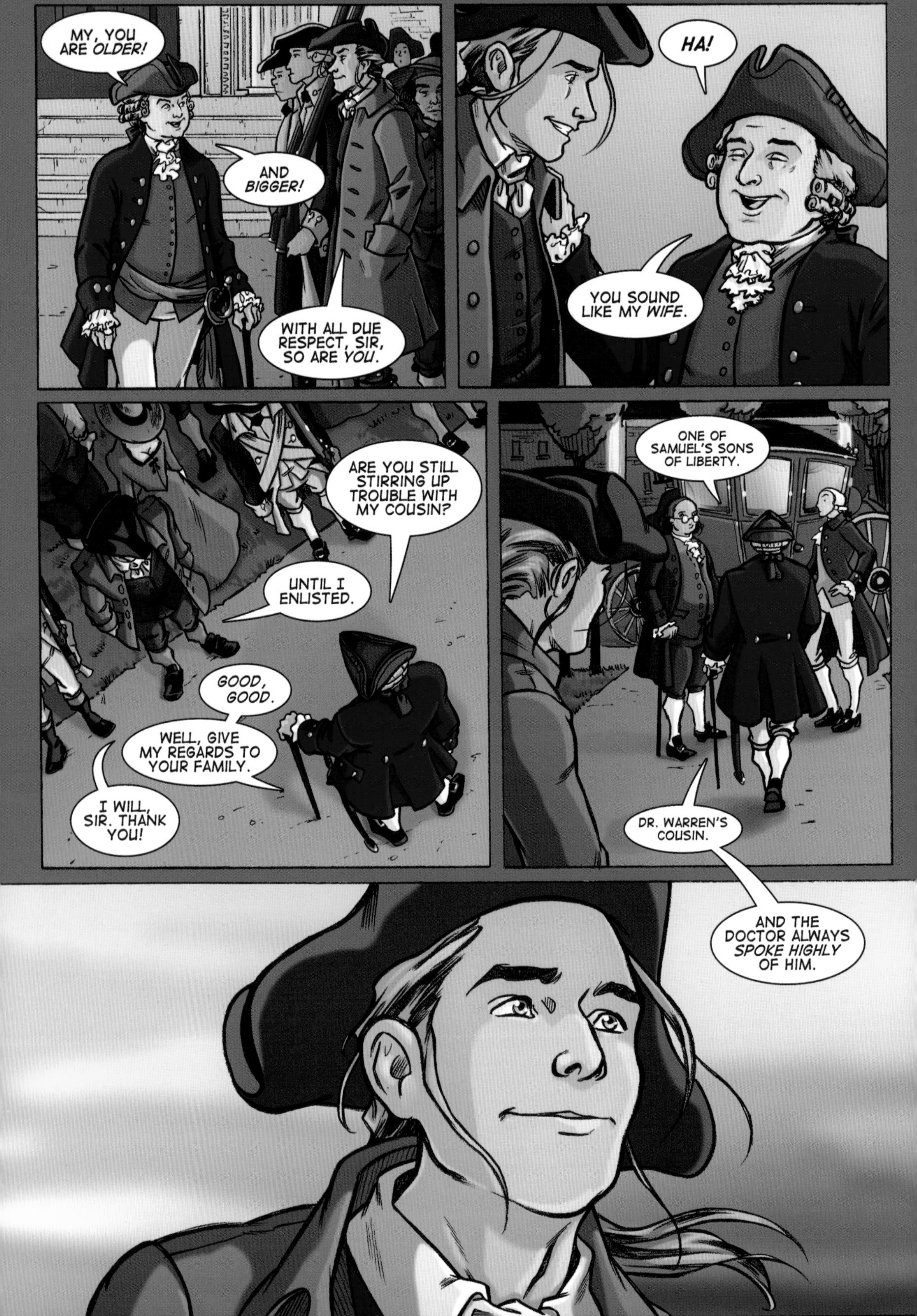
MY, YOU ARE *OLDER!*
AND *BIGGER!*
WITH ALL DUE RESPECT, SIR, SO ARE *YOU*.
HA!
YOU SOUND LIKE MY *WIFE*.
ARE YOU STILL STIRRING UP TROUBLE WITH MY COUSIN?
UNTIL I ENLISTED.
GOOD, GOOD.
WELL, GIVE MY REGARDS TO YOUR FAMILY.
I WILL, SIR. THANK YOU!
ONE OF SAMUEL'S SONS OF LIBERTY.
DR. WARREN'S COUSIN.
AND THE DOCTOR ALWAYS *SPOKE HIGHLY* OF HIM.

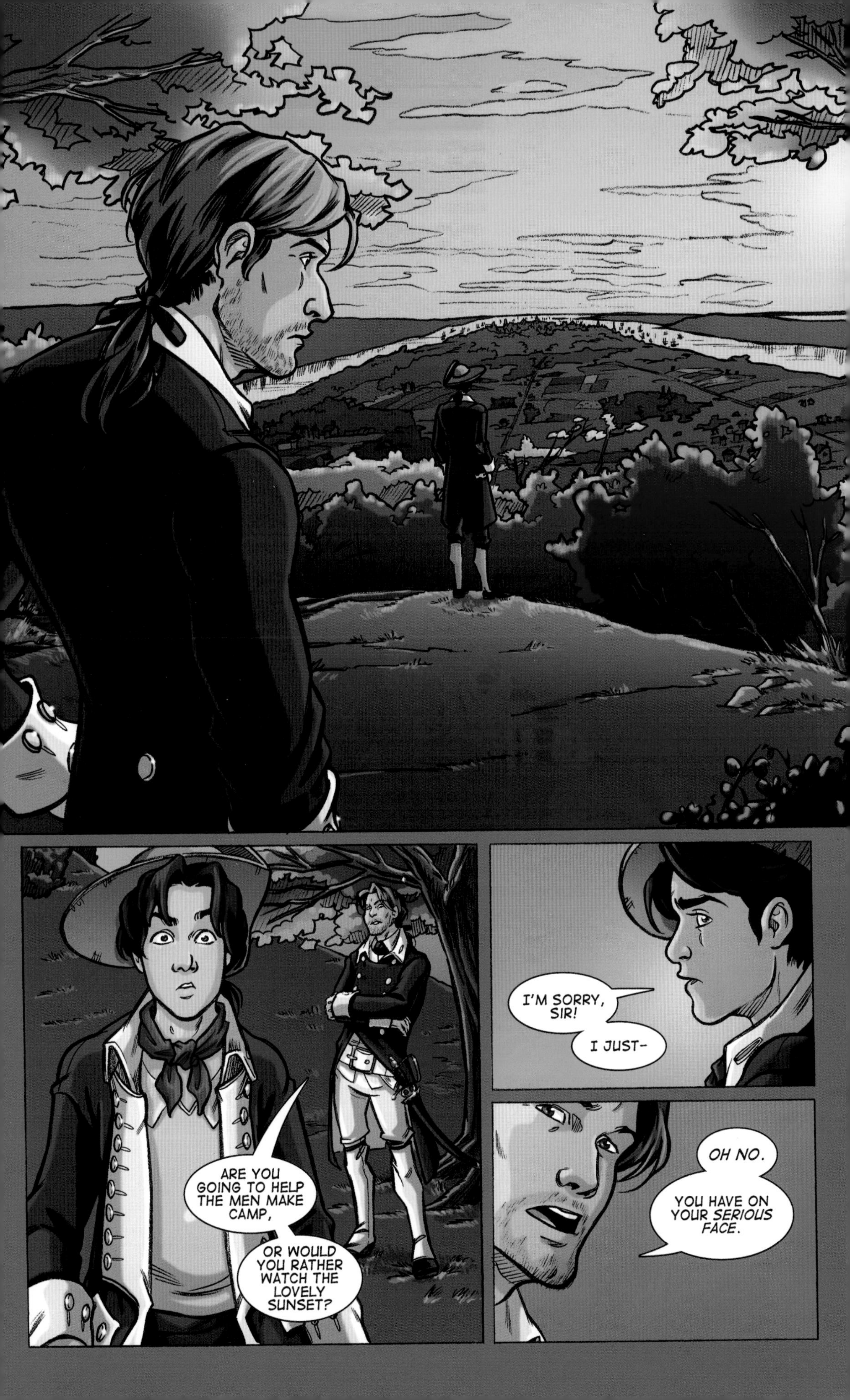
ARE YOU GOING TO HELP THE MEN MAKE CAMP,
OR WOULD YOU RATHER WATCH THE LOVELY SUNSET?
I'M SORRY, SIR!
I JUST-
OH NO.
YOU HAVE ON YOUR *SERIOUS* FACE.

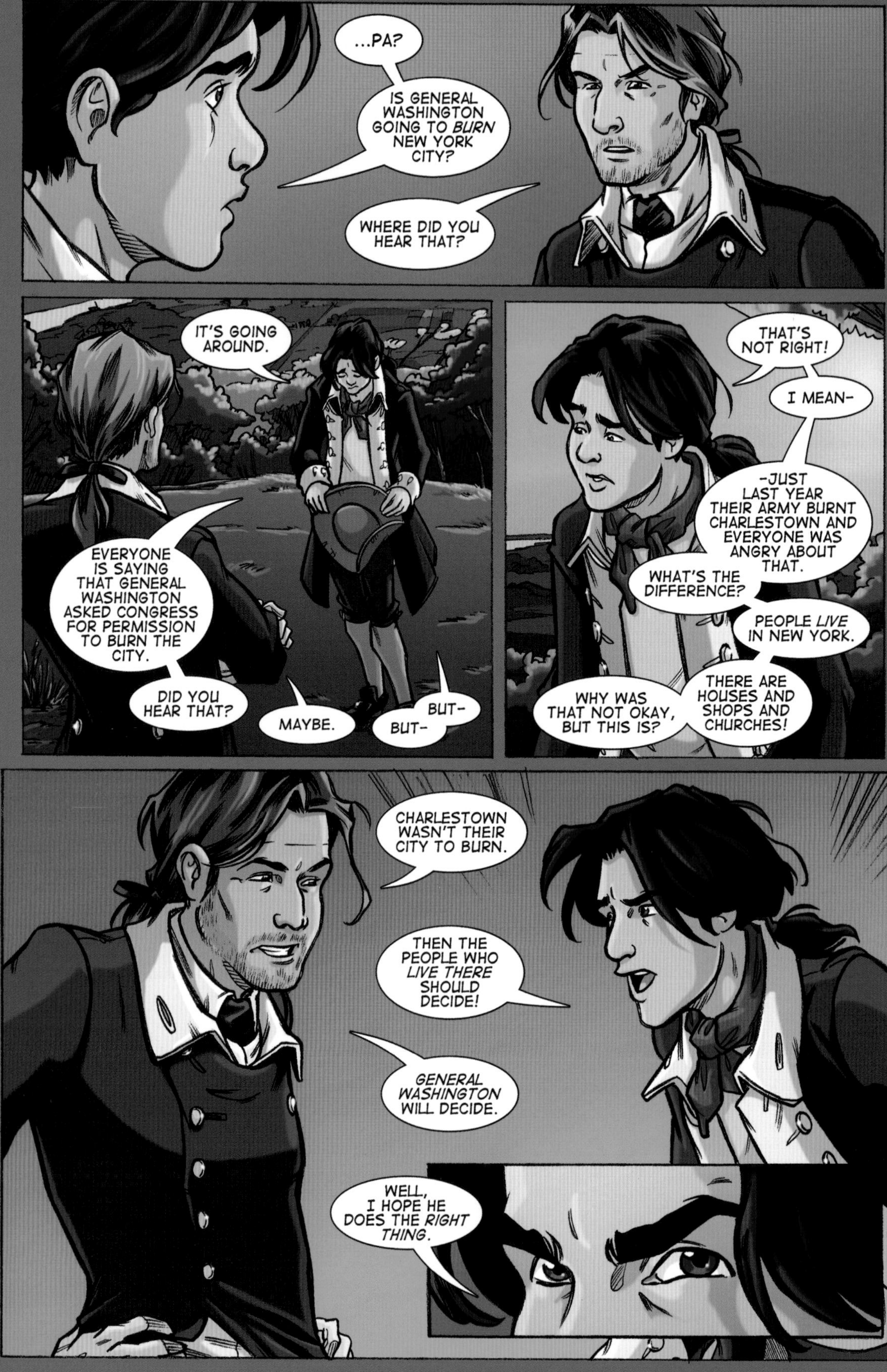
...PA?
IS GENERAL WASHINGTON GOING TO *BURN* NEW YORK CITY?
WHERE DID YOU HEAR THAT?
IT'S GOING AROUND.
EVERYONE IS SAYING THAT GENERAL WASHINGTON ASKED CONGRESS FOR PERMISSION TO BURN THE CITY.
DID YOU HEAR THAT?
MAYBE.
BUT-
BUT-
THAT'S NOT RIGHT!
I MEAN-
-JUST LAST YEAR THEIR ARMY BURNT CHARLESTOWN AND EVERYONE WAS ANGRY ABOUT THAT.
WHAT'S THE DIFFERENCE?
PEOPLE *LIVE* IN NEW YORK.
THERE ARE HOUSES AND SHOPS AND CHURCHES!
WHY WAS THAT NOT OKAY, BUT THIS IS?
CHARLESTOWN WASN'T THEIR CITY TO BURN.
THEN THE PEOPLE WHO *LIVE THERE* SHOULD DECIDE!
GENERAL WASHINGTON WILL DECIDE.
WELL, I HOPE HE DOES THE *RIGHT THING*.

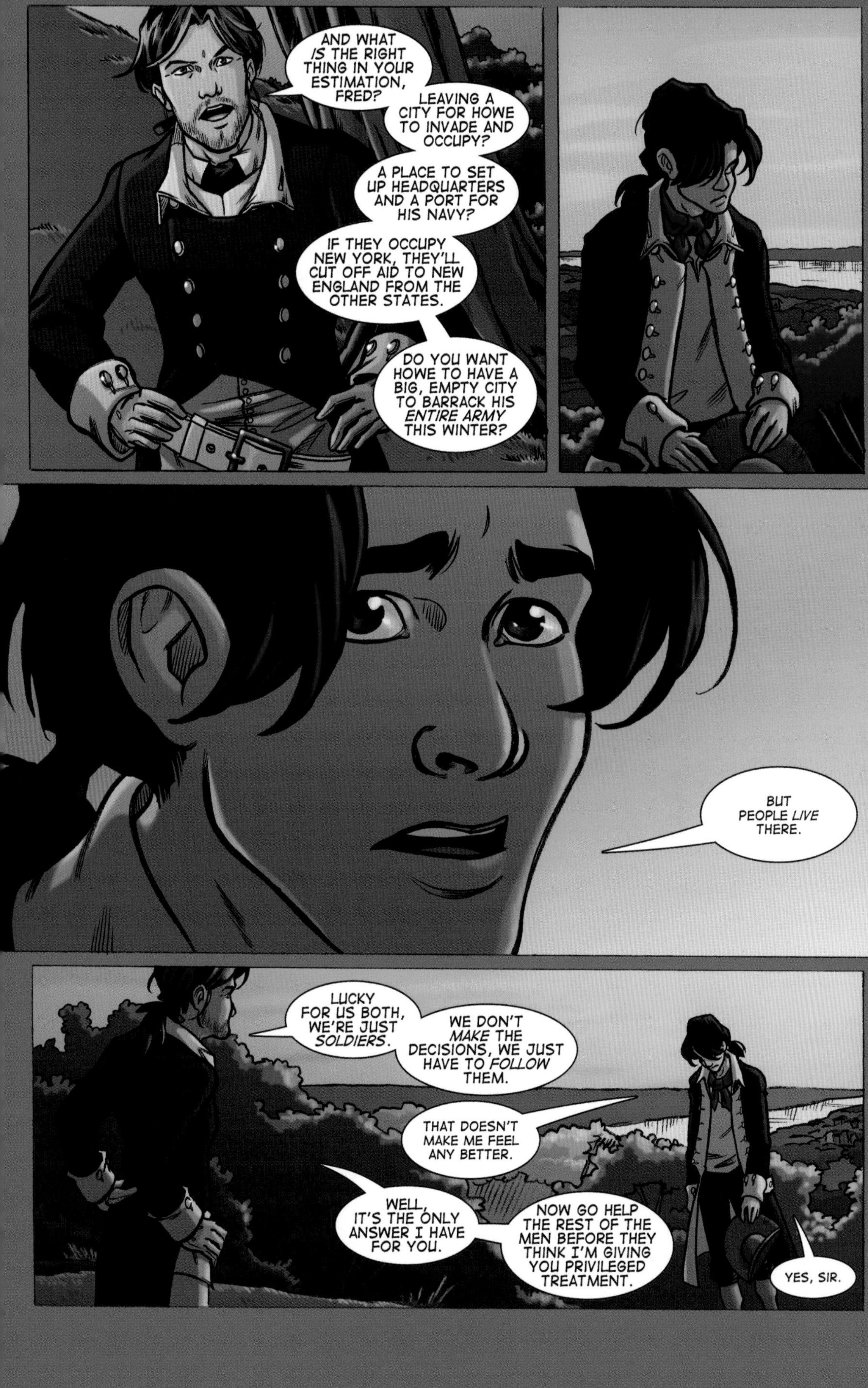

AND WHAT *IS* THE RIGHT THING IN YOUR ESTIMATION, FRED?
LEAVING A CITY FOR HOWE TO INVADE AND OCCUPY?
A PLACE TO SET UP HEADQUARTERS AND A PORT FOR HIS NAVY?
IF THEY OCCUPY NEW YORK, THEY'LL CUT OFF AID TO NEW ENGLAND FROM THE OTHER STATES.
DO YOU WANT HOWE TO HAVE A BIG, EMPTY CITY TO BARRACK HIS *ENTIRE ARMY* THIS WINTER?
BUT PEOPLE *LIVE* THERE.
LUCKY FOR US BOTH, WE'RE JUST *SOLDIERS*.
WE DON'T *MAKE* THE DECISIONS, WE JUST HAVE TO *FOLLOW* THEM.
THAT DOESN'T MAKE ME FEEL ANY BETTER.
WELL, IT'S THE ONLY ANSWER I HAVE FOR YOU.
NOW GO HELP THE REST OF THE MEN BEFORE THEY THINK I'M GIVING YOU PRIVILEGED TREATMENT.
YES, SIR.

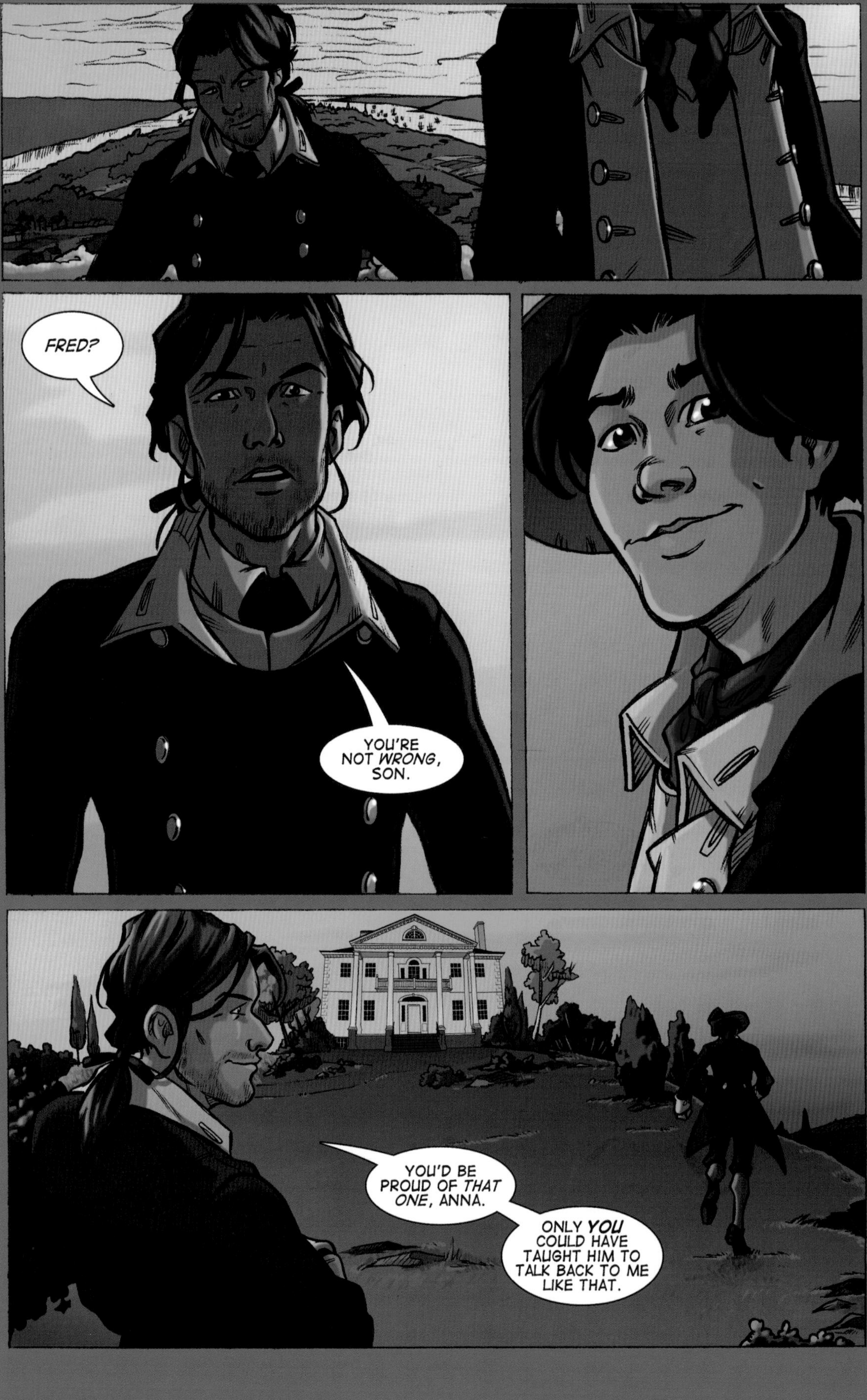
FRED?
YOU'RE NOT *WRONG*, SON.
YOU'D BE PROUD OF *THAT ONE*, ANNA.
ONLY ***YOU*** COULD HAVE TAUGHT HIM TO TALK BACK TO ME LIKE THAT.

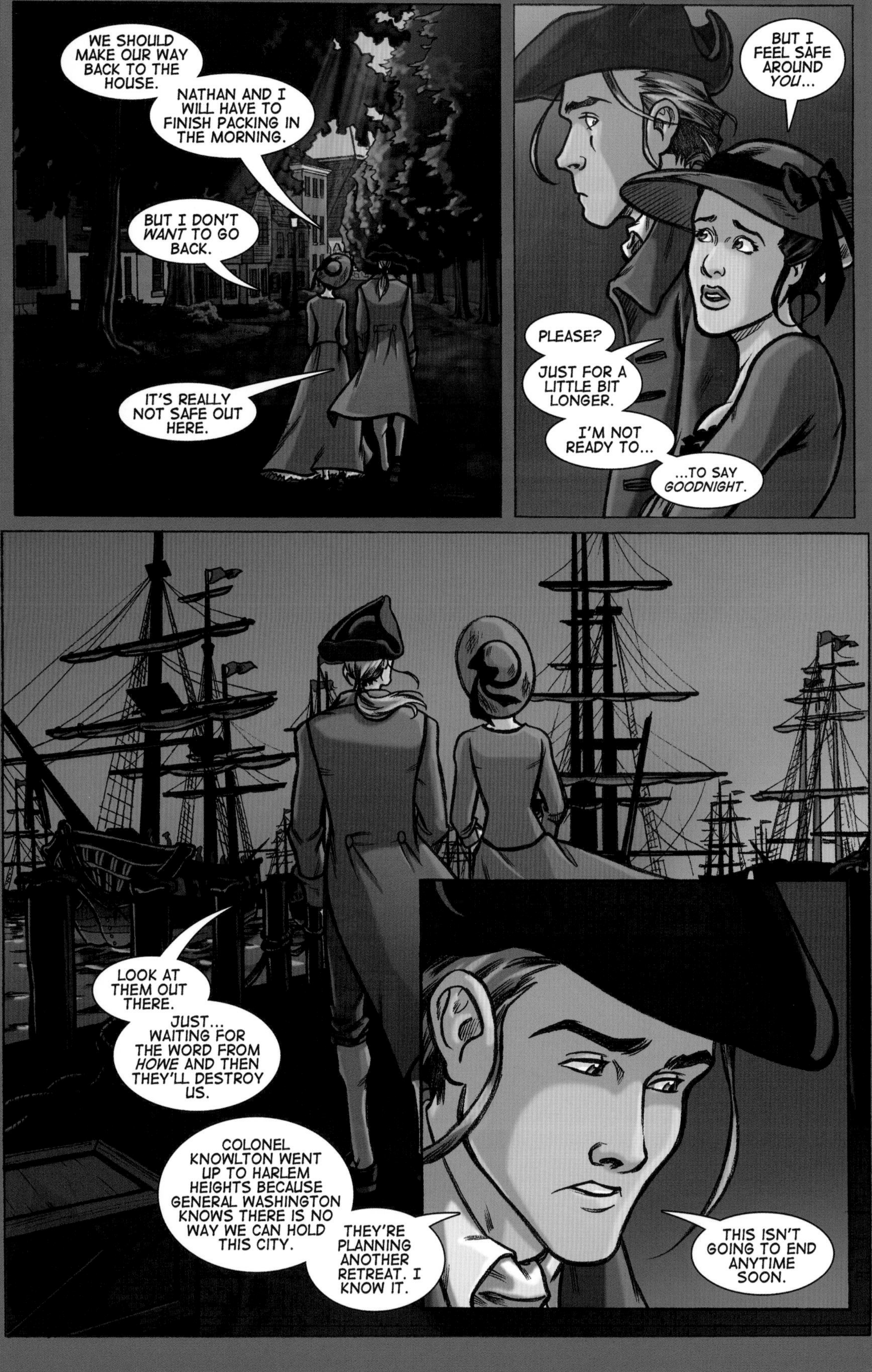
WE SHOULD MAKE OUR WAY BACK TO THE HOUSE.
NATHAN AND I WILL HAVE TO FINISH PACKING IN THE MORNING.
BUT I DON'T *WANT* TO GO BACK.
IT'S REALLY NOT SAFE OUT HERE.
BUT I FEEL SAFE AROUND *YOU*...
PLEASE?
JUST FOR A LITTLE BIT LONGER.
I'M NOT READY TO...
...TO SAY *GOODNIGHT*.
LOOK AT THEM OUT THERE.
JUST... WAITING FOR THE WORD FROM *HOWE* AND THEN THEY'LL DESTROY US.
COLONEL KNOWLTON WENT UP TO HARLEM HEIGHTS BECAUSE GENERAL WASHINGTON KNOWS THERE IS NO WAY WE CAN HOLD THIS CITY.
THEY'RE PLANNING ANOTHER RETREAT. I KNOW IT.
THIS ISN'T GOING TO END ANYTIME SOON.

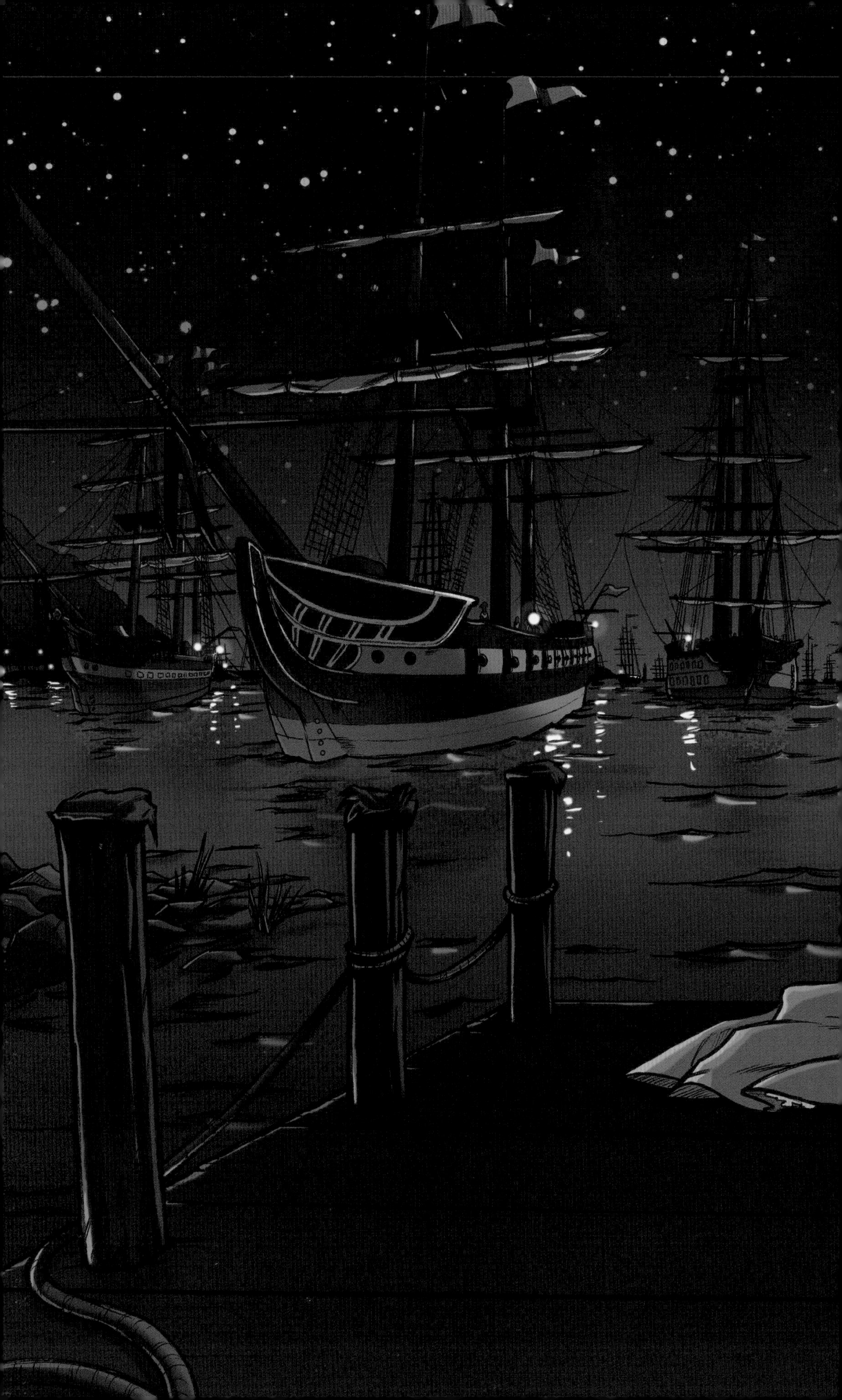

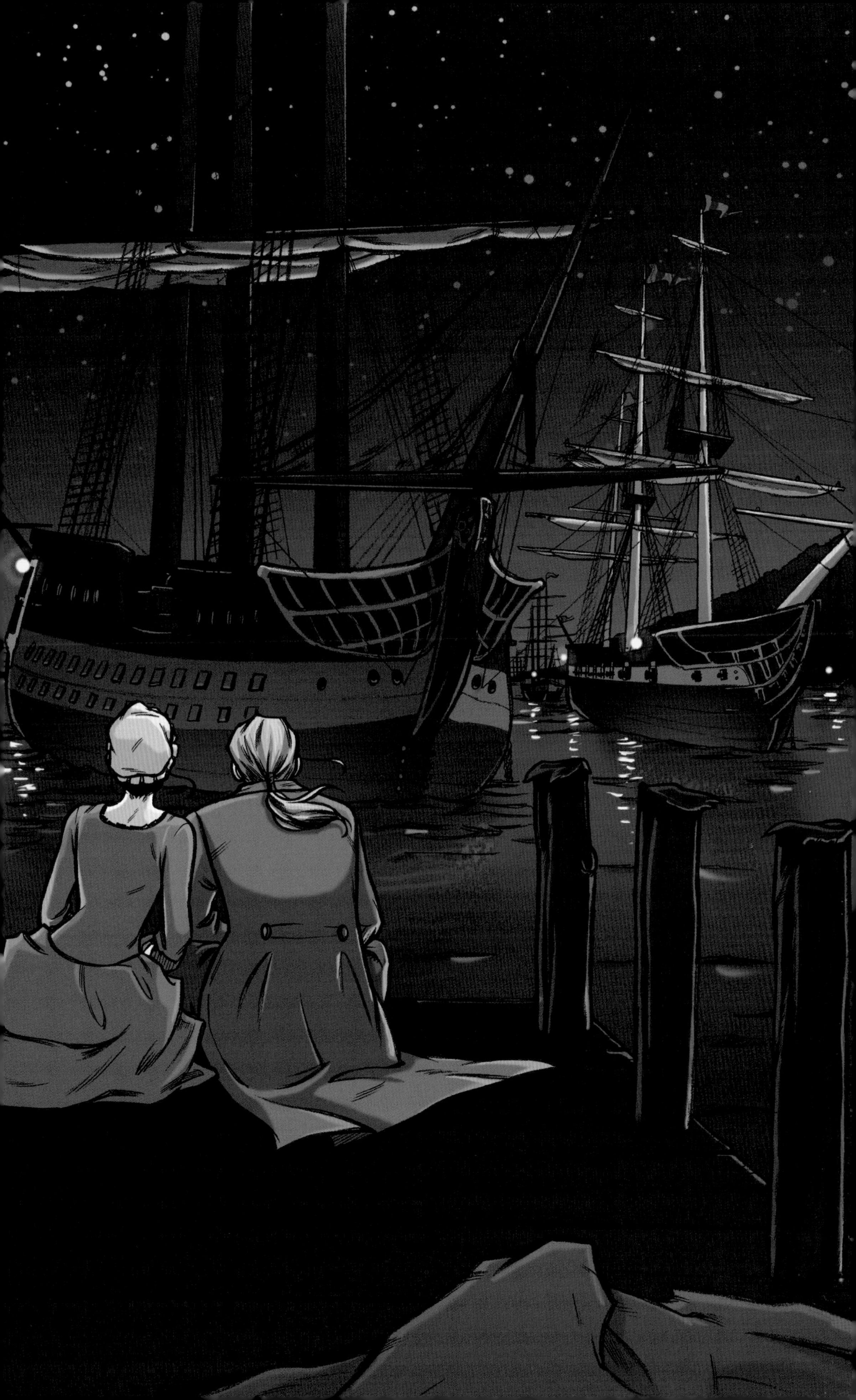

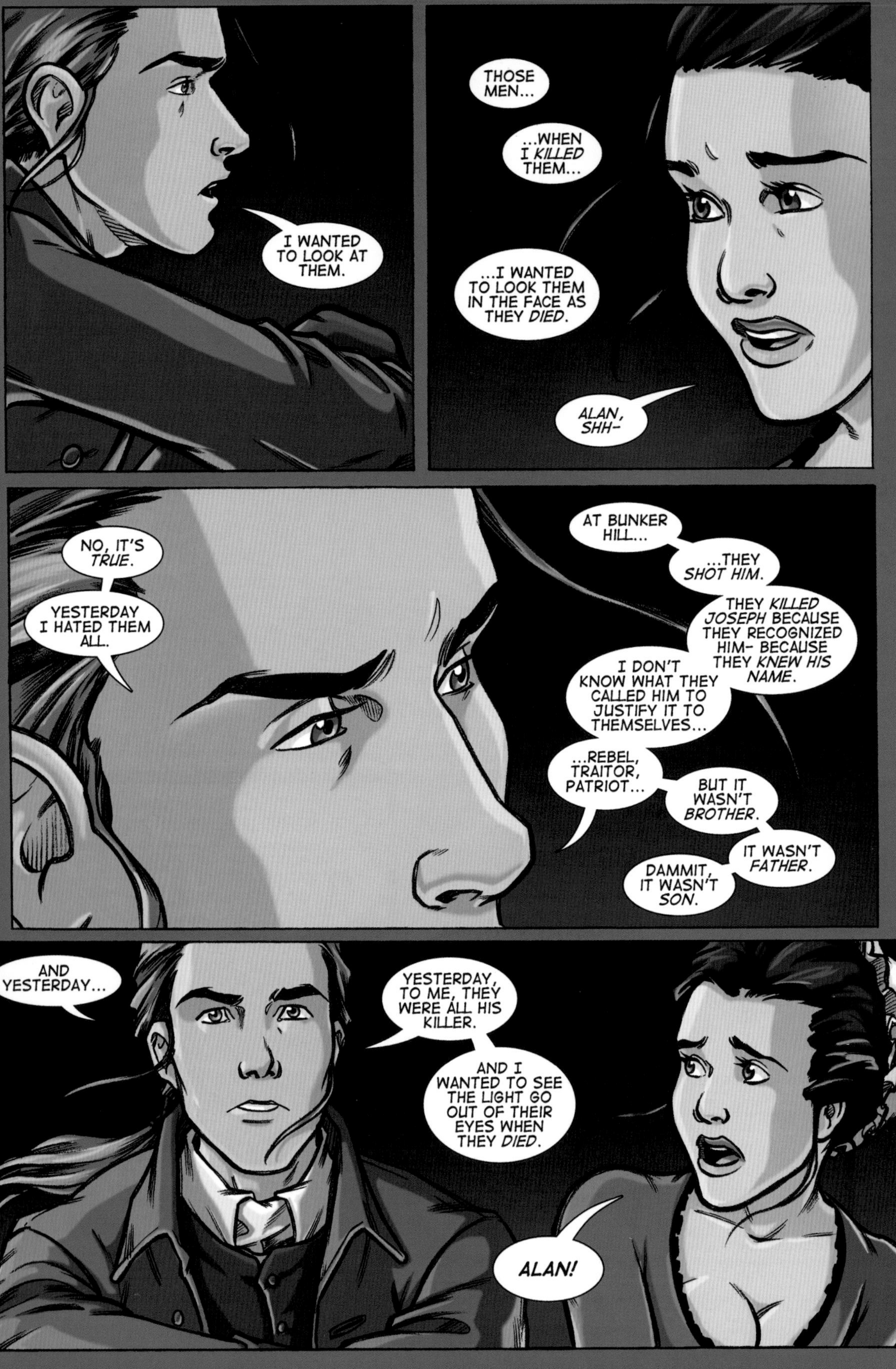
I WANTED TO LOOK AT THEM.
THOSE MEN...
...WHEN I KILLED THEM...
...I WANTED TO LOOK THEM IN THE FACE AS THEY DIED.
ALAN, SHH-
NO, IT'S TRUE.
YESTERDAY I HATED THEM ALL.
AT BUNKER HILL...
...THEY SHOT HIM.
THEY KILLED JOSEPH BECAUSE THEY RECOGNIZED HIM- BECAUSE THEY KNEW HIS NAME.
I DON'T KNOW WHAT THEY CALLED HIM TO JUSTIFY IT TO THEMSELVES...
...REBEL, TRAITOR, PATRIOT...
BUT IT WASN'T BROTHER.
IT WASN'T FATHER.
DAMMIT, IT WASN'T SON.
AND YESTERDAY...
YESTERDAY, TO ME, THEY WERE ALL HIS KILLER.
AND I WANTED TO SEE THE LIGHT GO OUT OF THEIR EYES WHEN THEY DIED.
ALAN!

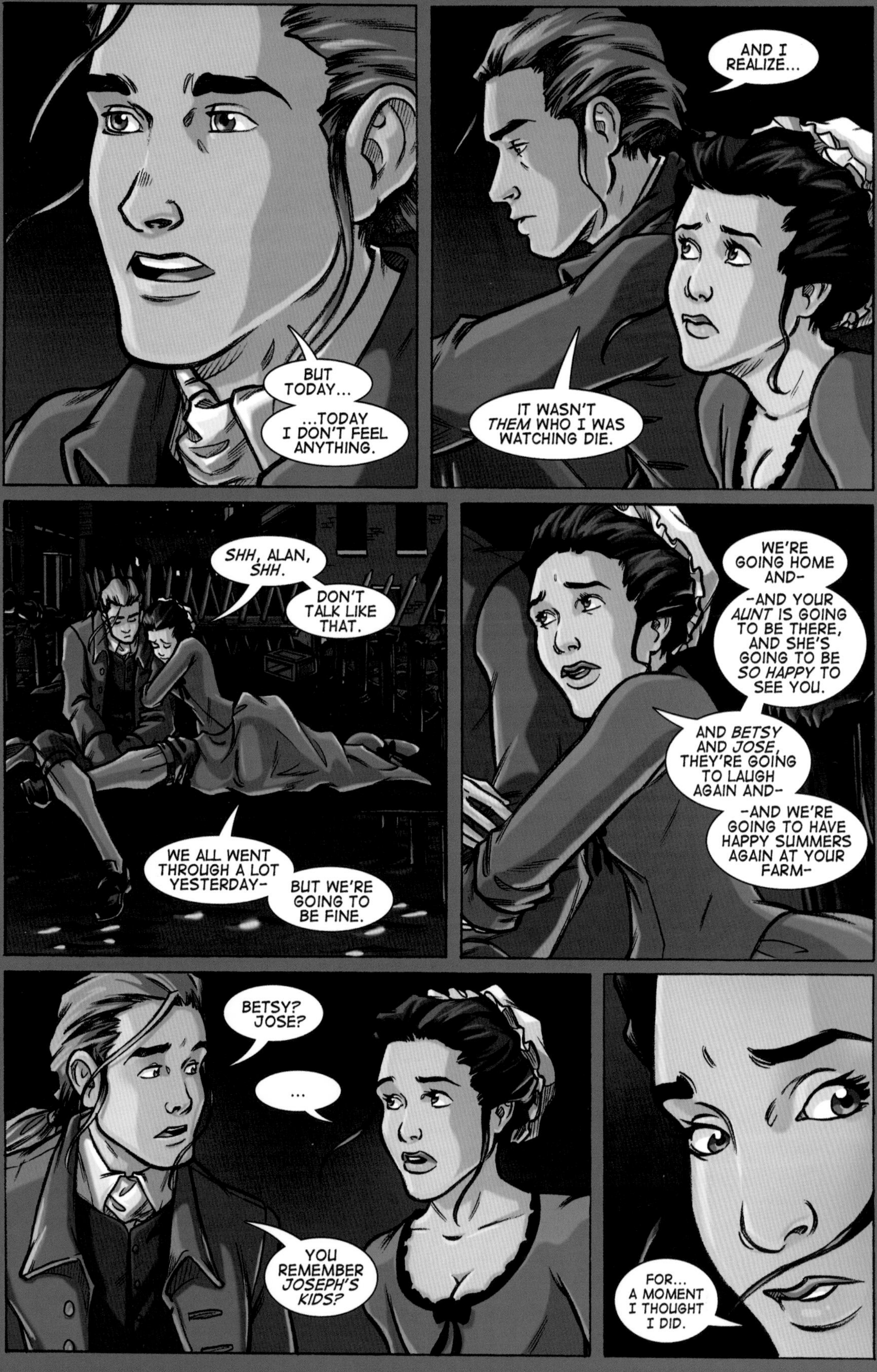
BUT TODAY...
...TODAY I DON'T FEEL ANYTHING.
AND I REALIZE...
IT WASN'T *THEM* WHO I WAS WATCHING DIE.
SHH, ALAN, *SHH*.
DON'T TALK LIKE THAT.
WE ALL WENT THROUGH A LOT YESTERDAY-
BUT WE'RE GOING TO BE FINE.
WE'RE GOING HOME AND-
-AND YOUR *AUNT* IS GOING TO BE THERE, AND SHE'S GOING TO BE *SO HAPPY* TO SEE YOU.
AND *BETSY* AND *JOSE*, THEY'RE GOING TO LAUGH AGAIN AND-
-AND WE'RE GOING TO HAVE HAPPY SUMMERS AGAIN AT YOUR FARM-
BETSY? JOSE?
...
YOU REMEMBER *JOSEPH'S KIDS*?
FOR... A MOMENT I THOUGHT I DID.

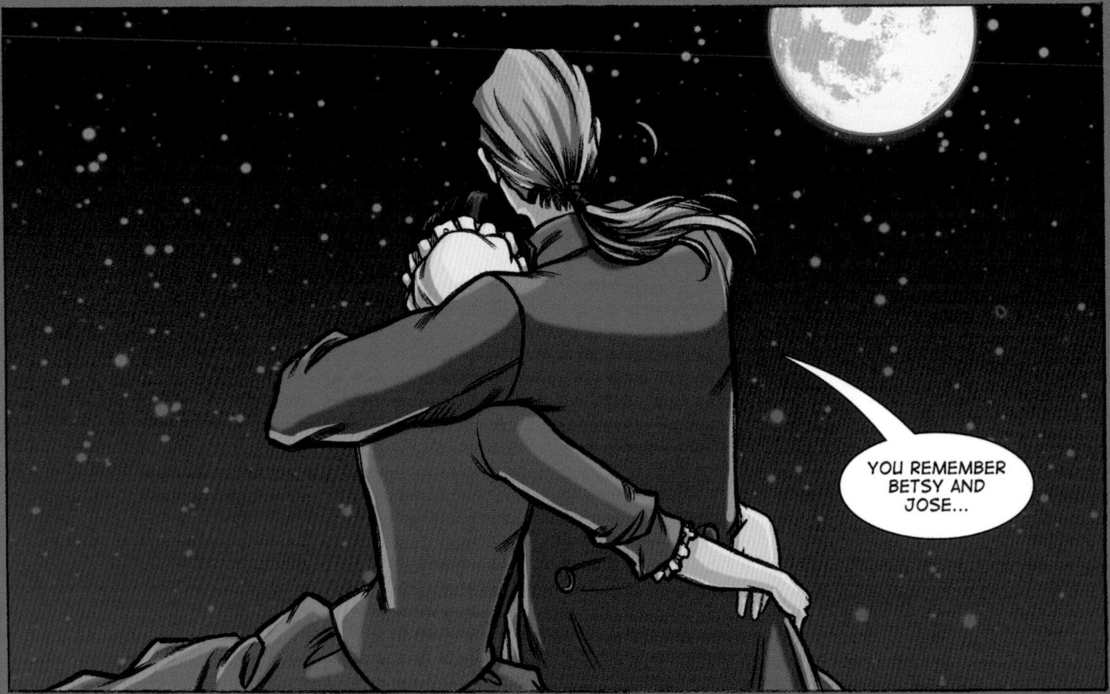
YOU REMEMBER BETSY AND JOSE...

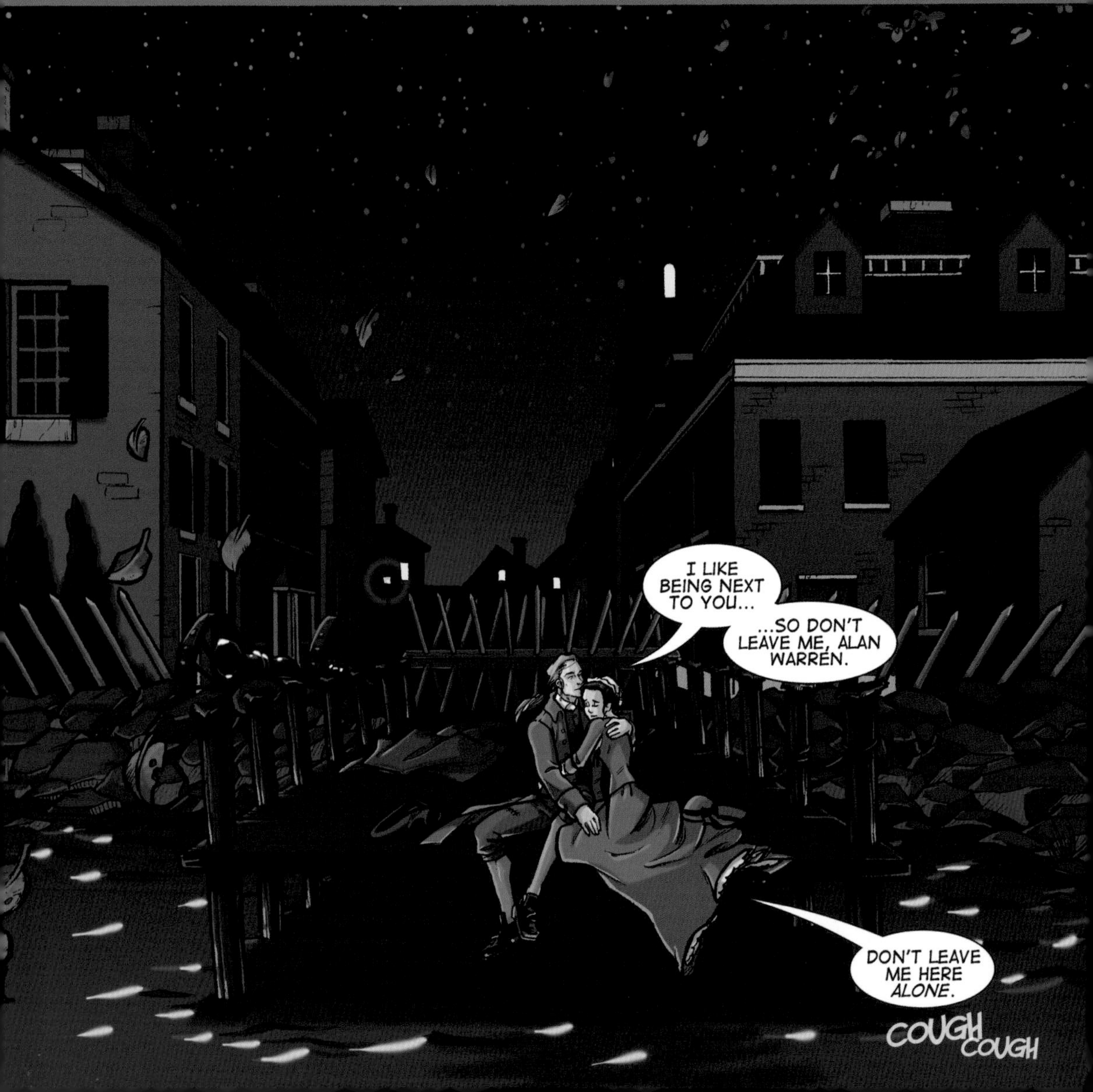
I LIKE BEING NEXT TO YOU...
...SO DON'T LEAVE ME, ALAN WARREN.
DON'T LEAVE ME HERE *ALONE*.
COUGH COUGH

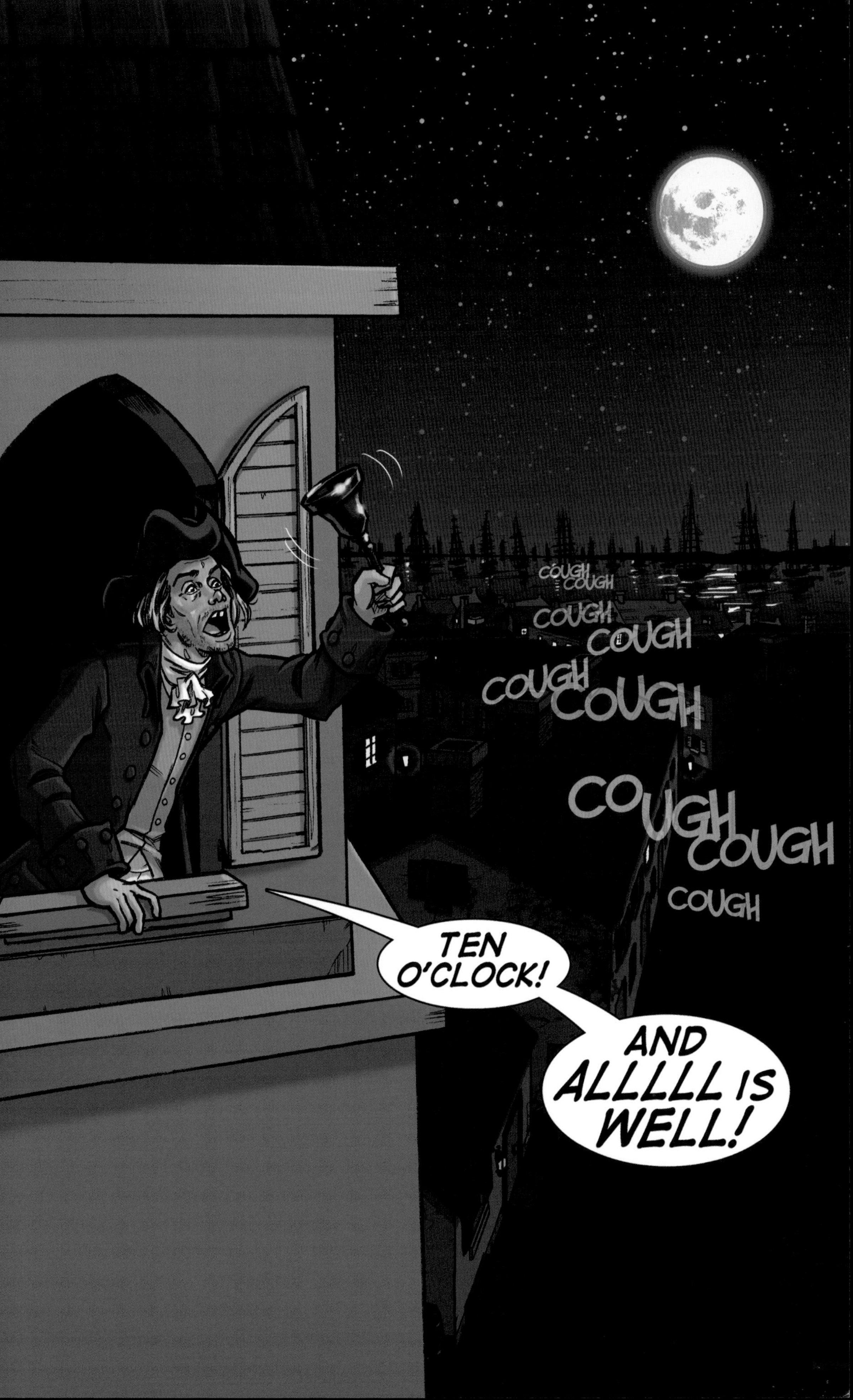
COUGH COUGH
COUGH
COUGH
COUGH COUGH
COUGH COUGH
COUGH
TEN O'CLOCK!
AND ALLLLL IS WELL!

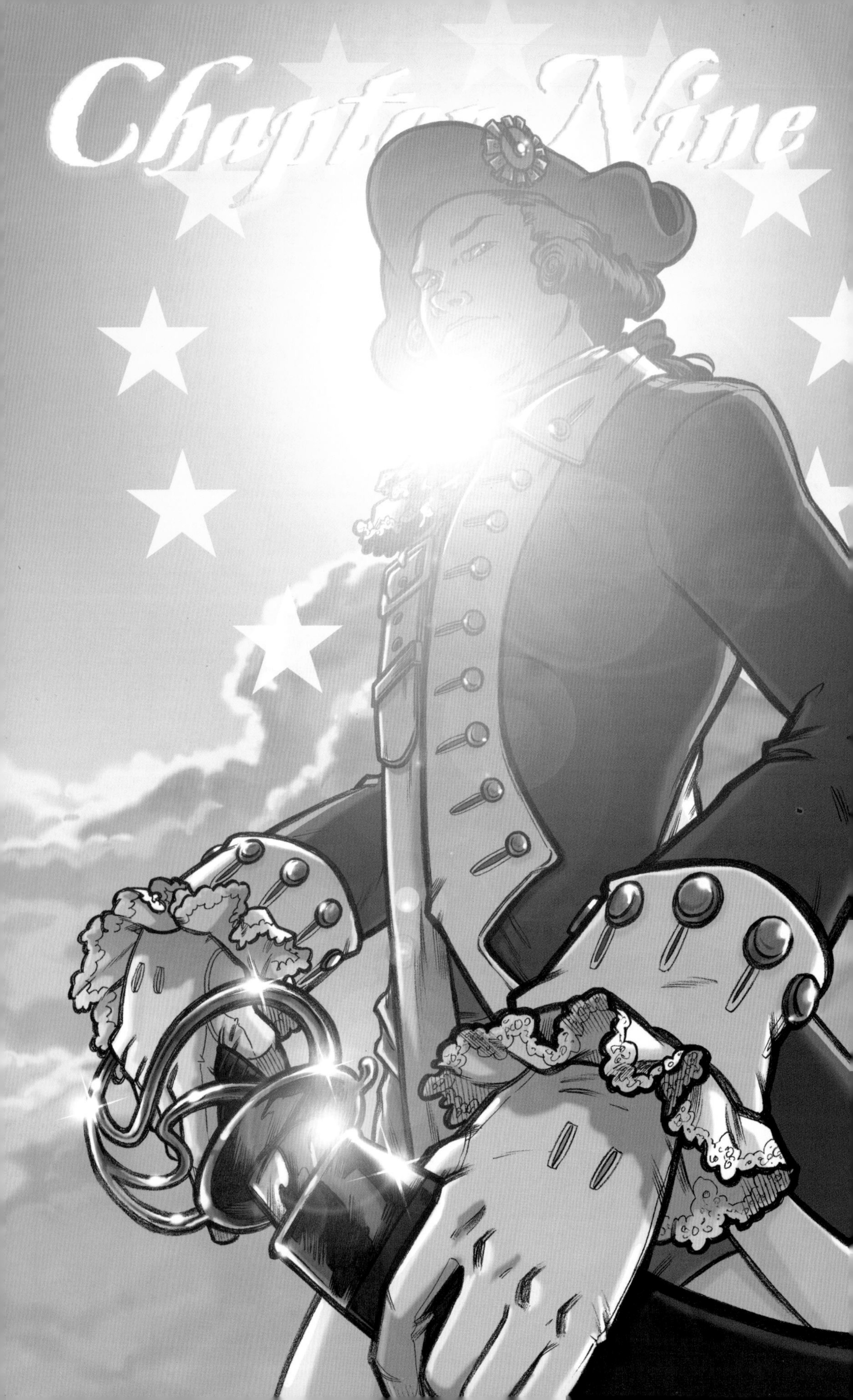
Chapter Nine

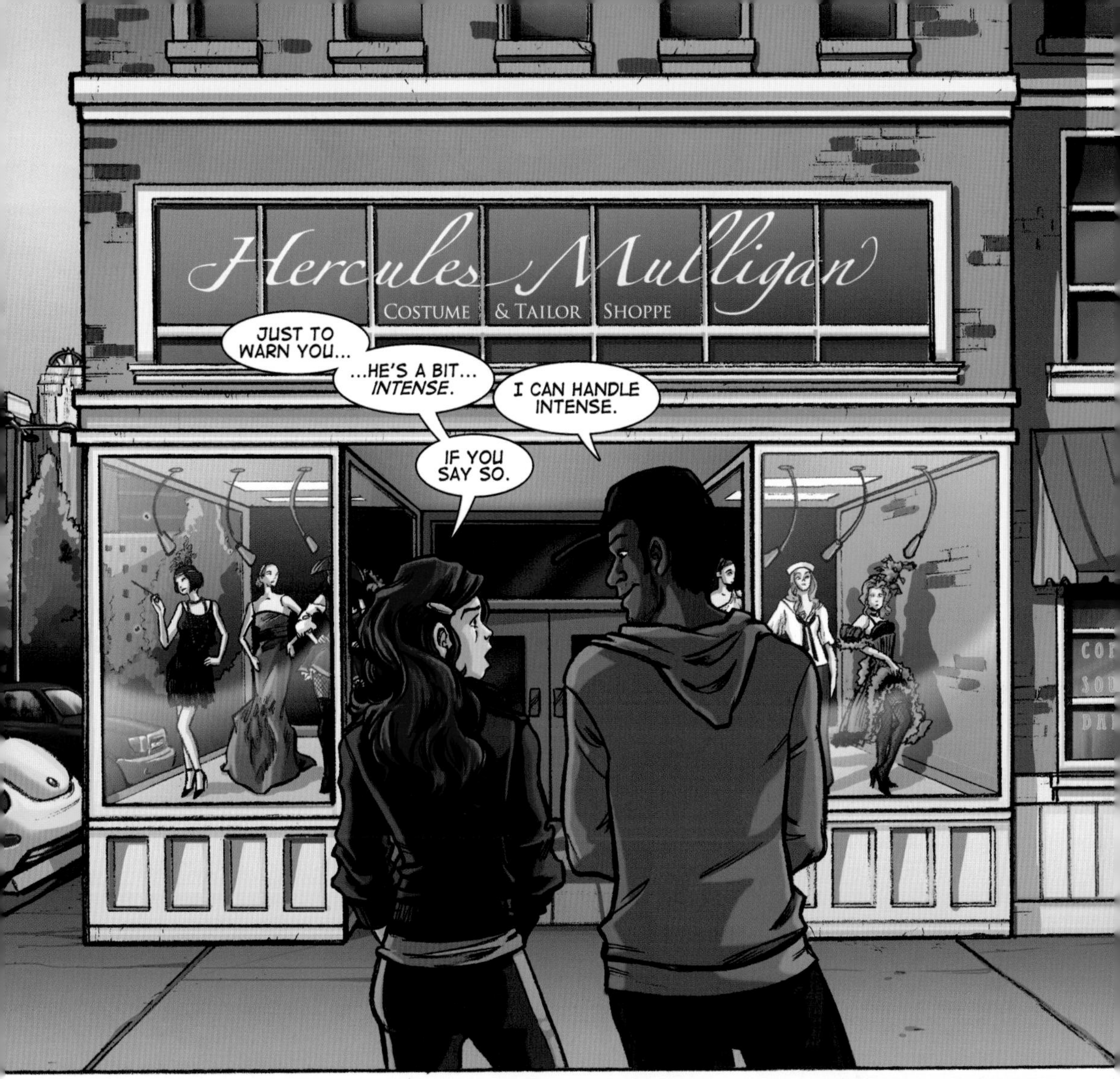
Hercules Mulligan
COSTUME & TAILOR SHOPPE
JUST TO WARN YOU...
...HE'S A BIT... *INTENSE*.
I CAN HANDLE INTENSE.
IF YOU SAY SO.

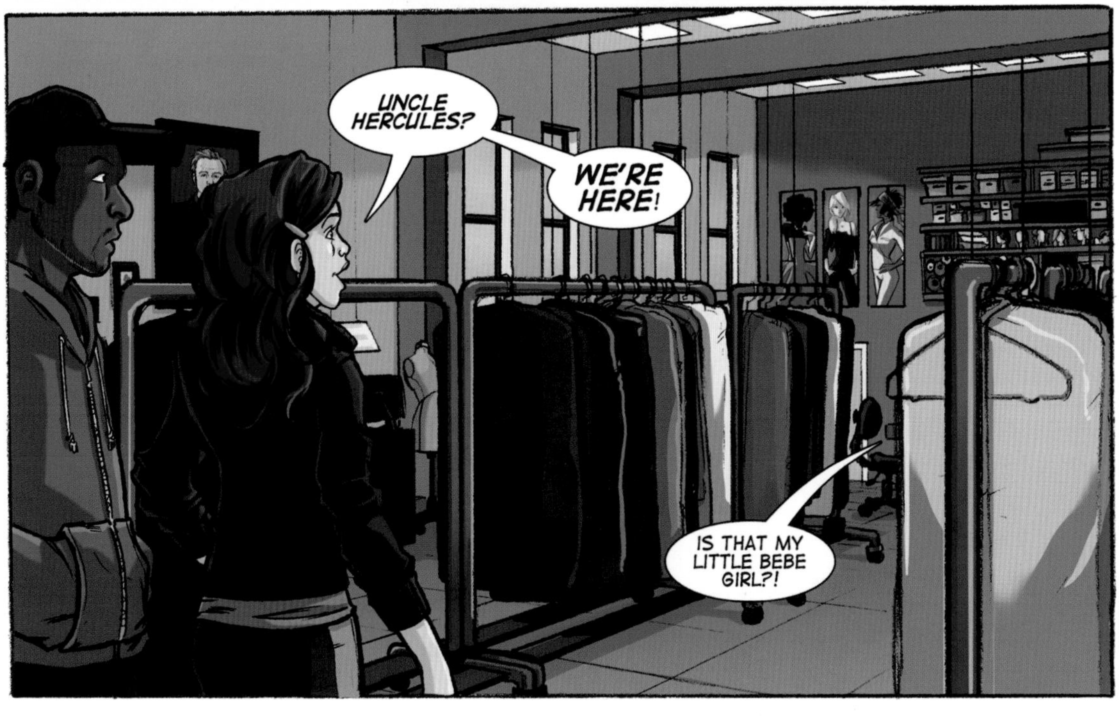
UNCLE HERCULES?
WE'RE HERE!
IS THAT MY LITTLE BEBE GIRL?!

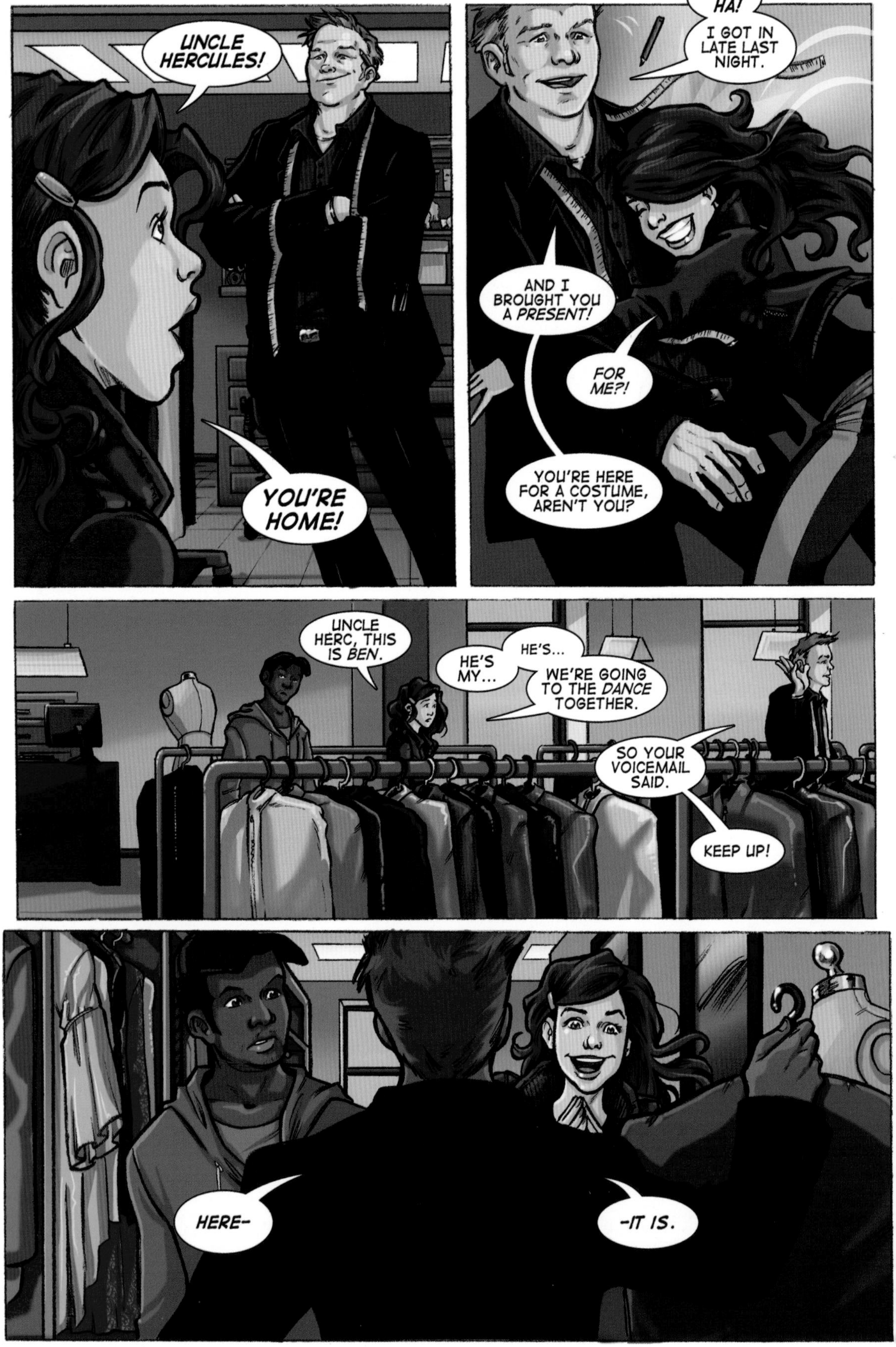
UNCLE HERCULES!
YOU'RE HOME!
HA! HA!
I GOT IN LATE LAST NIGHT.
AND I BROUGHT YOU A *PRESENT!*
FOR ME?!
YOU'RE HERE FOR A COSTUME, AREN'T YOU?
UNCLE HERC, THIS IS *BEN.*
HE'S MY...
HE'S...
WE'RE GOING TO THE *DANCE* TOGETHER.
SO YOUR VOICEMAIL SAID.
KEEP UP!
HERE-
-IT IS.

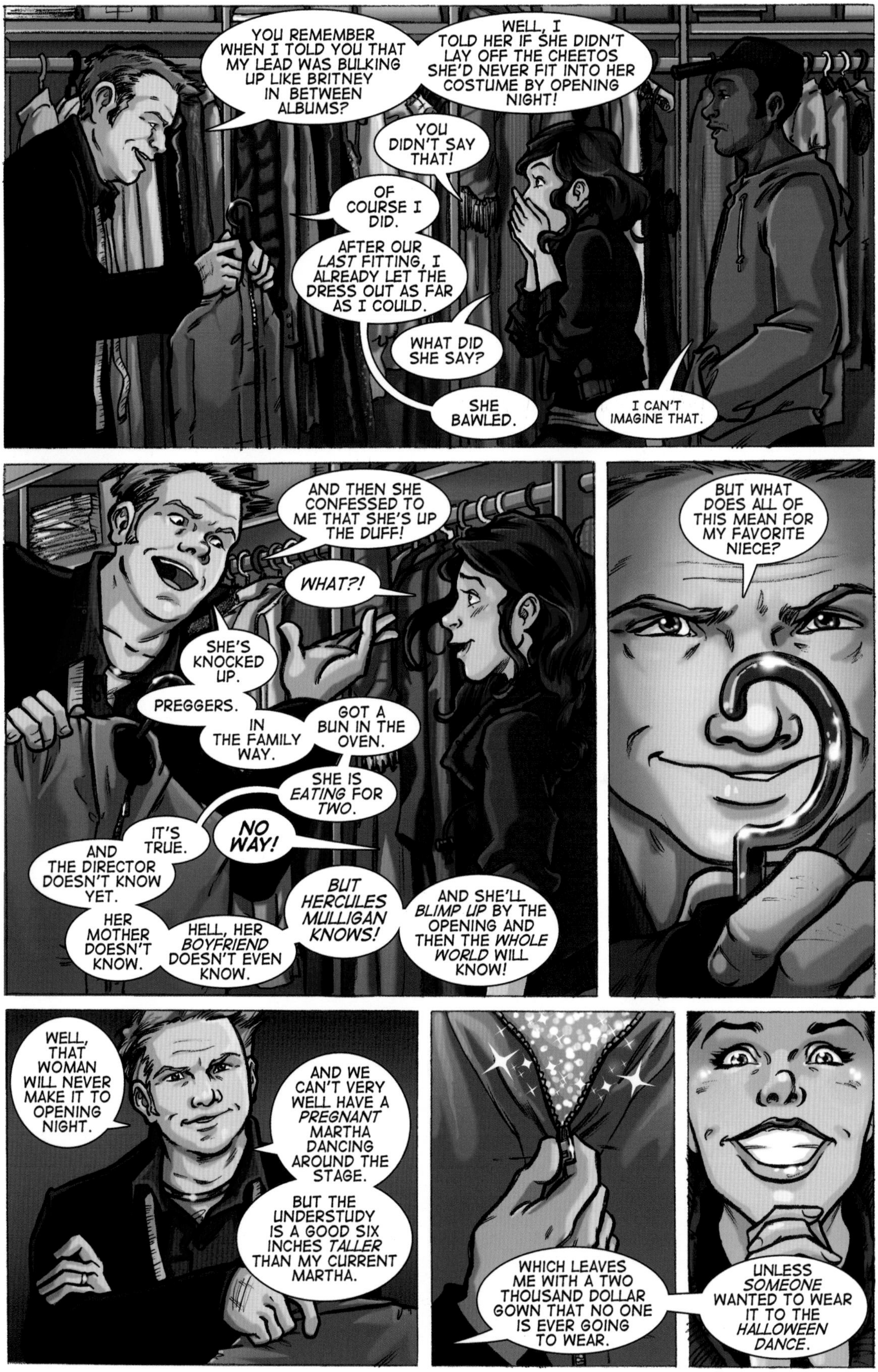

YOU REMEMBER WHEN I TOLD YOU THAT MY LEAD WAS BULKING UP LIKE BRITNEY IN BETWEEN ALBUMS?
WELL, I TOLD HER IF SHE DIDN'T LAY OFF THE CHEETOS SHE'D NEVER FIT INTO HER COSTUME BY OPENING NIGHT!
YOU DIDN'T SAY THAT!
OF COURSE I DID.
AFTER OUR *LAST* FITTING, I ALREADY LET THE DRESS OUT AS FAR AS I COULD.
WHAT DID SHE SAY?
SHE BAWLED.
I CAN'T IMAGINE THAT.
AND THEN SHE CONFESSED TO ME THAT SHE'S UP THE DUFF!
WHAT?!
SHE'S KNOCKED UP.
PREGGERS.
IN THE FAMILY WAY.
GOT A BUN IN THE OVEN.
SHE IS *EATING* FOR *TWO*.
NO WAY!
IT'S TRUE.
AND THE DIRECTOR DOESN'T KNOW YET.
HER MOTHER DOESN'T KNOW.
HELL, HER *BOYFRIEND* DOESN'T EVEN KNOW.
BUT HERCULES MULLIGAN KNOWS!
AND SHE'LL *BLIMP UP* BY THE OPENING AND THEN THE *WHOLE WORLD* WILL KNOW!
BUT WHAT DOES ALL OF THIS MEAN FOR MY FAVORITE NIECE?
WELL, THAT WOMAN WILL NEVER MAKE IT TO OPENING NIGHT.
AND WE CAN'T VERY WELL HAVE A *PREGNANT* MARTHA DANCING AROUND THE STAGE.
BUT THE UNDERSTUDY IS A GOOD SIX INCHES *TALLER* THAN MY CURRENT MARTHA.
WHICH LEAVES ME WITH A TWO THOUSAND DOLLAR GOWN THAT NO ONE IS EVER GOING TO WEAR.
UNLESS *SOMEONE* WANTED TO WEAR IT TO THE *HALLOWEEN DANCE*.

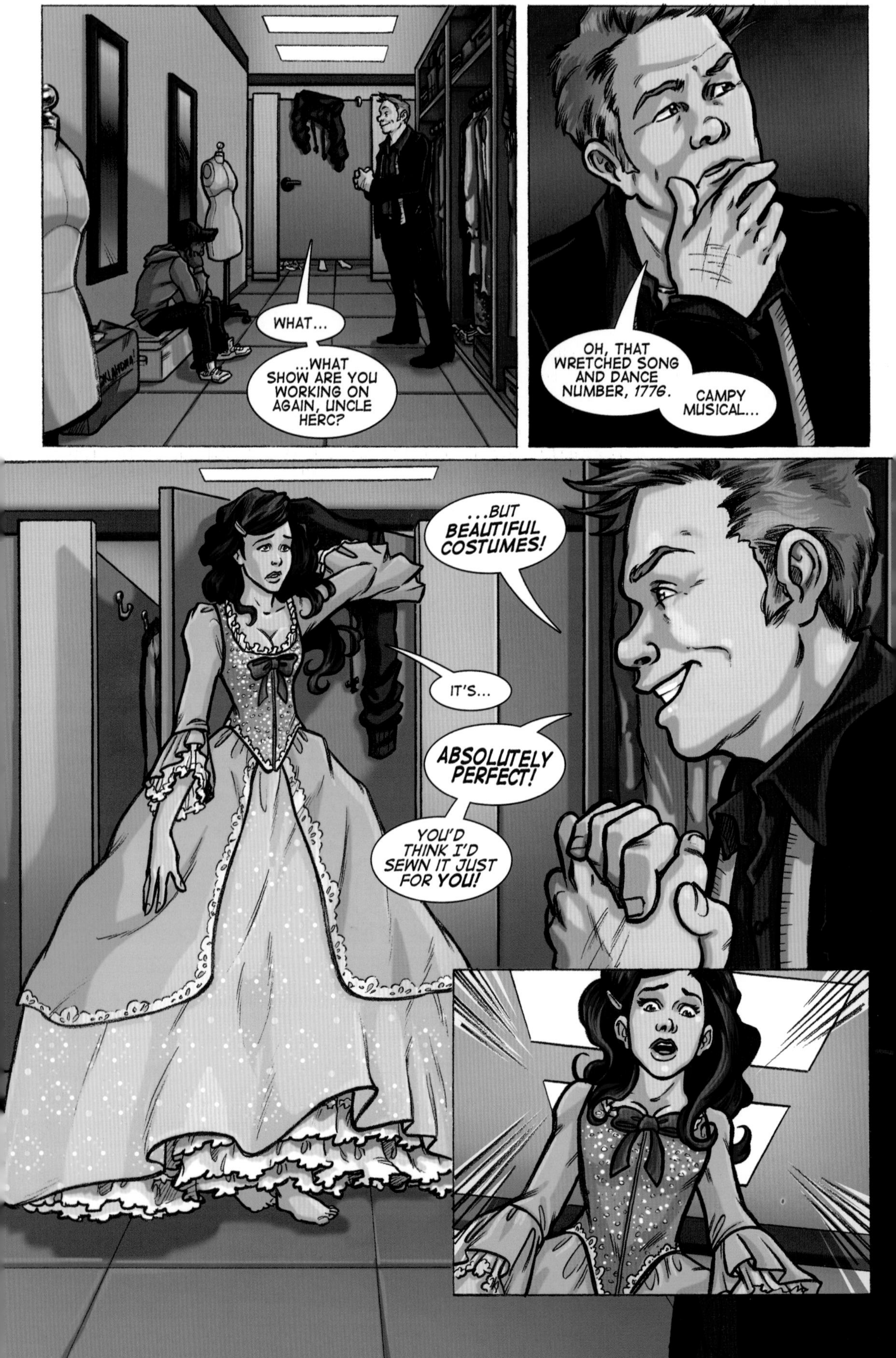
WHAT...
...WHAT SHOW ARE YOU WORKING ON AGAIN, UNCLE HERC?
OH, THAT WRETCHED SONG AND DANCE NUMBER, *1776*.
CAMPY MUSICAL...
...BUT **BEAUTIFUL COSTUMES!**
IT'S...
ABSOLUTELY PERFECT!
YOU'D THINK I'D SEWN IT JUST FOR ***YOU!***

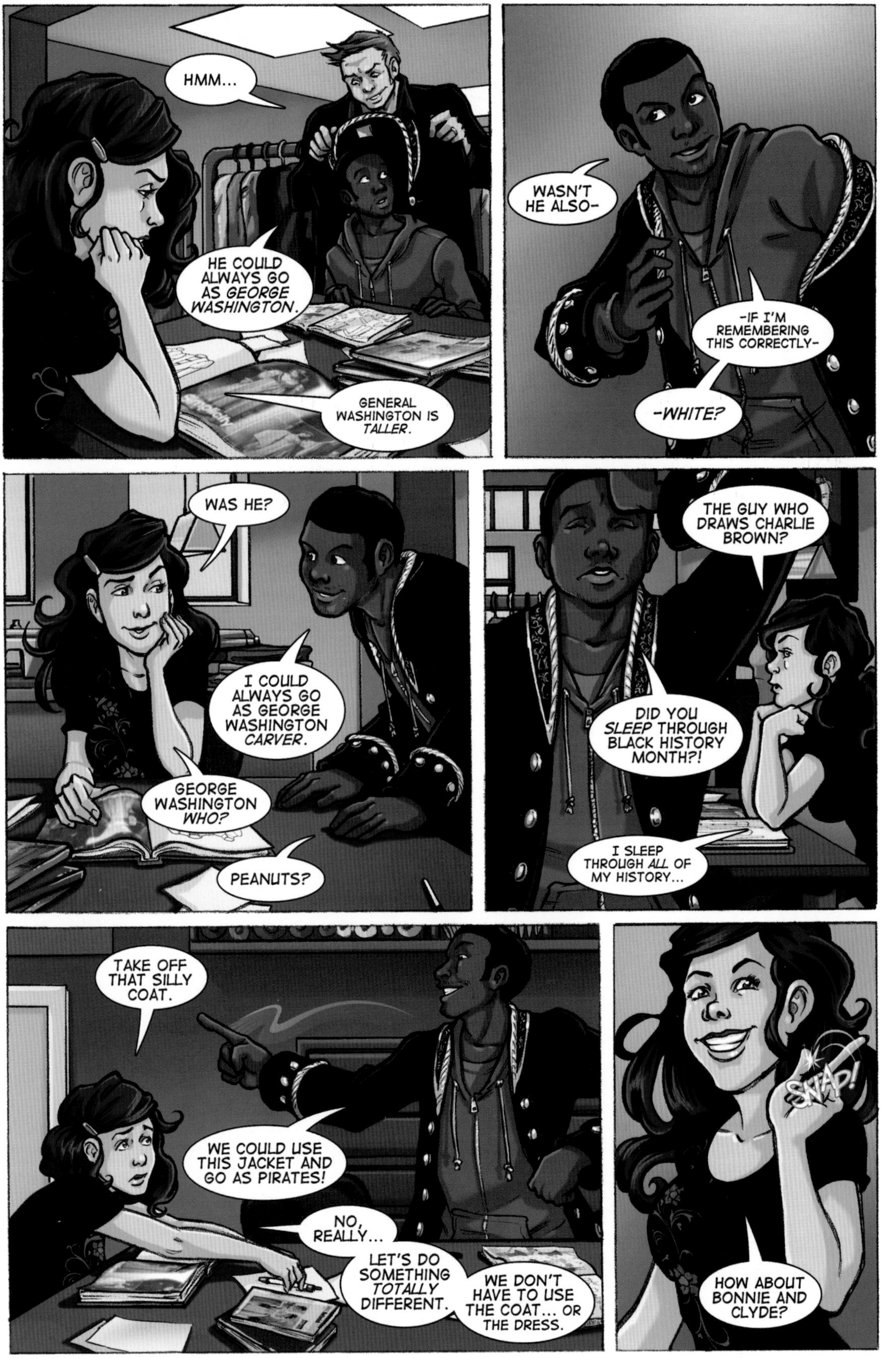
HMM...
HE COULD ALWAYS GO AS *GEORGE WASHINGTON*.
GENERAL WASHINGTON IS *TALLER*.
WASN'T HE ALSO-
-IF I'M REMEMBERING THIS CORRECTLY-
-WHITE?
WAS HE?
I COULD ALWAYS GO AS GEORGE WASHINGTON *CARVER*.
GEORGE WASHINGTON *WHO?*
PEANUTS?
THE GUY WHO DRAWS CHARLIE BROWN?
DID YOU *SLEEP* THROUGH BLACK HISTORY MONTH?!
I SLEEP THROUGH *ALL* OF MY HISTORY...
TAKE OFF THAT SILLY COAT.
WE COULD USE THIS JACKET AND GO AS PIRATES!
NO, REALLY...
LET'S DO SOMETHING *TOTALLY* DIFFERENT.
WE DON'T HAVE TO USE THE COAT... OR THE DRESS.
SNAP!
HOW ABOUT BONNIE AND CLYDE?

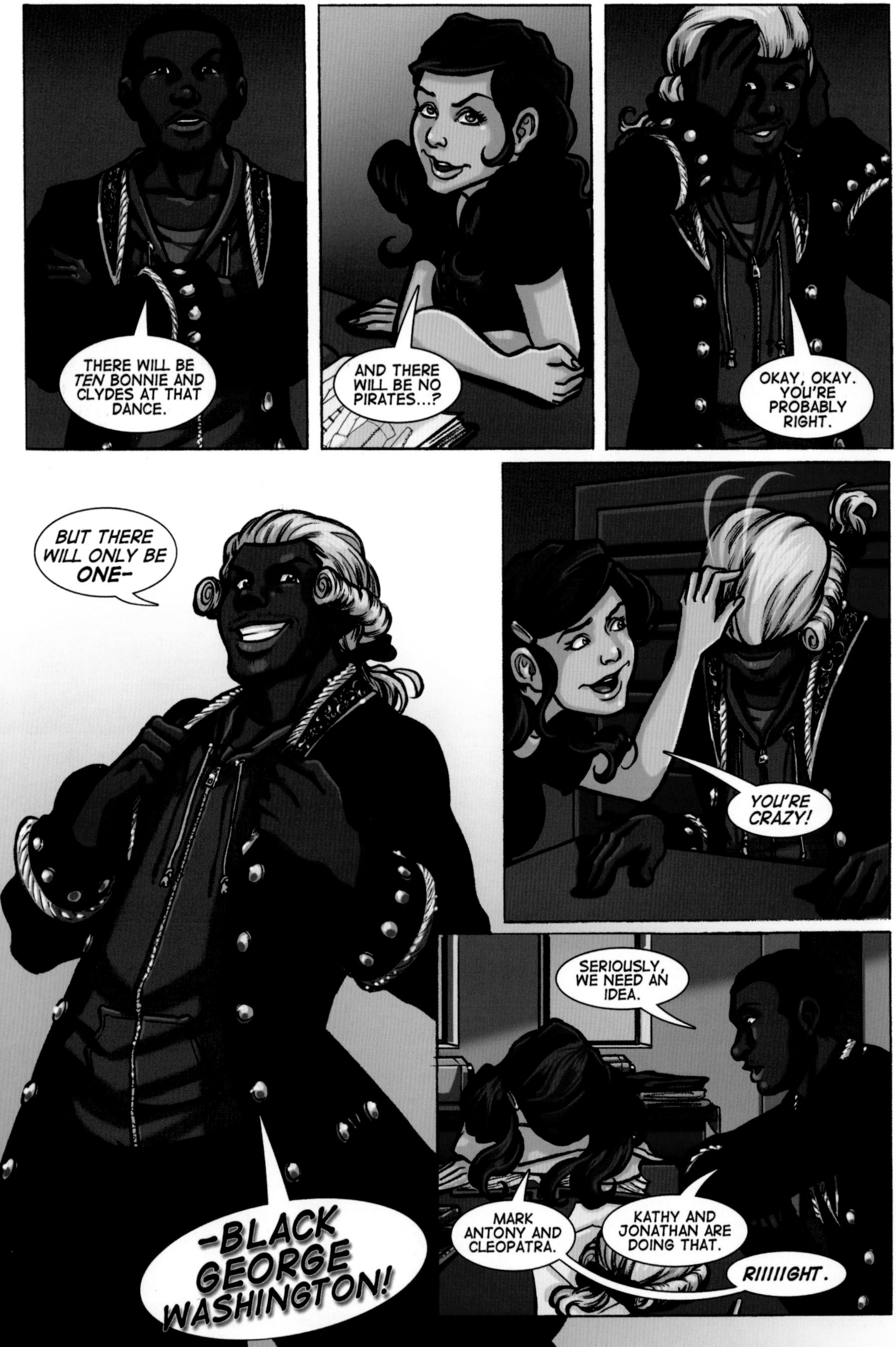
THERE WILL BE TEN BONNIE AND CLYDES AT THAT DANCE.
AND THERE WILL BE NO PIRATES...?
OKAY, OKAY. YOU'RE PROBABLY RIGHT.
BUT THERE WILL ONLY BE ONE-
-BLACK GEORGE WASHINGTON!
YOU'RE CRAZY!
SERIOUSLY, WE NEED AN IDEA.
MARK ANTONY AND CLEOPATRA.
KATHY AND JONATHAN ARE DOING THAT.
RIIIIIGHT.

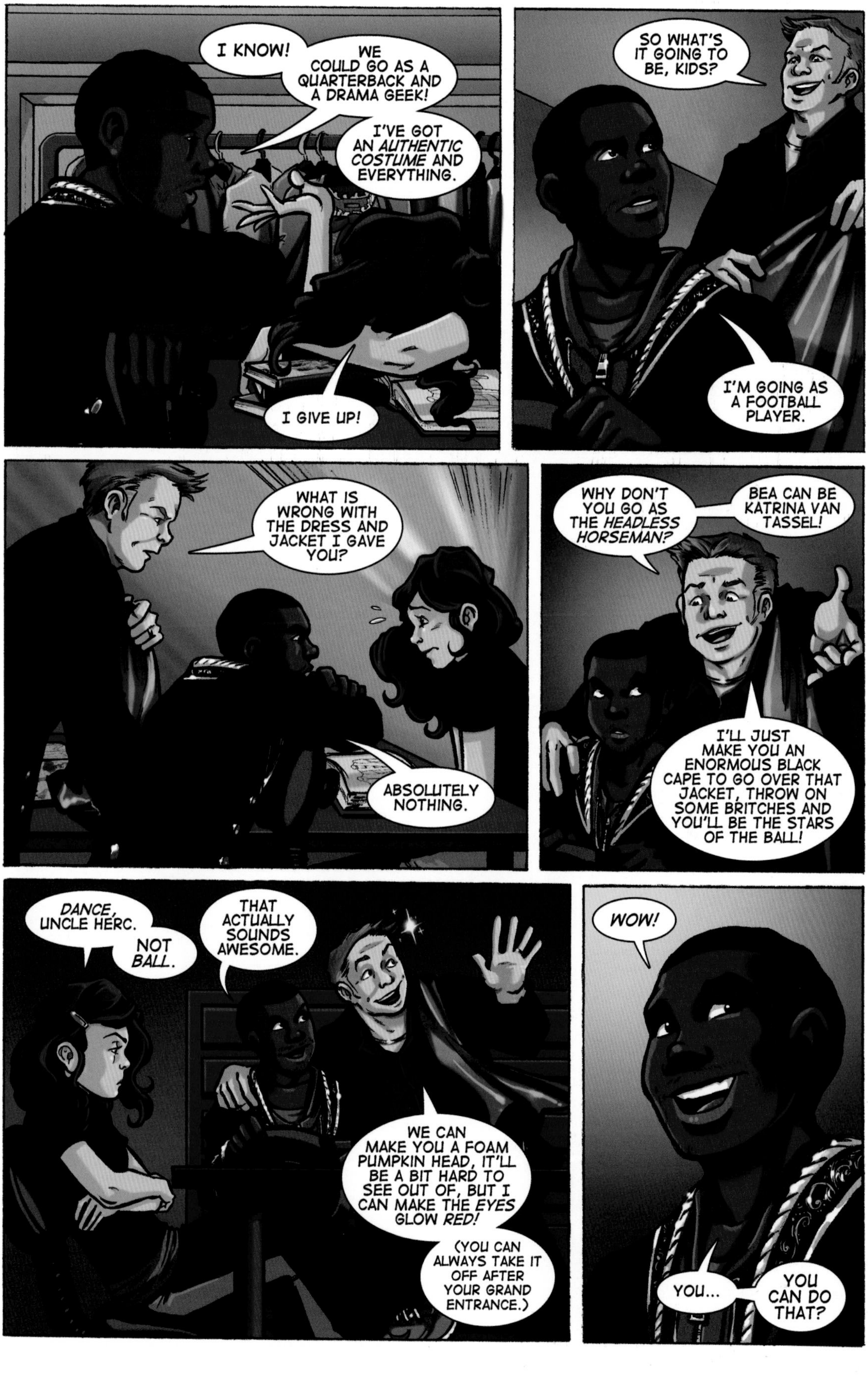
I KNOW!
WE COULD GO AS A QUARTERBACK AND A DRAMA GEEK!
I'VE GOT AN *AUTHENTIC COSTUME* AND EVERYTHING.
I GIVE UP!
SO WHAT'S IT GOING TO BE, KIDS?
I'M GOING AS A FOOTBALL PLAYER.
WHAT IS WRONG WITH THE DRESS AND JACKET I GAVE YOU?
ABSOLUTELY NOTHING.
WHY DON'T YOU GO AS THE *HEADLESS HORSEMAN?*
BEA CAN BE KATRINA VAN TASSEL!
I'LL JUST MAKE YOU AN ENORMOUS BLACK CAPE TO GO OVER THAT JACKET, THROW ON SOME BRITCHES AND YOU'LL BE THE STARS OF THE BALL!
DANCE, UNCLE HERC.
NOT *BALL*.
THAT ACTUALLY SOUNDS AWESOME.
WE CAN MAKE YOU A FOAM PUMPKIN HEAD, IT'LL BE A BIT HARD TO SEE OUT OF, BUT I CAN MAKE THE *EYES* GLOW *RED!*
(YOU CAN ALWAYS TAKE IT OFF AFTER YOUR GRAND ENTRANCE.)
WOW!
YOU...
YOU CAN DO THAT?

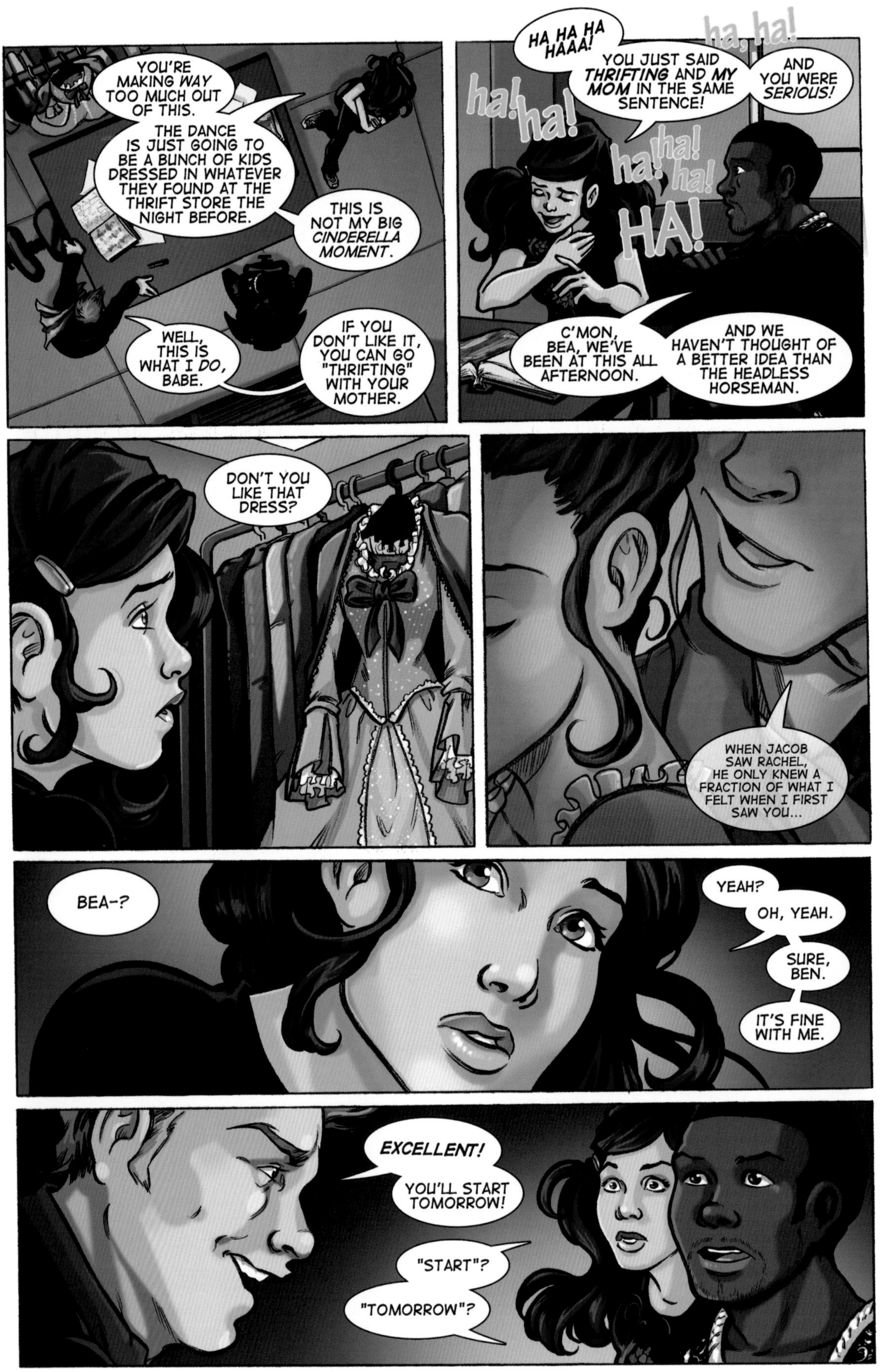
YOU'RE MAKING WAY TOO MUCH OUT OF THIS.
THE DANCE IS JUST GOING TO BE A BUNCH OF KIDS DRESSED IN WHATEVER THEY FOUND AT THE THRIFT STORE THE NIGHT BEFORE.
THIS IS NOT MY BIG CINDERELLA MOMENT.
WELL, THIS IS WHAT I DO, BABE.
IF YOU DON'T LIKE IT, YOU CAN GO "THRIFTING" WITH YOUR MOTHER.
HA HA HA HAAA!
YOU JUST SAID THRIFTING AND MY MOM IN THE SAME SENTENCE!
AND YOU WERE SERIOUS!
ha, ha!
ha! ha!
ha! ha! ha!
HA!
C'MON, BEA, WE'VE BEEN AT THIS ALL AFTERNOON.
AND WE HAVEN'T THOUGHT OF A BETTER IDEA THAN THE HEADLESS HORSEMAN.
DON'T YOU LIKE THAT DRESS?
WHEN JACOB SAW RACHEL, HE ONLY KNEW A FRACTION OF WHAT I FELT WHEN I FIRST SAW YOU...
BEA-?
YEAH?
OH, YEAH.
SURE, BEN.
IT'S FINE WITH ME.
EXCELLENT!
YOU'LL START TOMORROW!
"START"?
"TOMORROW"?

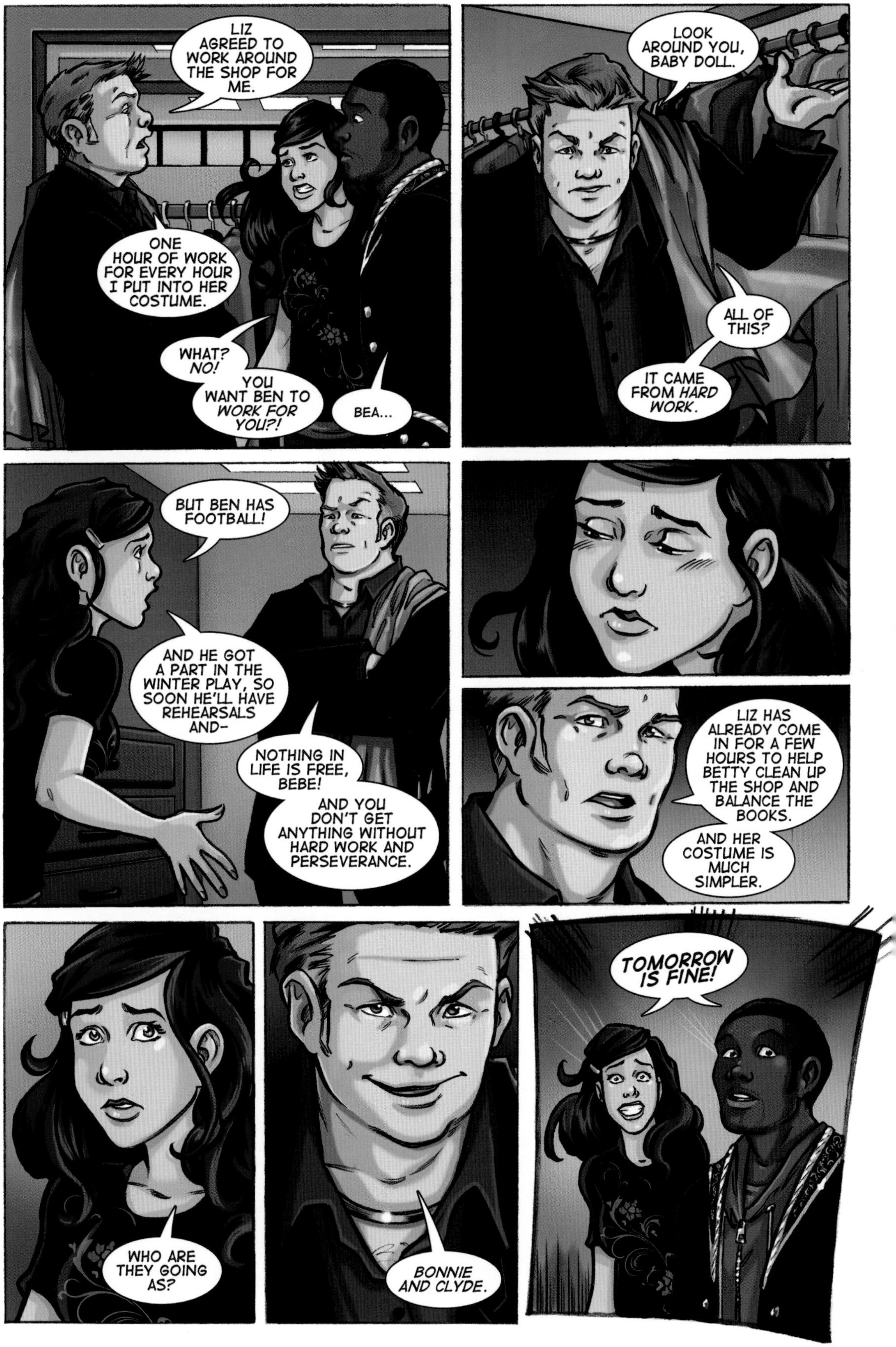
LIZ AGREED TO WORK AROUND THE SHOP FOR ME.
ONE HOUR OF WORK FOR EVERY HOUR I PUT INTO HER COSTUME.
WHAT? NO!
YOU WANT BEN TO WORK FOR YOU?!
BEA...
LOOK AROUND YOU, BABY DOLL.
ALL OF THIS?
IT CAME FROM HARD WORK.
BUT BEN HAS FOOTBALL!
AND HE GOT A PART IN THE WINTER PLAY, SO SOON HE'LL HAVE REHEARSALS AND-
NOTHING IN LIFE IS FREE, BEBE!
AND YOU DON'T GET ANYTHING WITHOUT HARD WORK AND PERSEVERANCE.
LIZ HAS ALREADY COME IN FOR A FEW HOURS TO HELP BETTY CLEAN UP THE SHOP AND BALANCE THE BOOKS.
AND HER COSTUME IS MUCH SIMPLER.
WHO ARE THEY GOING AS?
BONNIE AND CLYDE.
TOMORROW IS FINE!

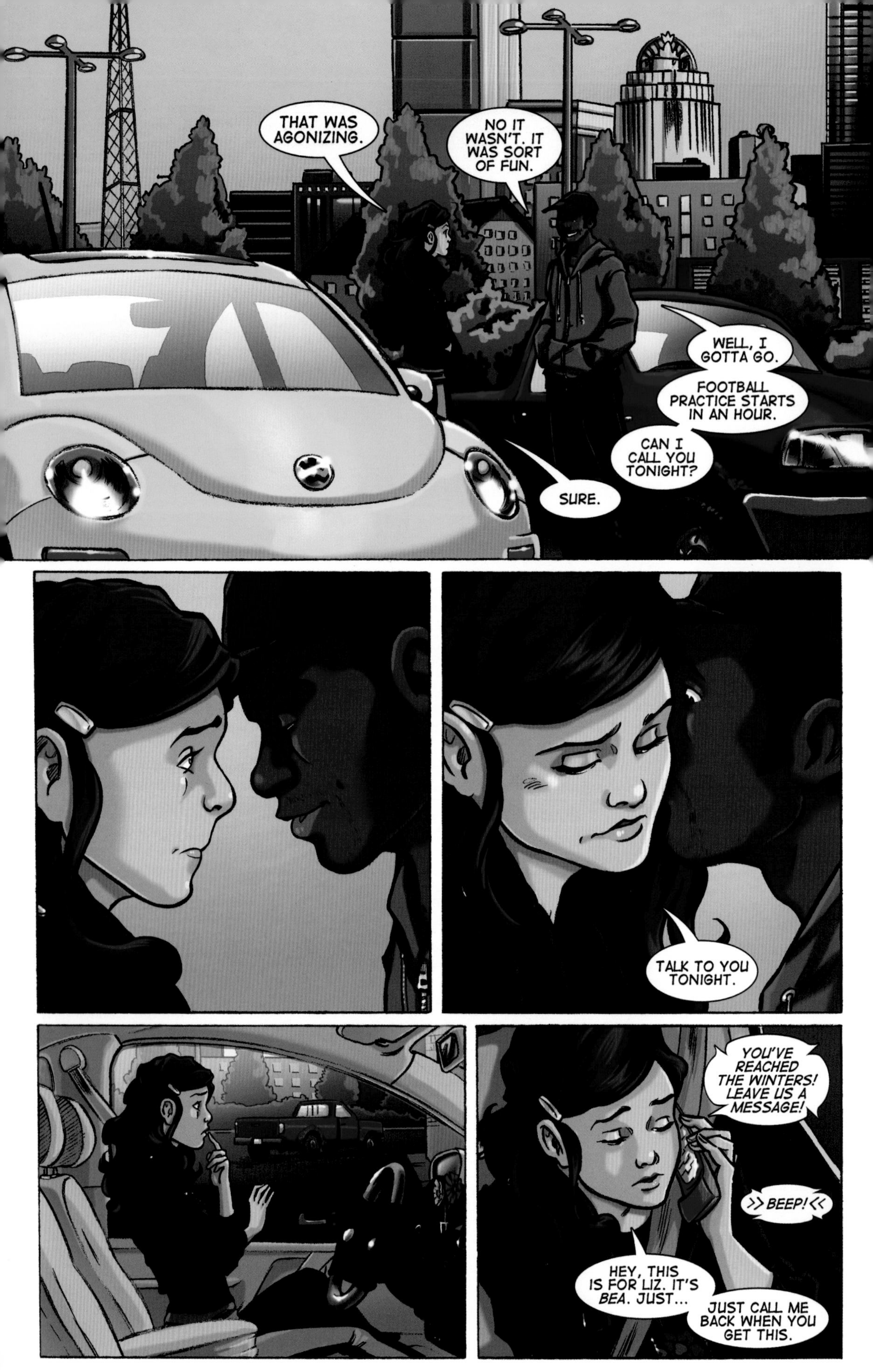
THAT WAS AGONIZING.
NO IT WASN'T. IT WAS SORT OF FUN.
WELL, I GOTTA GO.
FOOTBALL PRACTICE STARTS IN AN HOUR.
CAN I CALL YOU TONIGHT?
SURE.
TALK TO YOU TONIGHT.
YOU'VE REACHED THE WINTERS! LEAVE US A MESSAGE!
>> BEEP! <<
HEY, THIS IS FOR LIZ. IT'S BEA. JUST...
JUST CALL ME BACK WHEN YOU GET THIS.

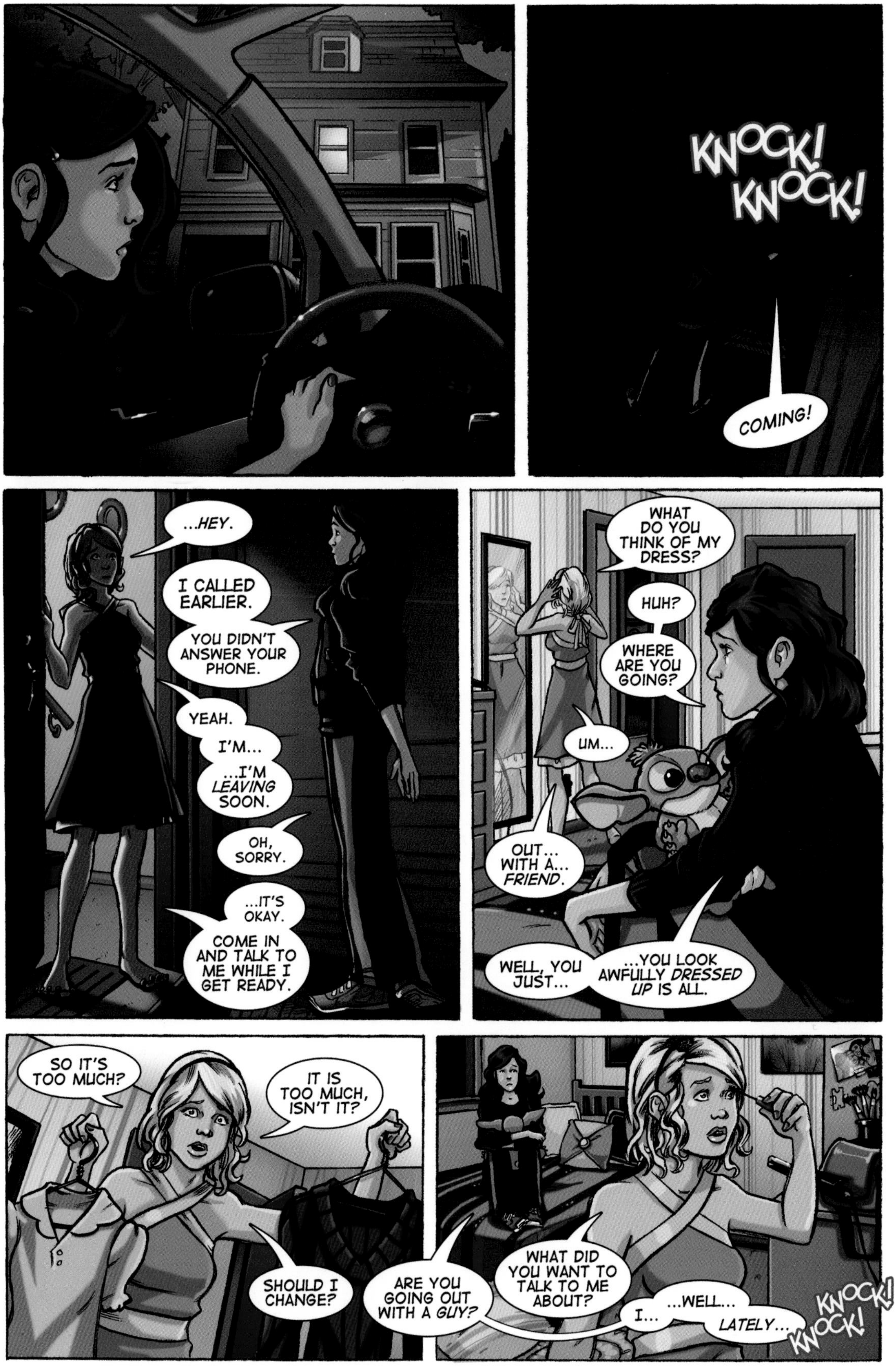
KNOCK! KNOCK!
COMING!
...HEY.
I CALLED EARLIER.
YOU DIDN'T ANSWER YOUR PHONE.
YEAH.
I'M...
...I'M *LEAVING* SOON.
OH, SORRY.
...IT'S OKAY.
COME IN AND TALK TO ME WHILE I GET READY.
WHAT DO YOU THINK OF MY DRESS?
HUH?
WHERE ARE YOU GOING?
UM...
OUT... WITH A... *FRIEND*.
WELL, YOU JUST...
...YOU LOOK AWFULLY *DRESSED UP* IS ALL.
SO IT'S TOO MUCH?
IT IS TOO MUCH, ISN'T IT?
SHOULD I CHANGE?
ARE YOU GOING OUT WITH A *GUY?*
WHAT DID YOU WANT TO TALK TO ME ABOUT?
I...
...WELL...
LATELY...
KNOCK! KNOCK!

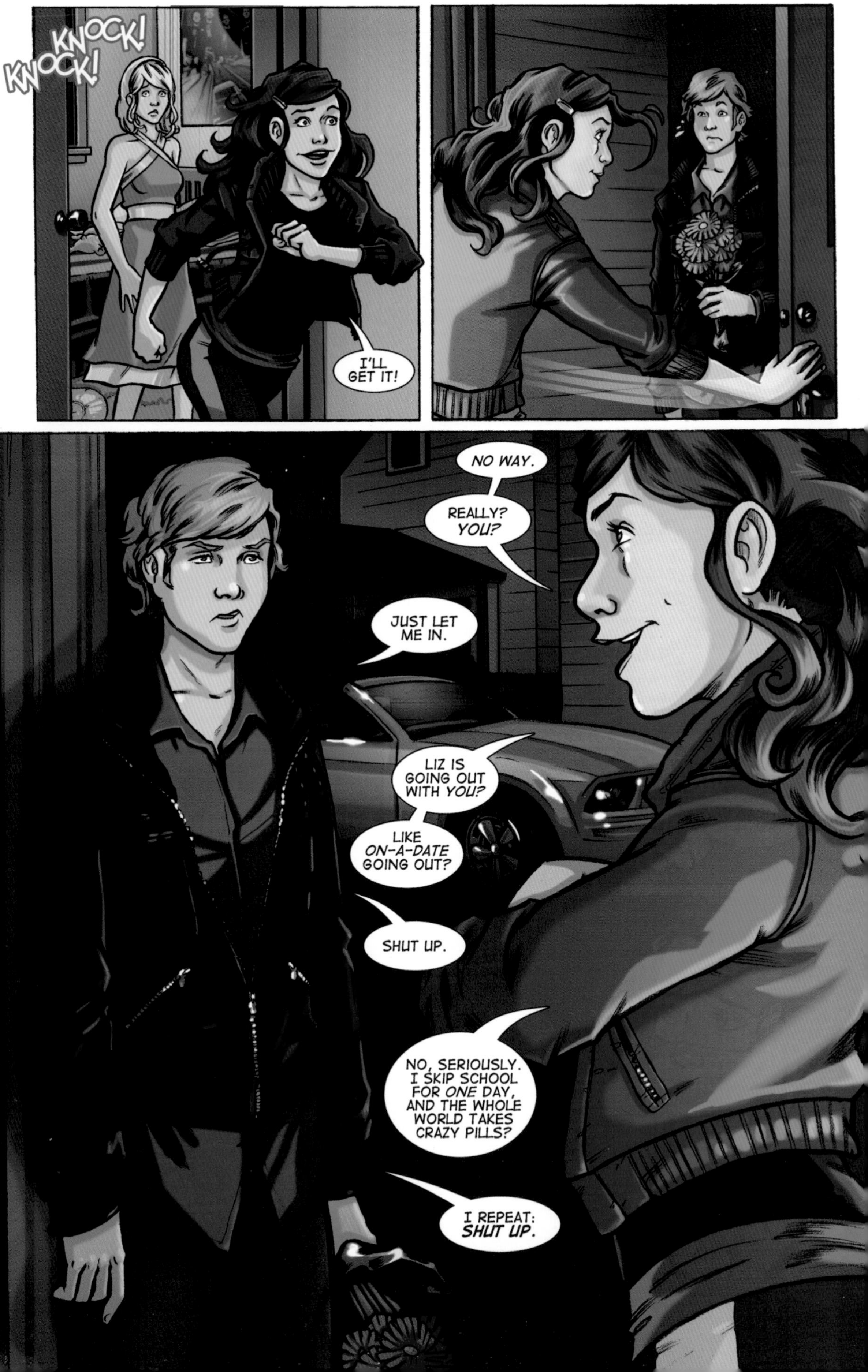
KNOCK! KNOCK!
I'LL GET IT!
NO WAY.
REALLY? *YOU?*
JUST LET ME IN.
LIZ IS GOING OUT WITH *YOU?*
LIKE *ON-A-DATE* GOING OUT?
SHUT UP.
NO, SERIOUSLY. I SKIP SCHOOL FOR *ONE* DAY, AND THE WHOLE WORLD TAKES CRAZY PILLS?
I REPEAT: ***SHUT UP.***

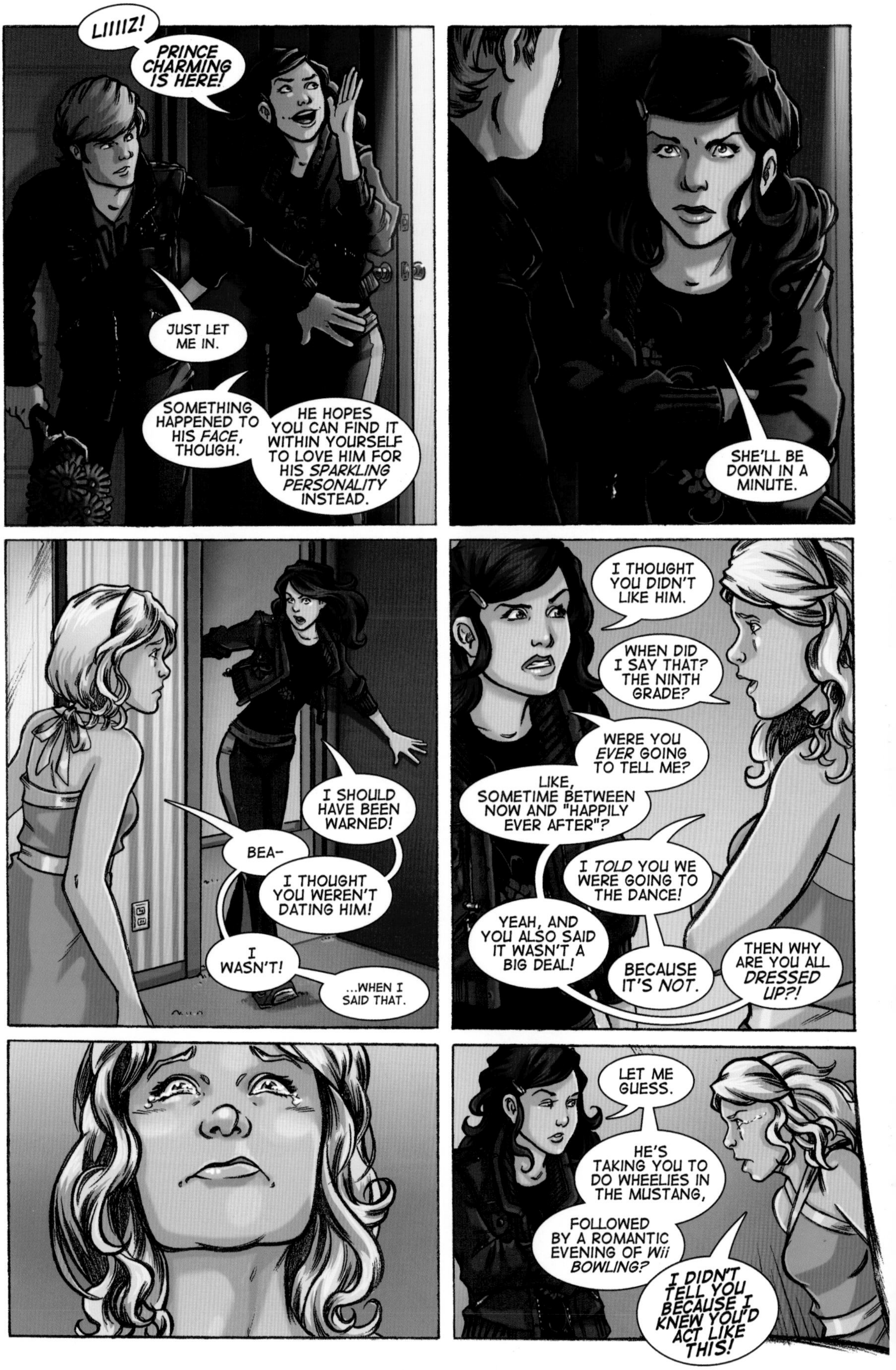
LIIIIZ!
PRINCE CHARMING IS HERE!
JUST LET ME IN.
SOMETHING HAPPENED TO HIS FACE, THOUGH.
HE HOPES YOU CAN FIND IT WITHIN YOURSELF TO LOVE HIM FOR HIS SPARKLING PERSONALITY INSTEAD.
SHE'LL BE DOWN IN A MINUTE.
I SHOULD HAVE BEEN WARNED!
BEA-
I THOUGHT YOU WEREN'T DATING HIM!
I WASN'T!
...WHEN I SAID THAT.
I THOUGHT YOU DIDN'T LIKE HIM.
WHEN DID I SAY THAT? THE NINTH GRADE?
WERE YOU EVER GOING TO TELL ME?
LIKE, SOMETIME BETWEEN NOW AND "HAPPILY EVER AFTER"?
I TOLD YOU WE WERE GOING TO THE DANCE!
YEAH, AND YOU ALSO SAID IT WASN'T A BIG DEAL!
BECAUSE IT'S NOT.
THEN WHY ARE YOU ALL DRESSED UP?!
LET ME GUESS.
HE'S TAKING YOU TO DO WHEELIES IN THE MUSTANG,
FOLLOWED BY A ROMANTIC EVENING OF Wii BOWLING?
I DIDN'T TELL YOU BECAUSE I KNEW YOU'D ACT LIKE THIS!

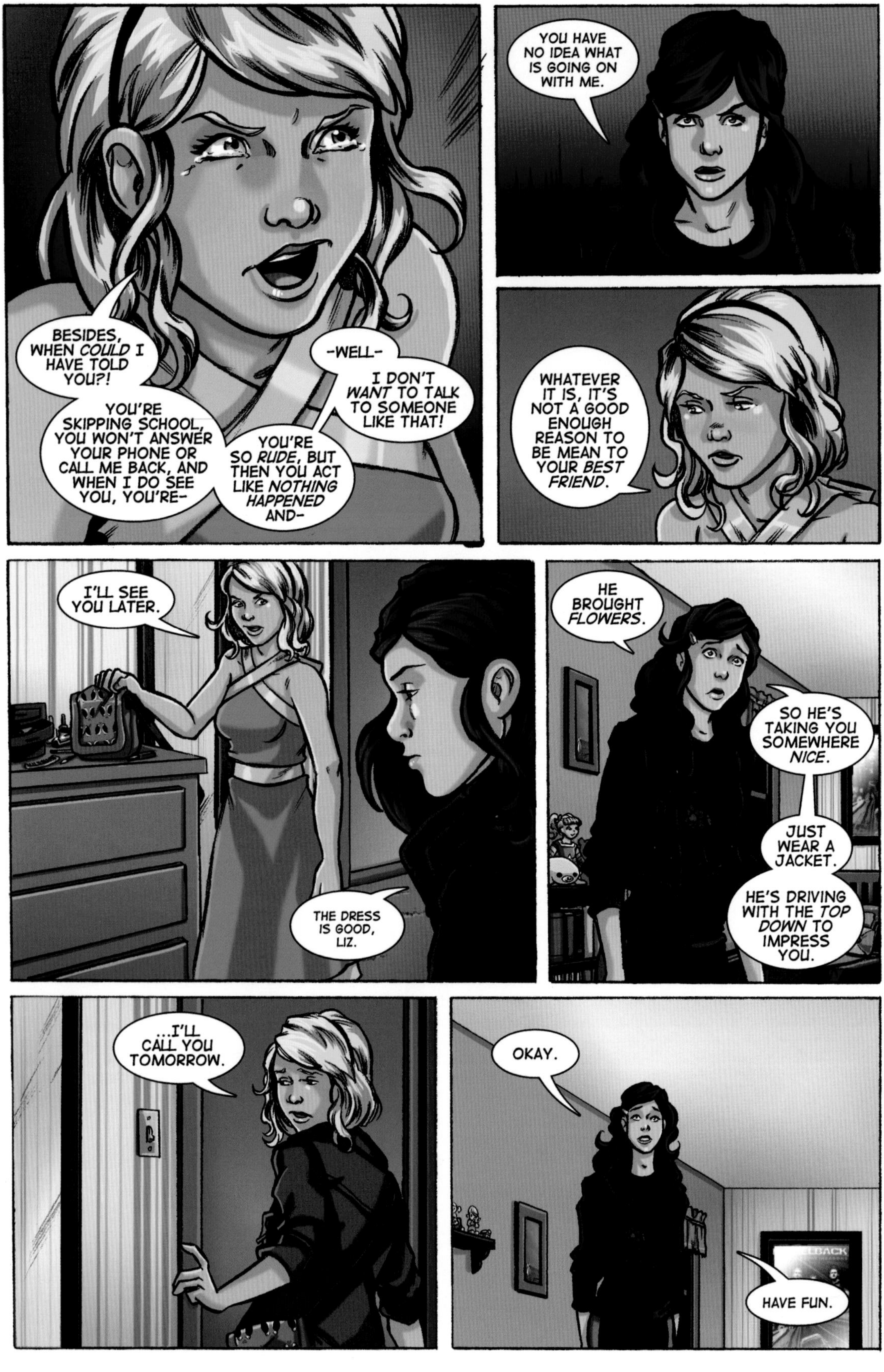
BESIDES, WHEN *COULD* I HAVE TOLD YOU?!
YOU'RE SKIPPING SCHOOL, YOU WON'T ANSWER YOUR PHONE OR CALL ME BACK, AND WHEN I DO SEE YOU, YOU'RE-
-WELL-
YOU'RE SO *RUDE*, BUT THEN YOU ACT LIKE *NOTHING HAPPENED* AND-
I DON'T *WANT* TO TALK TO SOMEONE LIKE THAT!
YOU HAVE NO IDEA WHAT IS GOING ON WITH ME.
WHATEVER IT IS, IT'S NOT A GOOD ENOUGH REASON TO BE MEAN TO YOUR *BEST FRIEND*.
I'LL SEE YOU LATER.
THE DRESS IS GOOD, LIZ.
HE BROUGHT *FLOWERS*.
SO HE'S TAKING YOU SOMEWHERE *NICE*.
JUST WEAR A JACKET.
HE'S DRIVING WITH THE *TOP DOWN* TO IMPRESS YOU.
...I'LL CALL YOU TOMORROW.
OKAY.
HAVE FUN.

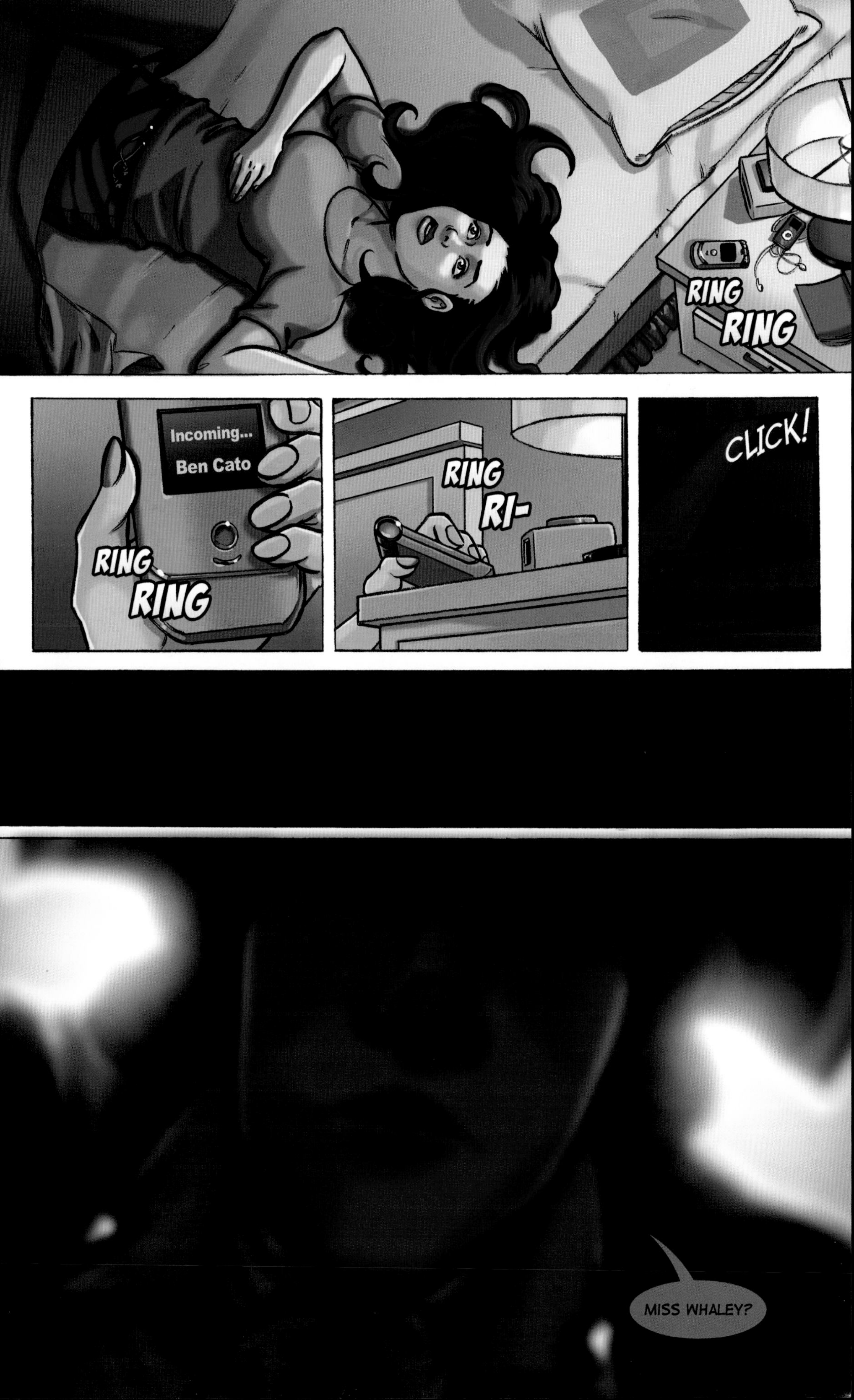
RING
RING
Incoming...
Ben Cato
RING
RING
RING
RI-
CLICK!
MISS WHALEY?

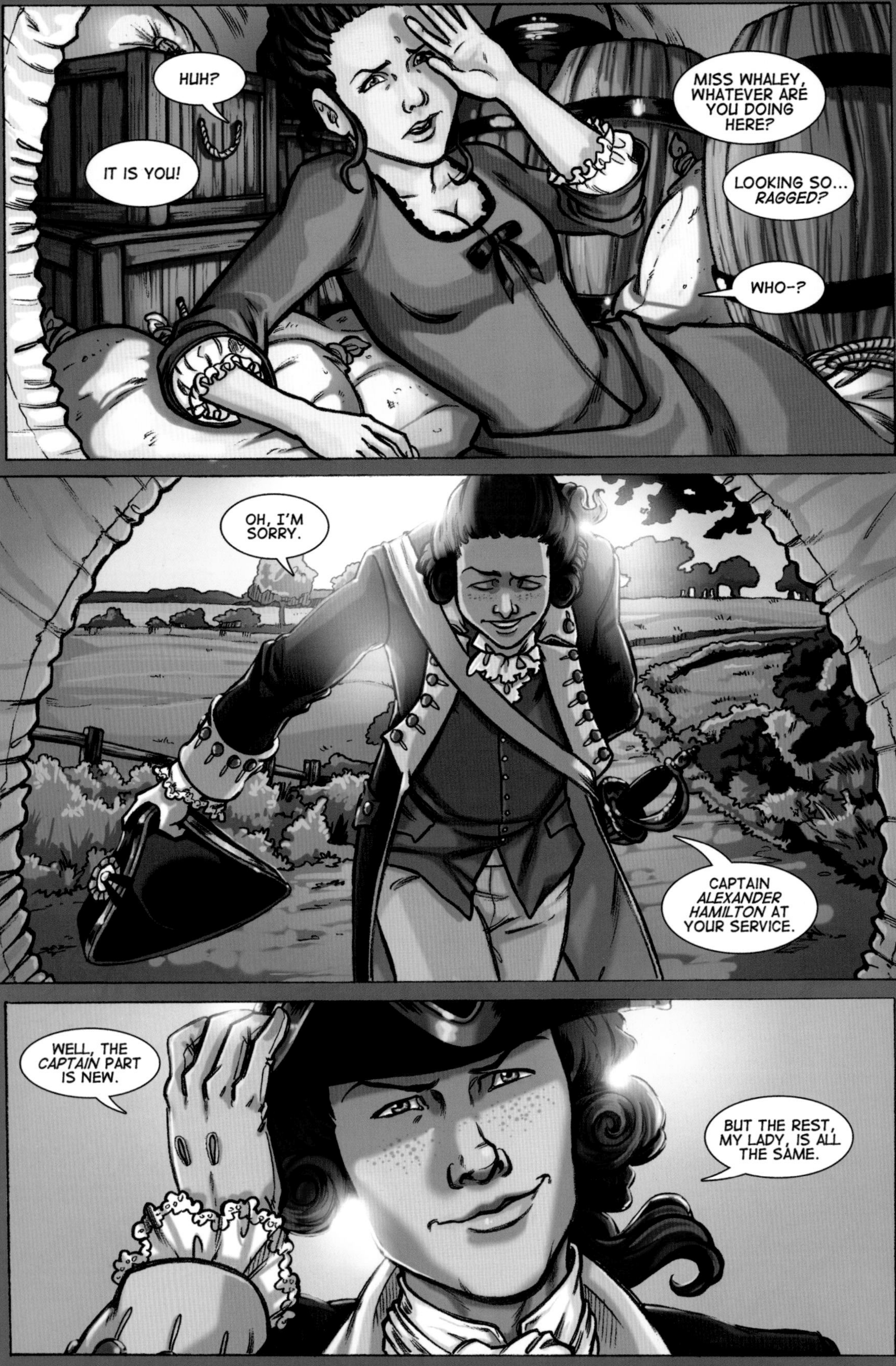
HUH?
IT IS YOU!
MISS WHALEY, WHATEVER ARE YOU DOING HERE?
LOOKING SO... *RAGGED?*
WHO-?
OH, I'M SORRY.
CAPTAIN *ALEXANDER HAMILTON* AT YOUR SERVICE.
WELL, THE *CAPTAIN* PART IS NEW.
BUT THE REST, MY LADY, IS ALL THE SAME.

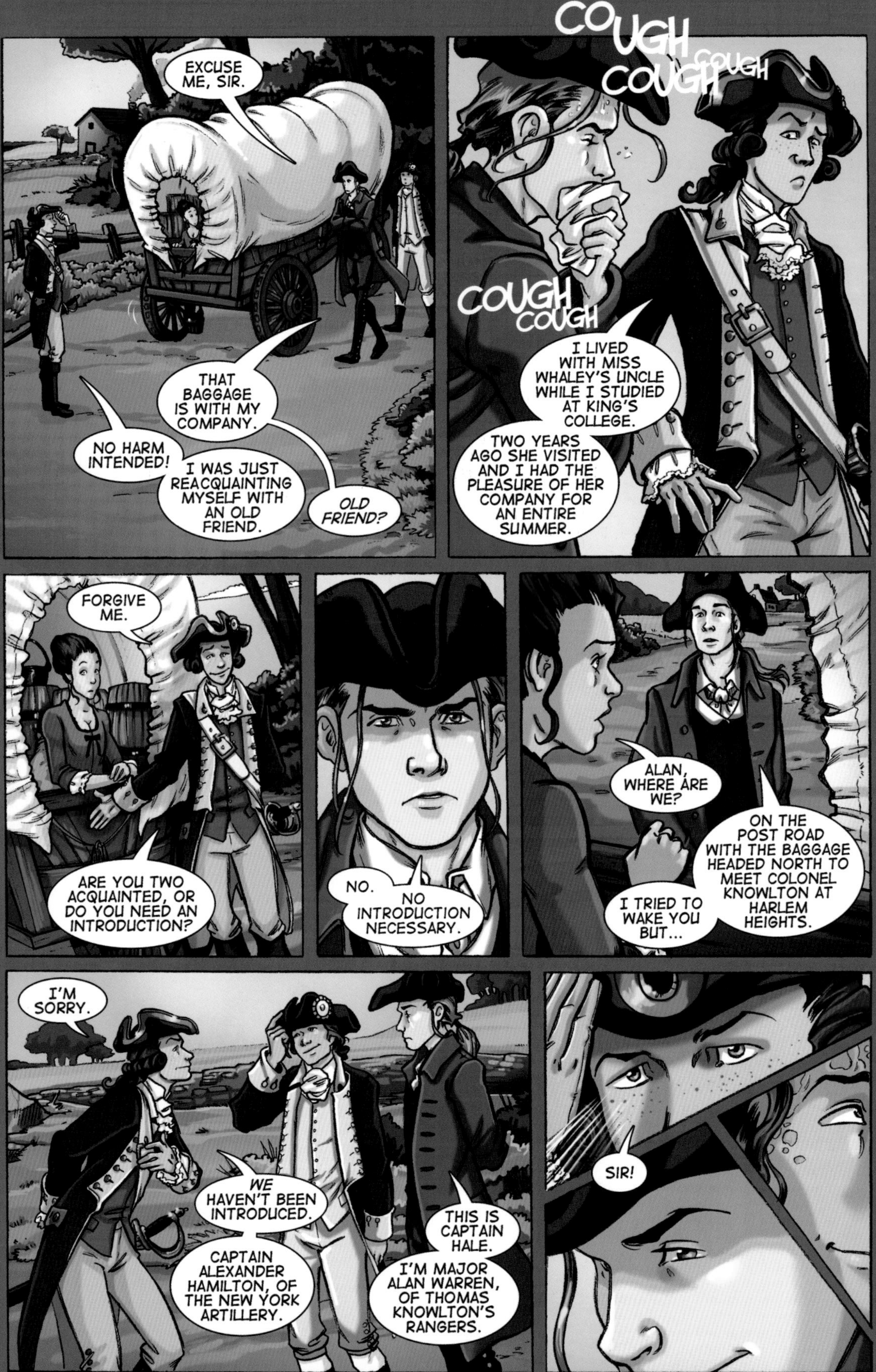
EXCUSE ME, SIR.
THAT BAGGAGE IS WITH MY COMPANY.
NO HARM INTENDED!
I WAS JUST REACQUAINTING MYSELF WITH AN OLD FRIEND.
OLD FRIEND?
COUGH COUGH COUGH
COUGH COUGH
I LIVED WITH MISS WHALEY'S UNCLE WHILE I STUDIED AT KING'S COLLEGE.
TWO YEARS AGO SHE VISITED AND I HAD THE PLEASURE OF HER COMPANY FOR AN ENTIRE SUMMER.
FORGIVE ME.
ARE YOU TWO ACQUAINTED, OR DO YOU NEED AN INTRODUCTION?
NO.
NO INTRODUCTION NECESSARY.
ALAN, WHERE ARE WE?
ON THE POST ROAD WITH THE BAGGAGE HEADED NORTH TO MEET COLONEL KNOWLTON AT HARLEM HEIGHTS.
I TRIED TO WAKE YOU BUT...
I'M SORRY.
WE HAVEN'T BEEN INTRODUCED.
CAPTAIN ALEXANDER HAMILTON, OF THE NEW YORK ARTILLERY.
THIS IS CAPTAIN HALE.
I'M MAJOR ALAN WARREN, OF THOMAS KNOWLTON'S RANGERS.
SIR!

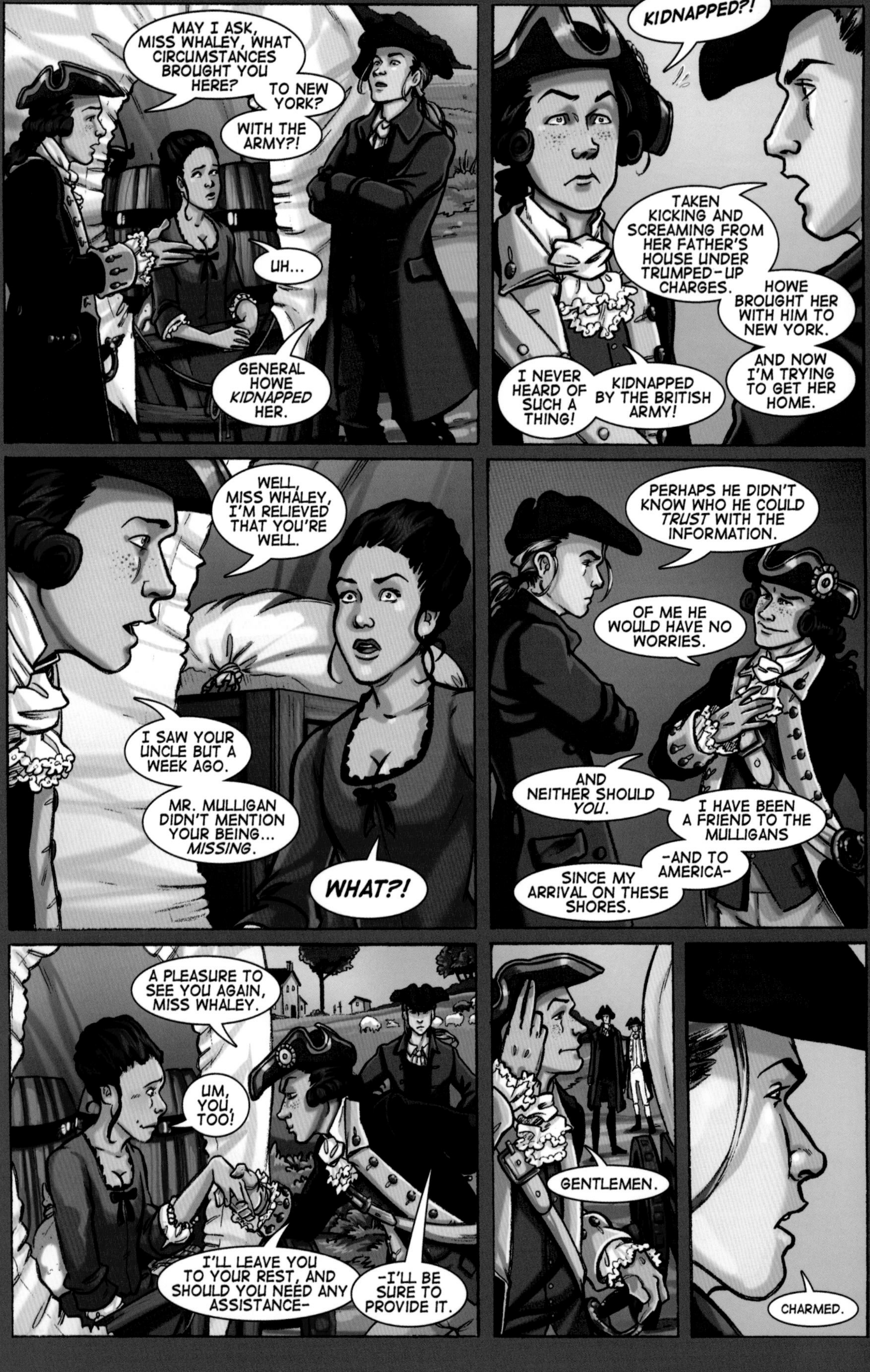

MAY I ASK, MISS WHALEY, WHAT CIRCUMSTANCES BROUGHT YOU HERE?
TO NEW YORK?
WITH THE ARMY?!
UH...
GENERAL HOWE *KIDNAPPED* HER.
KIDNAPPED?!
TAKEN KICKING AND SCREAMING FROM HER FATHER'S HOUSE UNDER TRUMPED-UP CHARGES.
HOWE BROUGHT HER WITH HIM TO NEW YORK.
AND NOW I'M TRYING TO GET HER HOME.
KIDNAPPED BY THE BRITISH ARMY!
I NEVER HEARD OF SUCH A THING!
WELL, MISS WHALEY, I'M RELIEVED THAT YOU'RE WELL.
I SAW YOUR UNCLE BUT A WEEK AGO.
MR. MULLIGAN DIDN'T MENTION YOUR BEING... *MISSING*.
WHAT?!
PERHAPS HE DIDN'T KNOW WHO HE COULD *TRUST* WITH THE INFORMATION.
OF ME HE WOULD HAVE NO WORRIES.
AND NEITHER SHOULD *YOU*.
I HAVE BEEN A FRIEND TO THE MULLIGANS
-AND TO AMERICA-
SINCE MY ARRIVAL ON THESE SHORES.
A PLEASURE TO SEE YOU AGAIN, MISS WHALEY.
UM, YOU, TOO!
I'LL LEAVE YOU TO YOUR REST, AND SHOULD YOU NEED ANY ASSISTANCE-
-I'LL BE SURE TO PROVIDE IT.
GENTLEMEN.
CHARMED.

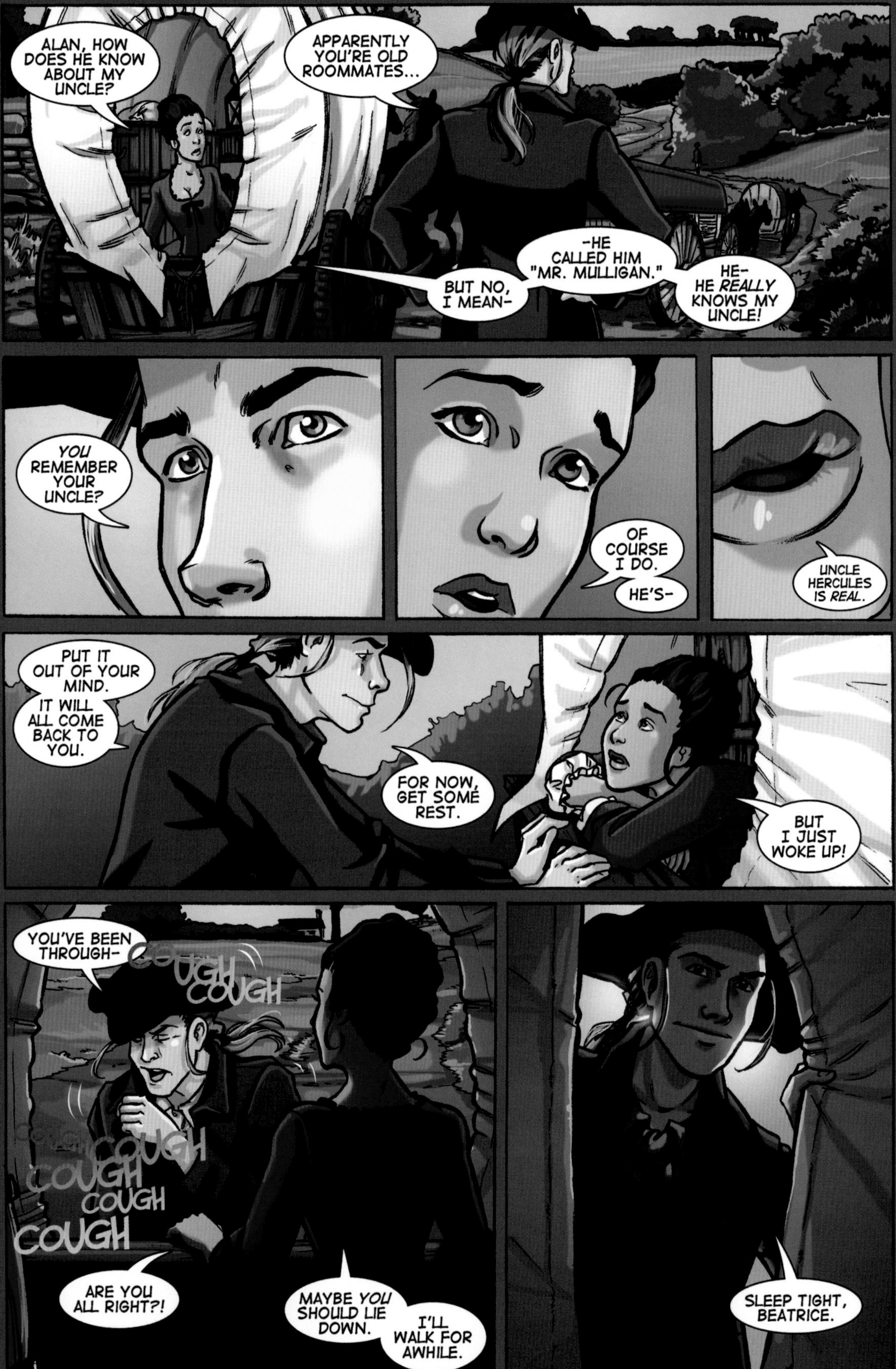

ALAN, HOW DOES HE KNOW ABOUT MY UNCLE?
APPARENTLY YOU'RE OLD ROOMMATES...
BUT NO, I MEAN-
-HE CALLED HIM "MR. MULLIGAN."
HE- HE *REALLY* KNOWS MY UNCLE!
YOU REMEMBER YOUR UNCLE?
OF COURSE I DO.
HE'S-
UNCLE HERCULES IS *REAL*.
PUT IT OUT OF YOUR MIND.
IT WILL ALL COME BACK TO YOU.
FOR NOW, GET SOME REST.
BUT I JUST WOKE UP!
YOU'VE BEEN THROUGH-
COUGH
COUGH
COUGH
COUGH
COUGH
COUGH
ARE YOU ALL RIGHT?!
MAYBE *YOU* SHOULD LIE DOWN.
I'LL WALK FOR AWHILE.
SLEEP TIGHT, BEATRICE.

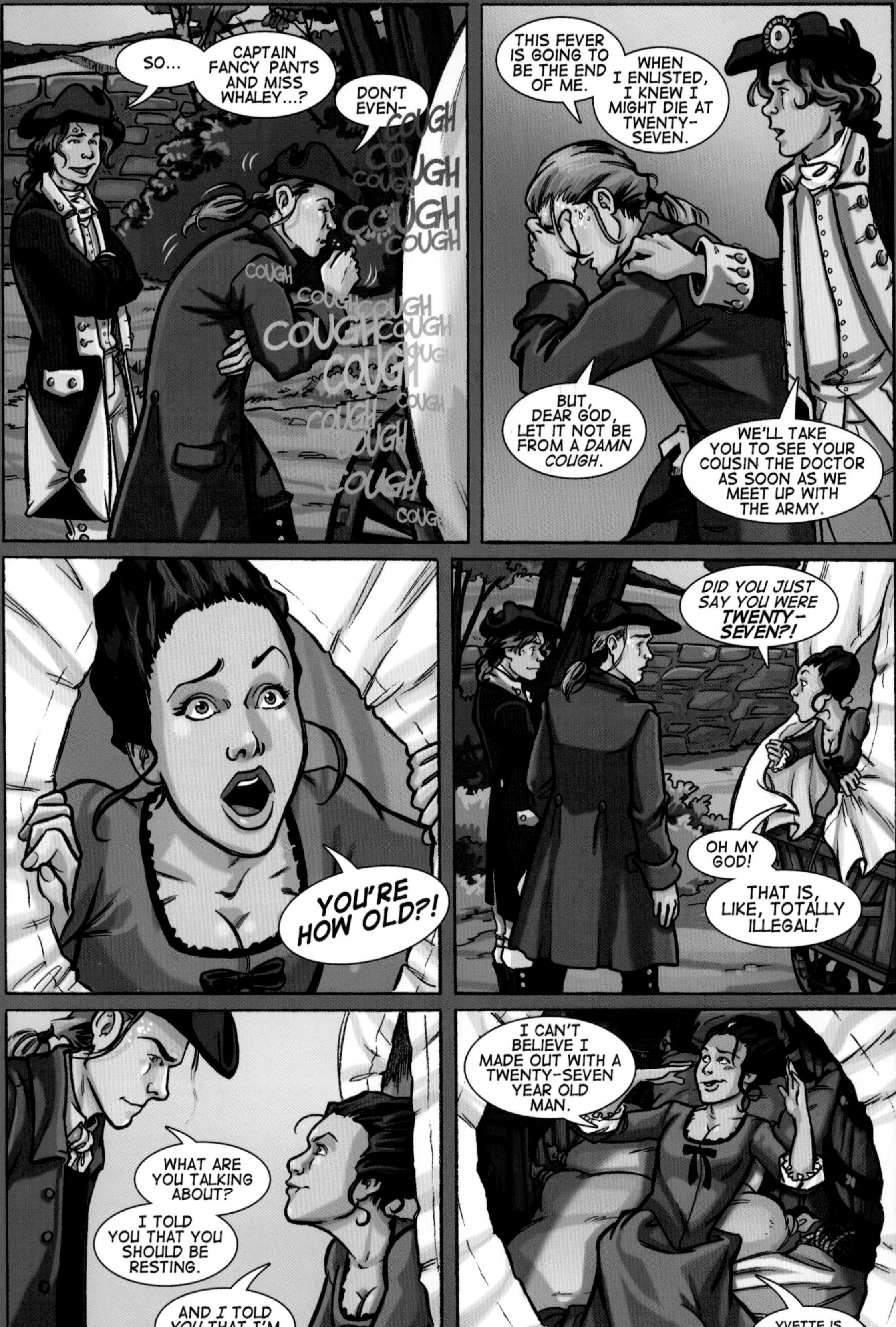

SO...
CAPTAIN FANCY PANTS AND MISS WHALEY...?
DON'T EVEN-
COUGH COUGH COUGH COUGH COUGH COUGH COUGH COUGH COUGH COUGH COUGH COUGH COUGH COUGH COUGH
THIS FEVER IS GOING TO BE THE END OF ME.
WHEN I ENLISTED, I KNEW I MIGHT DIE AT TWENTY-SEVEN.
BUT, DEAR GOD, LET IT NOT BE FROM A *DAMN COUGH*.
WE'LL TAKE YOU TO SEE YOUR COUSIN THE DOCTOR AS SOON AS WE MEET UP WITH THE ARMY.
YOU'RE HOW OLD?!
DID YOU JUST SAY YOU WERE ***TWENTY-SEVEN?!***
OH MY GOD!
THAT IS, LIKE, TOTALLY ILLEGAL!
WHAT ARE YOU TALKING ABOUT?
I TOLD YOU THAT YOU SHOULD BE RESTING.
AND *I* TOLD *YOU* THAT I'M NOT TIRED.
I CAN'T BELIEVE I MADE OUT WITH A TWENTY-SEVEN YEAR OLD MAN.
YVETTE IS GOING TO BE SO JEALOUS.

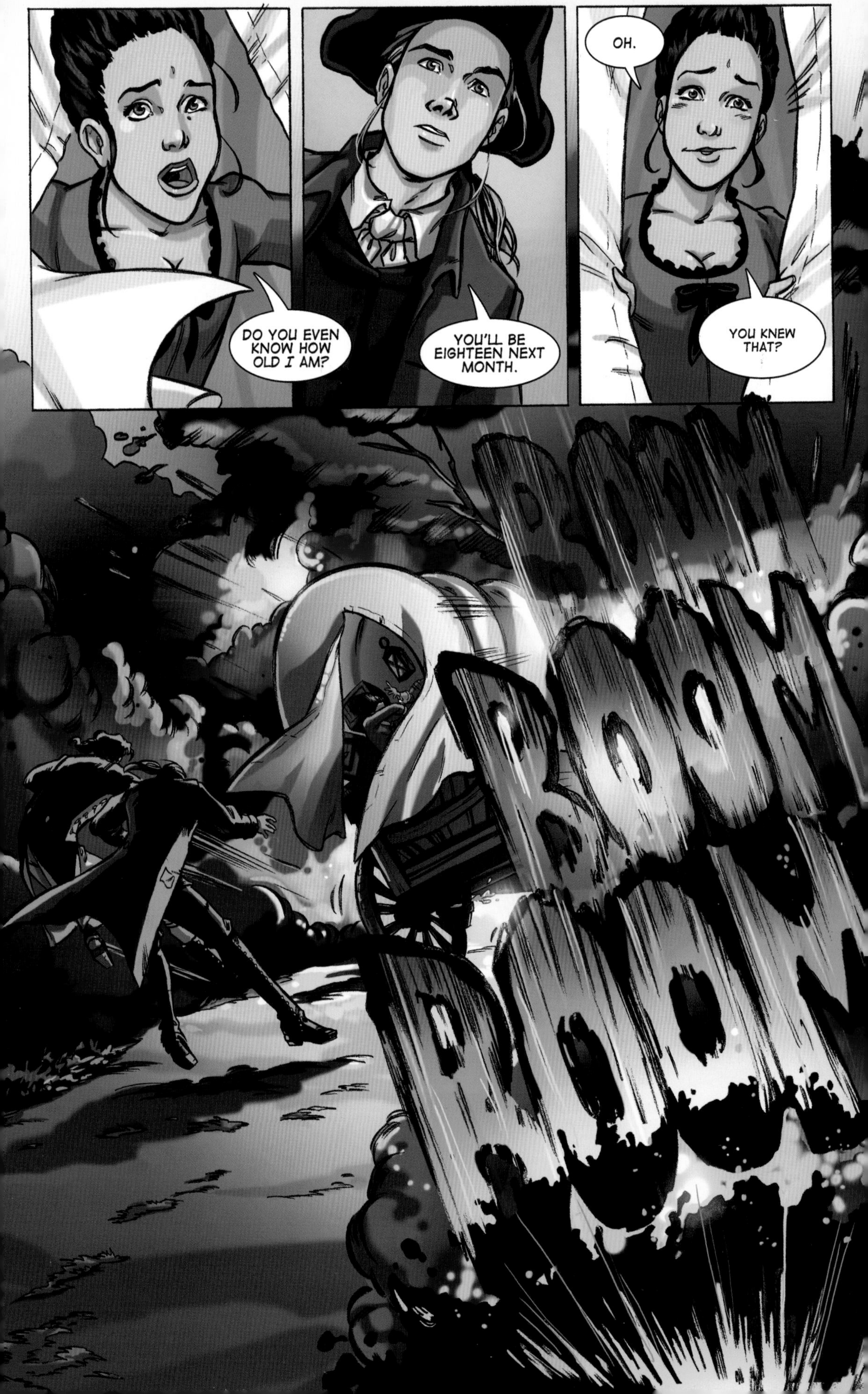
DO YOU EVEN KNOW HOW OLD I AM?
YOU'LL BE EIGHTEEN NEXT MONTH.
OH.
YOU KNEW THAT?

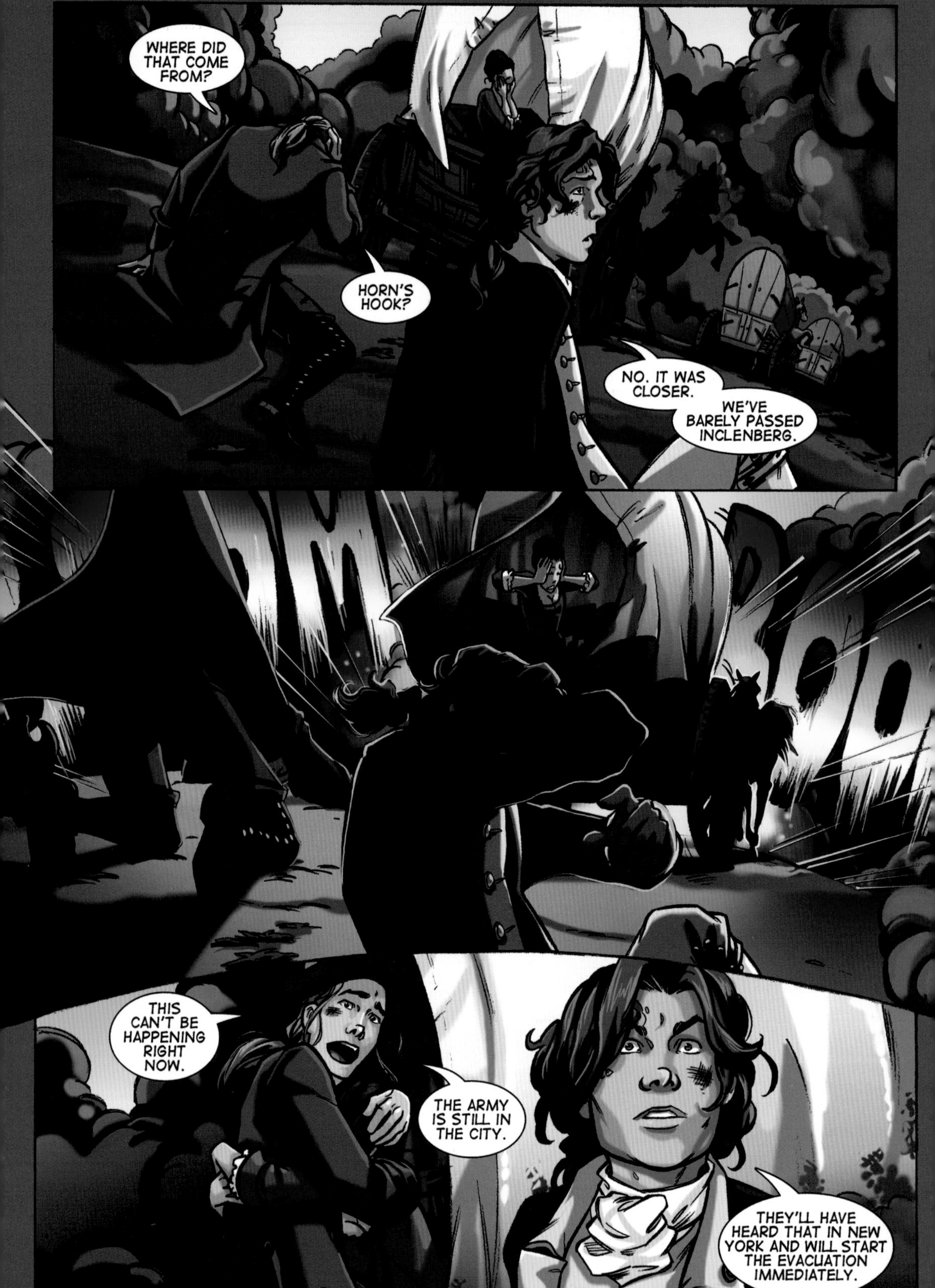
WHERE DID THAT COME FROM?
HORN'S HOOK?
NO. IT WAS CLOSER.
WE'VE BARELY PASSED INCLENBERG.
THIS CAN'T BE HAPPENING RIGHT NOW.
THE ARMY IS STILL IN THE CITY.
THEY'LL HAVE HEARD THAT IN NEW YORK AND WILL START THE EVACUATION IMMEDIATELY.

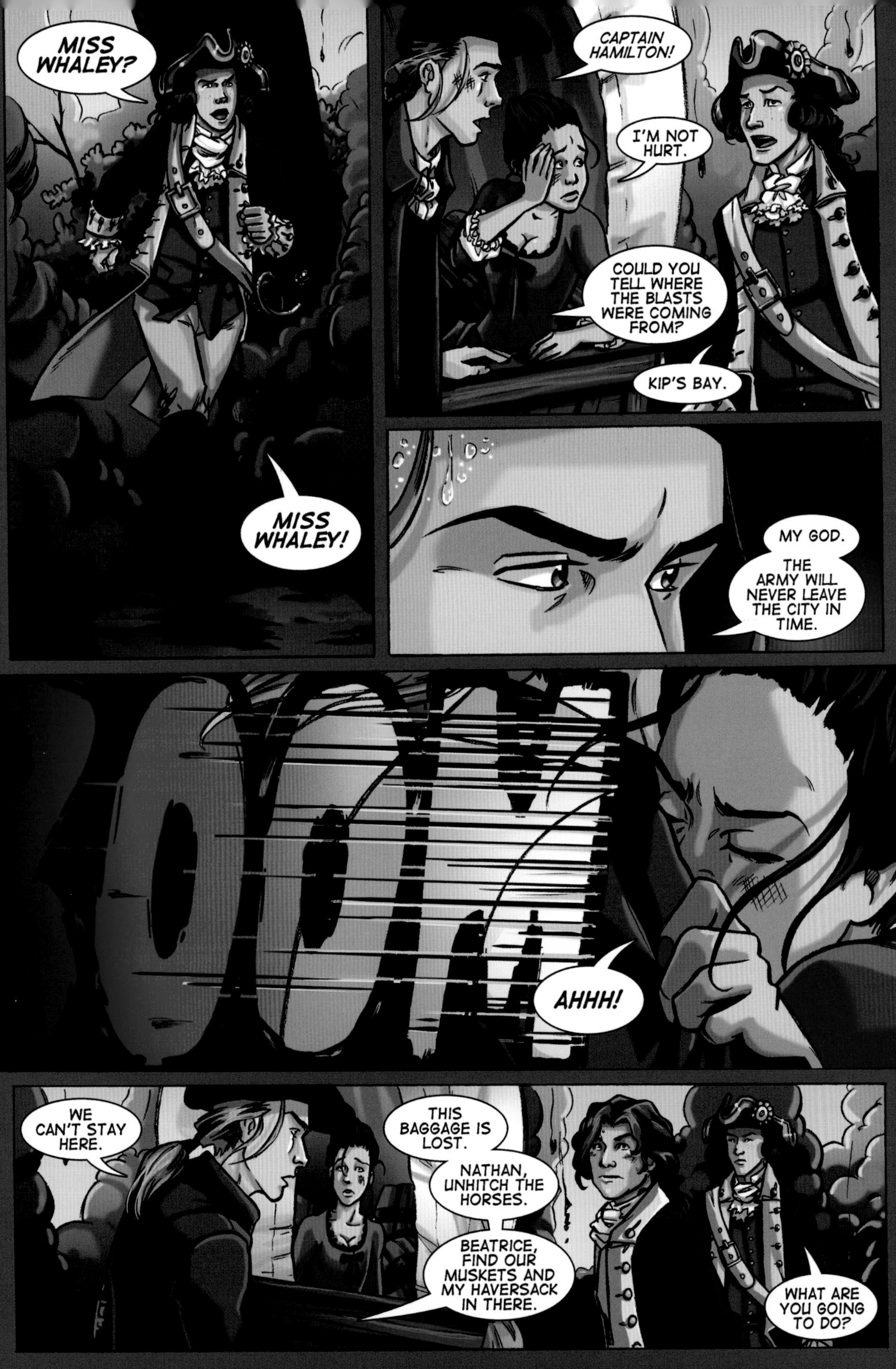
MISS WHALEY?
CAPTAIN HAMILTON!
I'M NOT HURT.
COULD YOU TELL WHERE THE BLASTS WERE COMING FROM?
KIP'S BAY.
MISS WHALEY!
MY GOD.
THE ARMY WILL NEVER LEAVE THE CITY IN TIME.
AHHH!
WE CAN'T STAY HERE.
THIS BAGGAGE IS LOST.
NATHAN, UNHITCH THE HORSES.
BEATRICE, FIND OUR MUSKETS AND MY HAVERSACK IN THERE.
WHAT ARE YOU GOING TO DO?

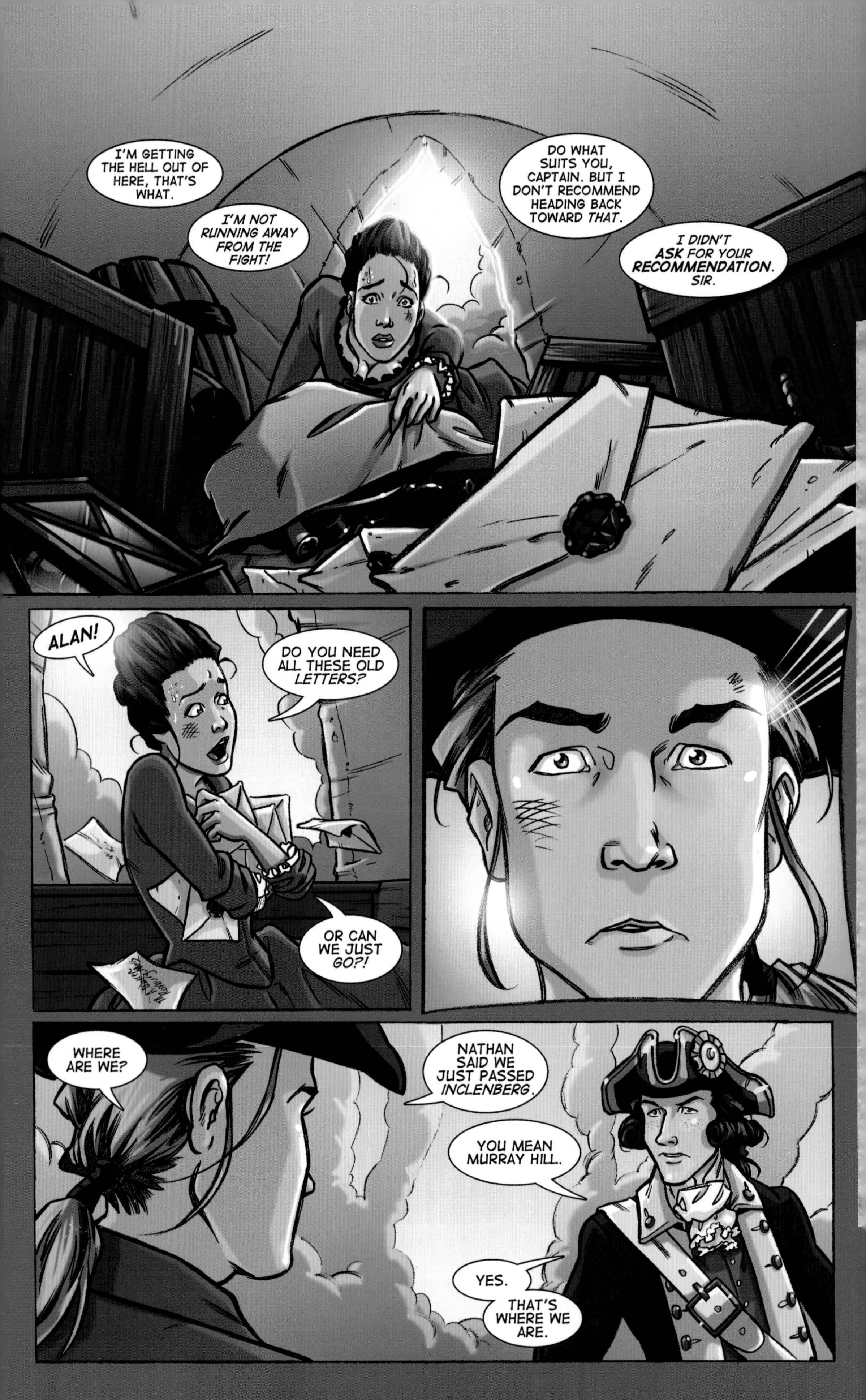
I'M GETTING THE HELL OUT OF HERE, THAT'S WHAT.
I'M NOT RUNNING AWAY FROM THE FIGHT!
DO WHAT SUITS YOU, CAPTAIN. BUT I DON'T RECOMMEND HEADING BACK TOWARD THAT.
I DIDN'T ASK FOR YOUR RECOMMENDATION. SIR.
ALAN!
DO YOU NEED ALL THESE OLD LETTERS?
OR CAN WE JUST GO?!
WHERE ARE WE?
NATHAN SAID WE JUST PASSED INCLENBERG.
YOU MEAN MURRAY HILL.
YES.
THAT'S WHERE WE ARE.

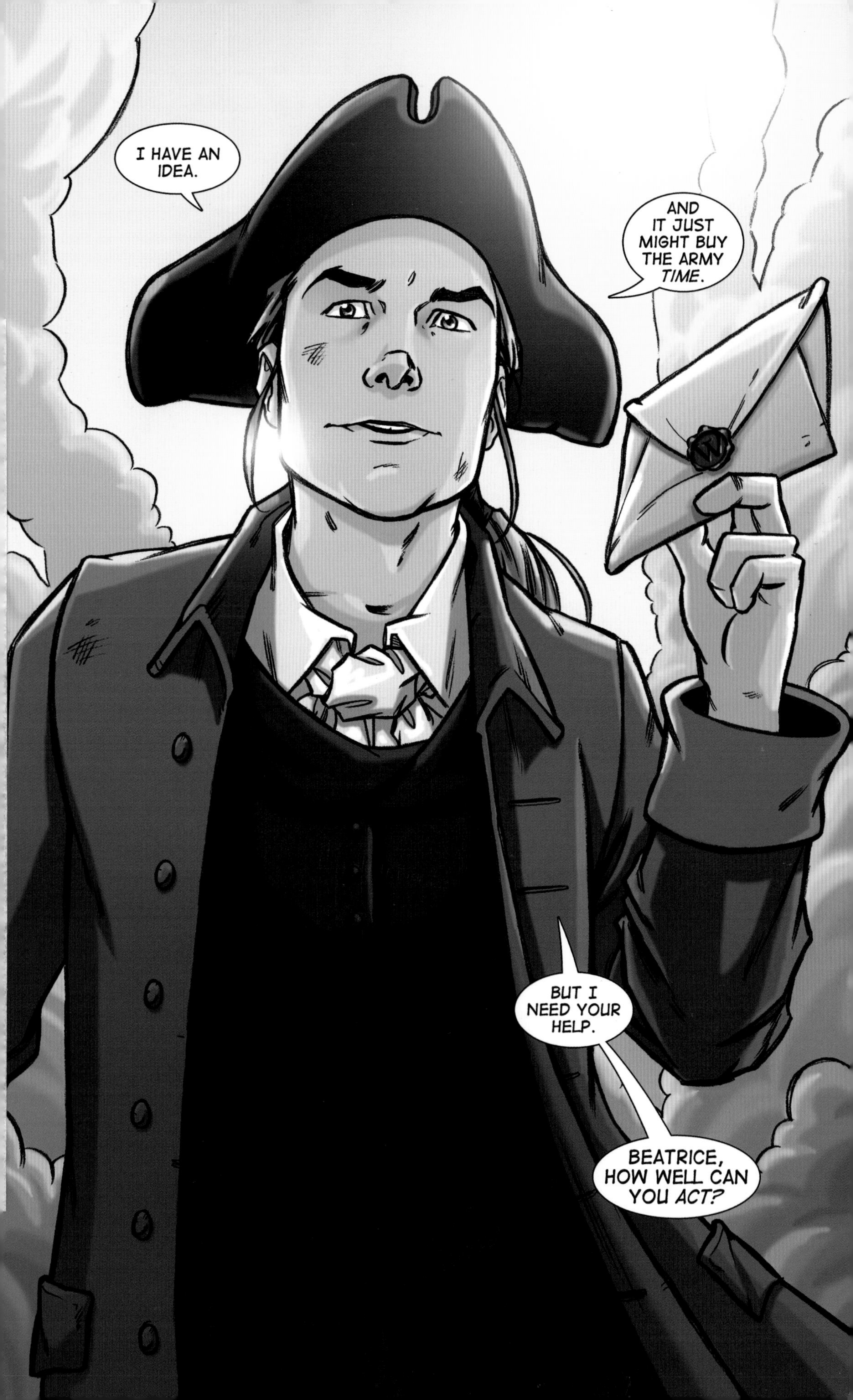
I HAVE AN IDEA.
AND IT JUST MIGHT BUY THE ARMY *TIME*.
BUT I NEED YOUR HELP.
BEATRICE, HOW WELL CAN YOU *ACT?*

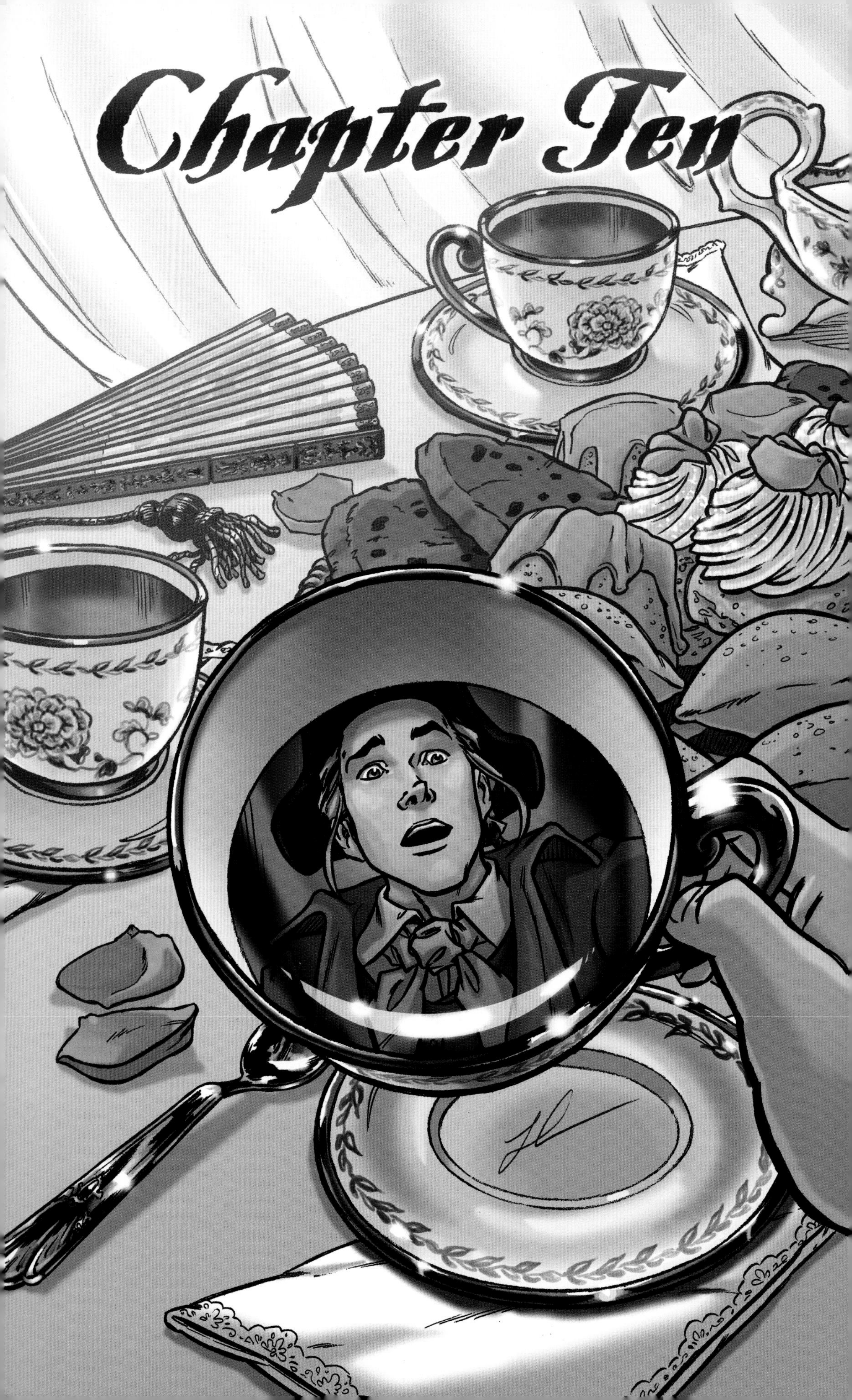
Chapter Ten

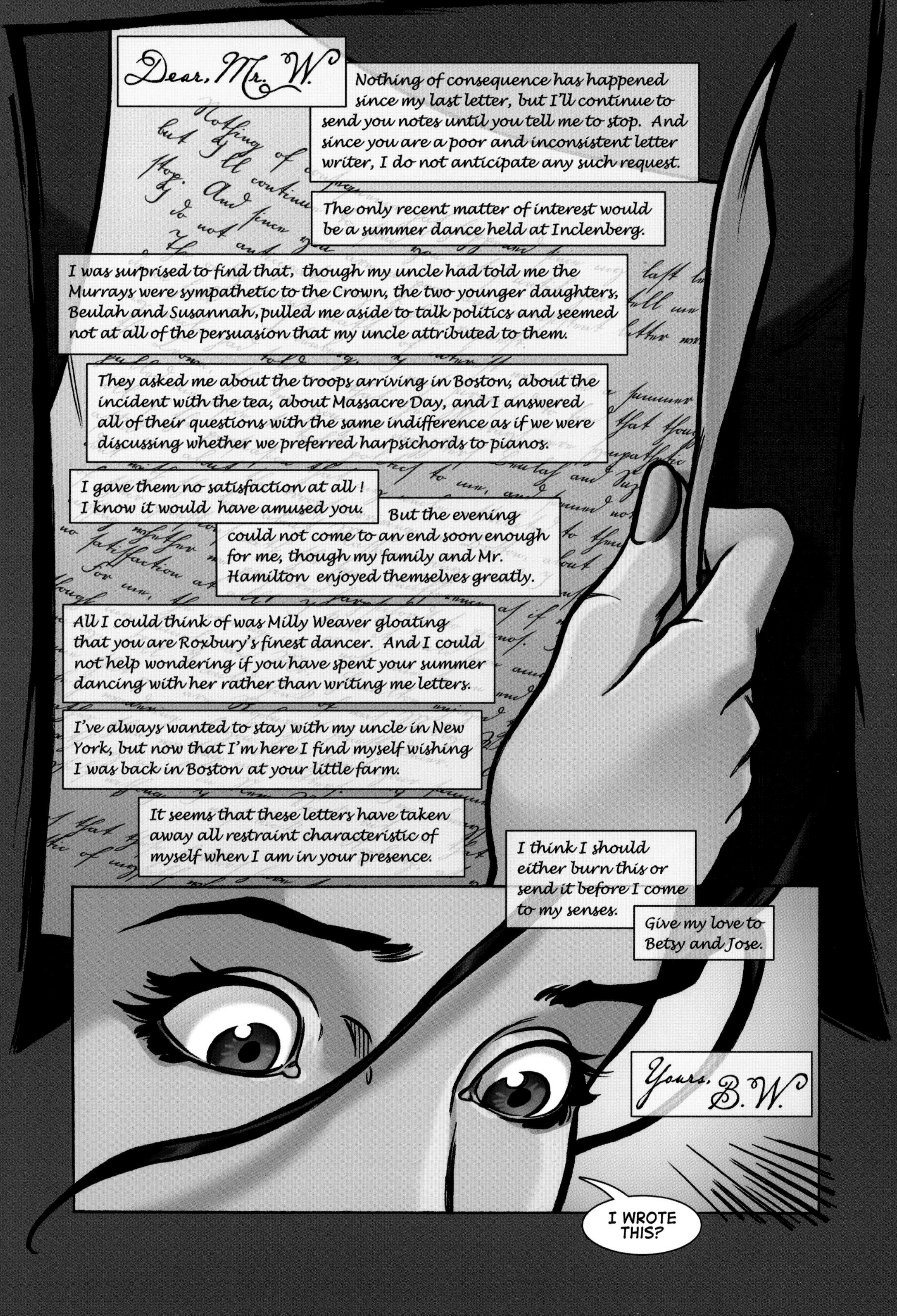
Dear, Mr. W.
Nothing of consequence has happened since my last letter, but I'll continue to send you notes until you tell me to stop. And since you are a poor and inconsistent letter writer, I do not anticipate any such request.
The only recent matter of interest would be a summer dance held at Inclenberg.
I was surprised to find that, though my uncle had told me the Murrays were sympathetic to the Crown, the two younger daughters, Beulah and Susannah, pulled me aside to talk politics and seemed not at all of the persuasion that my uncle attributed to them.
They asked me about the troops arriving in Boston, about the incident with the tea, about Massacre Day, and I answered all of their questions with the same indifference as if we were discussing whether we preferred harpsichords to pianos.
I gave them no satisfaction at all! I know it would have amused you.
But the evening could not come to an end soon enough for me, though my family and Mr. Hamilton enjoyed themselves greatly.
All I could think of was Milly Weaver gloating that you are Roxbury's finest dancer. And I could not help wondering if you have spent your summer dancing with her rather than writing me letters.
I've always wanted to stay with my uncle in New York, but now that I'm here I find myself wishing I was back in Boston at your little farm.
It seems that these letters have taken away all restraint characteristic of myself when I am in your presence.
I think I should either burn this or send it before I come to my senses.
Give my love to Betsy and Jose.
Yours, B.W.
I WROTE THIS?

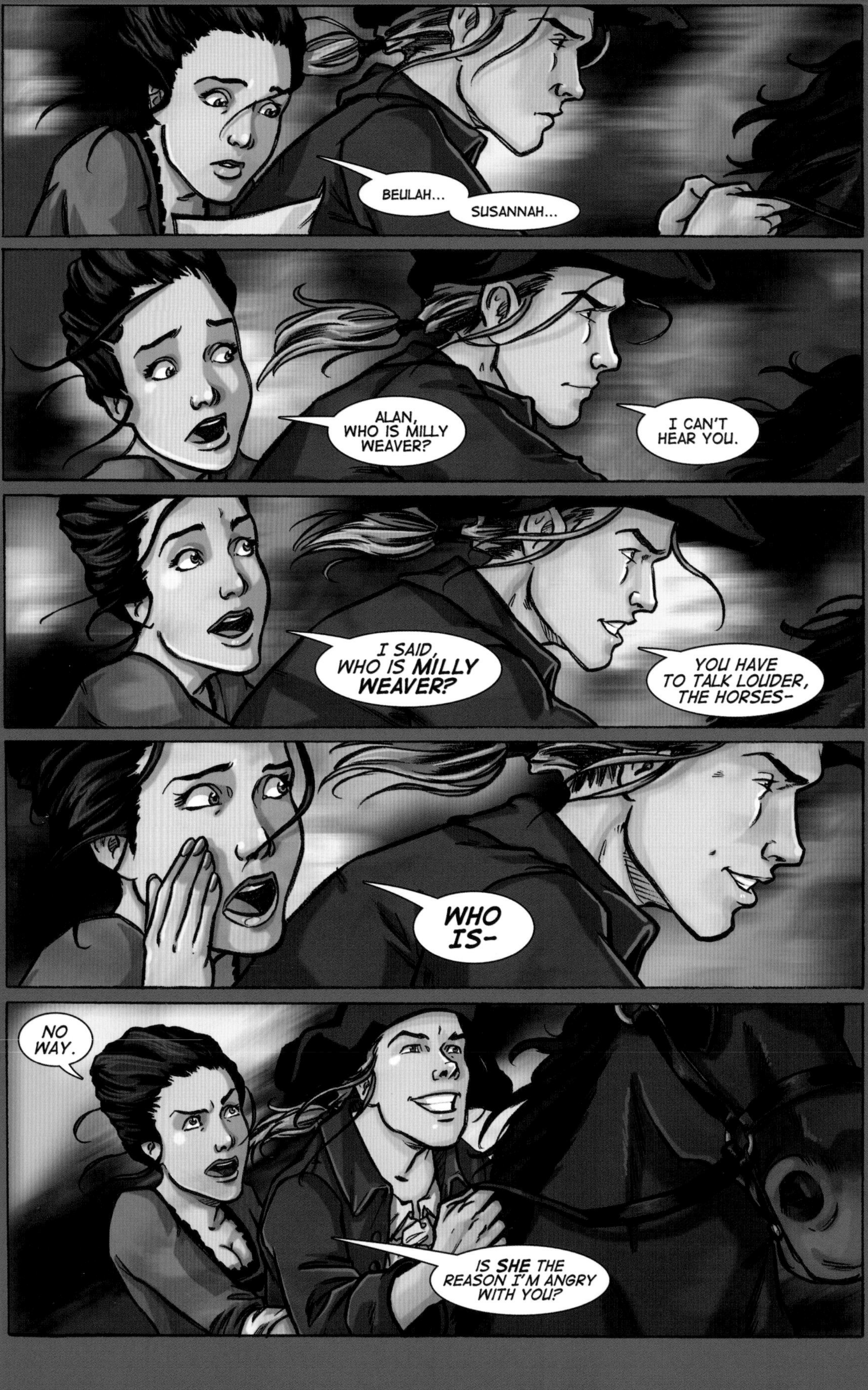
BEULAH...
SUSANNAH...
ALAN, WHO IS MILLY WEAVER?
I CAN'T HEAR YOU.
I SAID, WHO IS MILLY WEAVER?
YOU HAVE TO TALK LOUDER, THE HORSES-
WHO IS-
NO WAY.
IS SHE THE REASON I'M ANGRY WITH YOU?

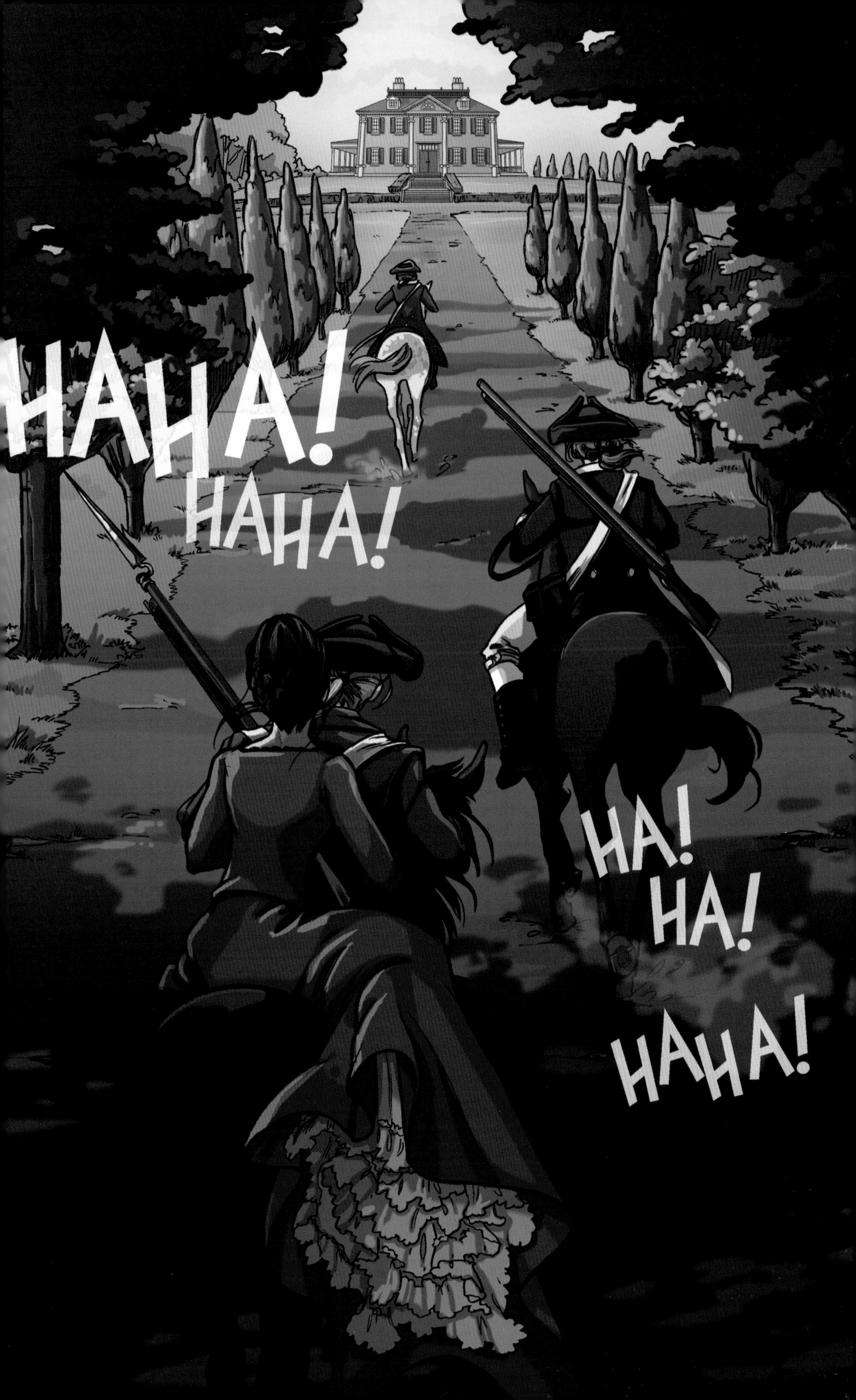
HAHA!
HAHA!
HA!
HA!
HAHA!

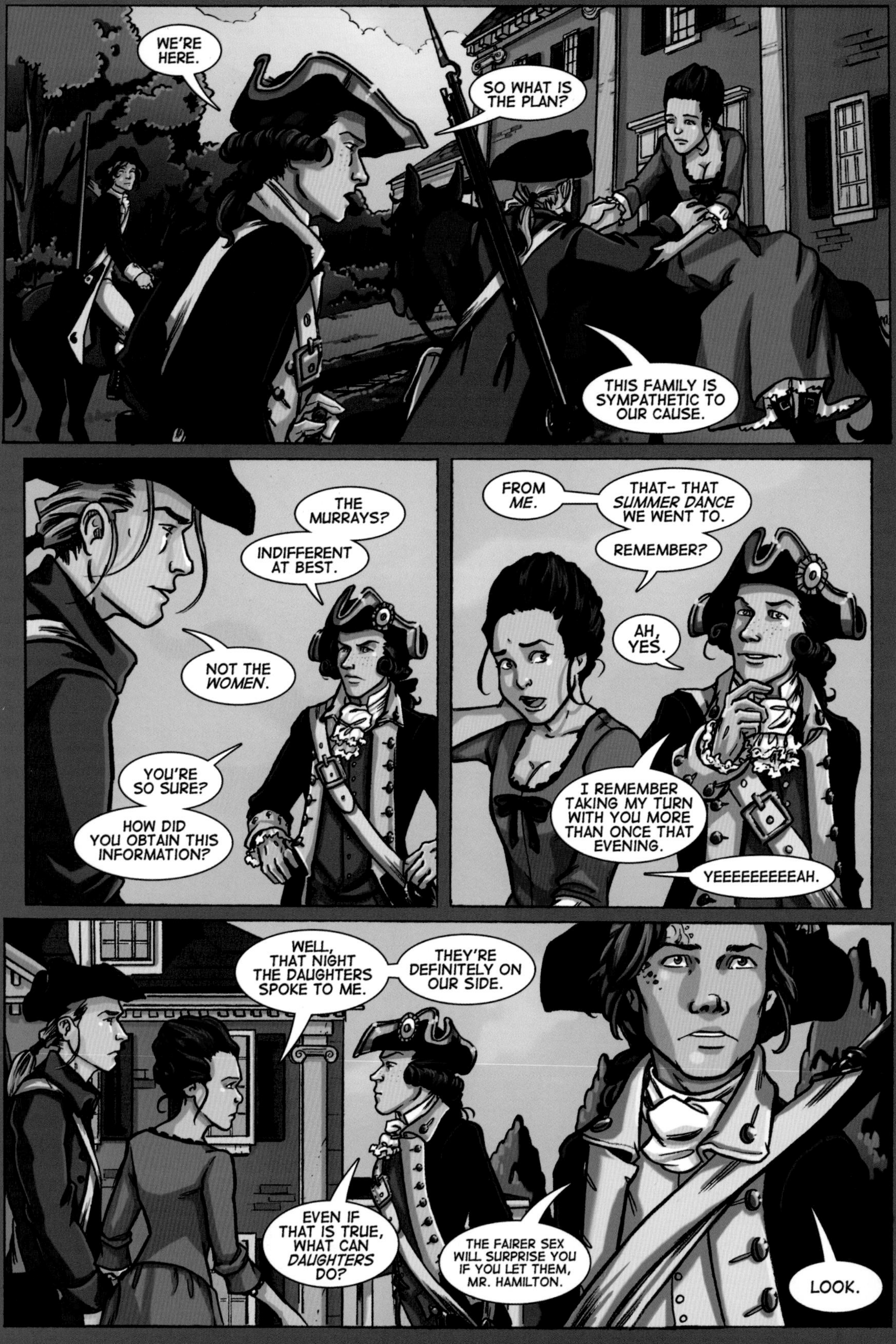
WE'RE HERE.
SO WHAT IS THE PLAN?
THIS FAMILY IS SYMPATHETIC TO OUR CAUSE.
THE MURRAYS?
INDIFFERENT AT BEST.
NOT THE *WOMEN*.
YOU'RE SO SURE?
HOW DID YOU OBTAIN THIS INFORMATION?
FROM *ME*.
THAT- THAT *SUMMER DANCE* WE WENT TO.
REMEMBER?
AH, YES.
I REMEMBER TAKING MY TURN WITH YOU MORE THAN ONCE THAT EVENING.
YEEEEEEEEEAH.
WELL, THAT NIGHT THE DAUGHTERS SPOKE TO ME.
THEY'RE DEFINITELY ON OUR SIDE.
EVEN IF THAT IS TRUE, WHAT CAN *DAUGHTERS* DO?
THE FAIRER SEX WILL SURPRISE YOU IF YOU LET THEM, MR. HAMILTON.
LOOK.

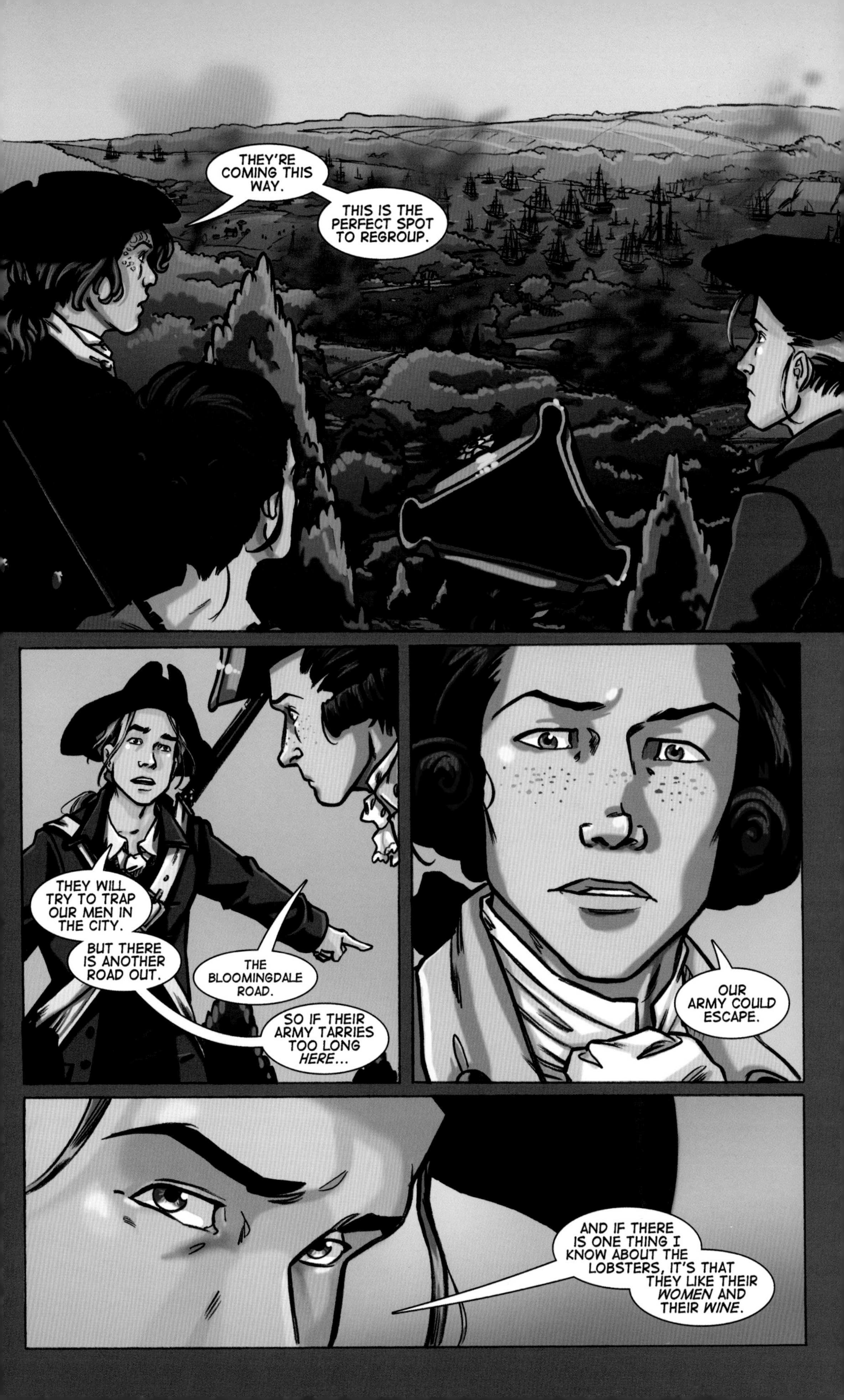
THEY'RE COMING THIS WAY.
THIS IS THE PERFECT SPOT TO REGROUP.
THEY WILL TRY TO TRAP OUR MEN IN THE CITY.
BUT THERE IS ANOTHER ROAD OUT.
THE BLOOMINGDALE ROAD.
SO IF THEIR ARMY TARRIES TOO LONG *HERE*...
OUR ARMY COULD ESCAPE.
AND IF THERE IS ONE THING I KNOW ABOUT THE LOBSTERS, IT'S THAT THEY LIKE THEIR *WOMEN* AND THEIR *WINE*.

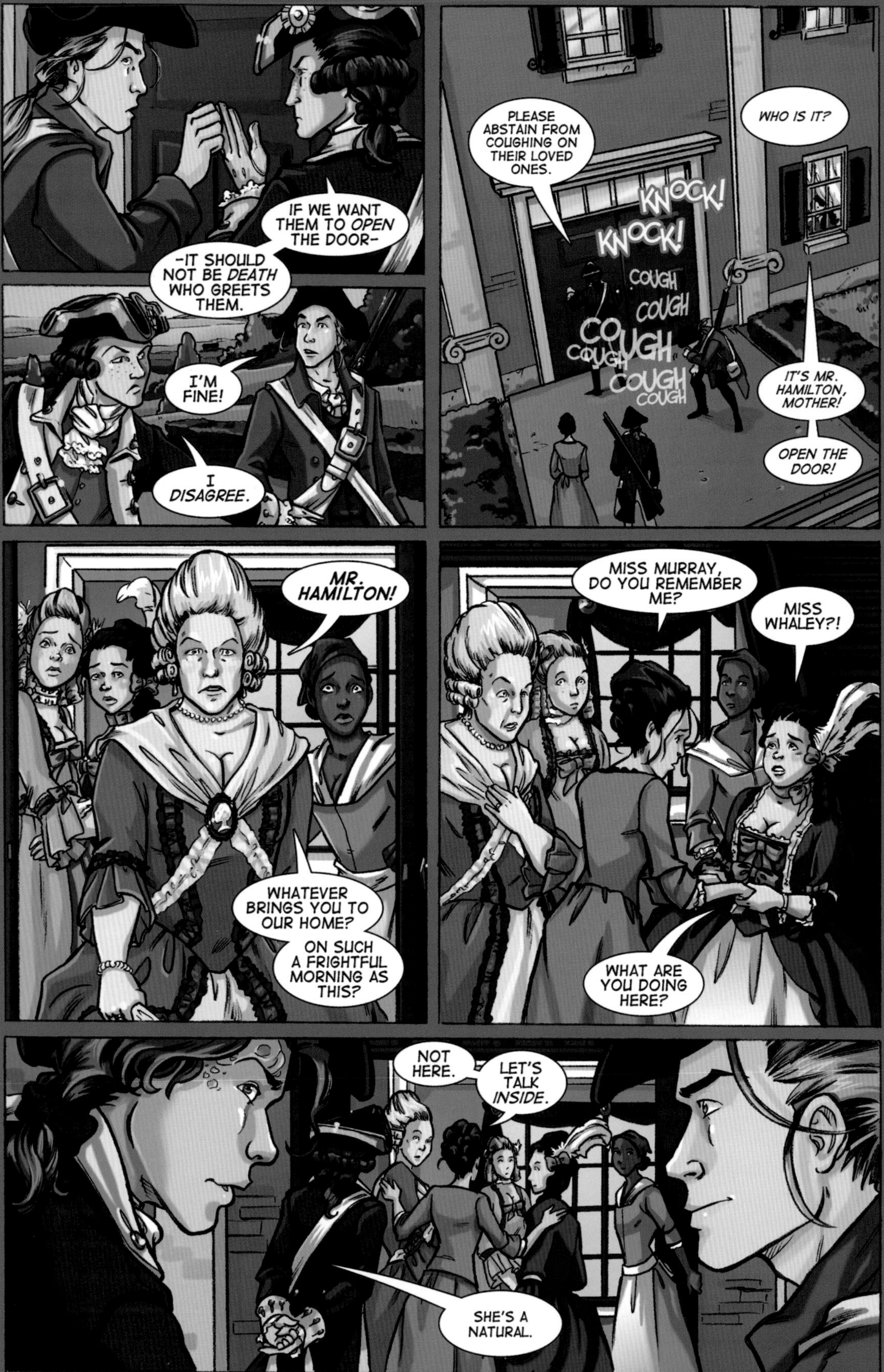
IF WE WANT THEM TO *OPEN* THE DOOR-
-IT SHOULD NOT BE *DEATH* WHO GREETS THEM.
I'M FINE!
I *DISAGREE*.
PLEASE ABSTAIN FROM COUGHING ON THEIR LOVED ONES.
KNOCK! KNOCK!
COUGH COUGH COUGH COUGH COUGH COUGH
WHO IS IT?
IT'S MR. HAMILTON, MOTHER!
OPEN THE DOOR!
MR. HAMILTON!
WHATEVER BRINGS YOU TO OUR HOME?
ON SUCH A FRIGHTFUL MORNING AS THIS?
MISS MURRAY, DO YOU REMEMBER ME?
MISS WHALEY?!
WHAT ARE YOU DOING HERE?
NOT HERE.
LET'S TALK *INSIDE*.
SHE'S A NATURAL.

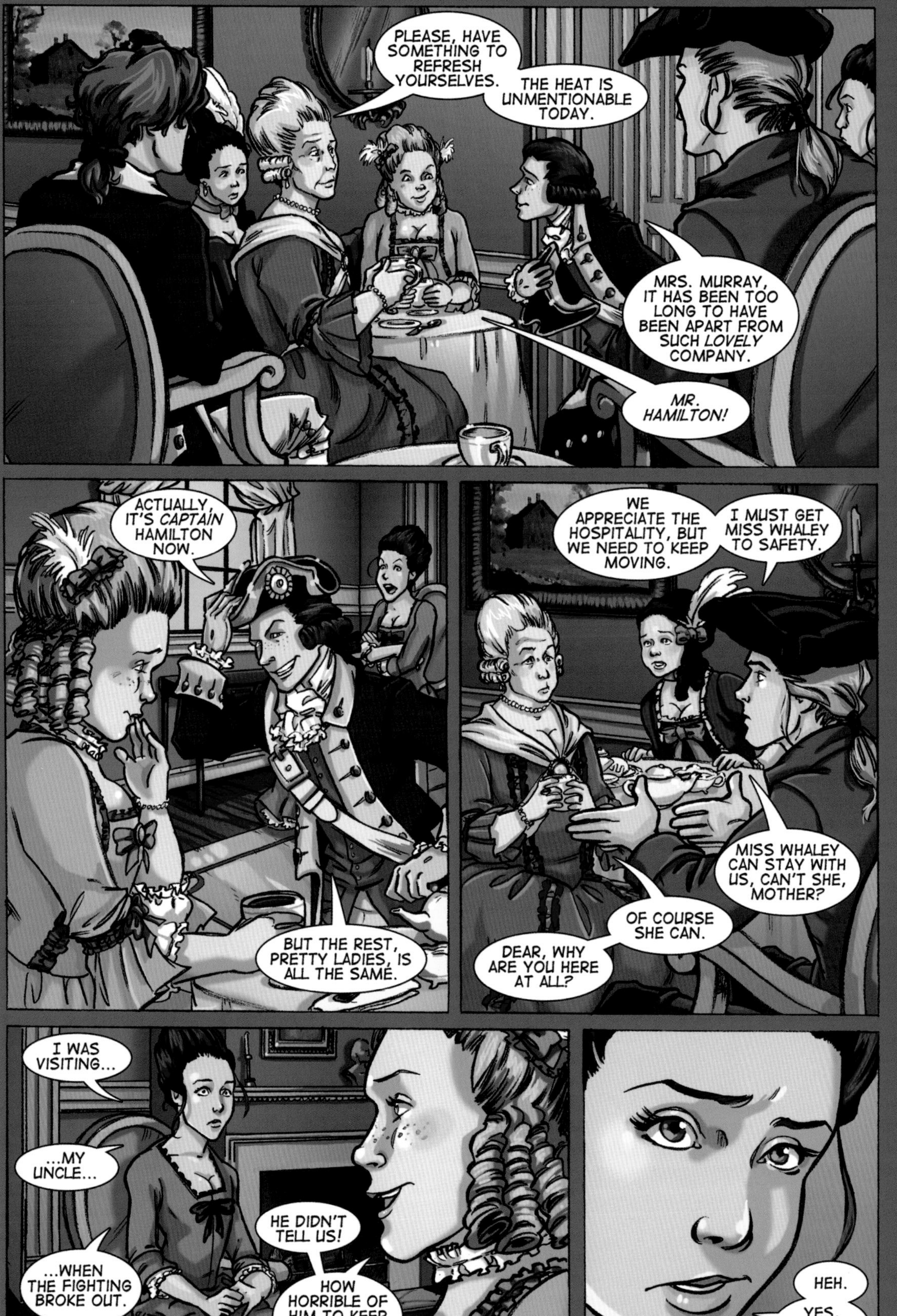
PLEASE, HAVE SOMETHING TO REFRESH YOURSELVES.
THE HEAT IS UNMENTIONABLE TODAY.
MRS. MURRAY, IT HAS BEEN TOO LONG TO HAVE BEEN APART FROM SUCH *LOVELY* COMPANY.
MR. HAMILTON!
ACTUALLY, IT'S *CAPTAIN* HAMILTON NOW.
BUT THE REST, PRETTY LADIES, IS ALL THE SAME.
WE APPRECIATE THE HOSPITALITY, BUT WE NEED TO KEEP MOVING.
I MUST GET MISS WHALEY TO SAFETY.
MISS WHALEY CAN STAY WITH US, CAN'T SHE, MOTHER?
OF COURSE SHE CAN.
DEAR, WHY ARE YOU HERE AT ALL?
I WAS VISITING...
...MY UNCLE...
...WHEN THE FIGHTING BROKE OUT.
HE DIDN'T TELL US!
HOW HORRIBLE OF HIM TO KEEP YOU ALL TO HIMSELF!
HEH.
YES, WICKED OF HIM.

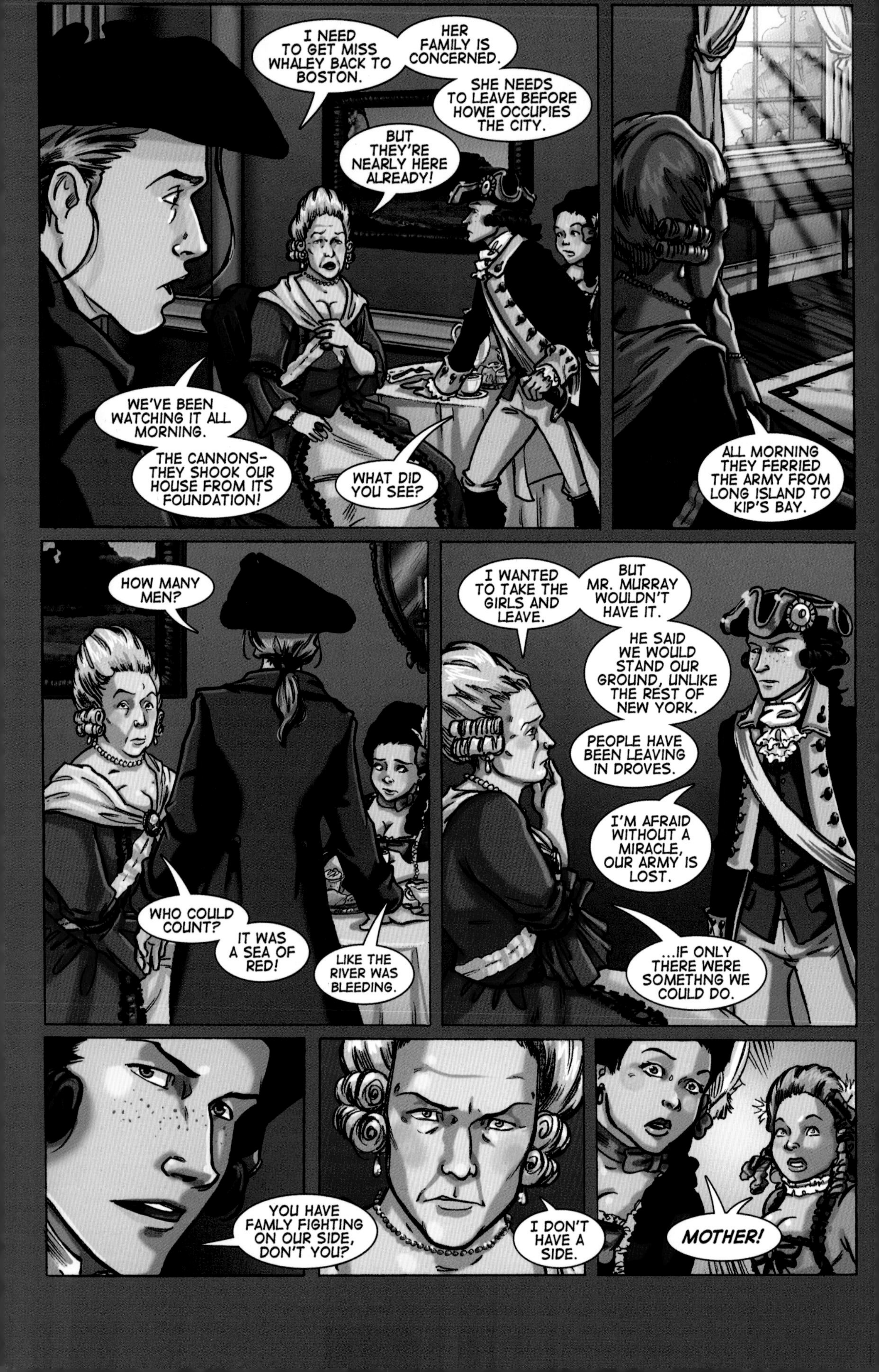
I NEED TO GET MISS WHALEY BACK TO BOSTON.
HER FAMILY IS CONCERNED.
SHE NEEDS TO LEAVE BEFORE HOWE OCCUPIES THE CITY.
BUT THEY'RE NEARLY HERE ALREADY!
WE'VE BEEN WATCHING IT ALL MORNING.
THE CANNONS- THEY SHOOK OUR HOUSE FROM ITS FOUNDATION!
WHAT DID YOU SEE?
ALL MORNING THEY FERRIED THE ARMY FROM LONG ISLAND TO KIP'S BAY.
HOW MANY MEN?
WHO COULD COUNT?
IT WAS A SEA OF RED!
LIKE THE RIVER WAS BLEEDING.
I WANTED TO TAKE THE GIRLS AND LEAVE.
BUT MR. MURRAY WOULDN'T HAVE IT.
HE SAID WE WOULD STAND OUR GROUND, UNLIKE THE REST OF NEW YORK.
PEOPLE HAVE BEEN LEAVING IN DROVES.
I'M AFRAID WITHOUT A MIRACLE, OUR ARMY IS LOST.
...IF ONLY THERE WERE SOMETHNG WE COULD DO.
YOU HAVE FAMLY FIGHTING ON OUR SIDE, DON'T YOU?
I DON'T HAVE A SIDE.
MOTHER!

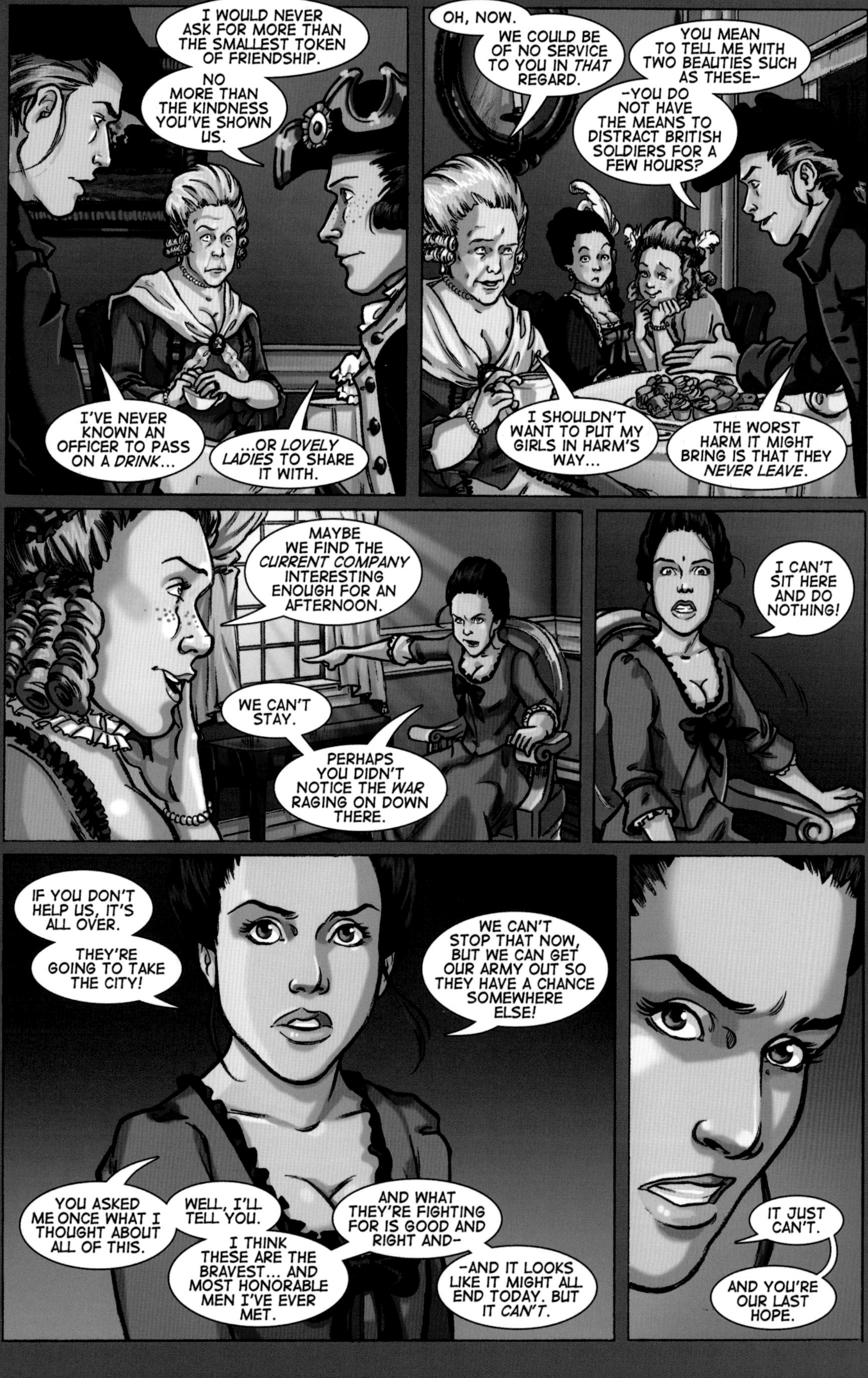
I WOULD NEVER ASK FOR MORE THAN THE SMALLEST TOKEN OF FRIENDSHIP.
NO MORE THAN THE KINDNESS YOU'VE SHOWN US.
I'VE NEVER KNOWN AN OFFICER TO PASS ON A *DRINK*...
...OR *LOVELY LADIES* TO SHARE IT WITH.
OH, NOW.
WE COULD BE OF NO SERVICE TO YOU IN *THAT* REGARD.
YOU MEAN TO TELL ME WITH TWO BEAUTIES SUCH AS THESE-
-YOU DO NOT HAVE THE MEANS TO DISTRACT BRITISH SOLDIERS FOR A FEW HOURS?
I SHOULDN'T WANT TO PUT MY GIRLS IN HARM'S WAY...
THE WORST HARM IT MIGHT BRING IS THAT THEY *NEVER LEAVE*.
MAYBE WE FIND THE *CURRENT COMPANY* INTERESTING ENOUGH FOR AN AFTERNOON.
WE CAN'T STAY.
PERHAPS YOU DIDN'T NOTICE THE *WAR* RAGING ON DOWN THERE.
I CAN'T SIT HERE AND DO NOTHING!
IF YOU DON'T HELP US, IT'S ALL OVER.
THEY'RE GOING TO TAKE THE CITY!
WE CAN'T STOP THAT NOW, BUT WE CAN GET OUR ARMY OUT SO THEY HAVE A CHANCE SOMEWHERE ELSE!
YOU ASKED ME ONCE WHAT I THOUGHT ABOUT ALL OF THIS.
WELL, I'LL TELL YOU.
I THINK THESE ARE THE BRAVEST... AND MOST HONORABLE MEN I'VE EVER MET.
AND WHAT THEY'RE FIGHTING FOR IS GOOD AND RIGHT AND-
-AND IT LOOKS LIKE IT MIGHT ALL END TODAY. BUT IT *CAN'T*.
IT JUST CAN'T.
AND YOU'RE OUR LAST HOPE.

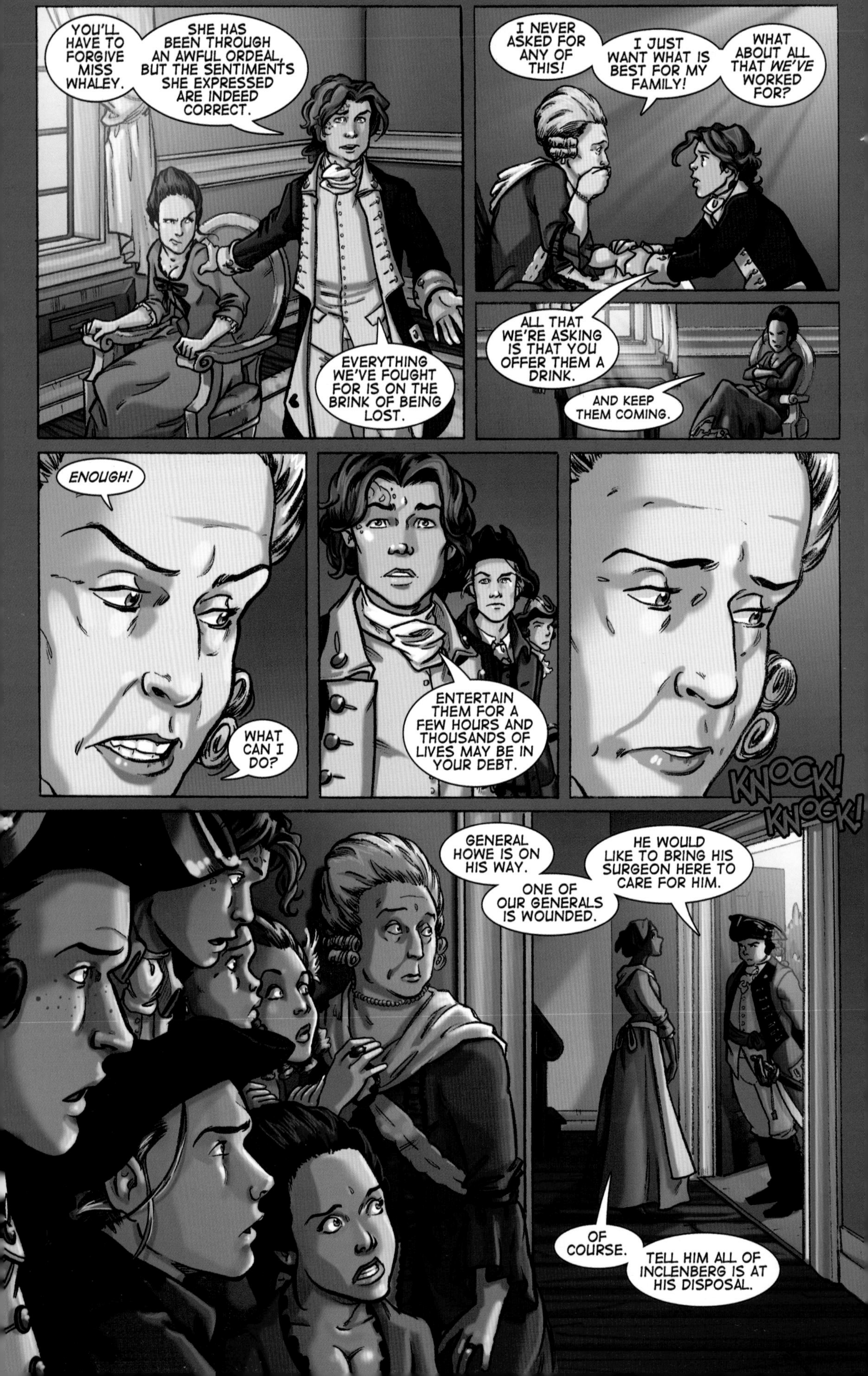
YOU'LL HAVE TO FORGIVE MISS WHALEY.
SHE HAS BEEN THROUGH AN AWFUL ORDEAL, BUT THE SENTIMENTS SHE EXPRESSED ARE INDEED CORRECT.
EVERYTHING WE'VE FOUGHT FOR IS ON THE BRINK OF BEING LOST.
I NEVER ASKED FOR ANY OF THIS!
I JUST WANT WHAT IS BEST FOR MY FAMILY!
WHAT ABOUT ALL THAT *WE'VE* WORKED FOR?
ALL THAT WE'RE ASKING IS THAT YOU OFFER THEM A DRINK.
AND KEEP THEM COMING.
ENOUGH!
WHAT CAN I DO?
ENTERTAIN THEM FOR A FEW HOURS AND THOUSANDS OF LIVES MAY BE IN YOUR DEBT.
KNOCK! KNOCK!
GENERAL HOWE IS ON HIS WAY.
ONE OF OUR GENERALS IS WOUNDED.
HE WOULD LIKE TO BRING HIS SURGEON HERE TO CARE FOR HIM.
OF COURSE.
TELL HIM ALL OF INCLENBERG IS AT HIS DISPOSAL.

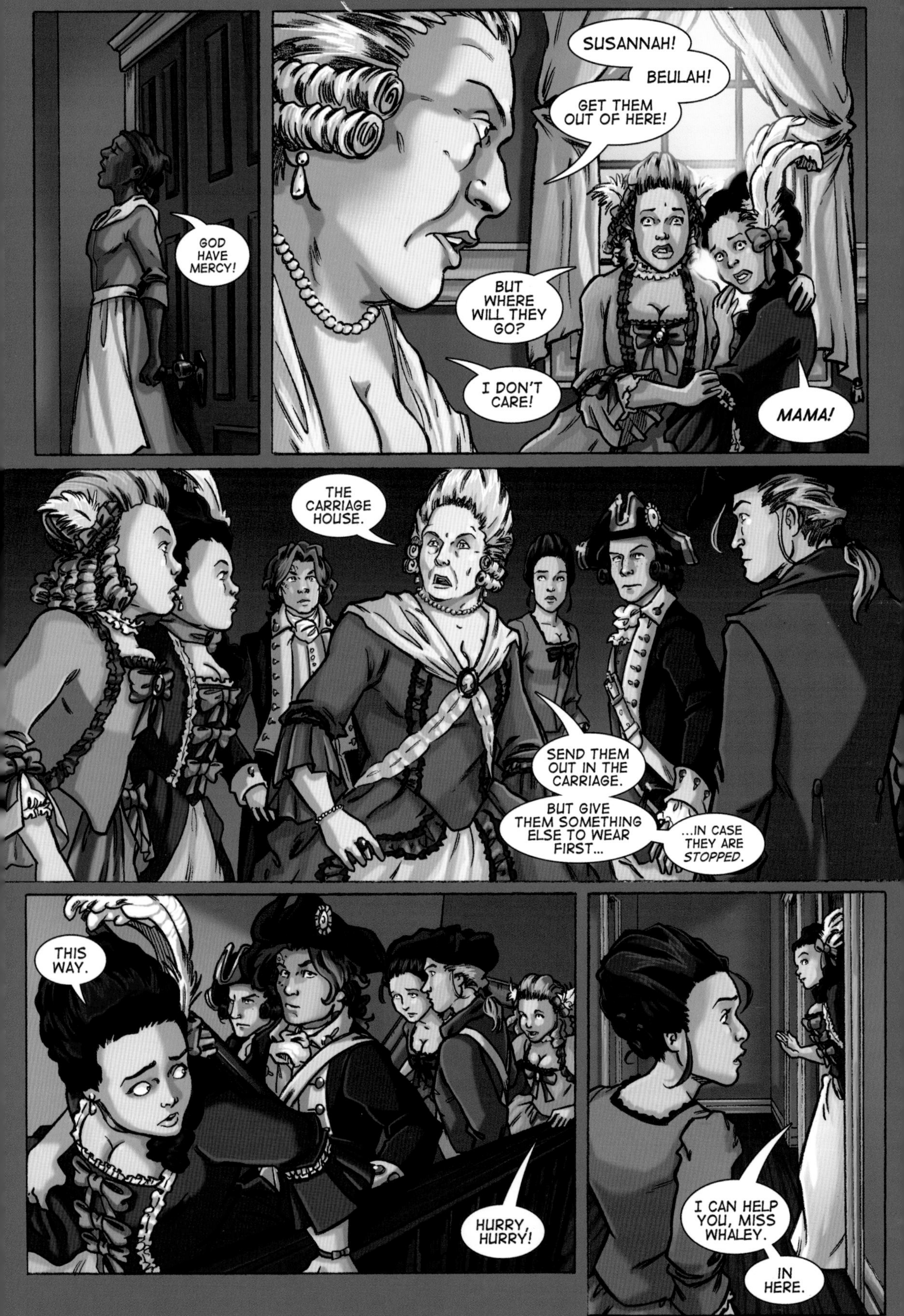
GOD HAVE MERCY!
SUSANNAH!
BEULAH!
GET THEM OUT OF HERE!
BUT WHERE WILL THEY GO?
I DON'T CARE!
MAMA!
THE CARRIAGE HOUSE.
SEND THEM OUT IN THE CARRIAGE.
BUT GIVE THEM SOMETHING ELSE TO WEAR FIRST...
...IN CASE THEY ARE STOPPED.
THIS WAY.
HURRY, HURRY!
I CAN HELP YOU, MISS WHALEY.
IN HERE.

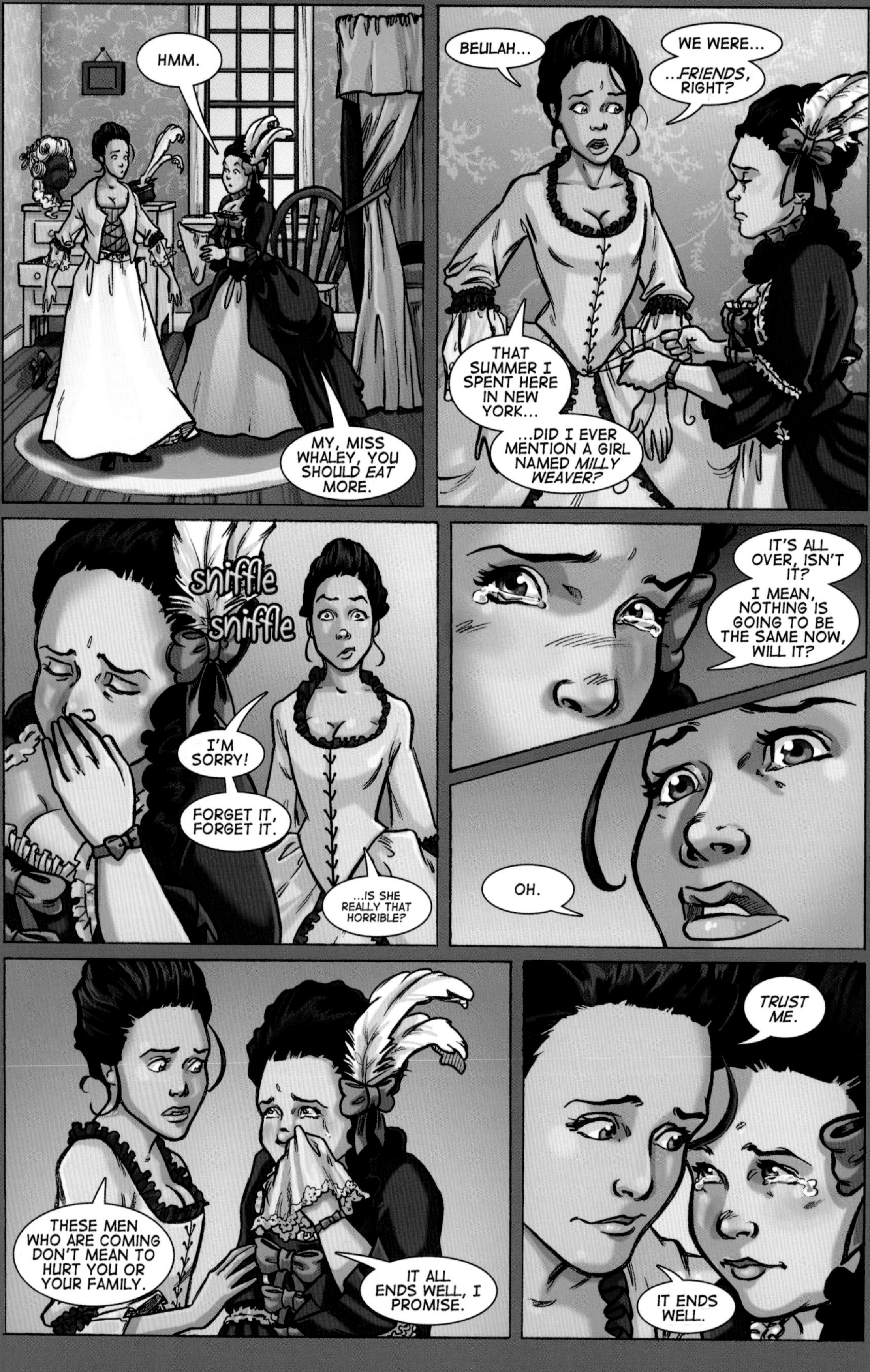
HMM.
MY, MISS WHALEY, YOU SHOULD *EAT* MORE.
BEULAH...
WE WERE...
...*FRIENDS*, RIGHT?
THAT SUMMER I SPENT HERE IN NEW YORK...
...DID I EVER MENTION A GIRL NAMED *MILLY WEAVER?*
sniffle
sniffle
I'M SORRY!
FORGET IT, FORGET IT.
...IS SHE REALLY THAT HORRIBLE?
IT'S ALL OVER, ISN'T IT?
I MEAN, NOTHING IS GOING TO BE THE SAME NOW, WILL IT?
OH.
THESE MEN WHO ARE COMING DON'T MEAN TO HURT YOU OR YOUR FAMILY.
IT ALL ENDS WELL, I PROMISE.
TRUST ME.
IT ENDS WELL.

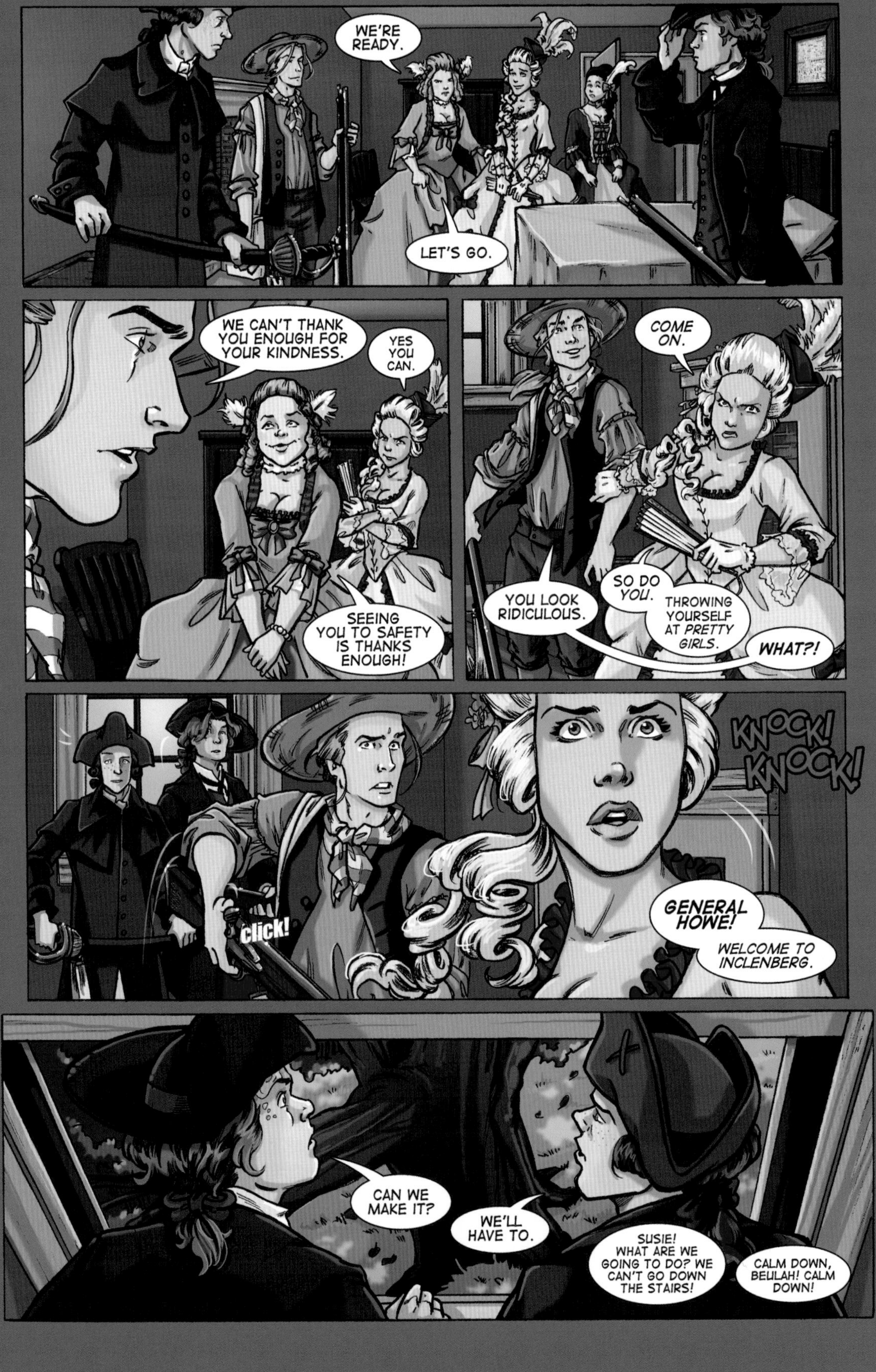
WE'RE READY.
LET'S GO.
WE CAN'T THANK YOU ENOUGH FOR YOUR KINDNESS.
YES YOU CAN.
SEEING YOU TO SAFETY IS THANKS ENOUGH!
COME ON.
YOU LOOK RIDICULOUS.
SO DO YOU.
THROWING YOURSELF AT *PRETTY GIRLS*.
WHAT?!
KNOCK! KNOCK!
click!
GENERAL HOWE!
WELCOME TO INCLENBERG.
CAN WE MAKE IT?
WE'LL HAVE TO.
SUSIE! WHAT ARE WE GOING TO DO? WE CAN'T GO DOWN THE STAIRS!
CALM DOWN, BEULAH! CALM DOWN!

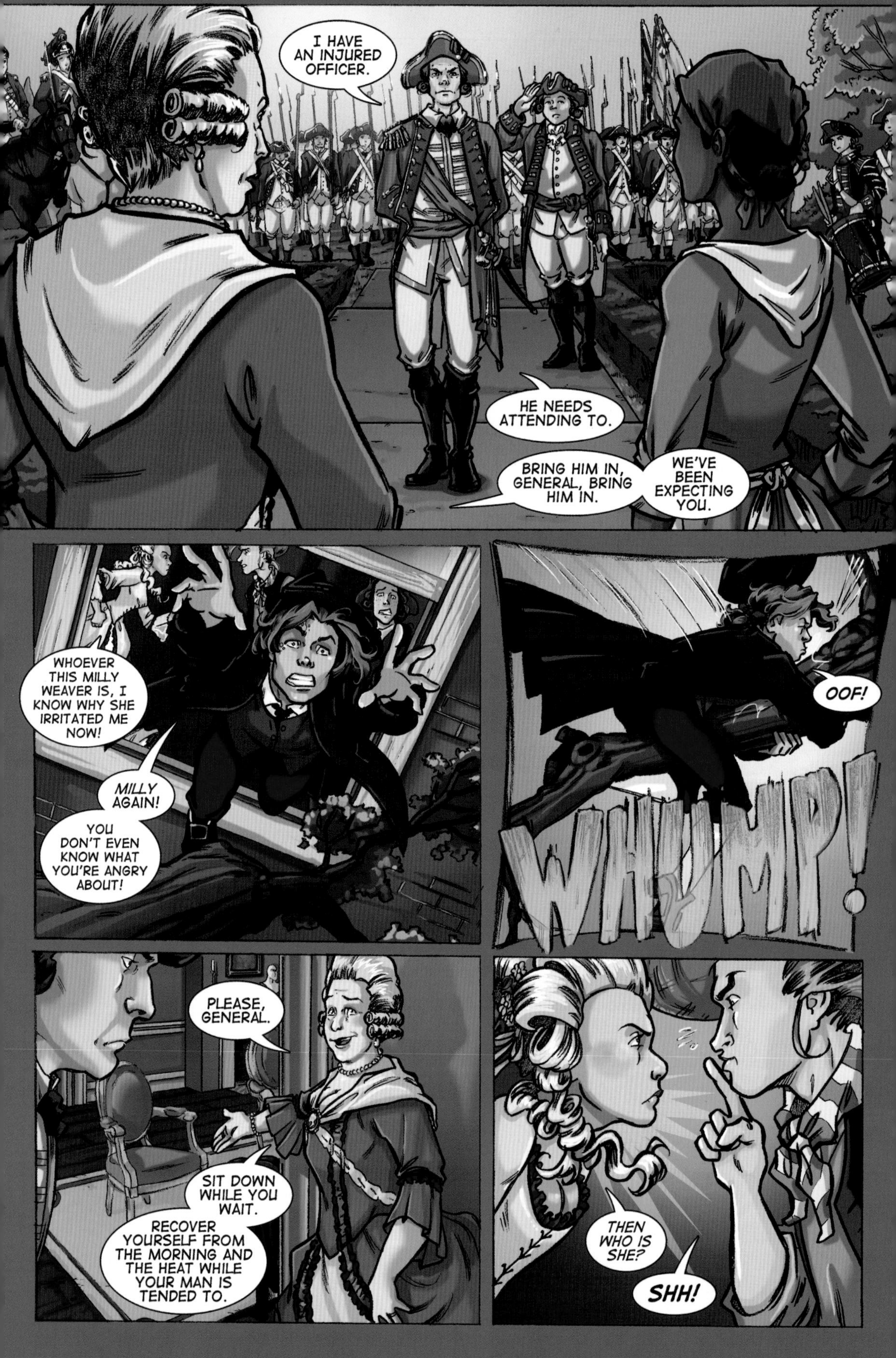
I HAVE AN INJURED OFFICER.
HE NEEDS ATTENDING TO.
BRING HIM IN, GENERAL, BRING HIM IN.
WE'VE BEEN EXPECTING YOU.
WHOEVER THIS MILLY WEAVER IS, I KNOW WHY SHE IRRITATED ME NOW!
MILLY AGAIN!
YOU DON'T EVEN KNOW WHAT YOU'RE ANGRY ABOUT!
OOF!
WHUMP!
PLEASE, GENERAL.
SIT DOWN WHILE YOU WAIT.
RECOVER YOURSELF FROM THE MORNING AND THE HEAT WHILE YOUR MAN IS TENDED TO.
THEN WHO IS SHE?
SHH!

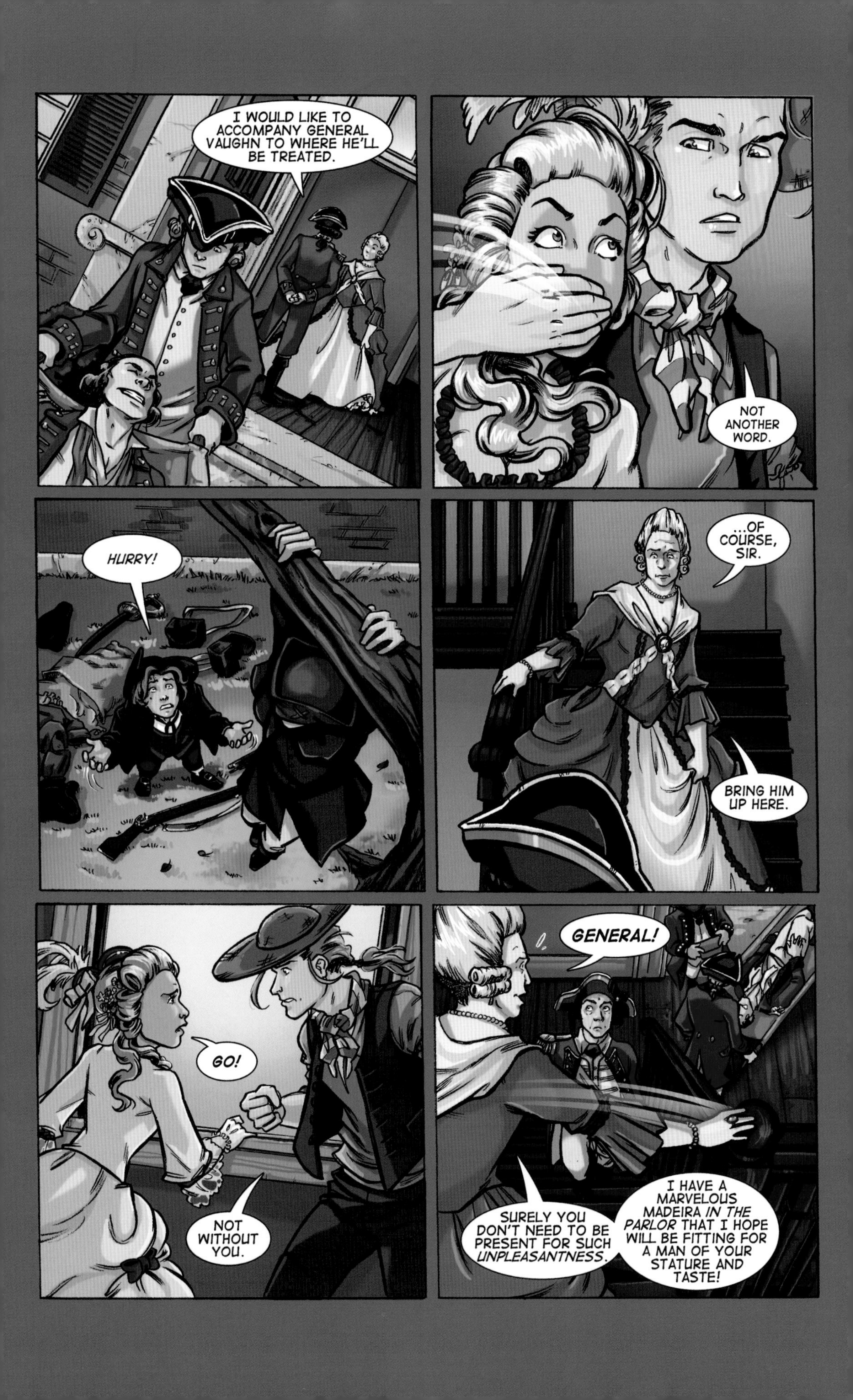
I WOULD LIKE TO ACCOMPANY GENERAL VAUGHN TO WHERE HE'LL BE TREATED.
NOT ANOTHER WORD.
HURRY!
...OF COURSE, SIR.
BRING HIM UP HERE.
GO!
NOT WITHOUT YOU.
GENERAL!
SURELY YOU DON'T NEED TO BE PRESENT FOR SUCH *UNPLEASANTNESS*.
I HAVE A MARVELOUS MADEIRA *IN THE PARLOR* THAT I HOPE WILL BE FITTING FOR A MAN OF YOUR STATURE AND TASTE!

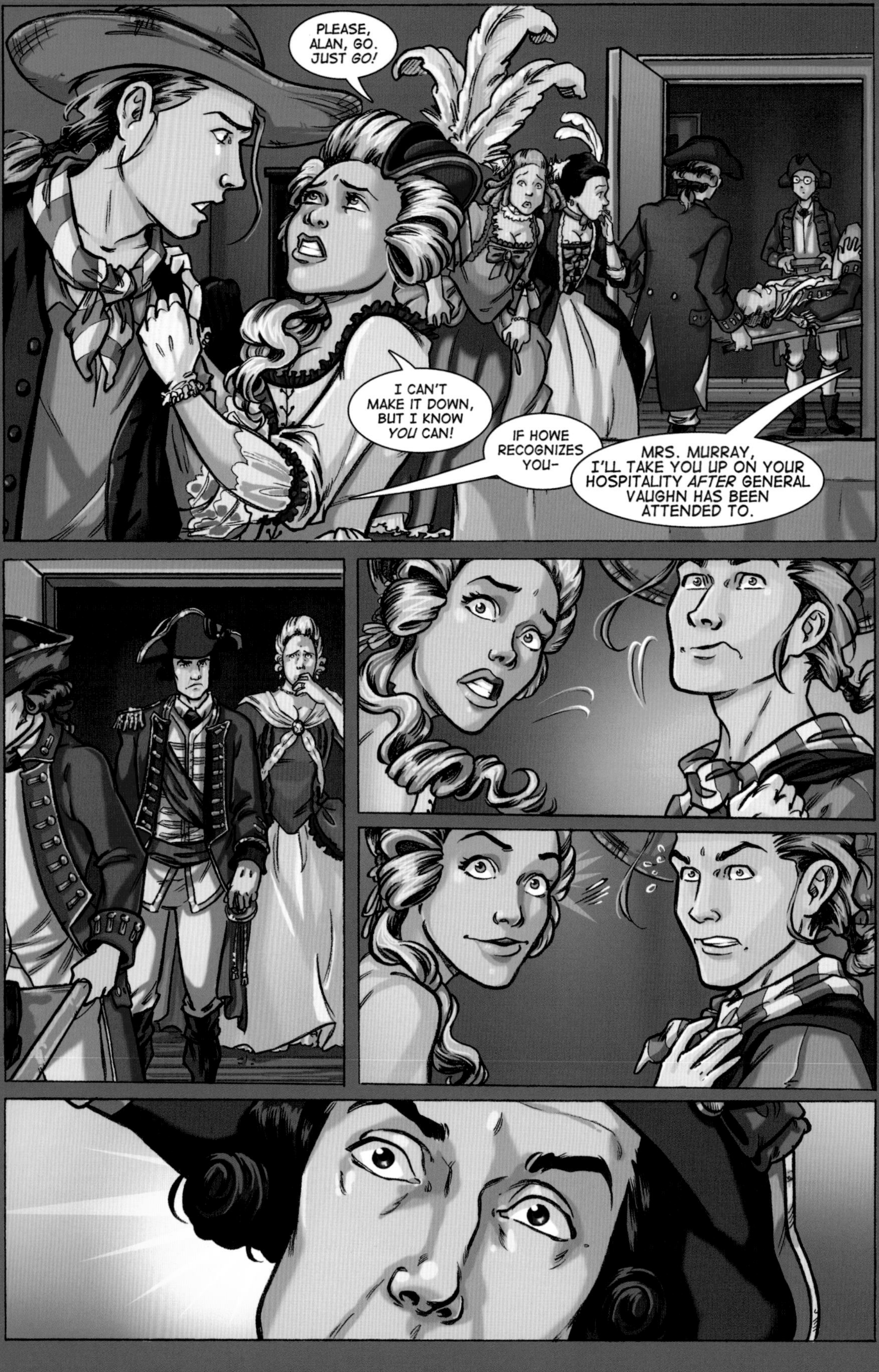
PLEASE, ALAN, GO. JUST GO!
I CAN'T MAKE IT DOWN, BUT I KNOW YOU CAN!
IF HOWE RECOGNIZES YOU-
MRS. MURRAY, I'LL TAKE YOU UP ON YOUR HOSPITALITY AFTER GENERAL VAUGHN HAS BEEN ATTENDED TO.

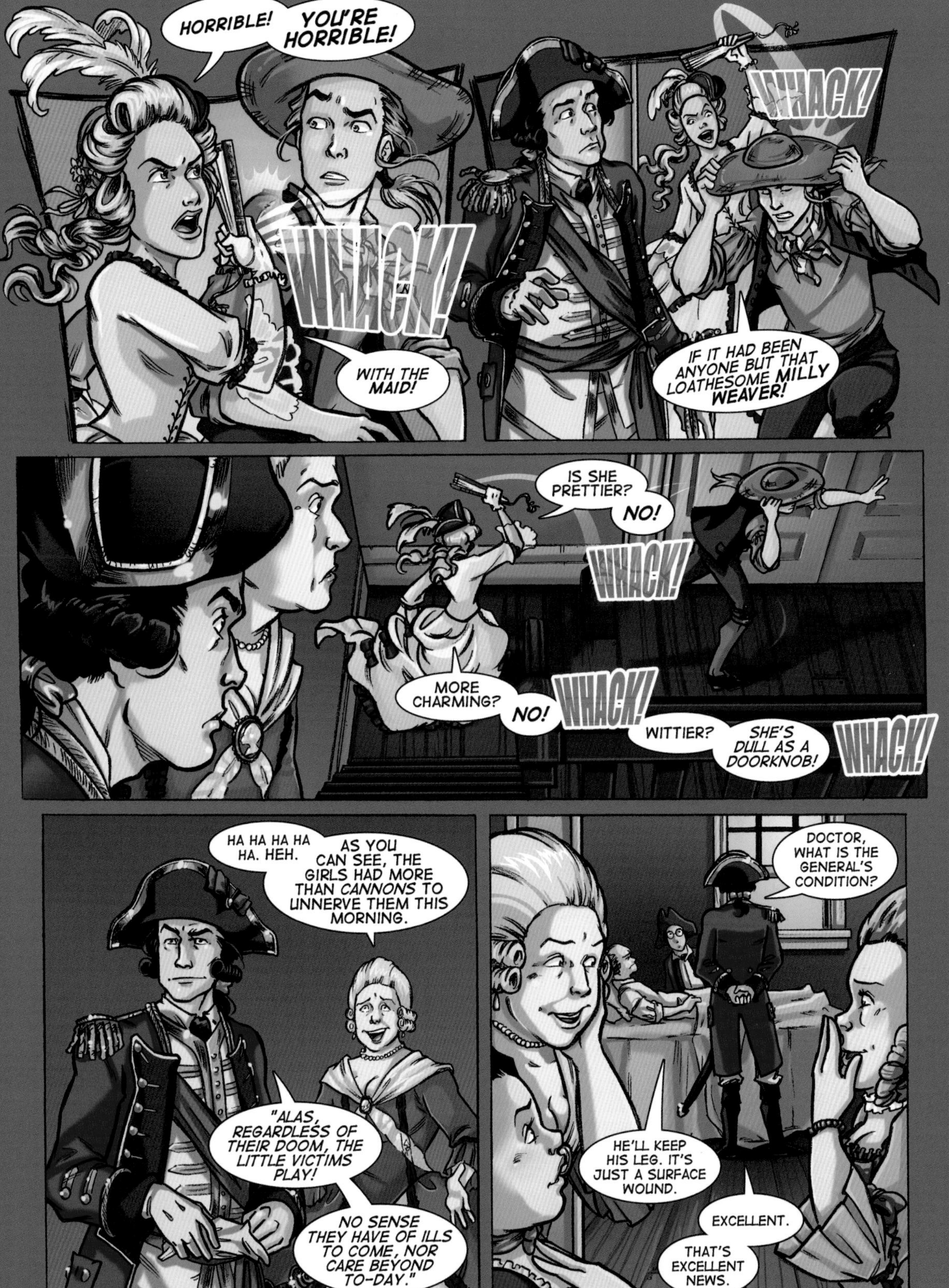
HORRIBLE!
YOU'RE HORRIBLE!
WHACK!
WITH THE MAID!
WHACK!
IF IT HAD BEEN ANYONE BUT THAT LOATHESOME MILLY WEAVER!
IS SHE PRETTIER?
NO!
WHACK!
MORE CHARMING?
NO!
WHACK!
WITTIER?
SHE'S DULL AS A DOORKNOB!
WHACK!
HA HA HA HA HA. HEH.
AS YOU CAN SEE, THE GIRLS HAD MORE THAN CANNONS TO UNNERVE THEM THIS MORNING.
"ALAS, REGARDLESS OF THEIR DOOM, THE LITTLE VICTIMS PLAY!
NO SENSE THEY HAVE OF ILLS TO COME, NOR CARE BEYOND TO-DAY."
DOCTOR, WHAT IS THE GENERAL'S CONDITION?
HE'LL KEEP HIS LEG. IT'S JUST A SURFACE WOUND.
EXCELLENT.
THAT'S EXCELLENT NEWS.

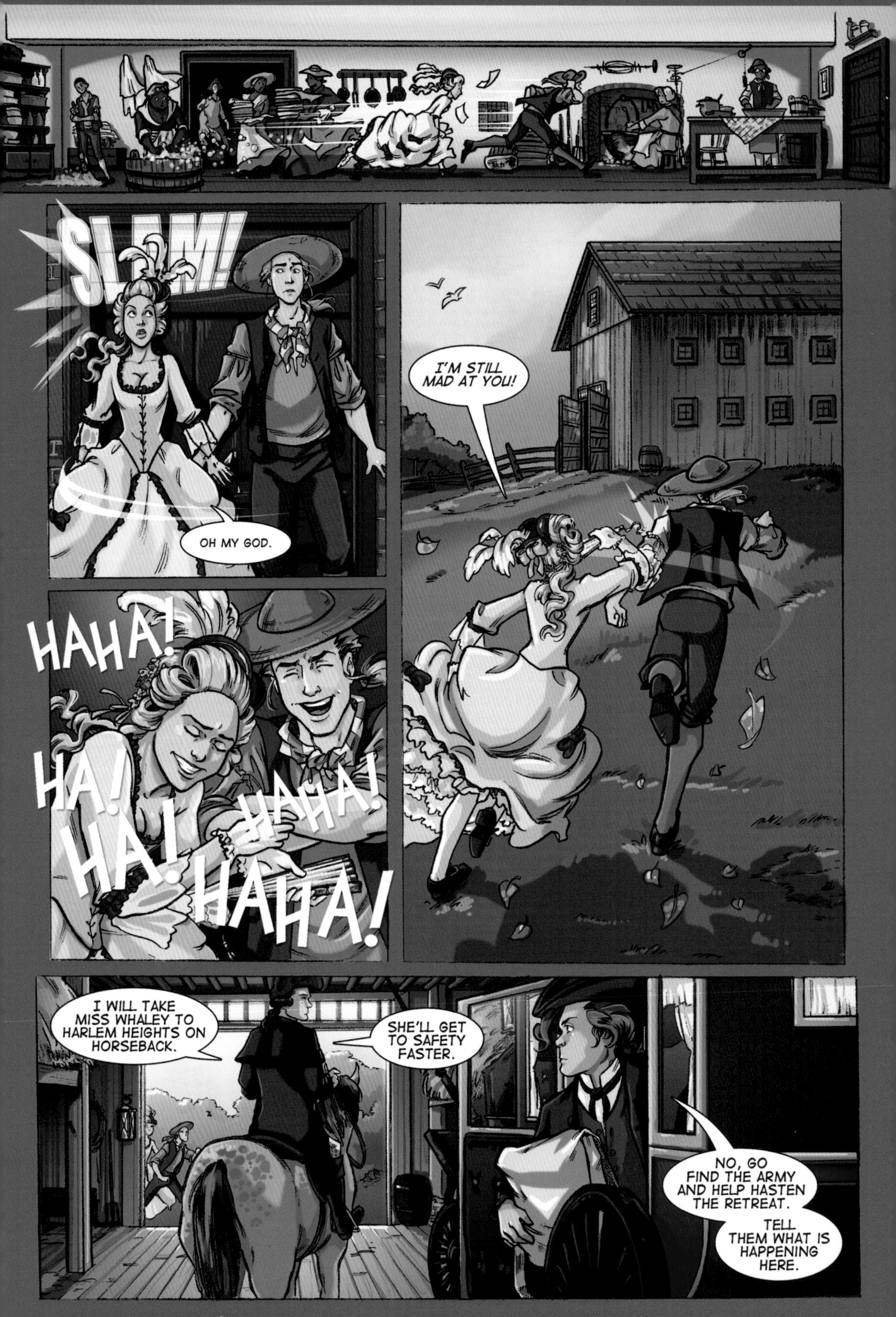
SLAM!
OH MY GOD.
HAHA!
HA!
HA!
HAHA!
HAHA!
I'M STILL MAD AT YOU!
I WILL TAKE MISS WHALEY TO HARLEM HEIGHTS ON HORSEBACK.
SHE'LL GET TO SAFETY FASTER.
NO, GO FIND THE ARMY AND HELP HASTEN THE RETREAT.
TELL THEM WHAT IS HAPPENING HERE.

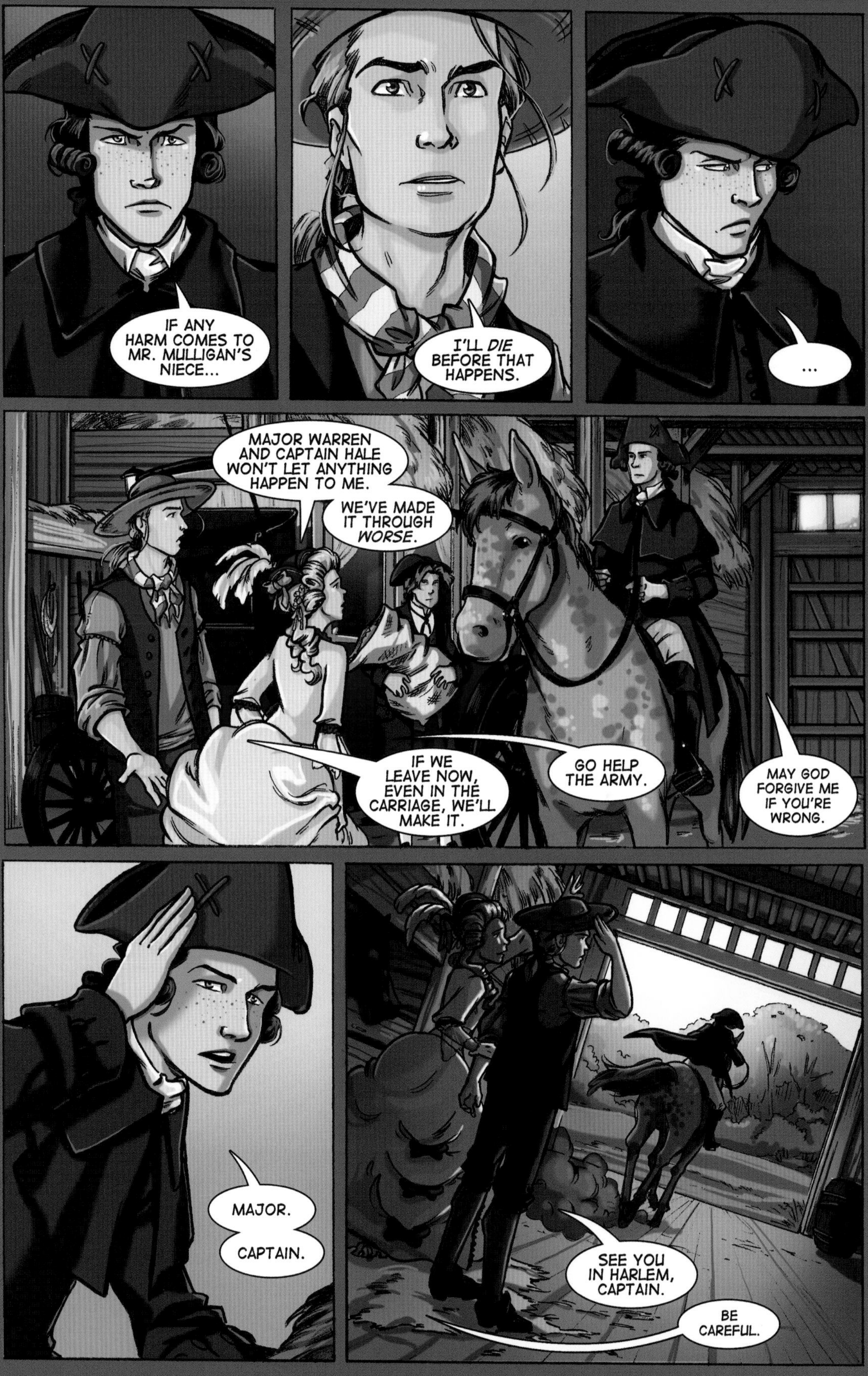

IF ANY HARM COMES TO MR. MULLIGAN'S NIECE...
I'LL *DIE* BEFORE THAT HAPPENS.
...
MAJOR WARREN AND CAPTAIN HALE WON'T LET ANYTHING HAPPEN TO ME.
WE'VE MADE IT THROUGH *WORSE*.
IF WE LEAVE NOW, EVEN IN THE CARRIAGE, WE'LL MAKE IT.
GO HELP THE ARMY.
MAY GOD FORGIVE ME IF YOU'RE WRONG.
MAJOR.
CAPTAIN.
SEE YOU IN HARLEM, CAPTAIN.
BE CAREFUL.

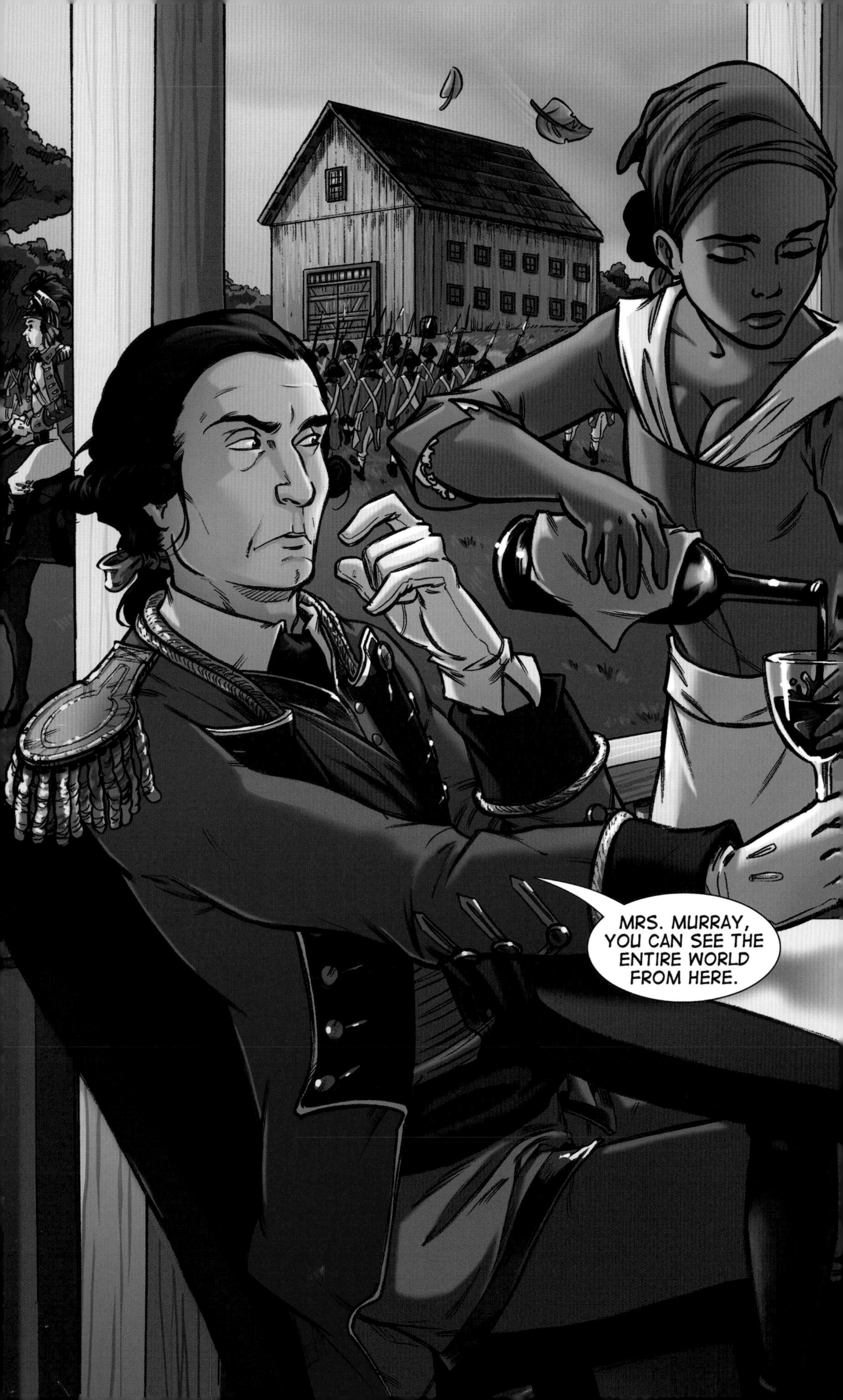
MRS. MURRAY, YOU CAN SEE THE ENTIRE WORLD FROM HERE.

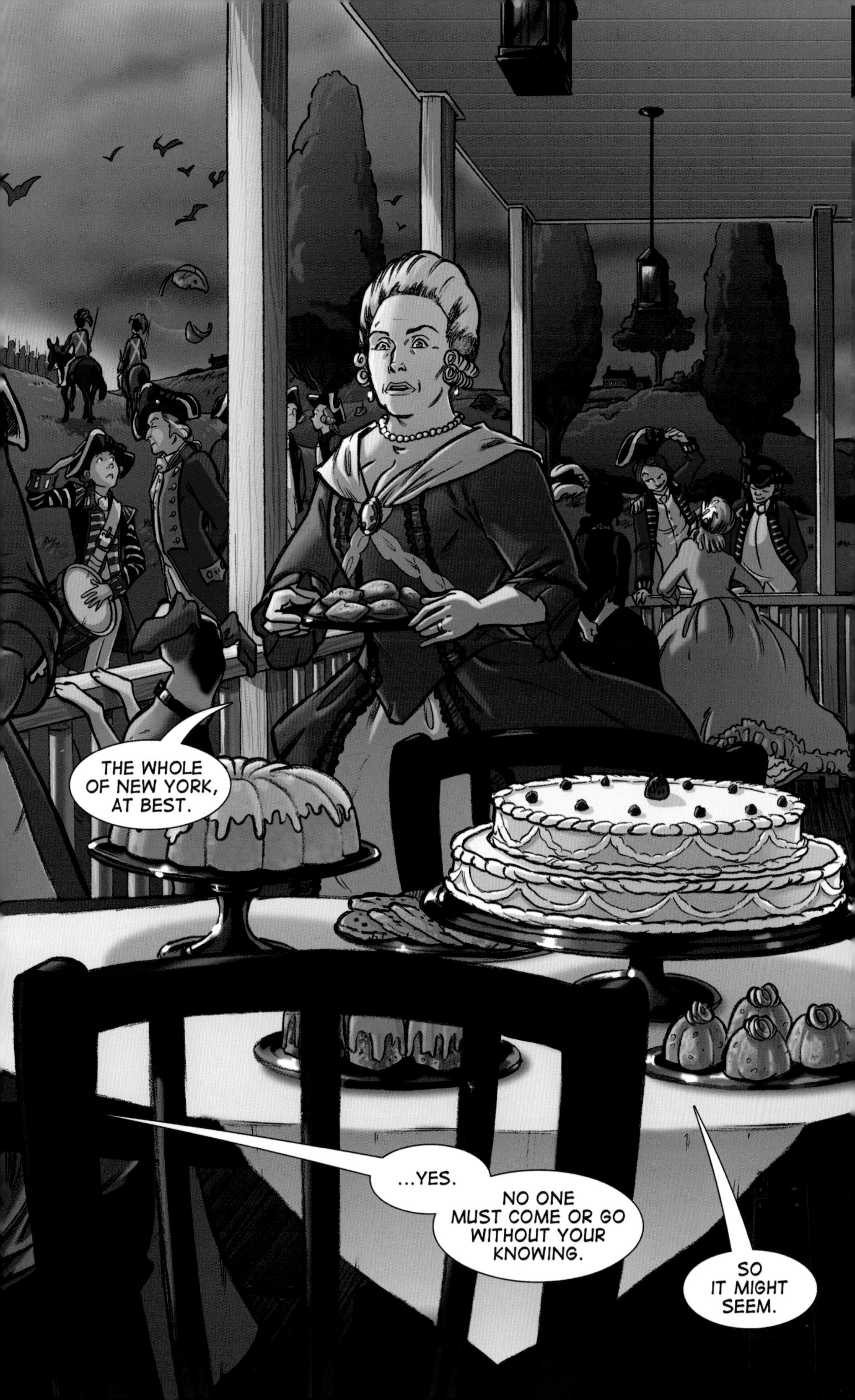
THE WHOLE OF NEW YORK, AT BEST.
...YES.
NO ONE MUST COME OR GO WITHOUT YOUR KNOWING.
SO IT MIGHT SEEM.

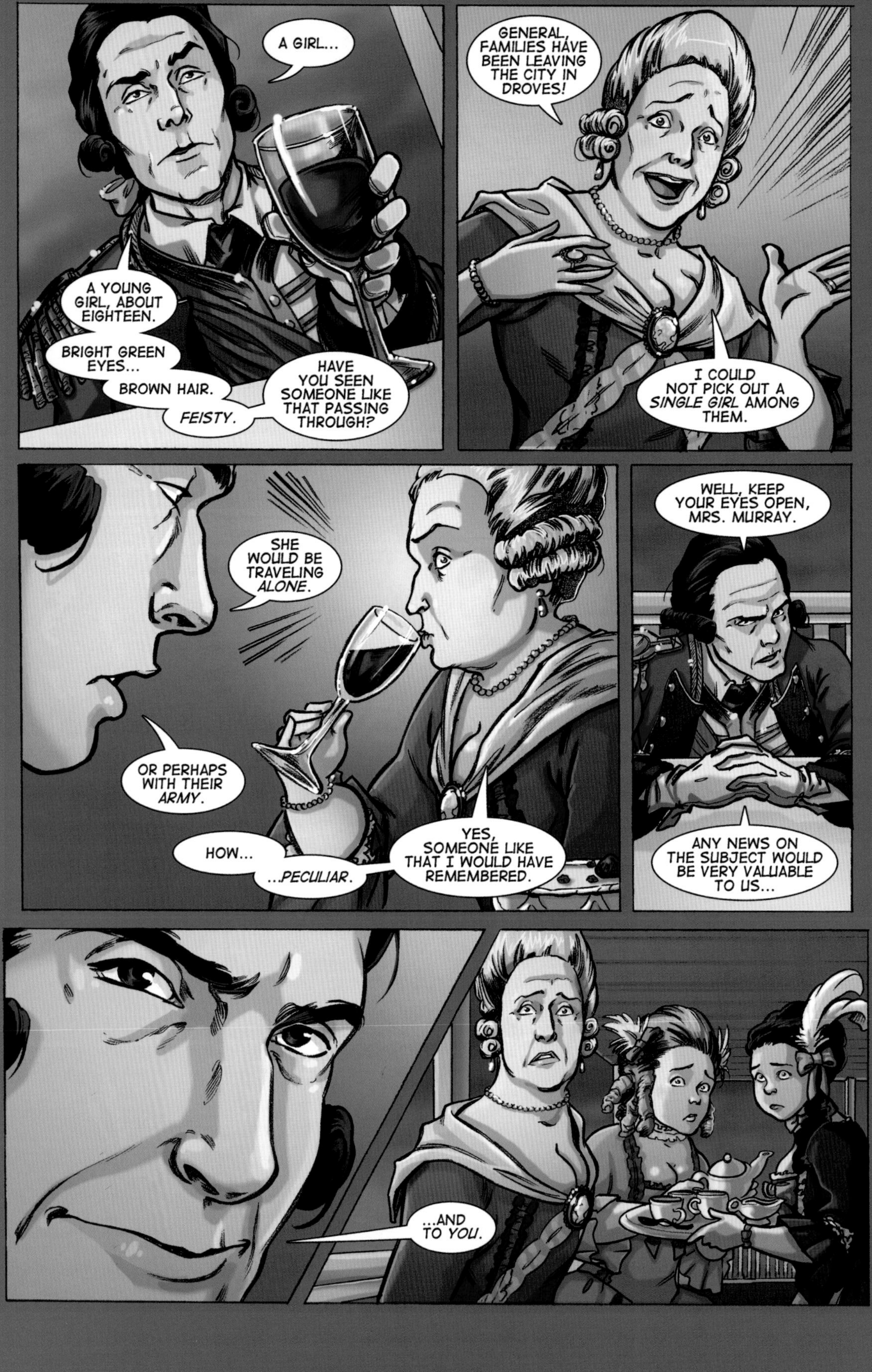
A GIRL...
A YOUNG GIRL, ABOUT EIGHTEEN.
BRIGHT GREEN EYES...
BROWN HAIR.
FEISTY.
HAVE YOU SEEN SOMEONE LIKE THAT PASSING THROUGH?
GENERAL, FAMILIES HAVE BEEN LEAVING THE CITY IN DROVES!
I COULD NOT PICK OUT A SINGLE GIRL AMONG THEM.
SHE WOULD BE TRAVELING ALONE.
OR PERHAPS WITH THEIR ARMY.
HOW...
...PECULIAR.
YES, SOMEONE LIKE THAT I WOULD HAVE REMEMBERED.
WELL, KEEP YOUR EYES OPEN, MRS. MURRAY.
ANY NEWS ON THE SUBJECT WOULD BE VERY VALUABLE TO US...
...AND TO YOU.

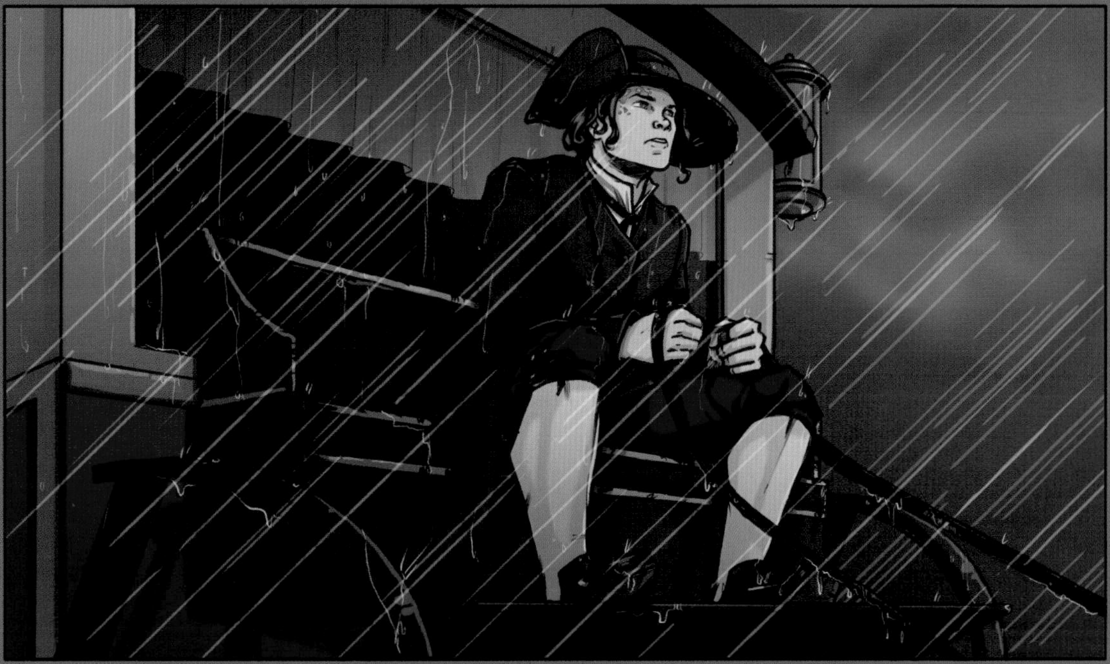

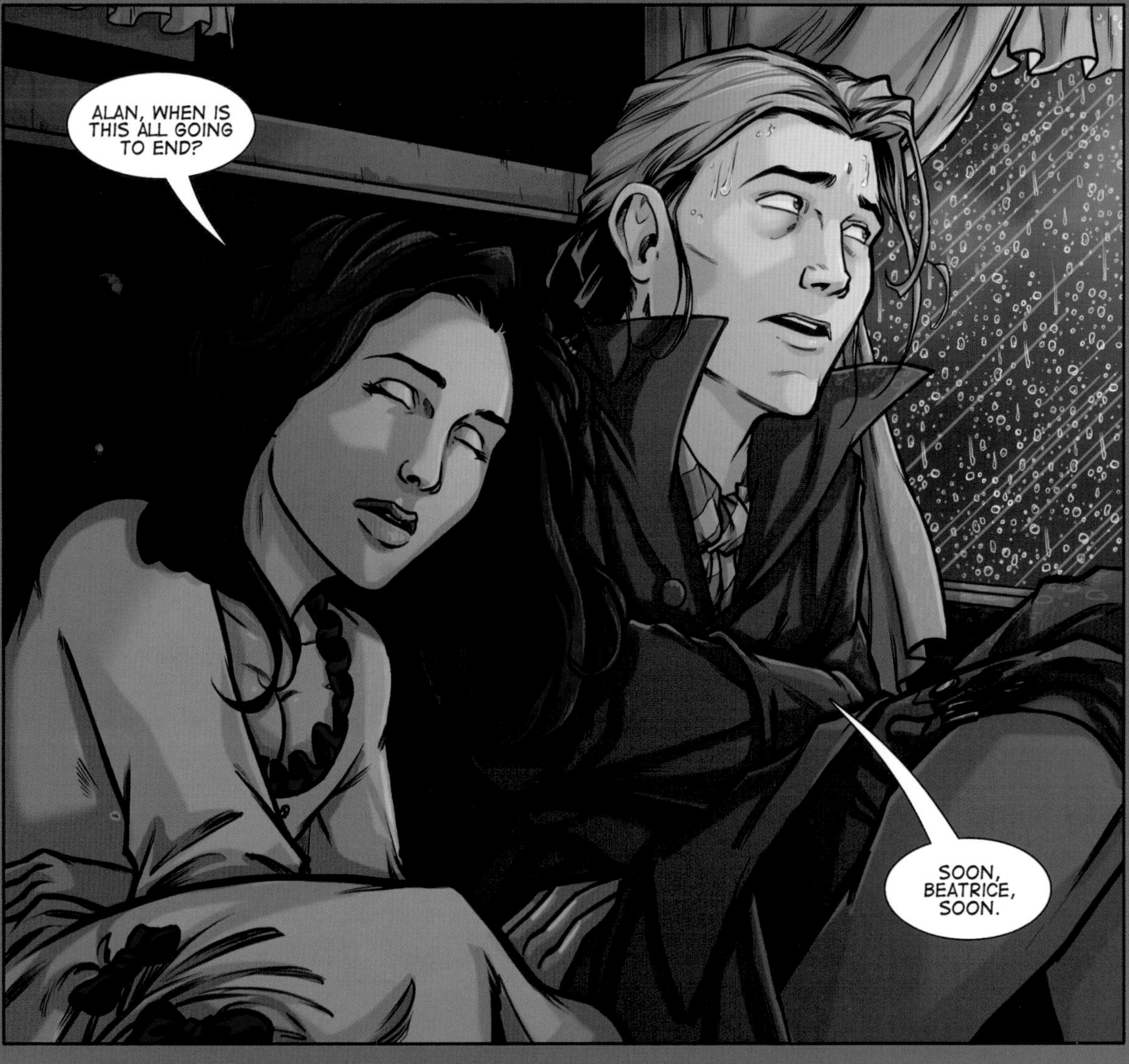
ALAN, WHEN IS THIS ALL GOING TO END?
SOON, BEATRICE, SOON.

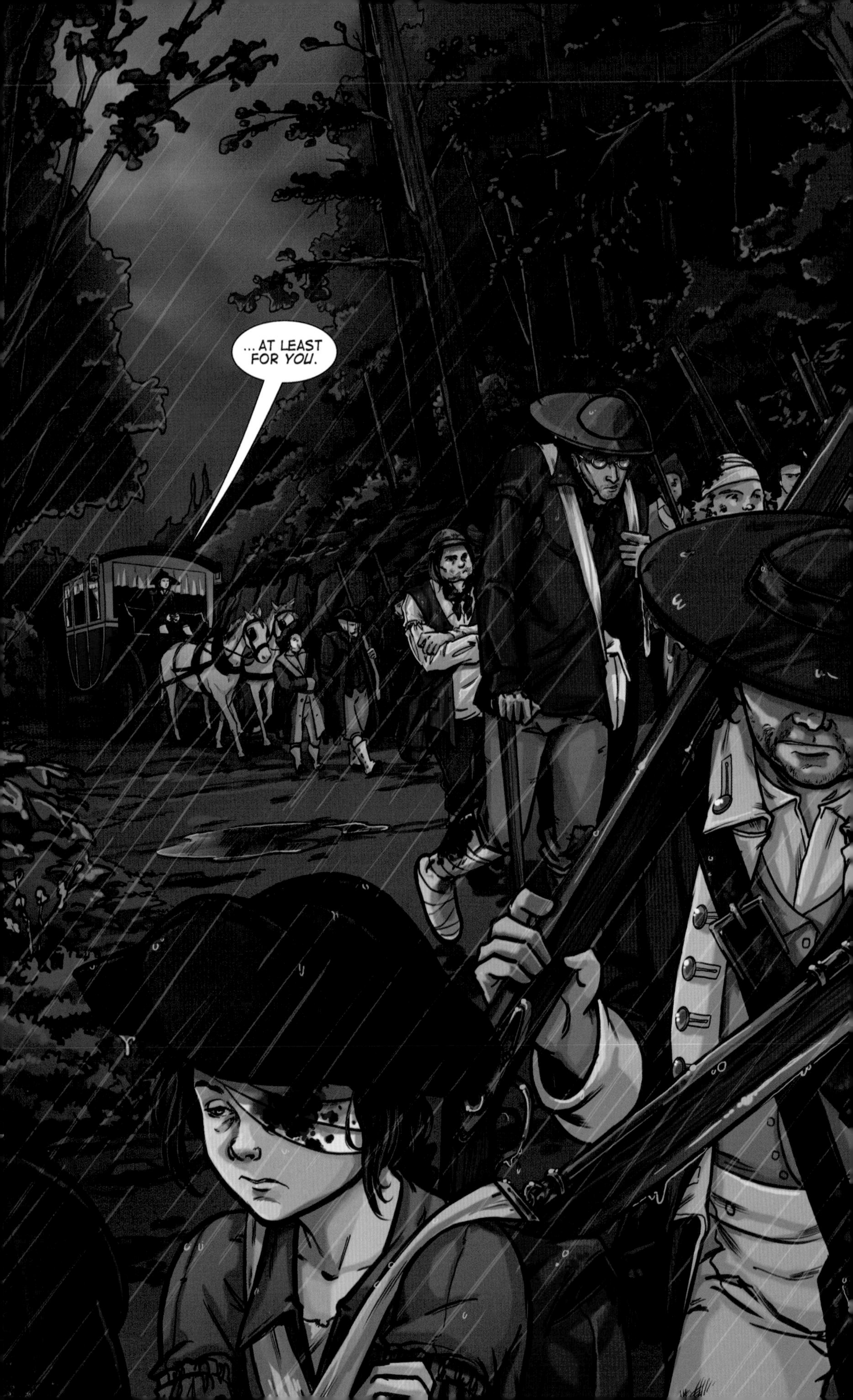
...AT LEAST FOR *YOU*.

Chapter Eleven

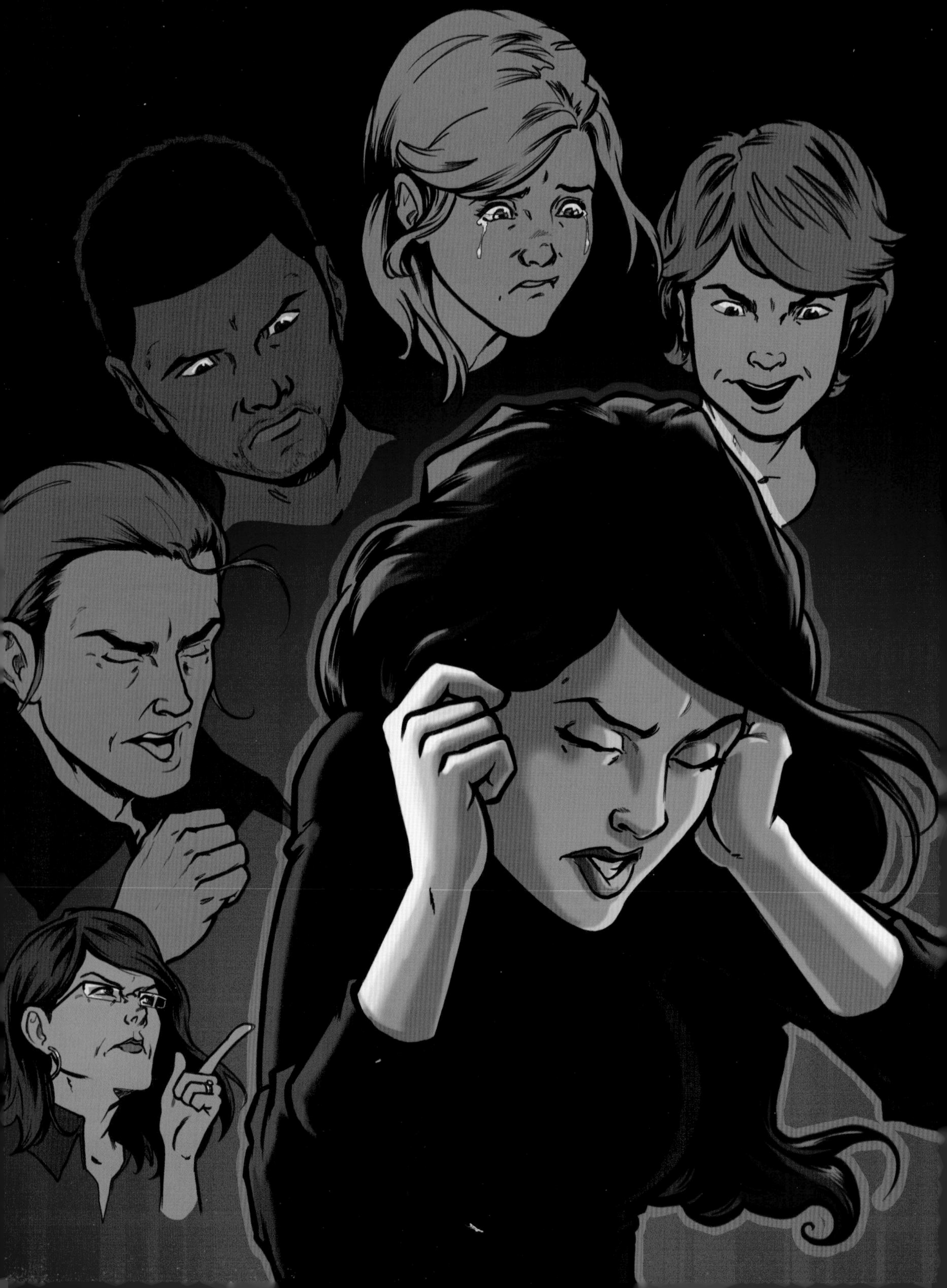

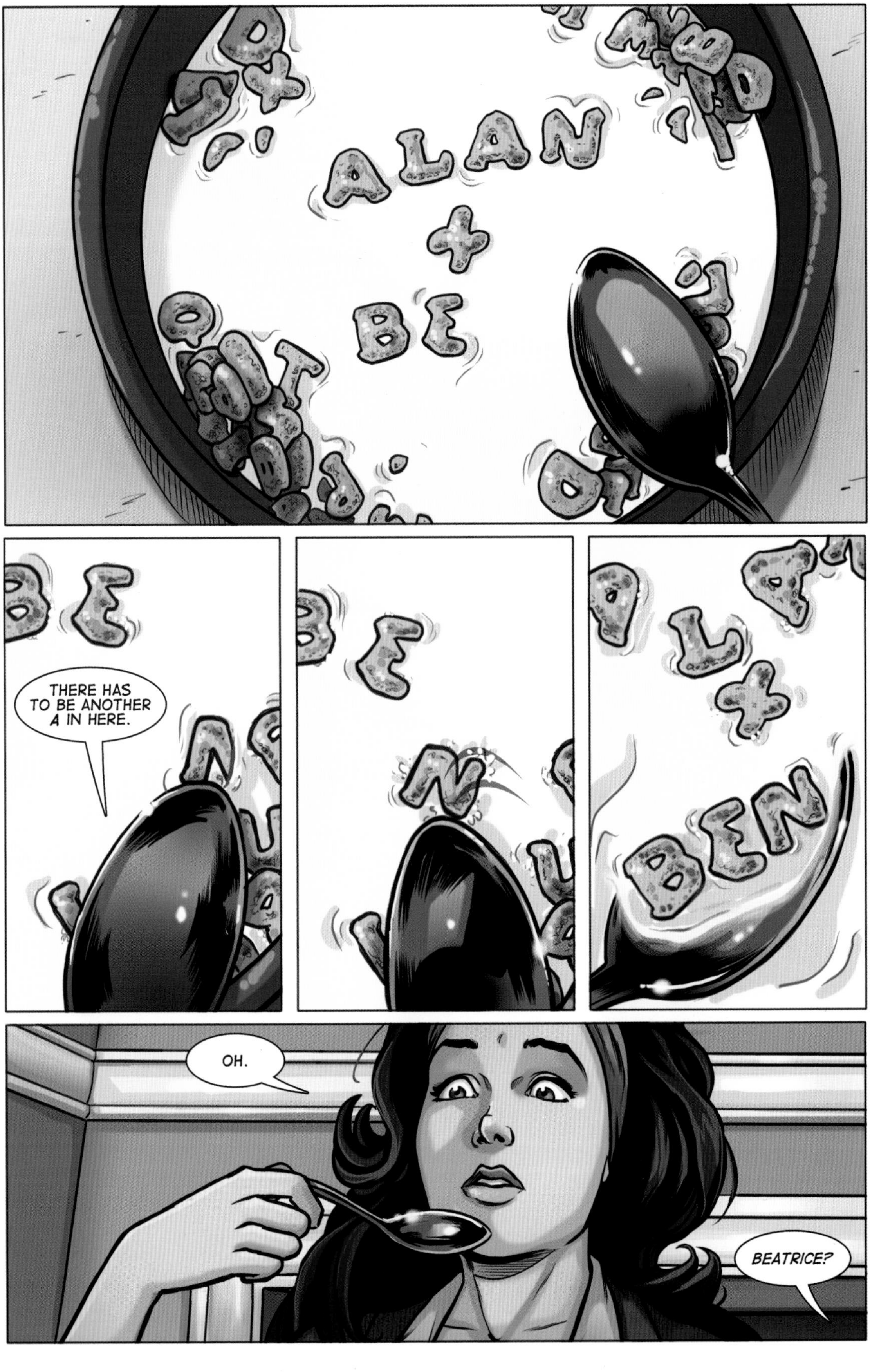
ALAN
+
BE
THERE HAS TO BE ANOTHER *A* IN HERE.
BEN
OH.
BEATRICE?

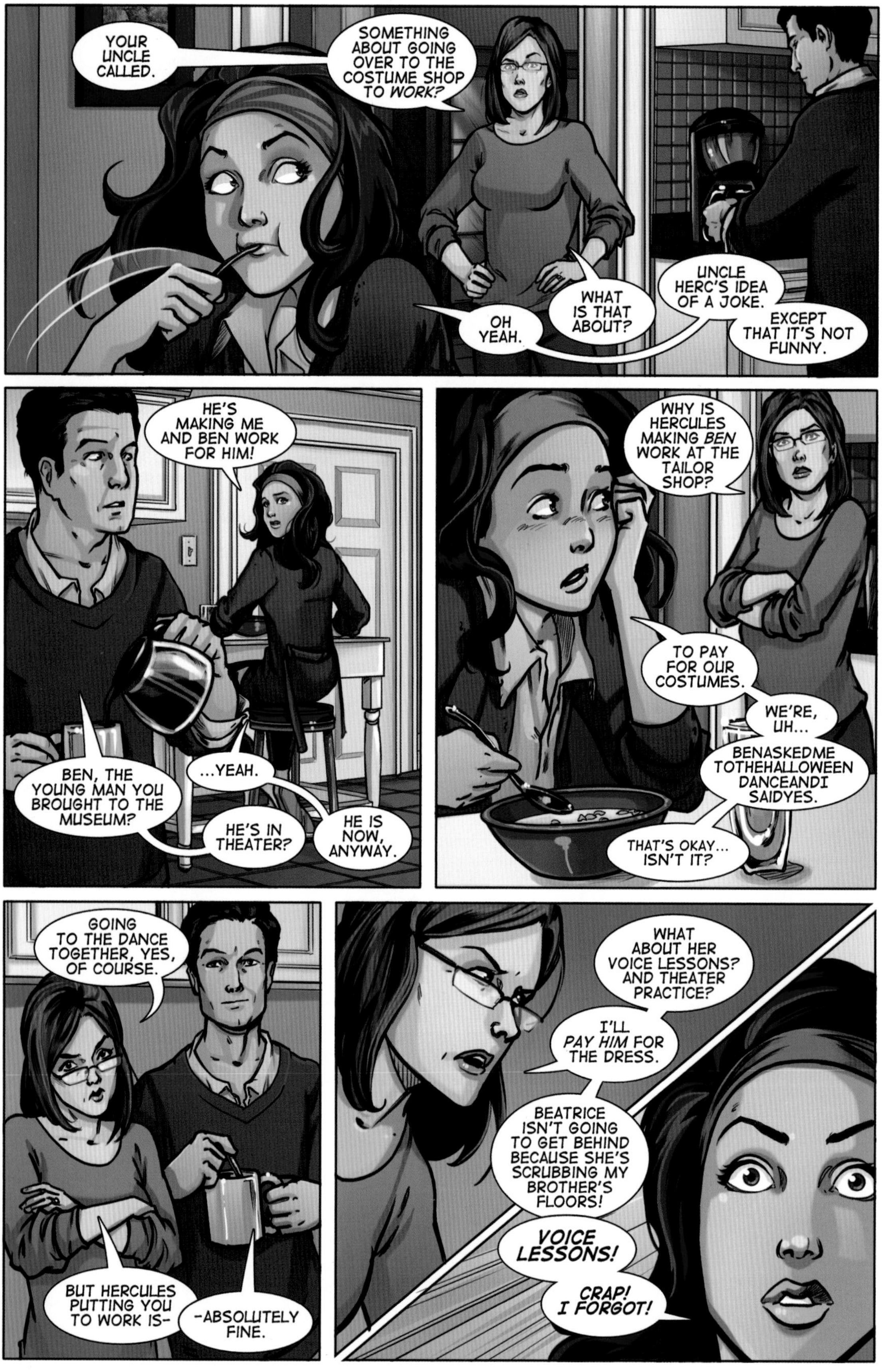
YOUR UNCLE CALLED.
SOMETHING ABOUT GOING OVER TO THE COSTUME SHOP TO *WORK?*
OH YEAH.
WHAT IS THAT ABOUT?
UNCLE HERC'S IDEA OF A JOKE.
EXCEPT THAT IT'S NOT FUNNY.
HE'S MAKING ME AND BEN WORK FOR HIM!
BEN, THE YOUNG MAN YOU BROUGHT TO THE MUSEUM?
...YEAH.
HE'S IN THEATER?
HE IS NOW, ANYWAY.
WHY IS HERCULES MAKING *BEN* WORK AT THE TAILOR SHOP?
TO PAY FOR OUR COSTUMES.
WE'RE, UH...
BENASKEDME TOTHEHALLOWEEN DANCEANDI SAIDYES.
THAT'S OKAY... ISN'T IT?
GOING TO THE DANCE TOGETHER, YES, OF COURSE.
BUT HERCULES PUTTING YOU TO WORK IS-
-ABSOLUTELY FINE.
WHAT ABOUT HER VOICE LESSONS? AND THEATER PRACTICE?
I'LL *PAY HIM* FOR THE DRESS.
BEATRICE ISN'T GOING TO GET BEHIND BECAUSE SHE'S SCRUBBING MY BROTHER'S FLOORS!
VOICE LESSONS!
CRAP! I FORGOT!

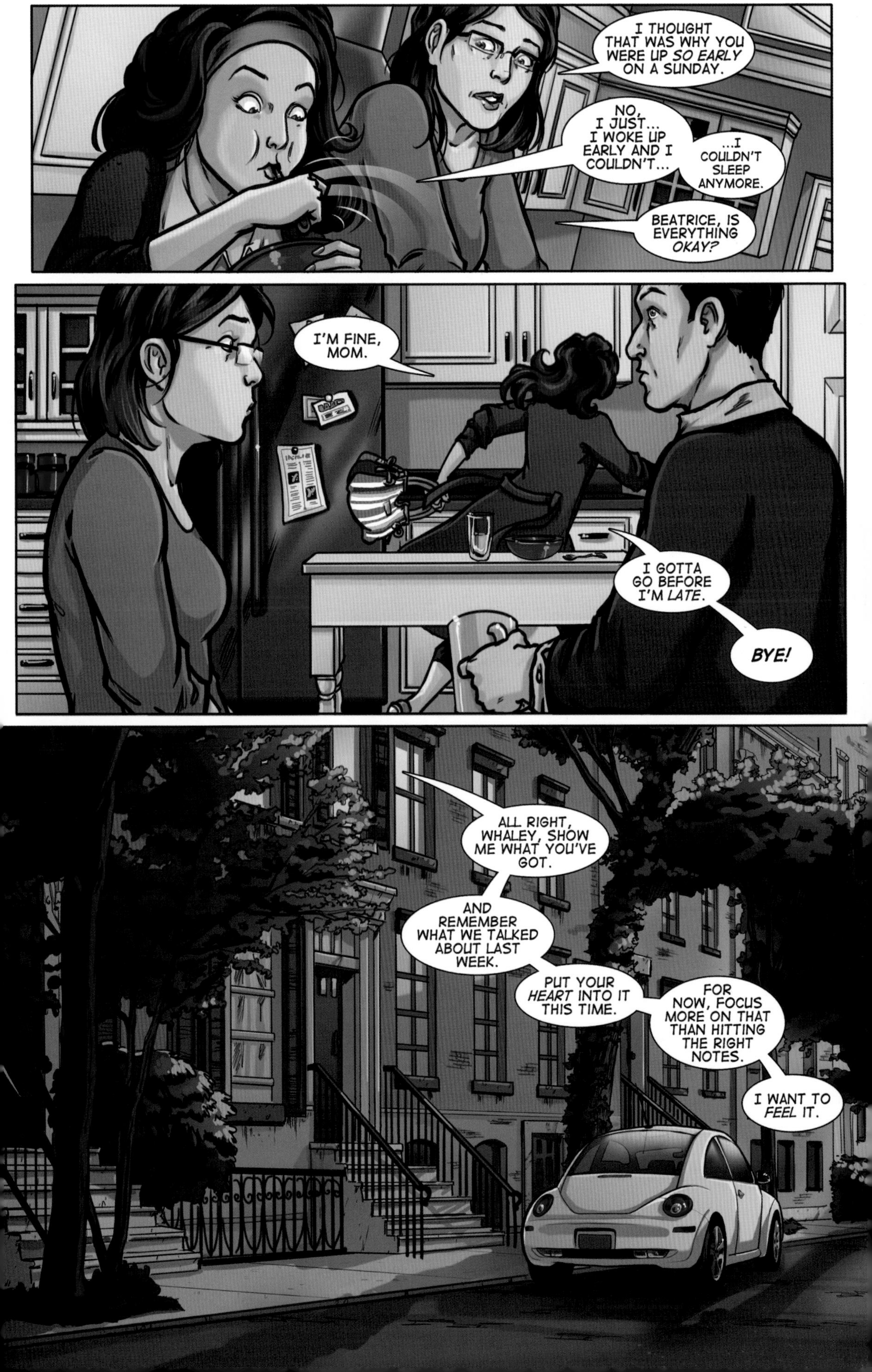
I THOUGHT THAT WAS WHY YOU WERE UP SO EARLY ON A SUNDAY.
NO, I JUST... I WOKE UP EARLY AND I COULDN'T...
...I COULDN'T SLEEP ANYMORE.
BEATRICE, IS EVERYTHING OKAY?
I'M FINE, MOM.
I GOTTA GO BEFORE I'M LATE.
BYE!
ALL RIGHT, WHALEY, SHOW ME WHAT YOU'VE GOT.
AND REMEMBER WHAT WE TALKED ABOUT LAST WEEK.
PUT YOUR HEART INTO IT THIS TIME.
FOR NOW, FOCUS MORE ON THAT THAN HITTING THE RIGHT NOTES.
I WANT TO FEEL IT.

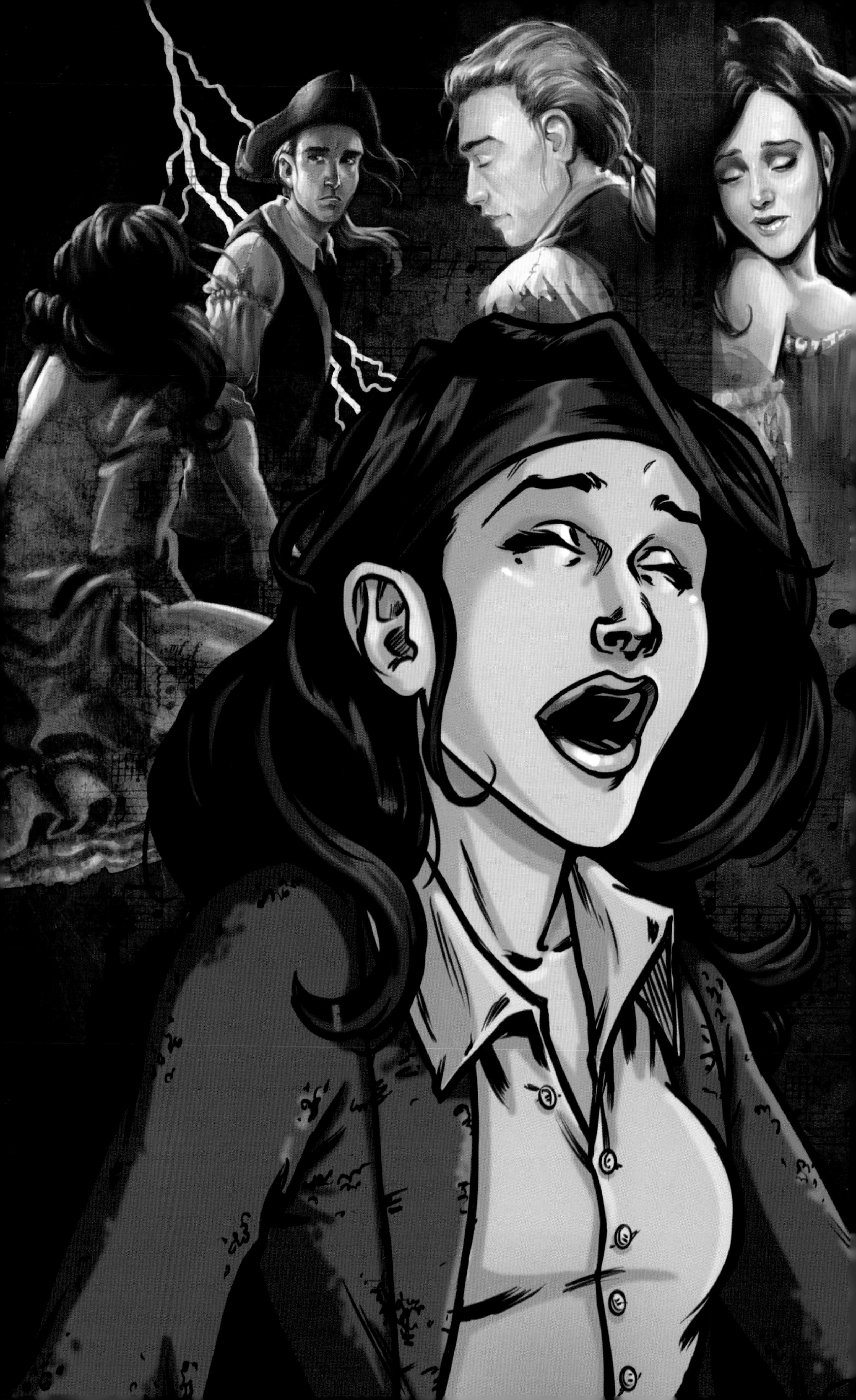

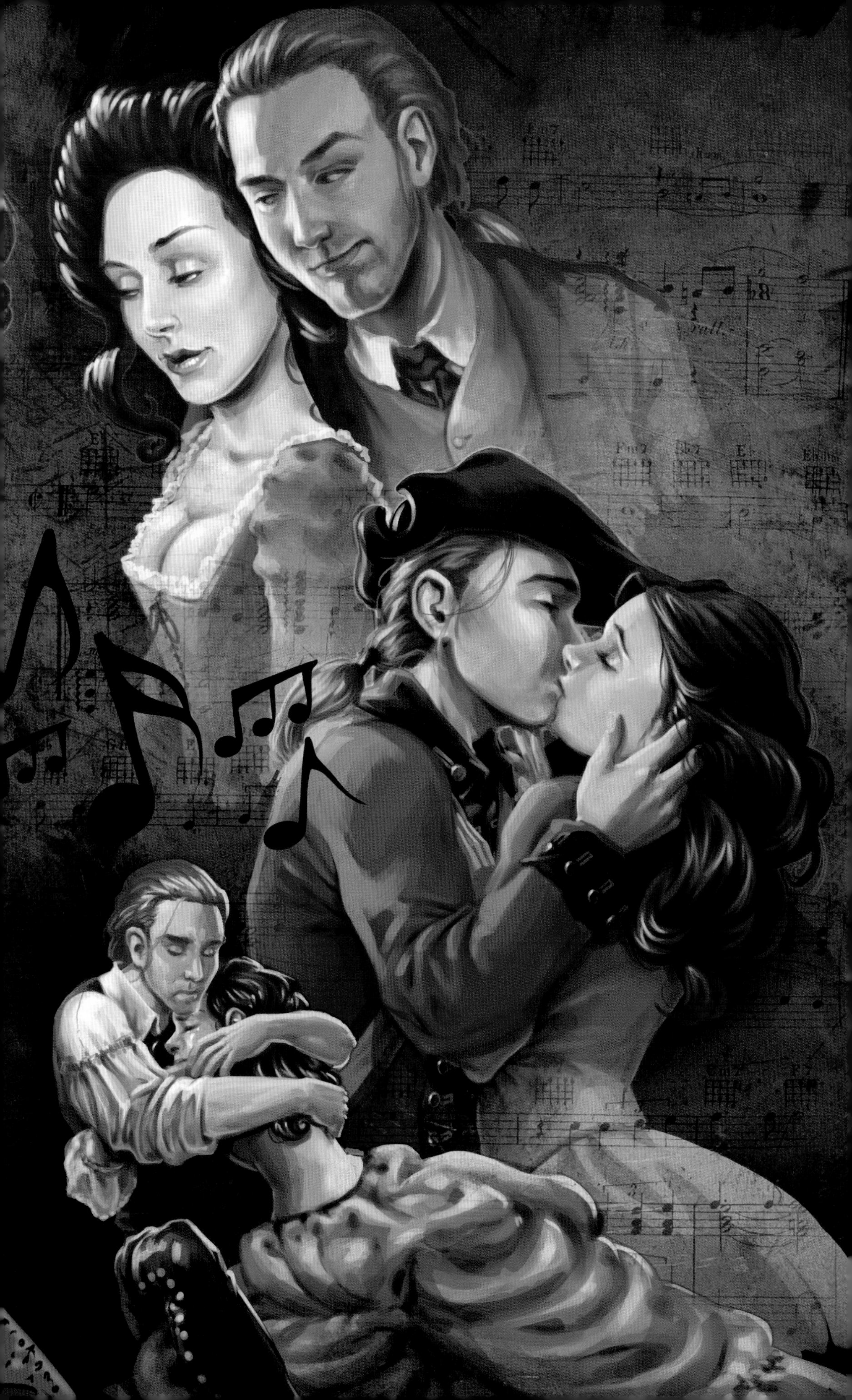

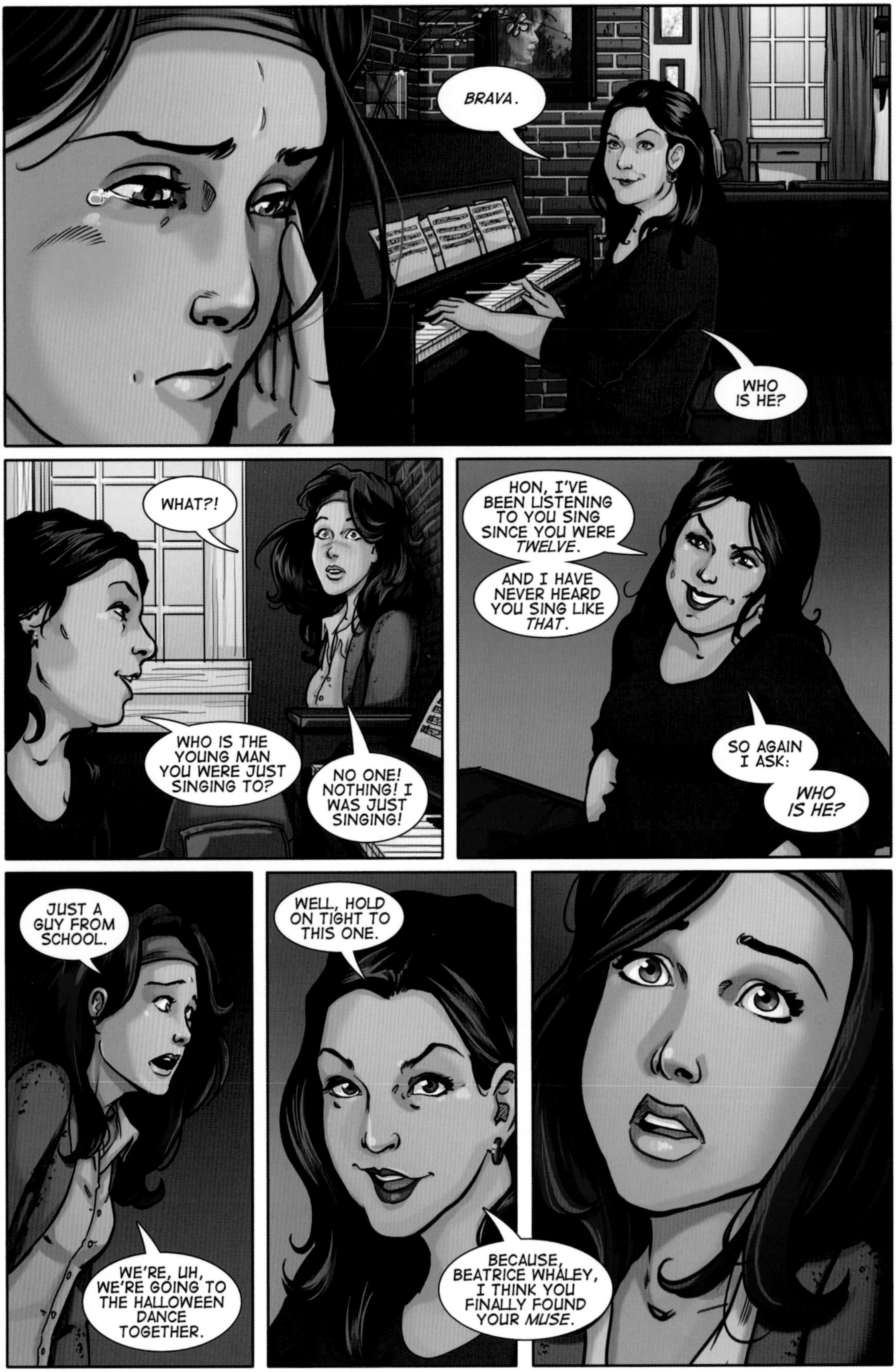
BRAVA.
WHO IS HE?
WHAT?!
WHO IS THE YOUNG MAN YOU WERE JUST SINGING TO?
NO ONE! NOTHING! I WAS JUST SINGING!
HON, I'VE BEEN LISTENING TO YOU SING SINCE YOU WERE TWELVE.
AND I HAVE NEVER HEARD YOU SING LIKE THAT.
SO AGAIN I ASK:
WHO IS HE?
JUST A GUY FROM SCHOOL.
WE'RE, UH, WE'RE GOING TO THE HALLOWEEN DANCE TOGETHER.
WELL, HOLD ON TIGHT TO THIS ONE.
BECAUSE, BEATRICE WHALEY, I THINK YOU FINALLY FOUND YOUR MUSE.

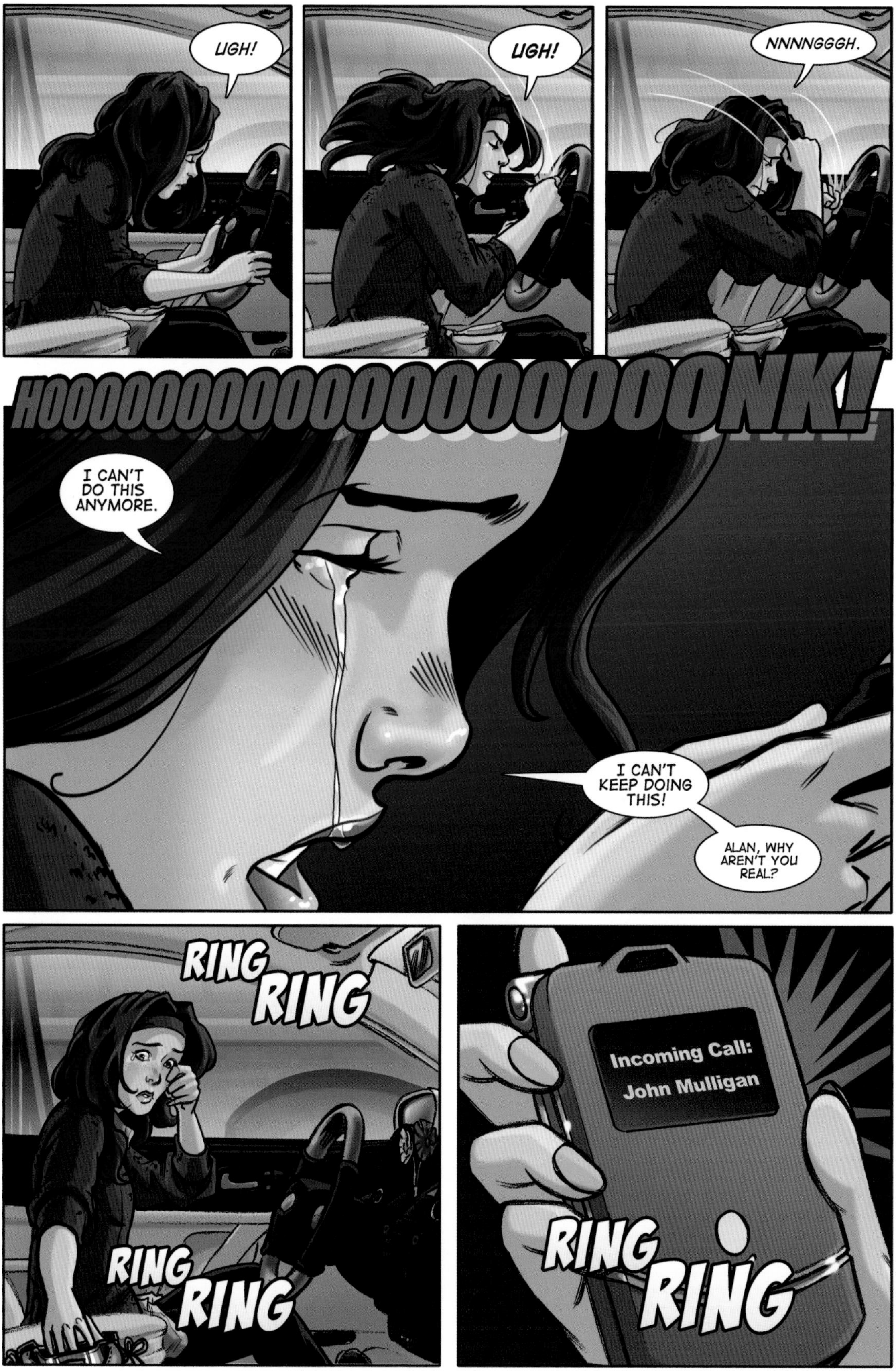

UGH!
UGH!
NNNNGGGH.
HOOOOOOOOOOOOOOOOOOONK!
I CAN'T DO THIS ANYMORE.
I CAN'T KEEP DOING THIS!
ALAN, WHY AREN'T YOU REAL?
RING RING
RING RING
Incoming Call: John Mulligan
RING RING

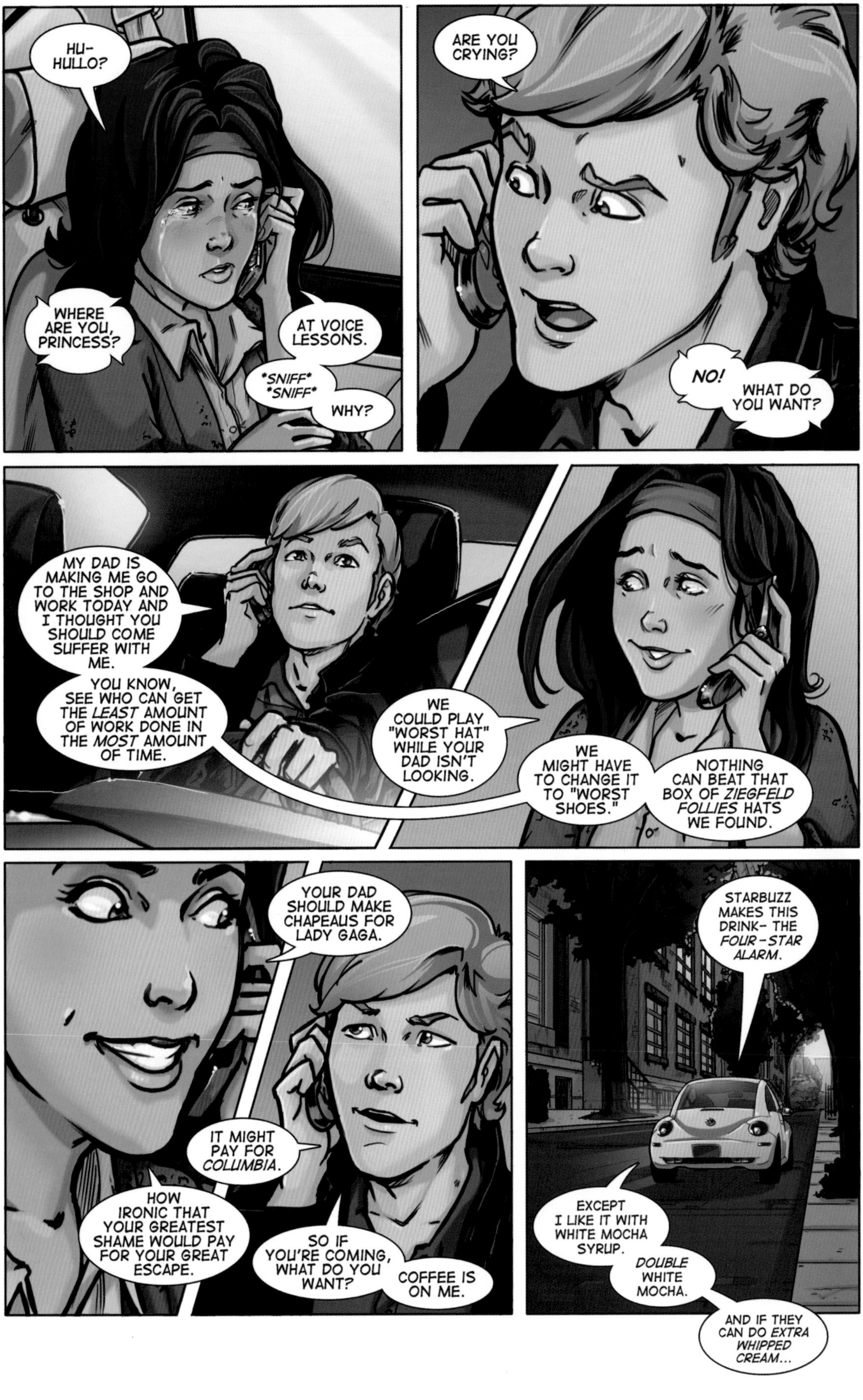
HU-HULLO?
ARE YOU CRYING?
WHERE ARE YOU, PRINCESS?
AT VOICE LESSONS.
SNIFF *SNIFF*
WHY?
NO!
WHAT DO YOU WANT?
MY DAD IS MAKING ME GO TO THE SHOP AND WORK TODAY AND I THOUGHT YOU SHOULD COME SUFFER WITH ME.
YOU KNOW, SEE WHO CAN GET THE LEAST AMOUNT OF WORK DONE IN THE MOST AMOUNT OF TIME.
WE COULD PLAY "WORST HAT" WHILE YOUR DAD ISN'T LOOKING.
WE MIGHT HAVE TO CHANGE IT TO "WORST SHOES."
NOTHING CAN BEAT THAT BOX OF ZIEGFELD FOLLIES HATS WE FOUND.
YOUR DAD SHOULD MAKE CHAPEAUS FOR LADY GAGA.
IT MIGHT PAY FOR COLUMBIA.
HOW IRONIC THAT YOUR GREATEST SHAME WOULD PAY FOR YOUR GREAT ESCAPE.
SO IF YOU'RE COMING, WHAT DO YOU WANT?
COFFEE IS ON ME.
STARBUZZ MAKES THIS DRINK- THE FOUR-STAR ALARM.
EXCEPT I LIKE IT WITH WHITE MOCHA SYRUP.
DOUBLE WHITE MOCHA.
AND IF THEY CAN DO EXTRA WHIPPED CREAM...

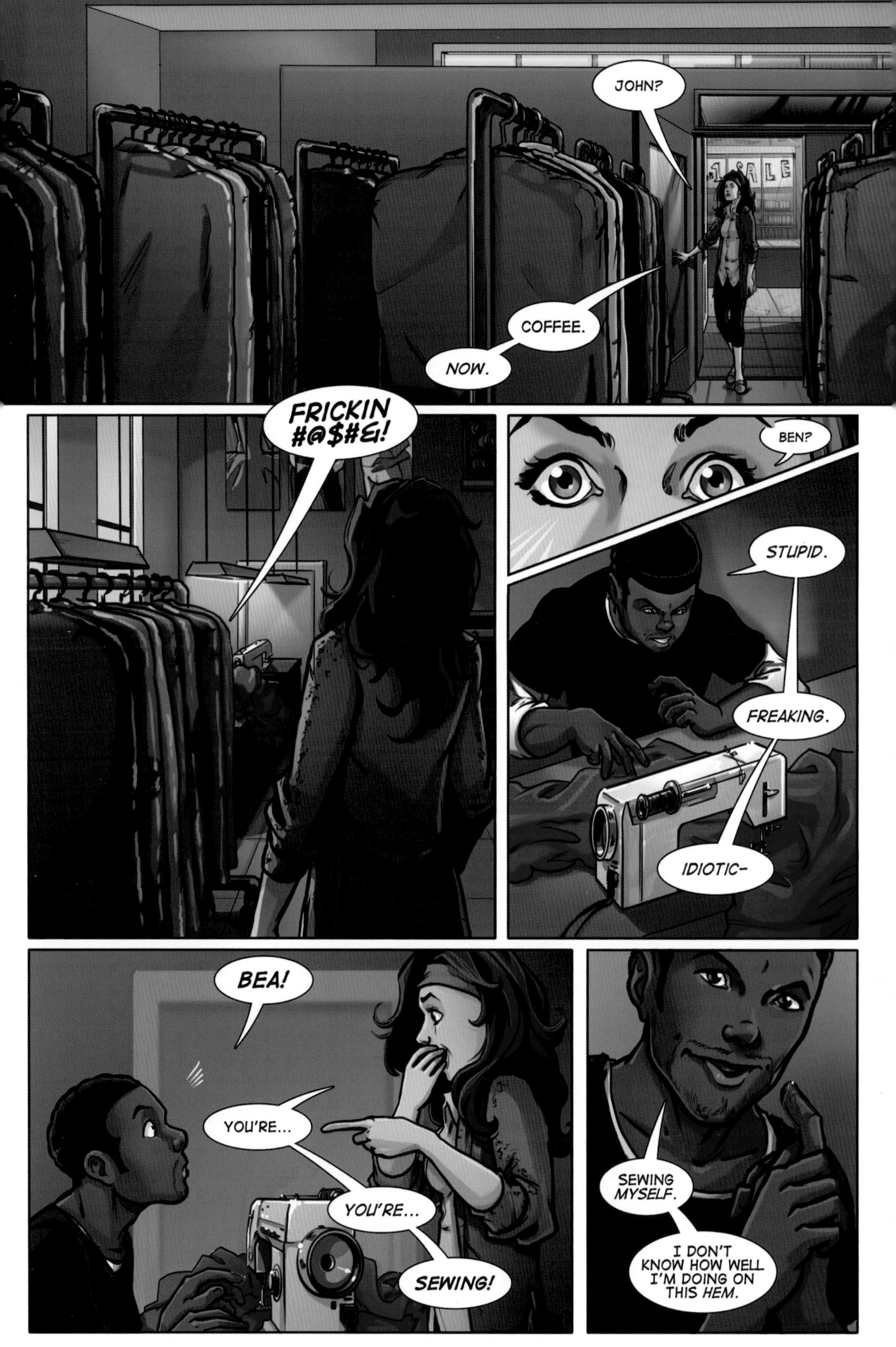

JOHN?
COFFEE.
NOW.
FRICKIN #@$#&!
BEN?
STUPID.
FREAKING.
IDIOTIC-
BEA!
YOU'RE...
YOU'RE...
SEWING!
SEWING MYSELF.
I DON'T KNOW HOW WELL I'M DOING ON THIS HEM.

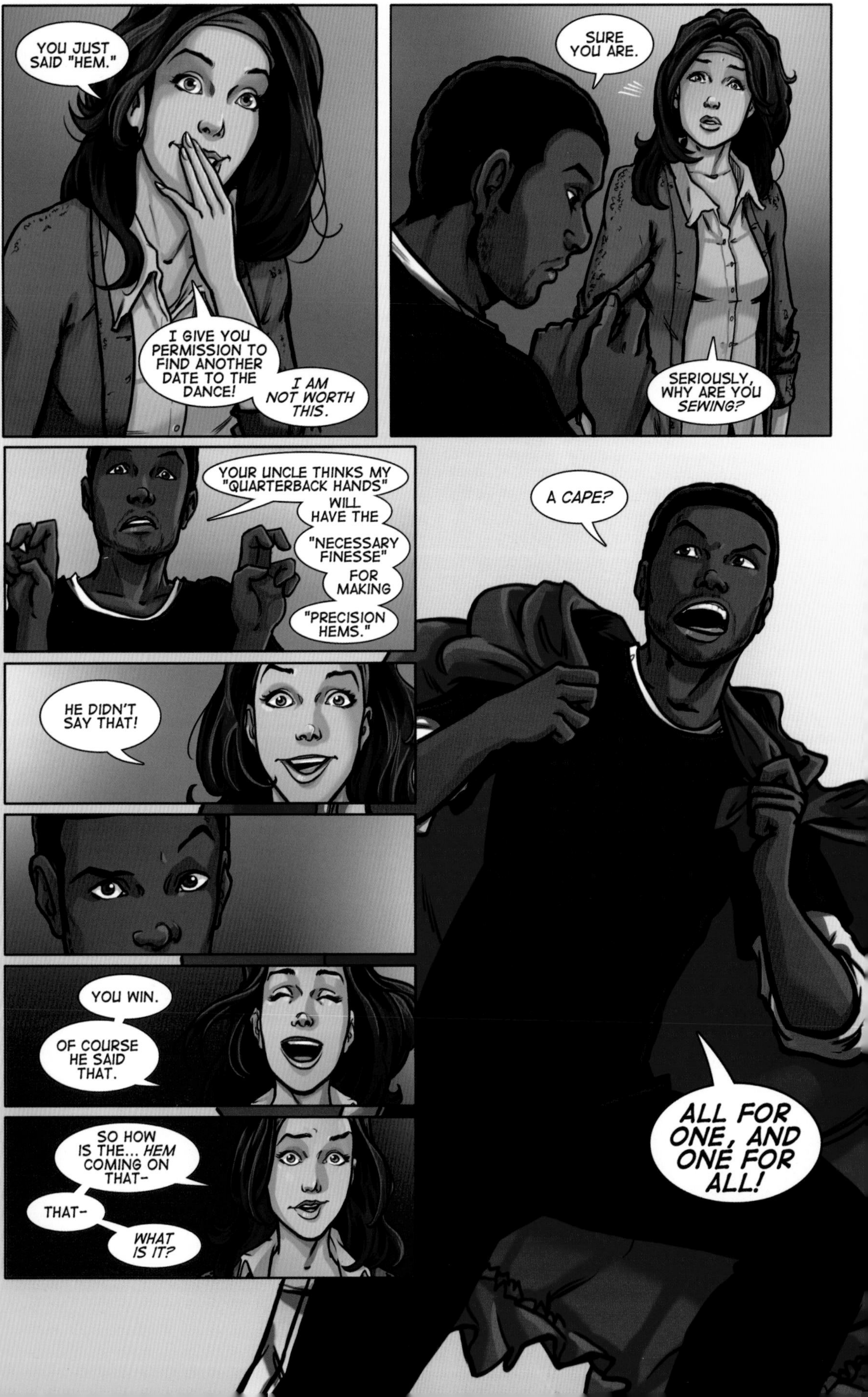
YOU JUST SAID "HEM."
I GIVE YOU PERMISSION TO FIND ANOTHER DATE TO THE DANCE!
I AM NOT WORTH THIS.
SURE YOU ARE.
SERIOUSLY, WHY ARE YOU SEWING?
YOUR UNCLE THINKS MY "QUARTERBACK HANDS"
WILL HAVE THE
"NECESSARY FINESSE"
FOR MAKING
"PRECISION HEMS."
HE DIDN'T SAY THAT!
YOU WIN.
OF COURSE HE SAID THAT.
SO HOW IS THE... HEM COMING ON THAT-
THAT-
WHAT IS IT?
A CAPE?
ALL FOR ONE, AND ONE FOR ALL!

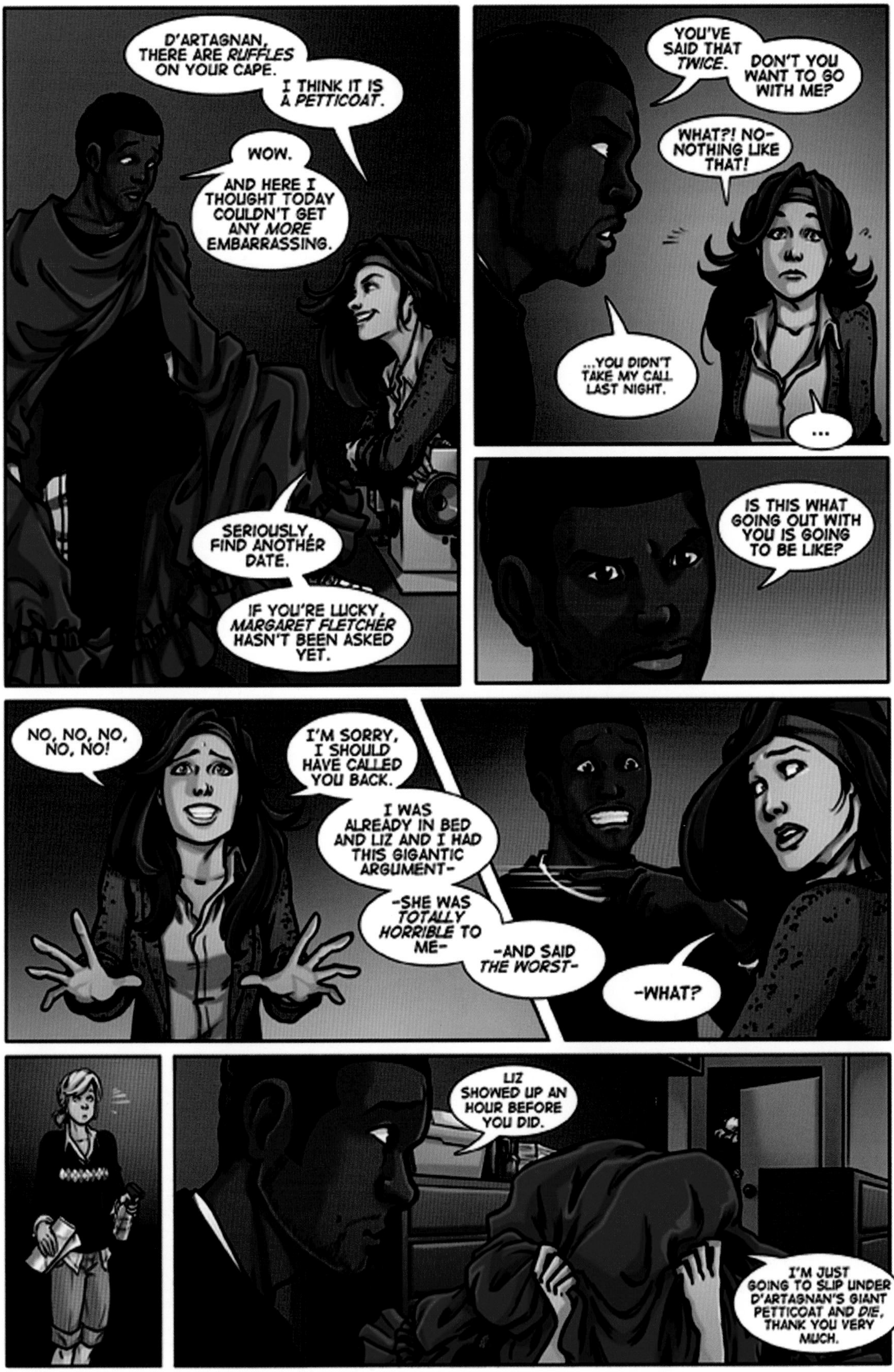
D'ARTAGNAN, THERE ARE *RUFFLES* ON YOUR CAPE.
I THINK IT IS A *PETTICOAT*.
WOW.
AND HERE I THOUGHT TODAY COULDN'T GET ANY *MORE* EMBARRASSING.
SERIOUSLY, FIND ANOTHER DATE.
IF YOU'RE LUCKY, *MARGARET FLETCHER* HASN'T BEEN ASKED YET.
YOU'VE SAID THAT *TWICE*.
DON'T YOU WANT TO GO WITH ME?
WHAT?! NO- NOTHING LIKE THAT!
...YOU DIDN'T TAKE MY CALL LAST NIGHT.
...
IS THIS WHAT GOING OUT WITH YOU IS GOING TO BE LIKE?
NO, NO, NO, NO, NO!
I'M SORRY, I SHOULD HAVE CALLED YOU BACK.
I WAS ALREADY IN BED AND LIZ AND I HAD THIS GIGANTIC ARGUMENT-
-SHE WAS *TOTALLY HORRIBLE* TO ME-
-AND SAID *THE WORST*-
-WHAT?
LIZ SHOWED UP AN HOUR BEFORE YOU DID.
I'M JUST GOING TO SLIP UNDER D'ARTAGNAN'S GIANT PETTICOAT AND *DIE*, THANK YOU VERY MUCH.

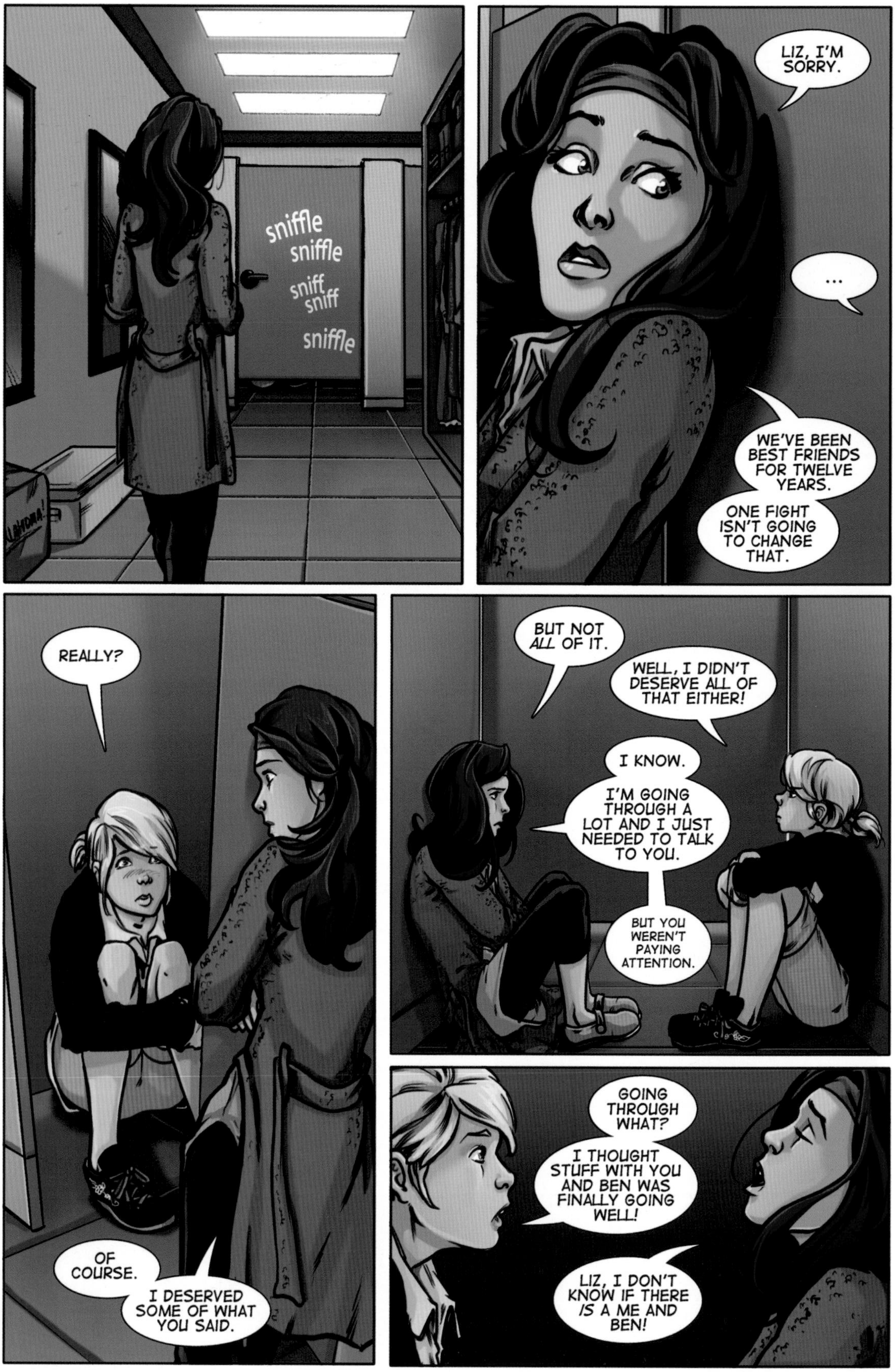
sniffle
sniffle
sniff
sniff
sniffle
LIZ, I'M SORRY.
...
WE'VE BEEN BEST FRIENDS FOR TWELVE YEARS.
ONE FIGHT ISN'T GOING TO CHANGE THAT.
REALLY?
OF COURSE.
I DESERVED SOME OF WHAT YOU SAID.
BUT NOT *ALL* OF IT.
WELL, I DIDN'T DESERVE ALL OF THAT EITHER!
I KNOW.
I'M GOING THROUGH A LOT AND I JUST NEEDED TO TALK TO YOU.
BUT YOU WEREN'T PAYING ATTENTION.
GOING THROUGH WHAT?
I THOUGHT STUFF WITH YOU AND BEN WAS FINALLY GOING WELL!
LIZ, I DON'T KNOW IF THERE *IS* A ME AND BEN!

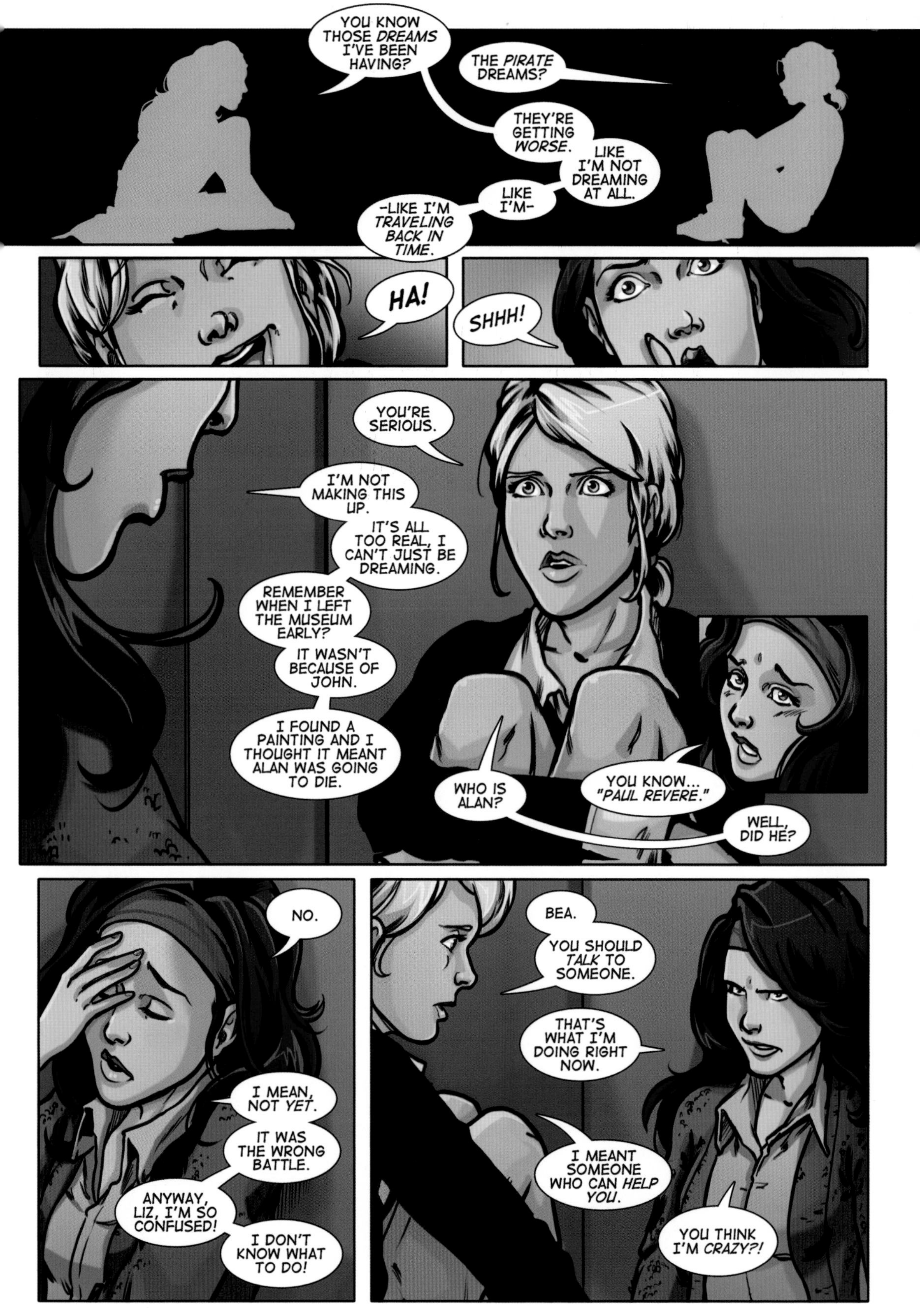

YOU KNOW THOSE *DREAMS* I'VE BEEN HAVING?
THE *PIRATE* DREAMS?
THEY'RE GETTING *WORSE*.
LIKE I'M NOT DREAMING AT ALL.
LIKE I'M-
-LIKE I'M *TRAVELING* *BACK IN* *TIME*.
HA!
SHHH!
YOU'RE SERIOUS.
I'M NOT MAKING THIS UP.
IT'S ALL TOO REAL, I CAN'T JUST BE DREAMING.
REMEMBER WHEN I LEFT THE MUSEUM EARLY?
IT WASN'T BECAUSE OF JOHN.
I FOUND A PAINTING AND I THOUGHT IT MEANT ALAN WAS GOING TO DIE.
WHO IS ALAN?
YOU KNOW... *"PAUL REVERE."*
WELL, DID HE?
NO.
I MEAN, NOT *YET*.
IT WAS THE WRONG BATTLE.
ANYWAY, LIZ, I'M SO CONFUSED!
I DON'T KNOW WHAT TO DO!
BEA.
YOU SHOULD *TALK* TO SOMEONE.
THAT'S WHAT I'M DOING RIGHT NOW.
I MEANT SOMEONE WHO CAN *HELP* *YOU*.
YOU THINK I'M *CRAZY?!*

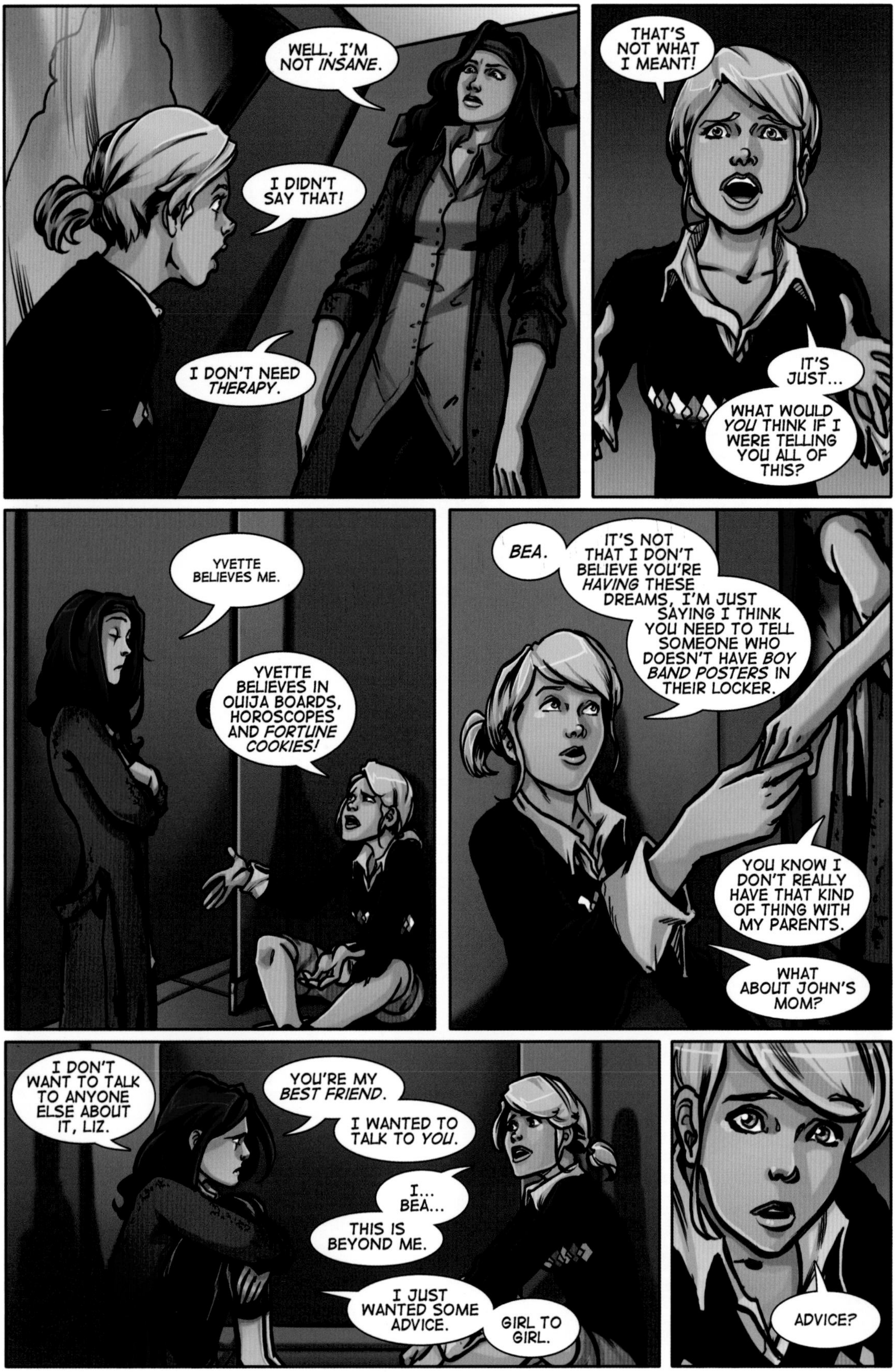
WELL, I'M NOT *INSANE*.
I DIDN'T SAY THAT!
I DON'T NEED *THERAPY*.
THAT'S NOT WHAT I MEANT!
IT'S JUST...
WHAT WOULD *YOU* THINK IF I WERE TELLING YOU ALL OF THIS?
YVETTE BELIEVES ME.
YVETTE BELIEVES IN OUIJA BOARDS, HOROSCOPES AND *FORTUNE COOKIES*!
BEA.
IT'S NOT THAT I DON'T BELIEVE YOU'RE *HAVING* THESE DREAMS, I'M JUST SAYING I THINK YOU NEED TO TELL SOMEONE WHO DOESN'T HAVE *BOY BAND POSTERS* IN THEIR LOCKER.
YOU KNOW I DON'T REALLY HAVE THAT KIND OF THING WITH MY PARENTS.
WHAT ABOUT JOHN'S MOM?
I DON'T WANT TO TALK TO ANYONE ELSE ABOUT IT, LIZ.
YOU'RE MY *BEST FRIEND*.
I WANTED TO TALK TO *YOU*.
I... BEA...
THIS IS BEYOND ME.
I JUST WANTED SOME ADVICE.
GIRL TO GIRL.
ADVICE?

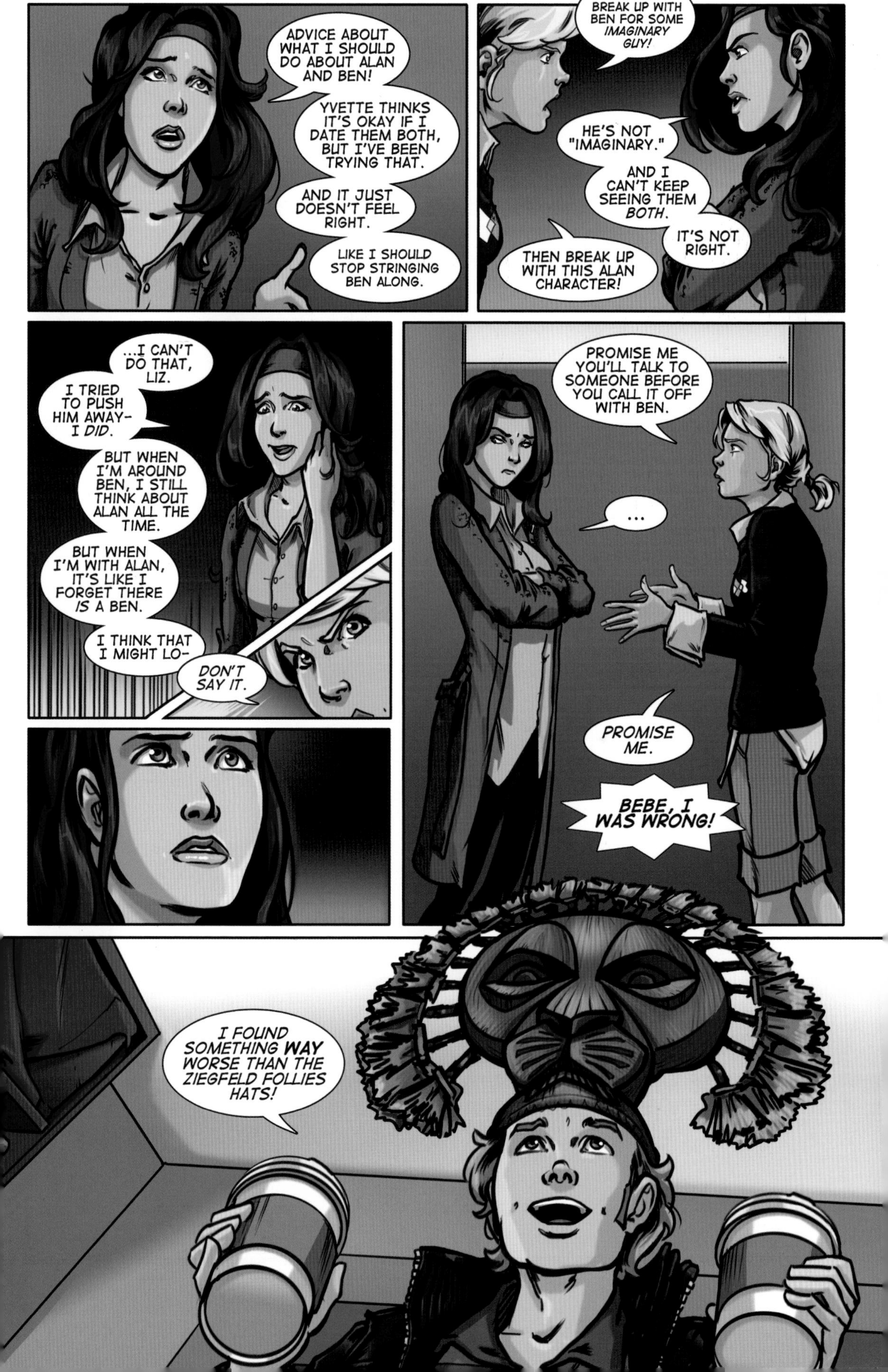

ADVICE ABOUT WHAT I SHOULD DO ABOUT ALAN AND BEN!
YVETTE THINKS IT'S OKAY IF I DATE THEM BOTH, BUT I'VE BEEN TRYING THAT.
AND IT JUST DOESN'T FEEL RIGHT.
LIKE I SHOULD STOP STRINGING BEN ALONG.
YOU CAN'T BREAK UP WITH BEN FOR SOME IMAGINARY GUY!
HE'S NOT "IMAGINARY."
AND I CAN'T KEEP SEEING THEM BOTH.
IT'S NOT RIGHT.
THEN BREAK UP WITH THIS ALAN CHARACTER!
...I CAN'T DO THAT, LIZ.
I TRIED TO PUSH HIM AWAY-I DID.
BUT WHEN I'M AROUND BEN, I STILL THINK ABOUT ALAN ALL THE TIME.
BUT WHEN I'M WITH ALAN, IT'S LIKE I FORGET THERE IS A BEN.
I THINK THAT I MIGHT LO-
DON'T SAY IT.
PROMISE ME YOU'LL TALK TO SOMEONE BEFORE YOU CALL IT OFF WITH BEN.
...
PROMISE ME.
BEBE, I WAS WRONG!
I FOUND SOMETHING WAY WORSE THAN THE ZIEGFELD FOLLIES HATS!

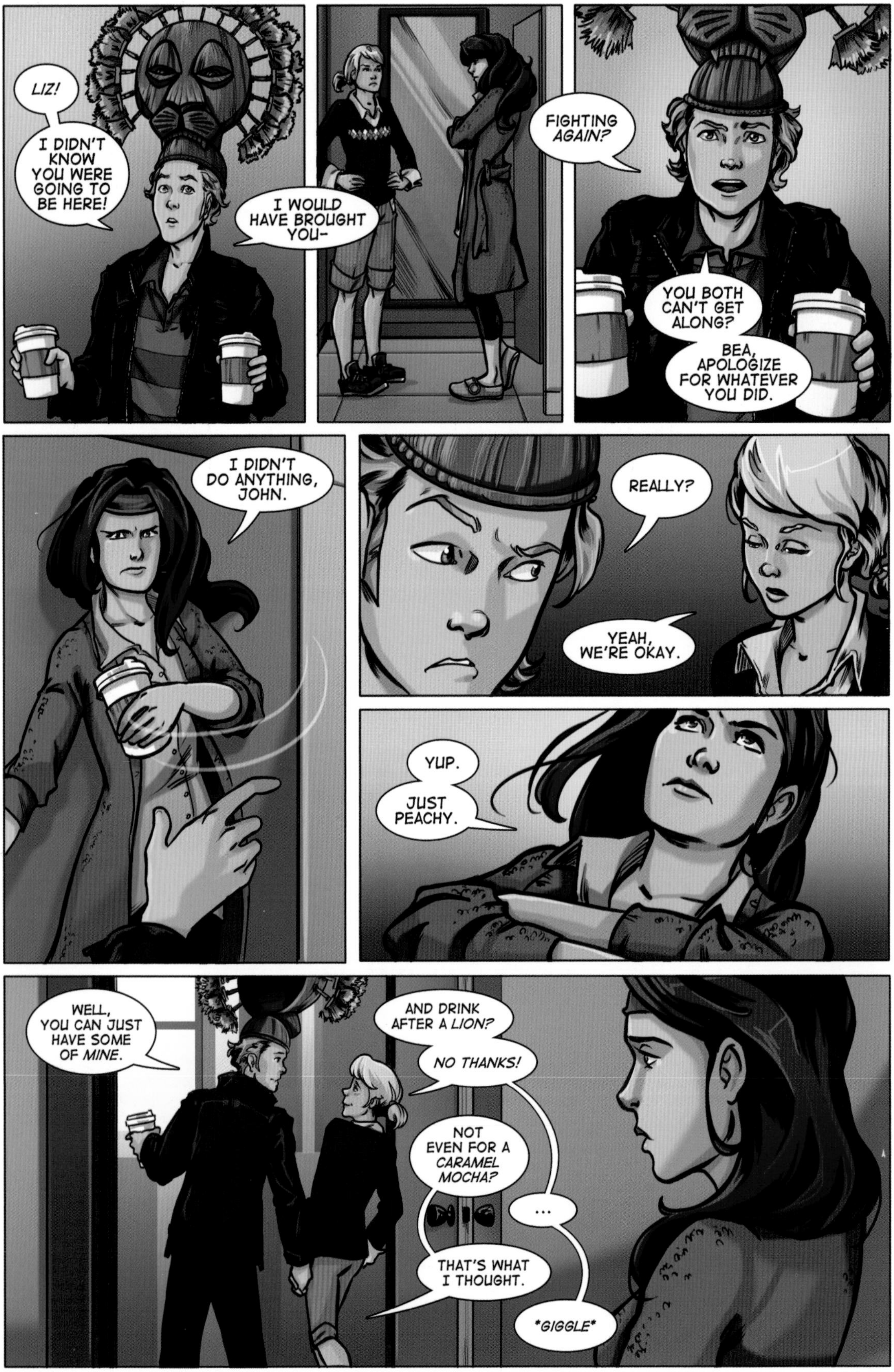
LIZ!
I DIDN'T KNOW YOU WERE GOING TO BE HERE!
I WOULD HAVE BROUGHT YOU-
FIGHTING AGAIN?
YOU BOTH CAN'T GET ALONG?
BEA, APOLOGIZE FOR WHATEVER YOU DID.
I DIDN'T DO ANYTHING, JOHN.
REALLY?
YEAH, WE'RE OKAY.
YUP.
JUST PEACHY.
WELL, YOU CAN JUST HAVE SOME OF MINE.
AND DRINK AFTER A LION?
NO THANKS!
NOT EVEN FOR A CARAMEL MOCHA?
...
THAT'S WHAT I THOUGHT.
GIGGLE

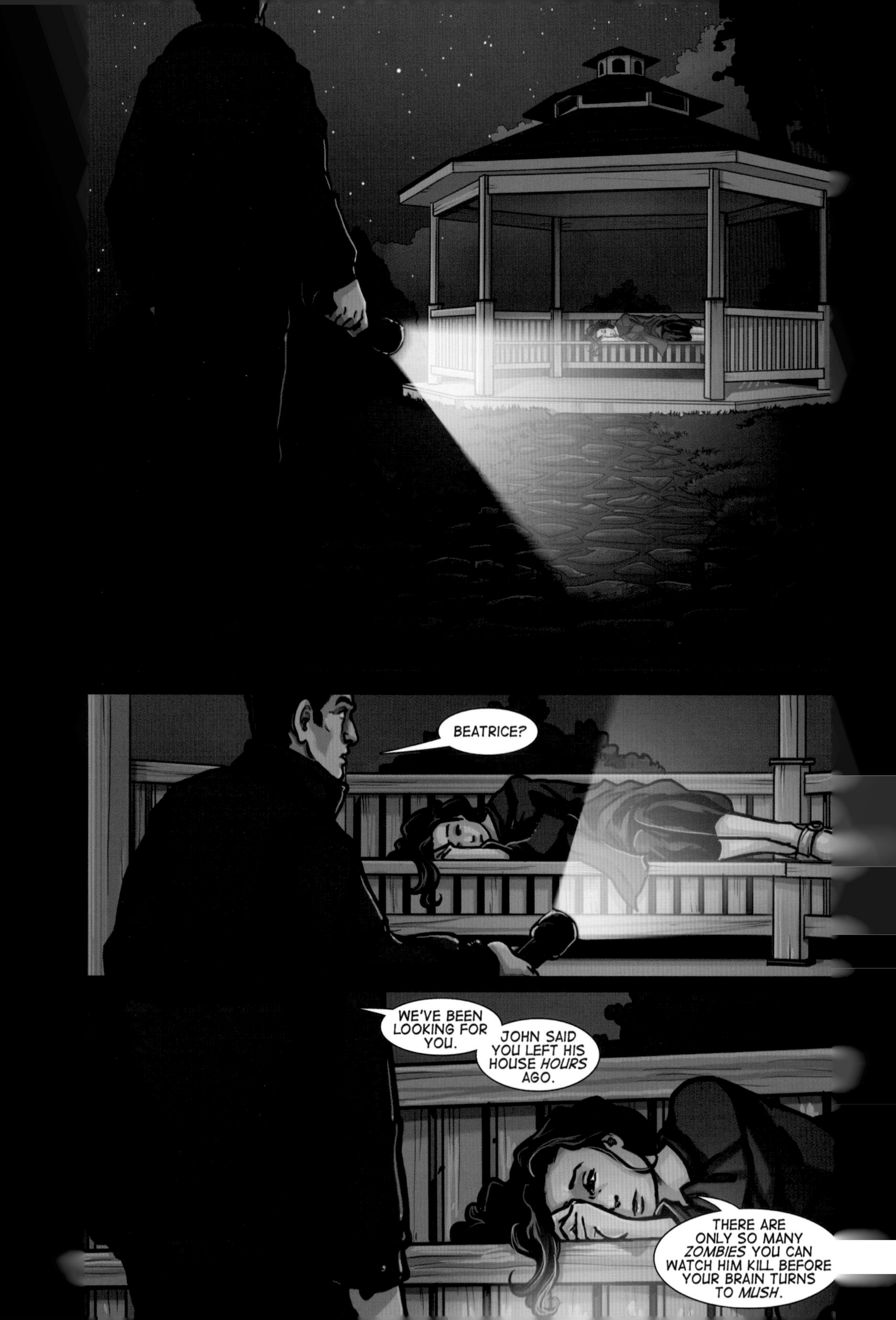
BEATRICE?
WE'VE BEEN LOOKING FOR YOU.
JOHN SAID YOU LEFT HIS HOUSE *HOURS* AGO.
THERE ARE ONLY SO MANY *ZOMBIES* YOU CAN WATCH HIM KILL BEFORE YOUR BRAIN TURNS TO *MUSH*.

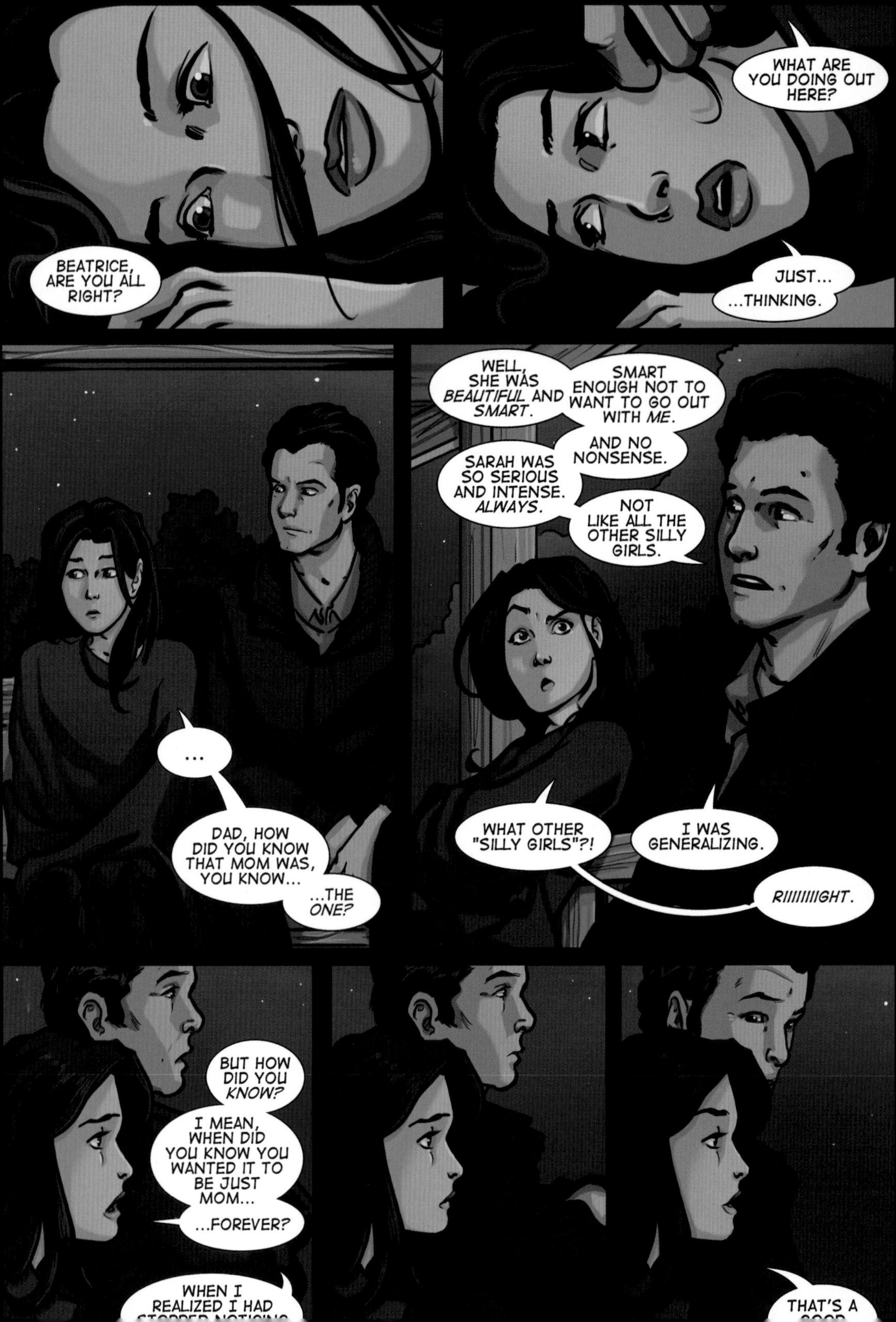
BEATRICE, ARE YOU ALL RIGHT?
WHAT ARE YOU DOING OUT HERE?
JUST...
...THINKING.
...
DAD, HOW DID YOU KNOW THAT MOM WAS, YOU KNOW...
...THE *ONE?*
WELL, SHE WAS *BEAUTIFUL* AND *SMART*.
SMART ENOUGH NOT TO WANT TO GO OUT WITH *ME*.
AND NO NONSENSE.
SARAH WAS SO SERIOUS AND INTENSE. *ALWAYS*.
NOT LIKE ALL THE OTHER SILLY GIRLS.
WHAT OTHER "SILLY GIRLS"?!
I WAS GENERALIZING.
RIIIIIIIGHT.
BUT HOW DID YOU *KNOW?*
I MEAN, WHEN DID YOU KNOW YOU WANTED IT TO BE JUST MOM...
...FOREVER?
WHEN I REALIZED I HAD
THAT'S A

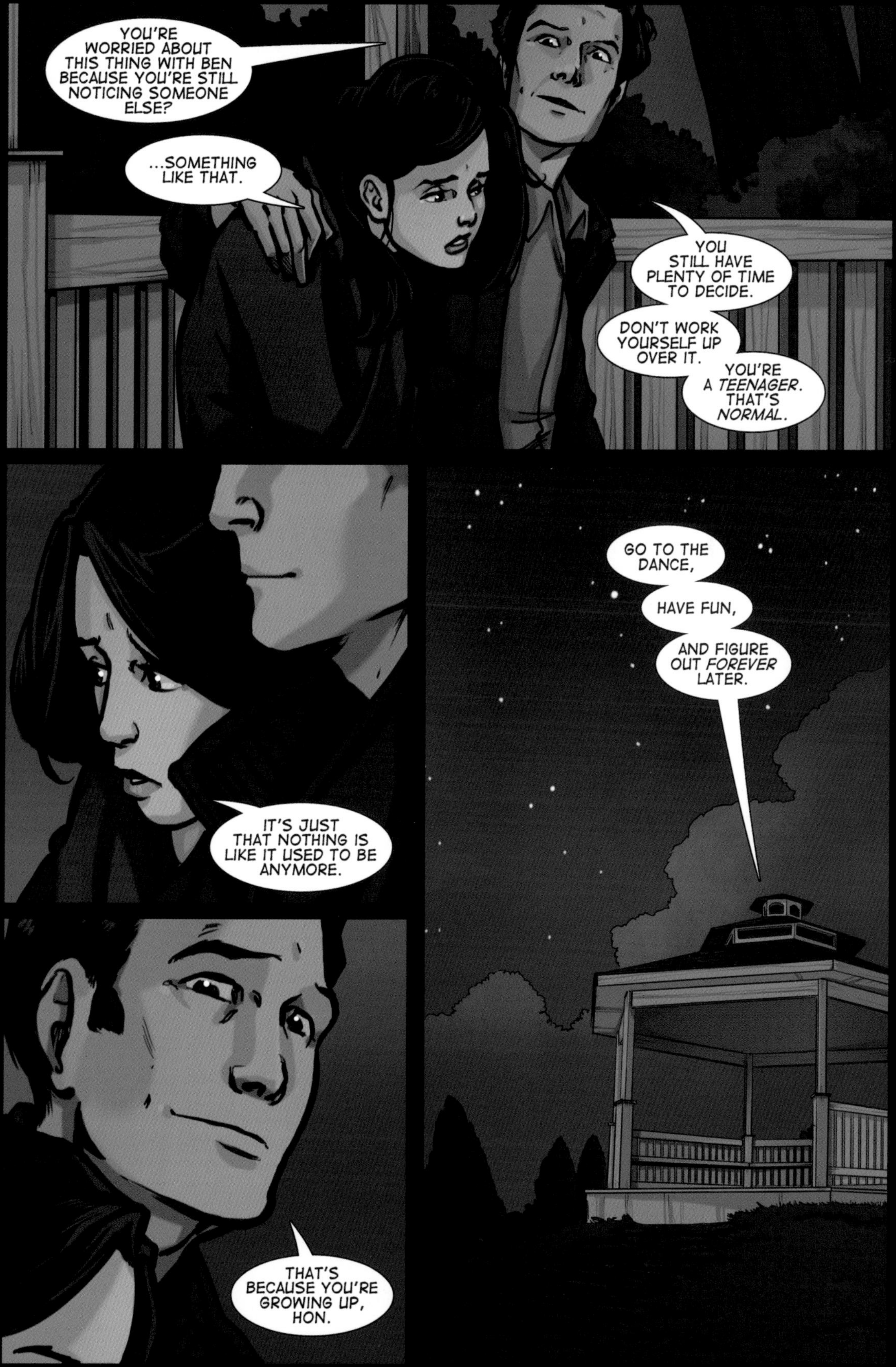
YOU'RE WORRIED ABOUT THIS THING WITH BEN BECAUSE YOU'RE STILL NOTICING SOMEONE ELSE?
...SOMETHING LIKE THAT.
YOU STILL HAVE PLENTY OF TIME TO DECIDE.
DON'T WORK YOURSELF UP OVER IT.
YOU'RE A *TEENAGER*. THAT'S *NORMAL*.
IT'S JUST THAT NOTHING IS LIKE IT USED TO BE ANYMORE.
THAT'S BECAUSE YOU'RE GROWING UP, HON.
GO TO THE DANCE,
HAVE FUN,
AND FIGURE OUT *FOREVER* LATER.

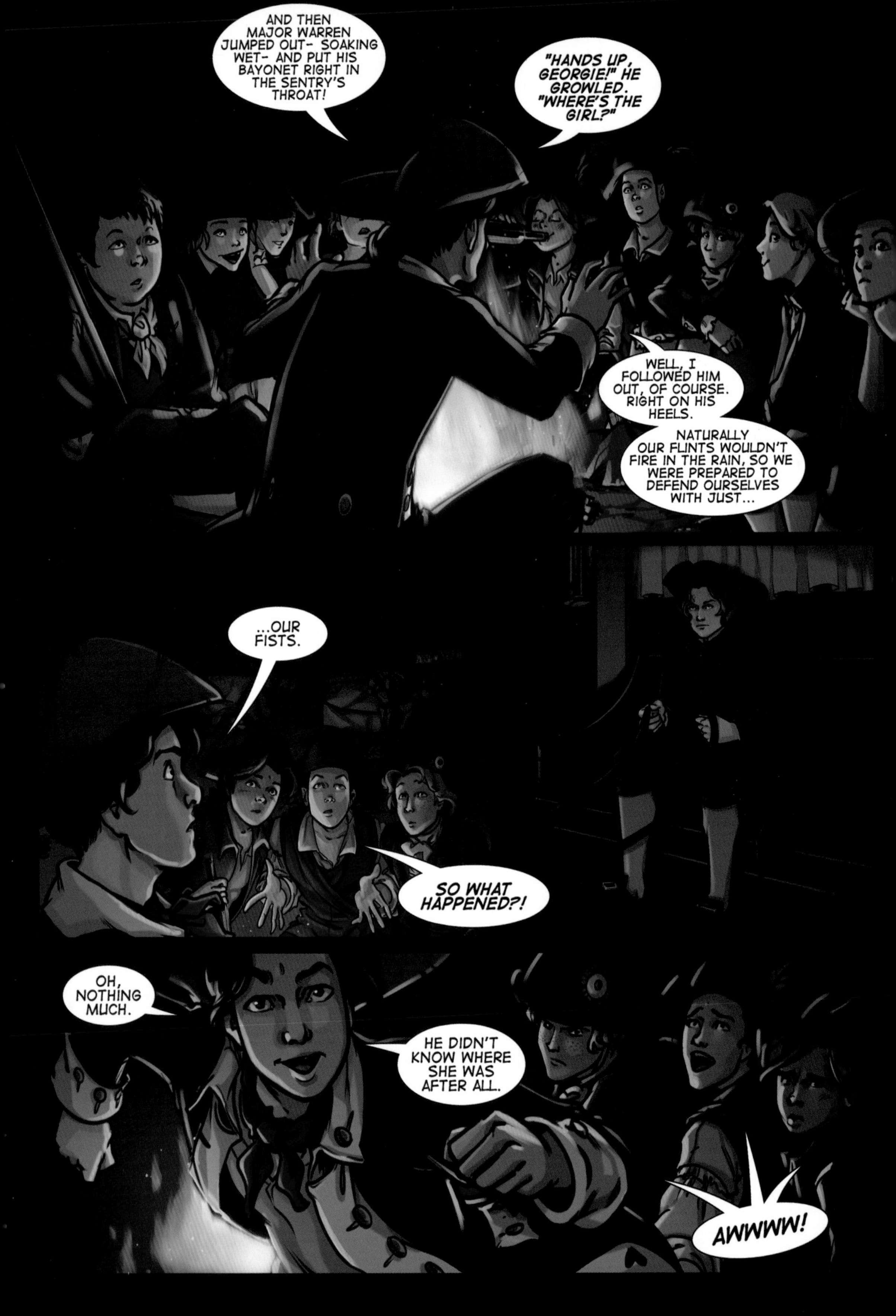
AND THEN MAJOR WARREN JUMPED OUT- SOAKING WET- AND PUT HIS BAYONET RIGHT IN THE SENTRY'S THROAT!
"HANDS UP, GEORGIE!" HE GROWLED. "WHERE'S THE GIRL?"
WELL, I FOLLOWED HIM OUT, OF COURSE. RIGHT ON HIS HEELS.
NATURALLY OUR FLINTS WOULDN'T FIRE IN THE RAIN, SO WE WERE PREPARED TO DEFEND OURSELVES WITH JUST...
...OUR FISTS.
SO WHAT HAPPENED?!
OH, NOTHING MUCH.
HE DIDN'T KNOW WHERE SHE WAS AFTER ALL.
AWWWW!

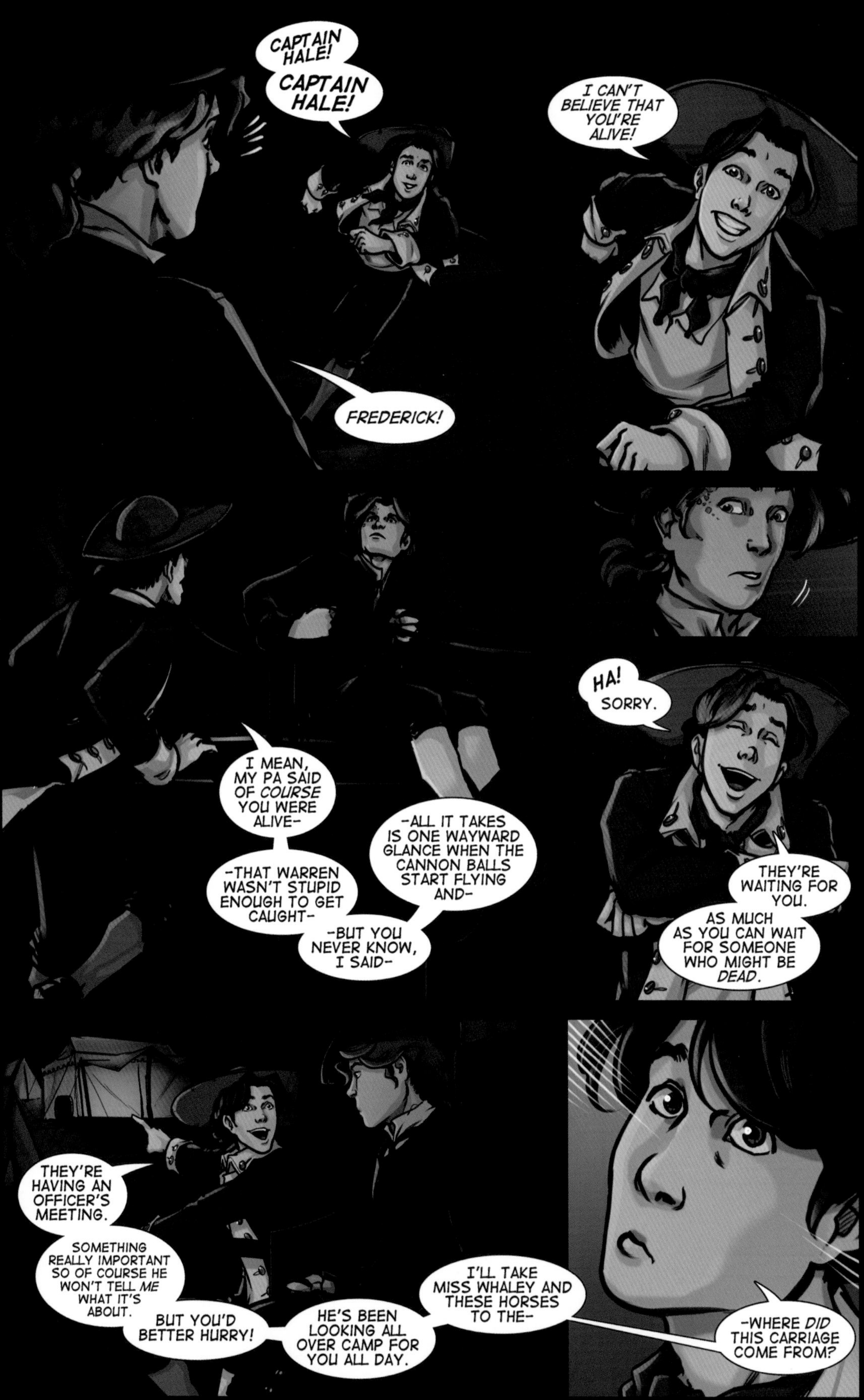
CAPTAIN HALE! CAPTAIN HALE!
FREDERICK!
I CAN'T BELIEVE THAT YOU'RE ALIVE!
I MEAN, MY PA SAID OF *COURSE* YOU WERE ALIVE-
-THAT WARREN WASN'T STUPID ENOUGH TO GET CAUGHT-
-BUT YOU NEVER KNOW, I SAID-
-ALL IT TAKES IS ONE WAYWARD GLANCE WHEN THE CANNON BALLS START FLYING AND-
HA! SORRY.
THEY'RE WAITING FOR YOU.
AS MUCH AS YOU CAN WAIT FOR SOMEONE WHO MIGHT BE *DEAD*.
THEY'RE HAVING AN OFFICER'S MEETING.
SOMETHING REALLY IMPORTANT SO OF COURSE HE WON'T TELL *ME* WHAT IT'S ABOUT.
BUT YOU'D BETTER HURRY!
HE'S BEEN LOOKING ALL OVER CAMP FOR YOU ALL DAY.
I'LL TAKE MISS WHALEY AND THESE HORSES TO THE-
-WHERE *DID* THIS CARRIAGE COME FROM?

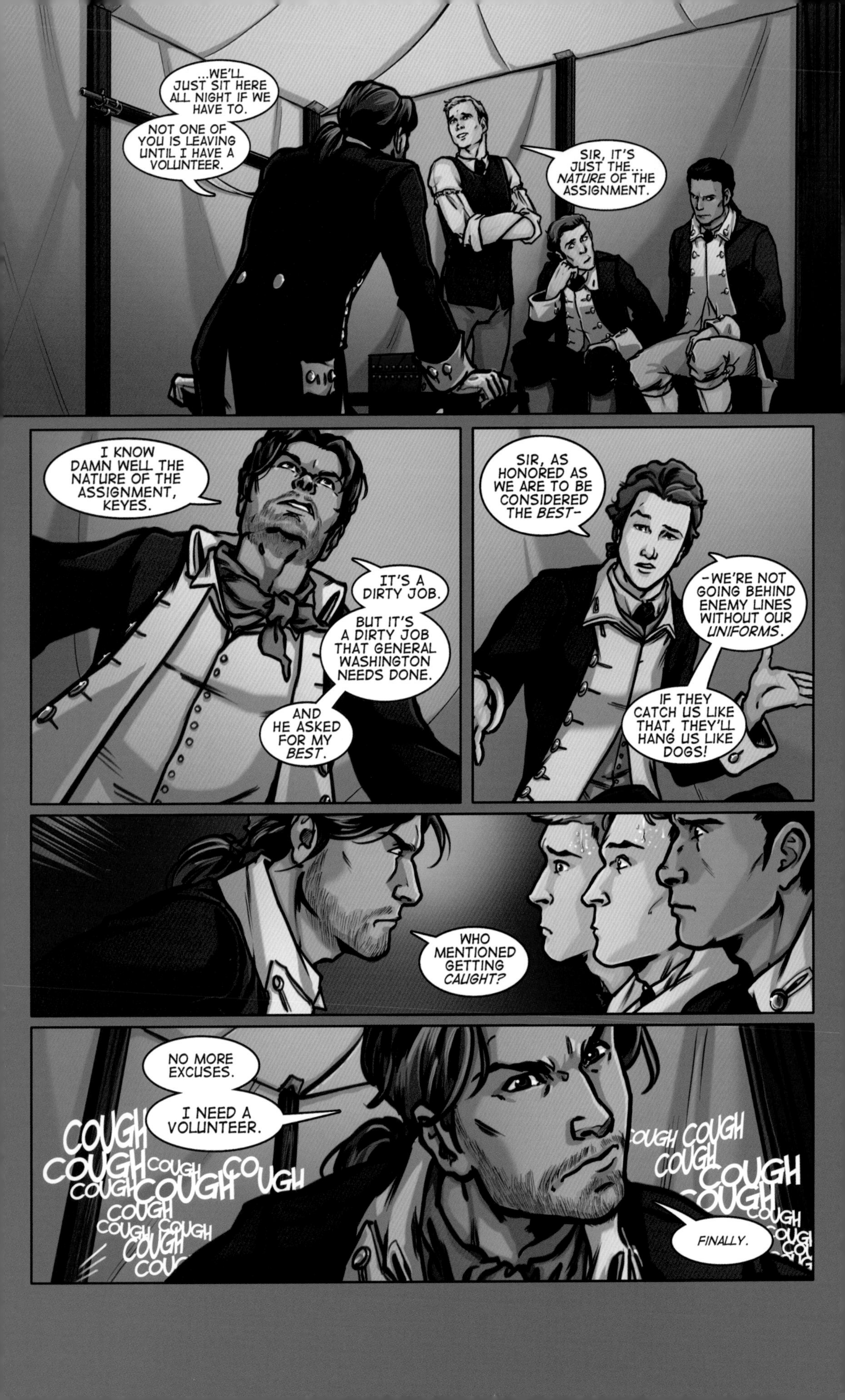
...WE'LL JUST SIT HERE ALL NIGHT IF WE HAVE TO.
NOT ONE OF YOU IS LEAVING UNTIL I HAVE A VOLUNTEER.
SIR, IT'S JUST THE... NATURE OF THE ASSIGNMENT.
I KNOW DAMN WELL THE NATURE OF THE ASSIGNMENT, KEYES.
IT'S A DIRTY JOB.
BUT IT'S A DIRTY JOB THAT GENERAL WASHINGTON NEEDS DONE.
AND HE ASKED FOR MY BEST.
SIR, AS HONORED AS WE ARE TO BE CONSIDERED THE BEST-
-WE'RE NOT GOING BEHIND ENEMY LINES WITHOUT OUR UNIFORMS.
IF THEY CATCH US LIKE THAT, THEY'LL HANG US LIKE DOGS!
WHO MENTIONED GETTING CAUGHT?
NO MORE EXCUSES.
I NEED A VOLUNTEER.
COUGH COUGH COUGH COUGH COUGH COUGH COUGH COUGH COUGH COUGH
COUGH COUGH COUGH COUGH COUGH COUGH
FINALLY.

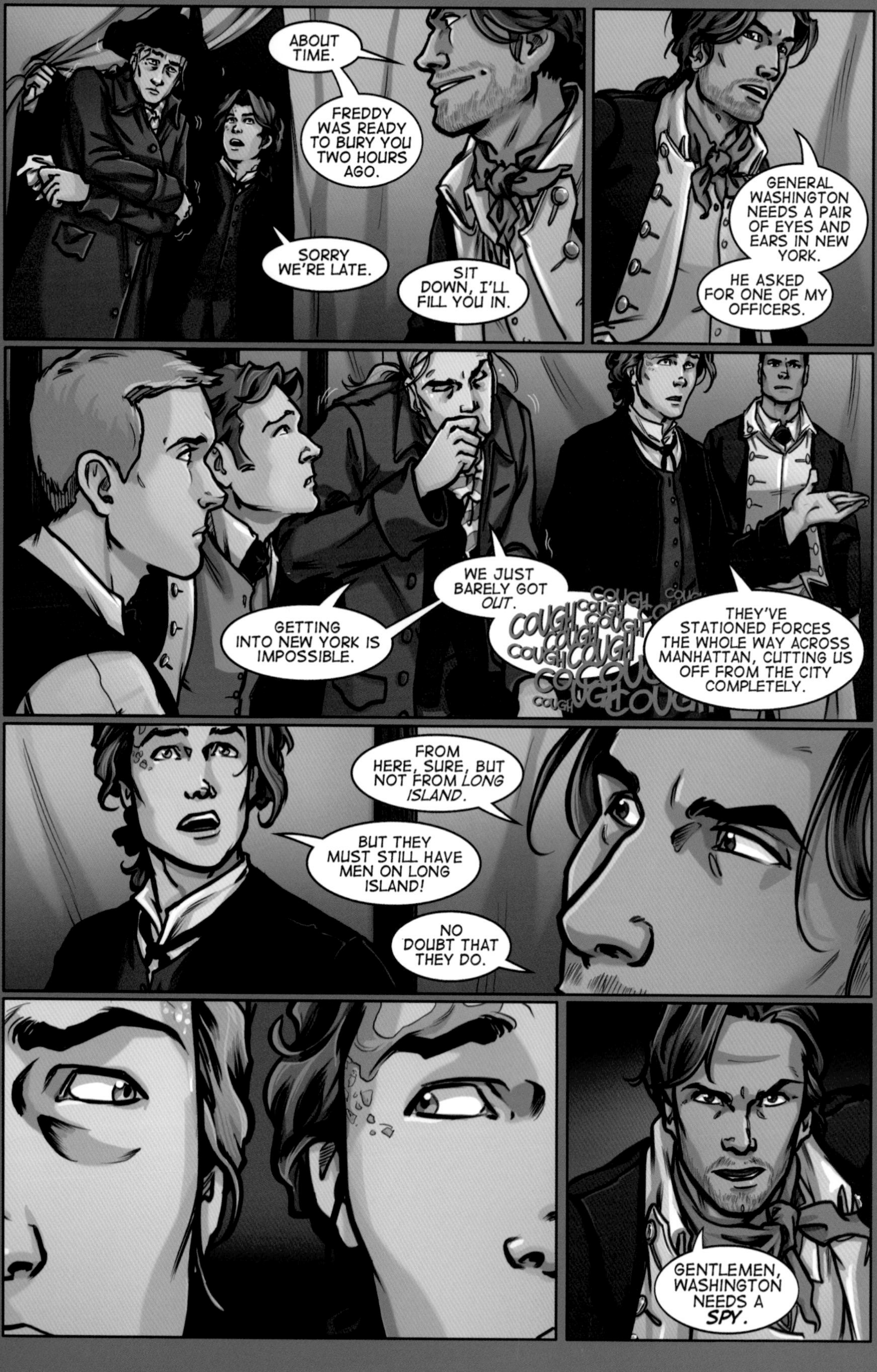

ABOUT TIME.
FREDDY WAS READY TO BURY YOU TWO HOURS AGO.
SORRY WE'RE LATE.
SIT DOWN, I'LL FILL YOU IN.
GENERAL WASHINGTON NEEDS A PAIR OF EYES AND EARS IN NEW YORK.
HE ASKED FOR ONE OF MY OFFICERS.
GETTING INTO NEW YORK IS IMPOSSIBLE.
WE JUST BARELY GOT *OUT*.
COUGH COUGH COUGH COUGH COUGH COUGH COUGH COUGH COUGH
THEY'VE STATIONED FORCES THE WHOLE WAY ACROSS MANHATTAN, CUTTING US OFF FROM THE CITY COMPLETELY.
FROM HERE, SURE, BUT NOT FROM *LONG ISLAND*.
BUT THEY MUST STILL HAVE MEN ON LONG ISLAND!
NO DOUBT THAT THEY DO.
GENTLEMEN, WASHINGTON NEEDS A ***SPY***.

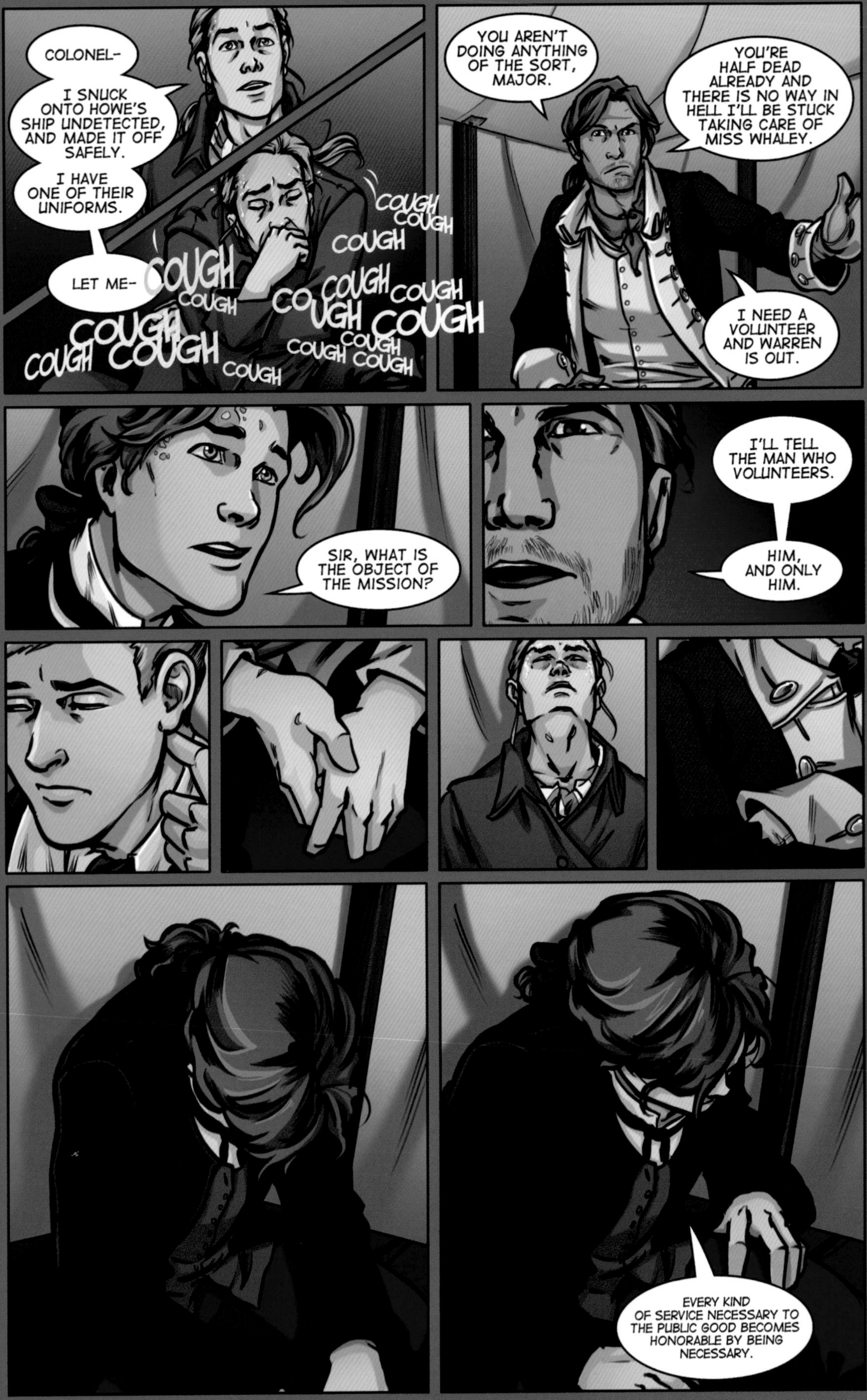
COLONEL-
I SNUCK ONTO HOWE'S SHIP UNDETECTED, AND MADE IT OFF SAFELY.
I HAVE ONE OF THEIR UNIFORMS.
LET ME-
COUGH COUGH COUGH COUGH COUGH COUGH COUGH COUGH COUGH COUGH COUGH COUGH COUGH COUGH COUGH COUGH
YOU AREN'T DOING ANYTHING OF THE SORT, MAJOR.
YOU'RE HALF DEAD ALREADY AND THERE IS NO WAY IN HELL I'LL BE STUCK TAKING CARE OF MISS WHALEY.
I NEED A VOLUNTEER AND WARREN IS OUT.
SIR, WHAT IS THE OBJECT OF THE MISSION?
I'LL TELL THE MAN WHO VOLUNTEERS.
HIM, AND ONLY HIM.
EVERY KIND OF SERVICE NECESSARY TO THE PUBLIC GOOD BECOMES HONORABLE BY BEING NECESSARY.

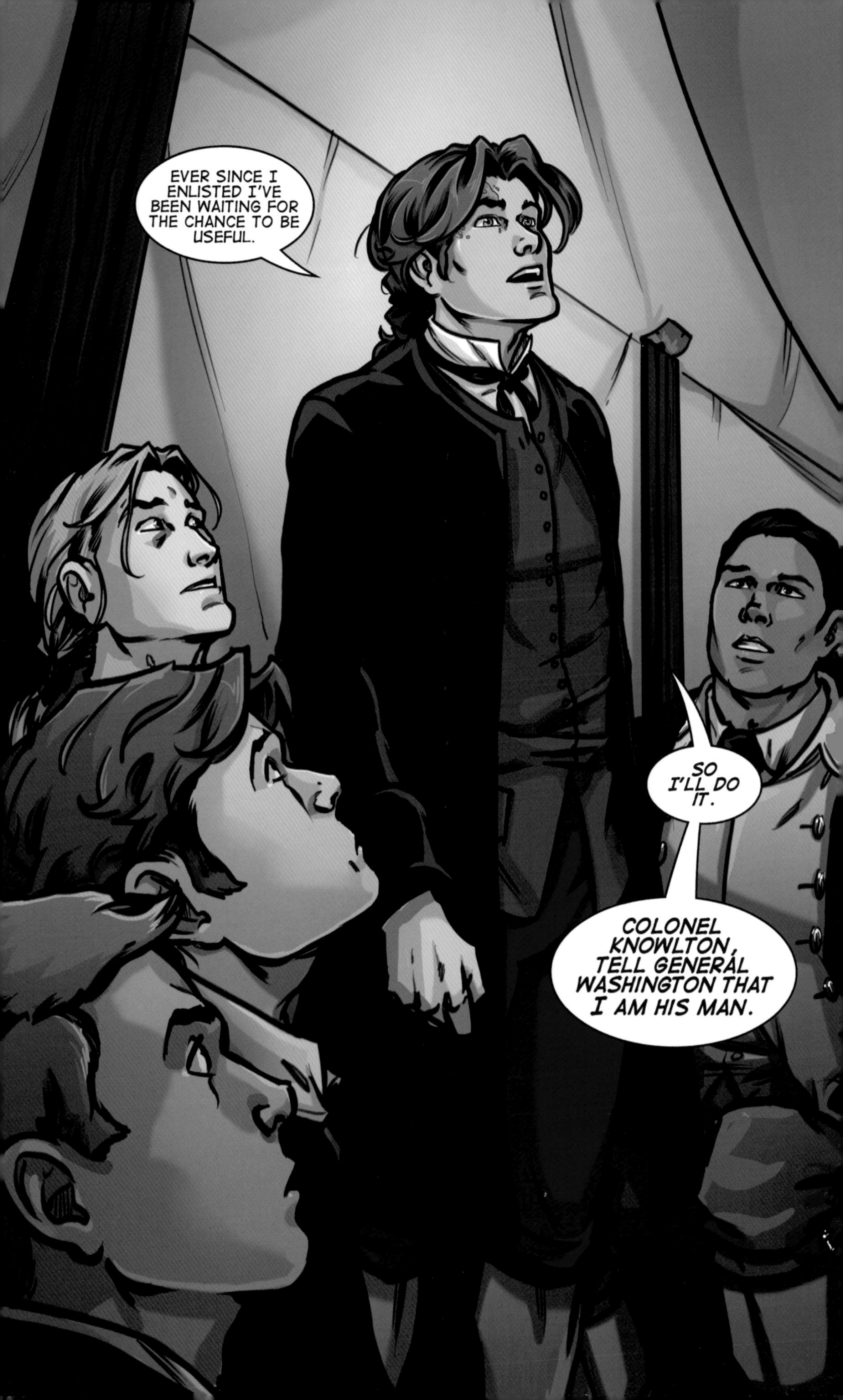
EVER SINCE I ENLISTED I'VE BEEN WAITING FOR THE CHANCE TO BE USEFUL.
SO I'LL DO IT.
COLONEL KNOWLTON, TELL GENERAL WASHINGTON THAT I AM HIS MAN.

Chapter Twelve

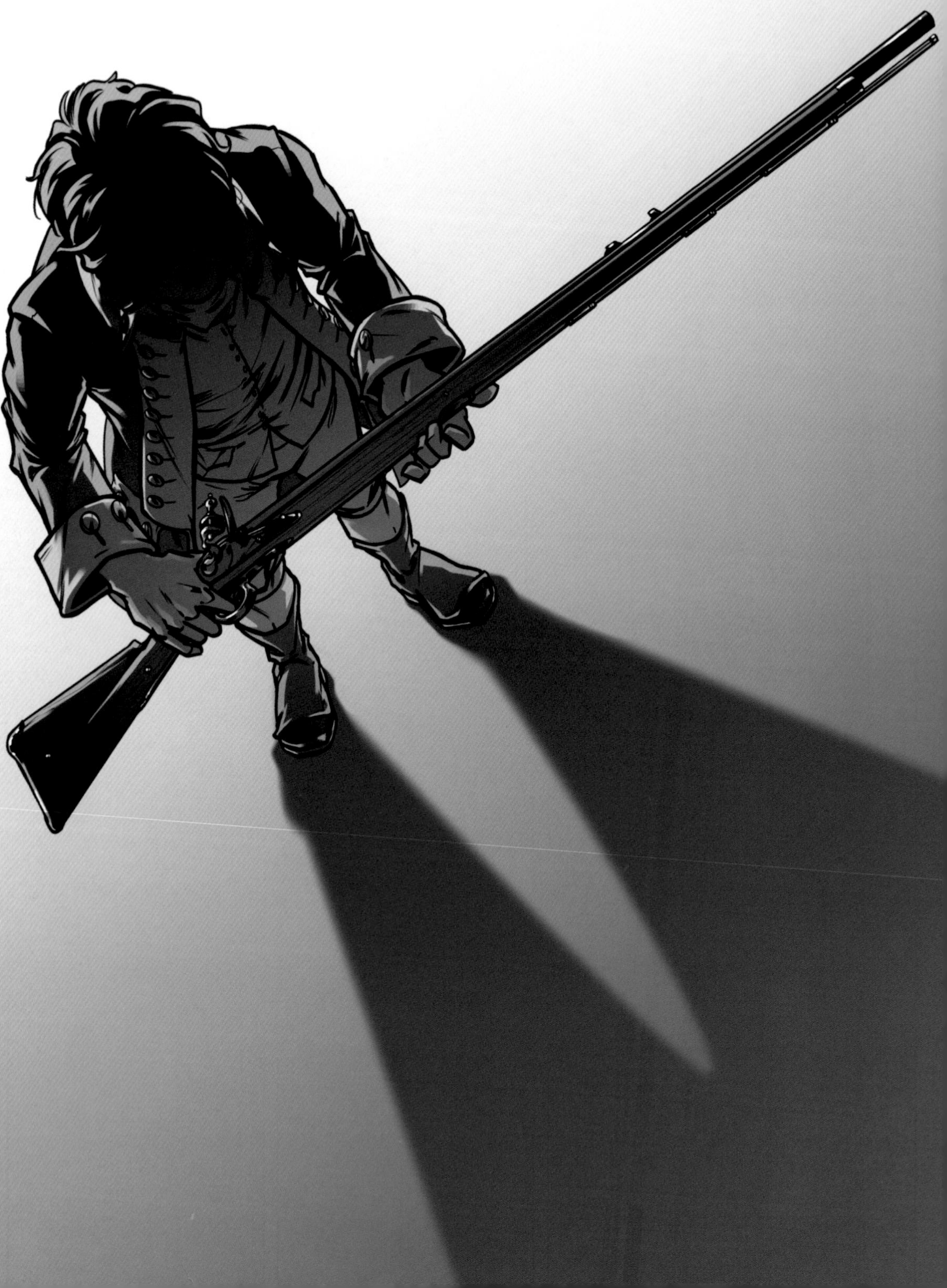

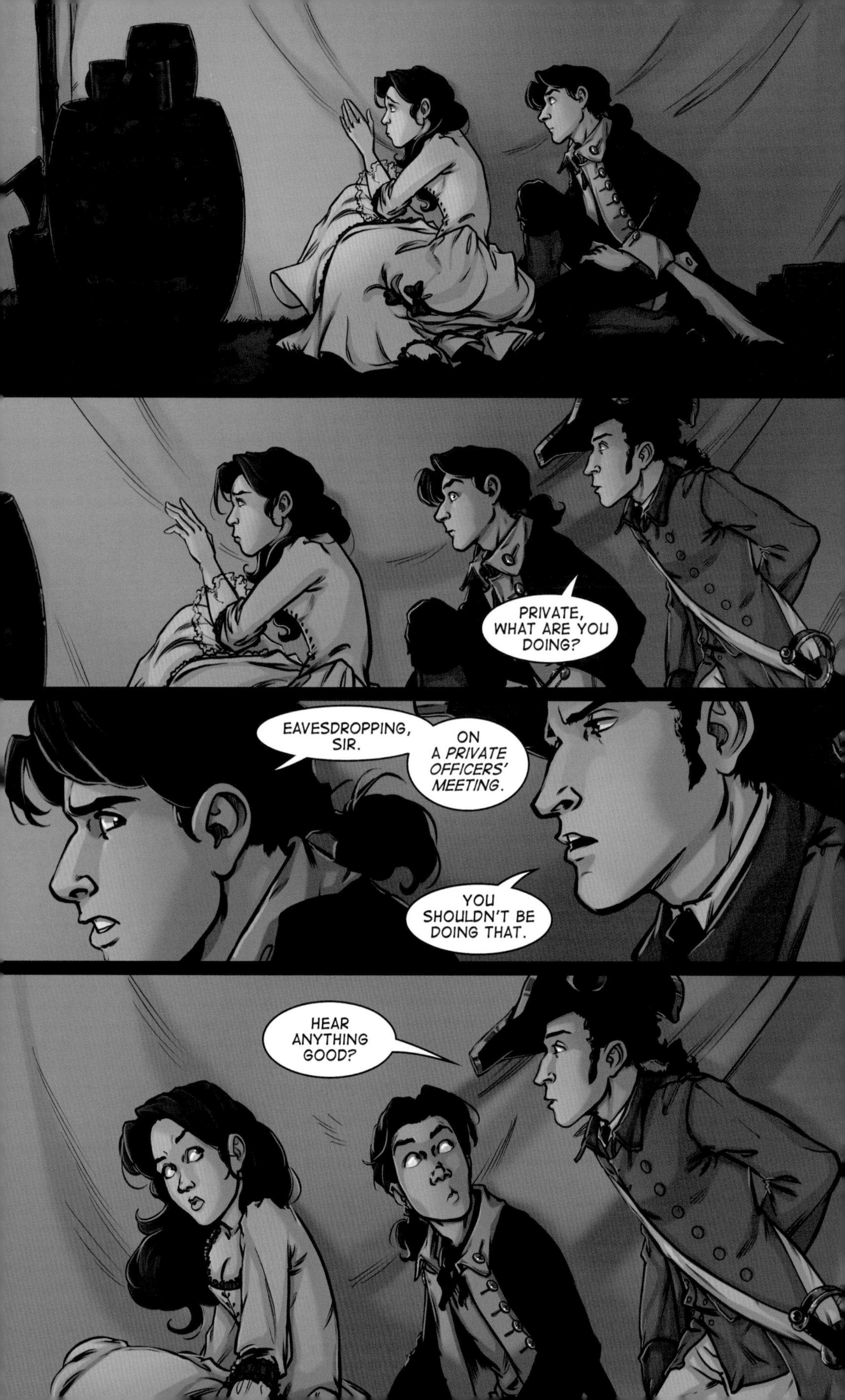
PRIVATE, WHAT ARE YOU DOING?
EAVESDROPPING, SIR.
ON A *PRIVATE* OFFICERS' *MEETING*.
YOU SHOULDN'T BE DOING THAT.
HEAR ANYTHING GOOD?

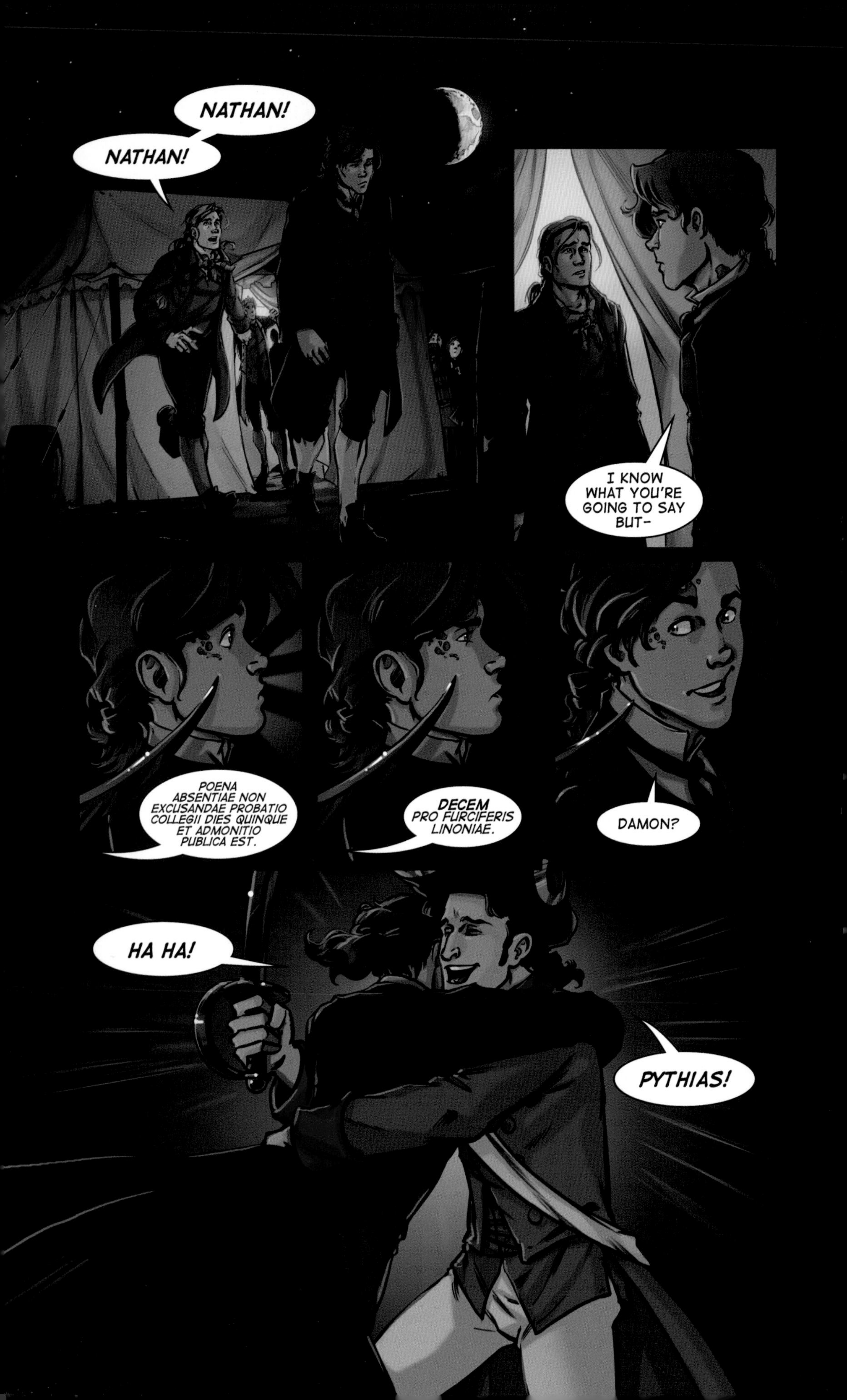
NATHAN!
NATHAN!
I KNOW WHAT YOU'RE GOING TO SAY BUT-
POENA ABSENTIAE NON EXCUSANDAE PROBATIO COLLEGII DIES QUINQUE ET ADMONITIO PUBLICA EST.
DECEM PRO FURCIFERIS LINONIAE.
DAMON?
HA HA!
PYTHIAS!

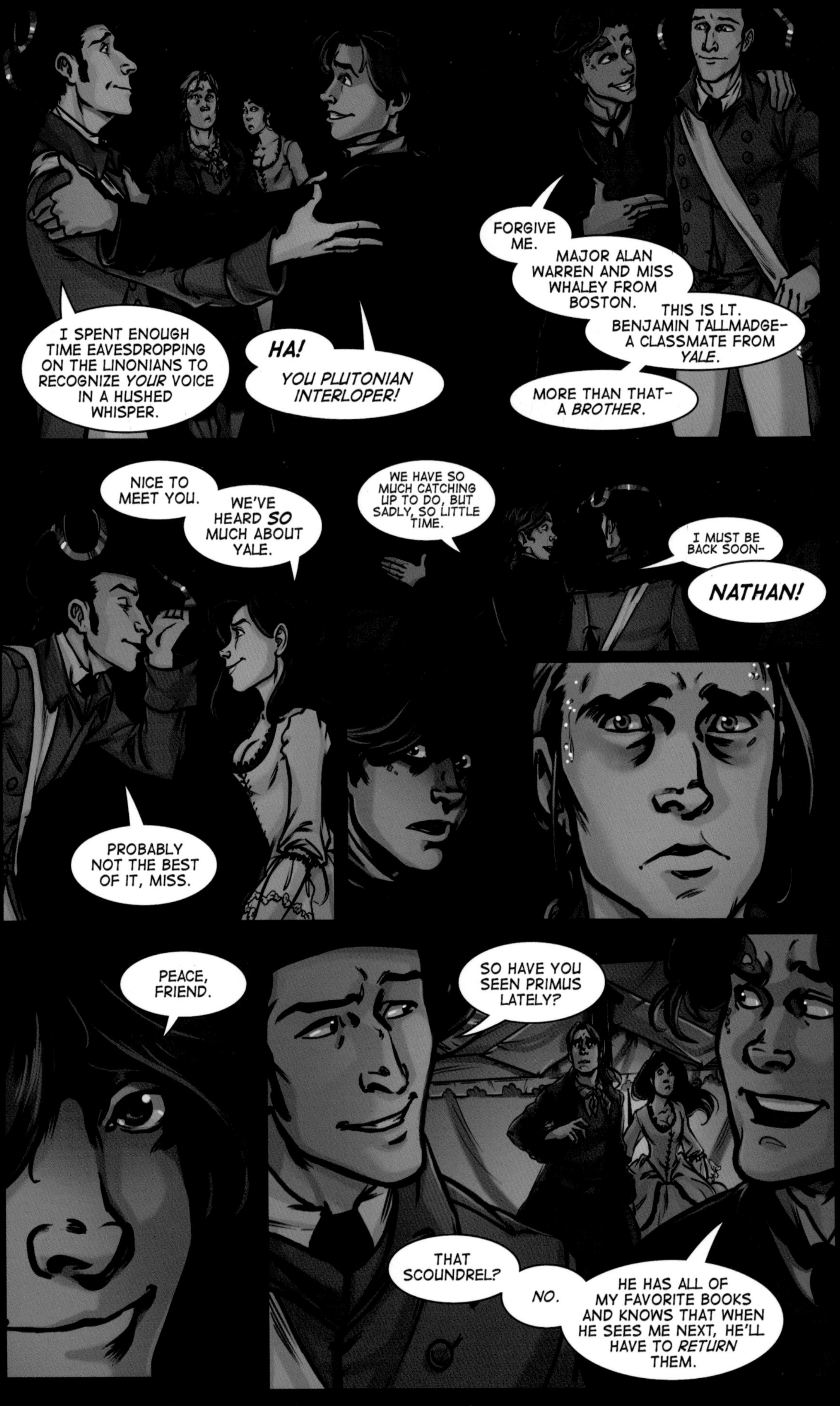
I SPENT ENOUGH TIME EAVESDROPPING ON THE LINONIANS TO RECOGNIZE *YOUR* VOICE IN A HUSHED WHISPER.
HA!
YOU PLUTONIAN INTERLOPER!
FORGIVE ME.
MAJOR ALAN WARREN AND MISS WHALEY FROM BOSTON.
THIS IS LT. BENJAMIN TALLMADGE- A CLASSMATE FROM *YALE*.
MORE THAN THAT- A *BROTHER*.
NICE TO MEET YOU.
WE'VE HEARD **SO** MUCH ABOUT YALE.
PROBABLY NOT THE BEST OF IT, MISS.
WE HAVE SO MUCH CATCHING UP TO DO, BUT SADLY, SO LITTLE TIME.
I MUST BE BACK SOON-
NATHAN!
PEACE, FRIEND.
SO HAVE YOU SEEN PRIMUS LATELY?
THAT SCOUNDREL?
NO.
HE HAS ALL OF MY FAVORITE BOOKS AND KNOWS THAT WHEN HE SEES ME NEXT, HE'LL HAVE TO *RETURN* THEM.

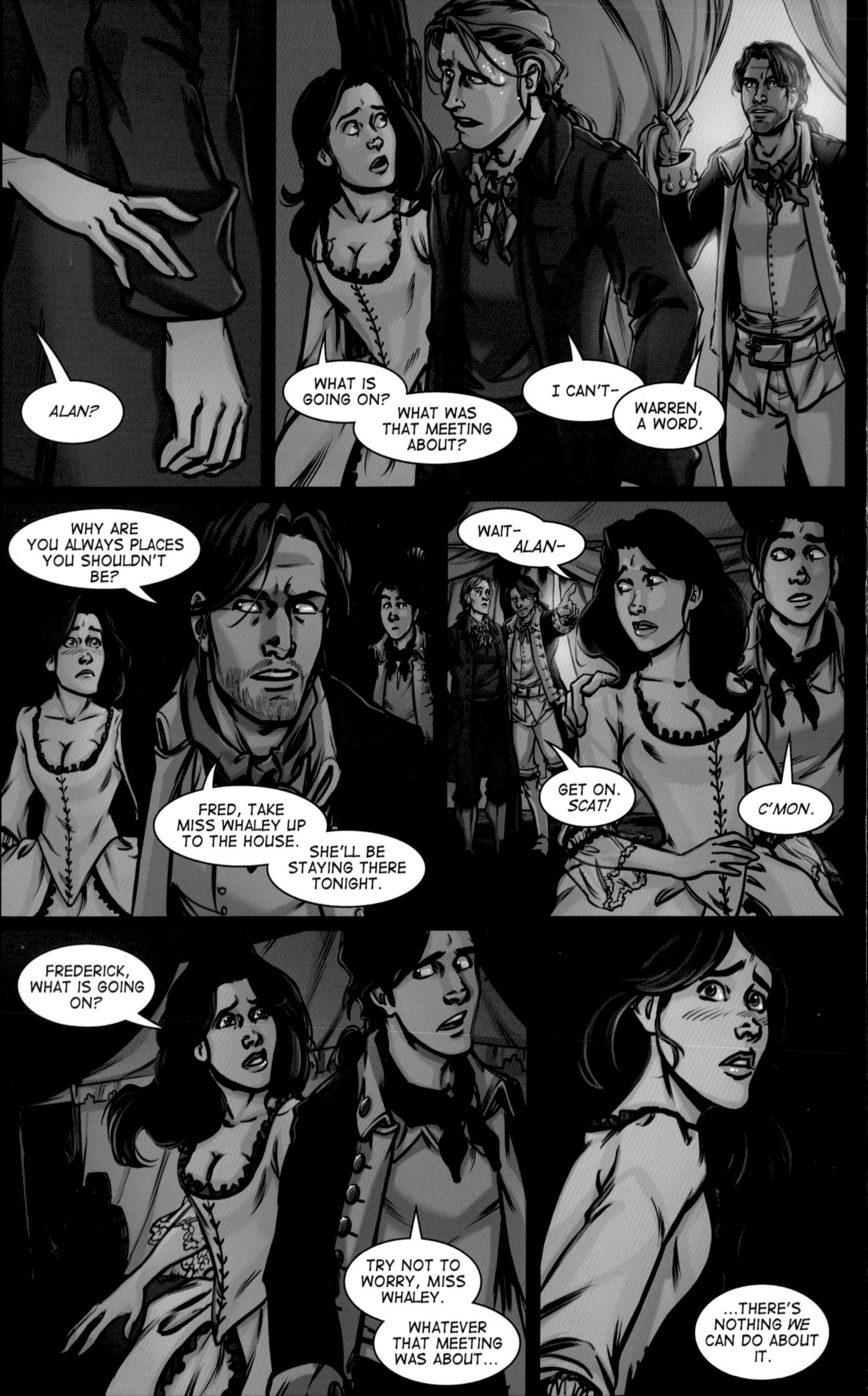
ALAN?
WHAT IS GOING ON?
WHAT WAS THAT MEETING ABOUT?
I CAN'T-
WARREN, A WORD.
WHY ARE YOU ALWAYS PLACES YOU SHOULDN'T BE?
FRED, TAKE MISS WHALEY UP TO THE HOUSE.
SHE'LL BE STAYING THERE TONIGHT.
WAIT- ALAN-
GET ON. SCAT!
C'MON.
FREDERICK, WHAT IS GOING ON?
TRY NOT TO WORRY, MISS WHALEY.
WHATEVER THAT MEETING WAS ABOUT...
...THERE'S NOTHING WE CAN DO ABOUT IT.

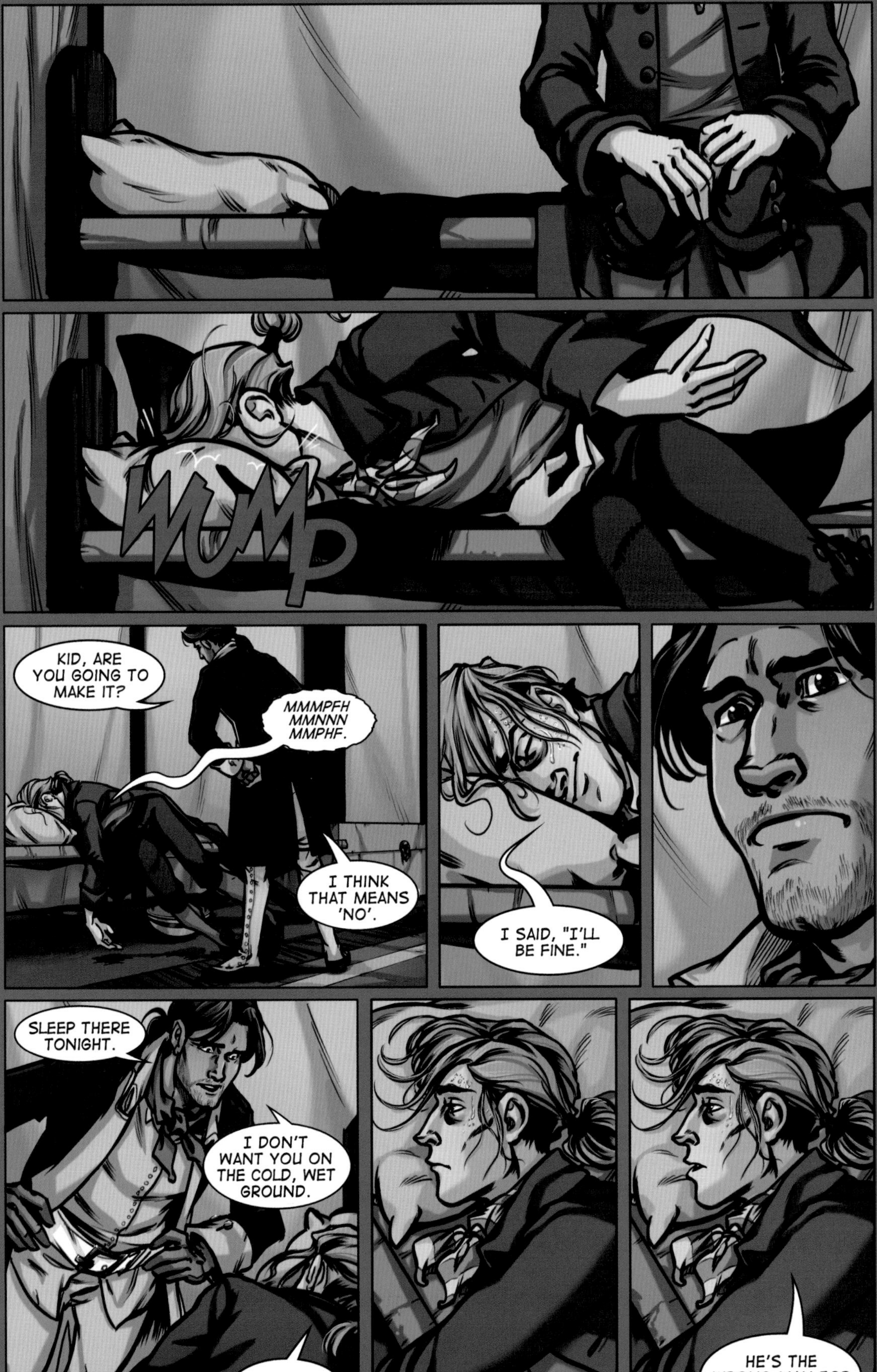
WUMP
KID, ARE YOU GOING TO MAKE IT?
MMMPFH MMNNN MMPHF.
I THINK THAT MEANS 'NO'.
I SAID, "I'LL BE FINE."
SLEEP THERE TONIGHT.
I DON'T WANT YOU ON THE COLD, WET GROUND.
THANK YOU, SIR.
HE'S THE WRONG MAN FOR THE JOB, SIR.

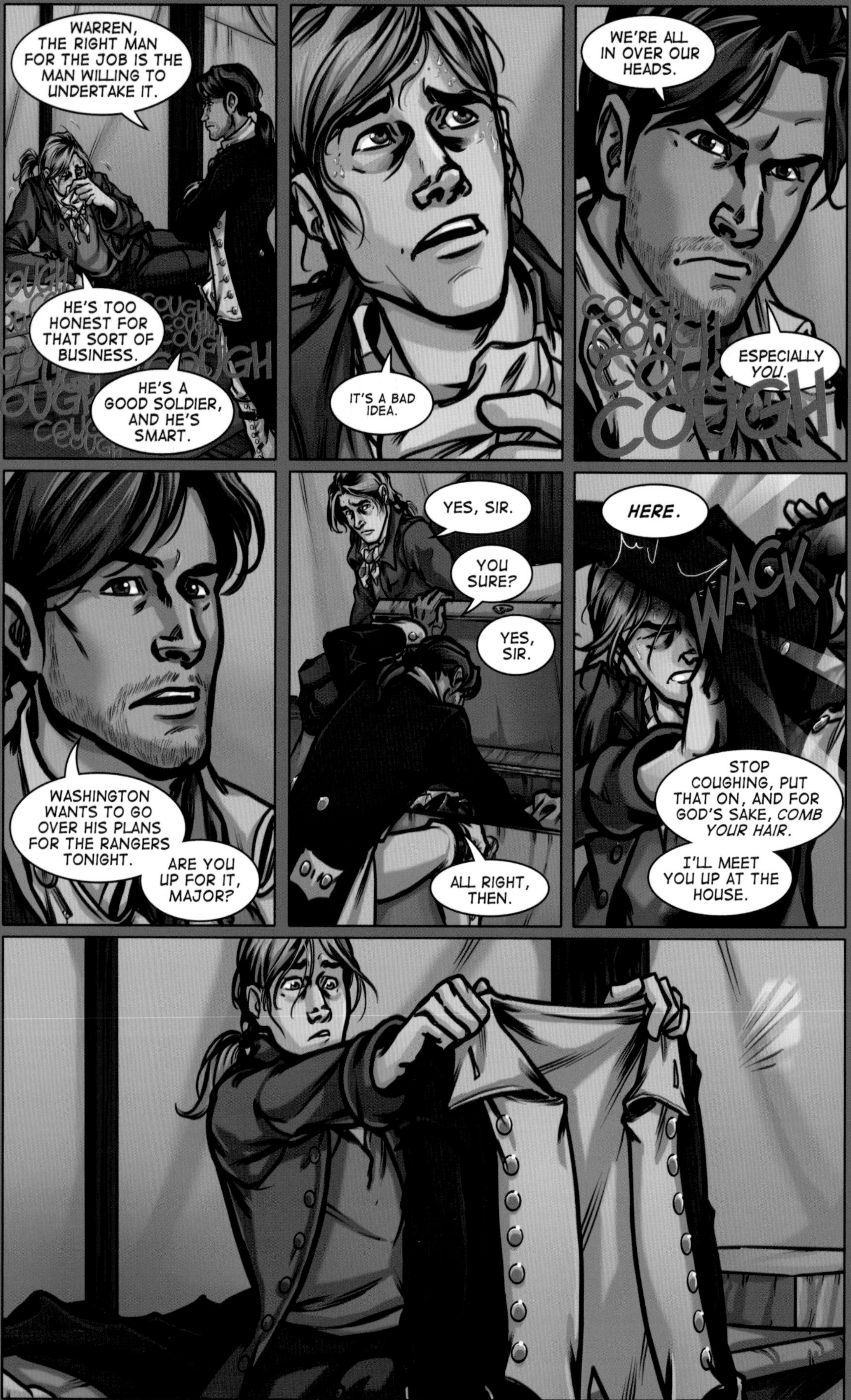
WARREN, THE RIGHT MAN FOR THE JOB IS THE MAN WILLING TO UNDERTAKE IT.
COUGH COUGH COUGH COUGH COUGH
HE'S TOO HONEST FOR THAT SORT OF BUSINESS.
HE'S A GOOD SOLDIER, AND HE'S SMART.
IT'S A BAD IDEA.
WE'RE ALL IN OVER OUR HEADS.
COUGH COUGH COUGH COUGH
ESPECIALLY *YOU*.
WASHINGTON WANTS TO GO OVER HIS PLANS FOR THE RANGERS TONIGHT.
ARE YOU UP FOR IT, MAJOR?
YES, SIR.
YOU SURE?
YES, SIR.
ALL RIGHT, THEN.
HERE.
WACK
STOP COUGHING, PUT THAT ON, AND FOR GOD'S SAKE, *COMB YOUR HAIR*.
I'LL MEET YOU UP AT THE HOUSE.

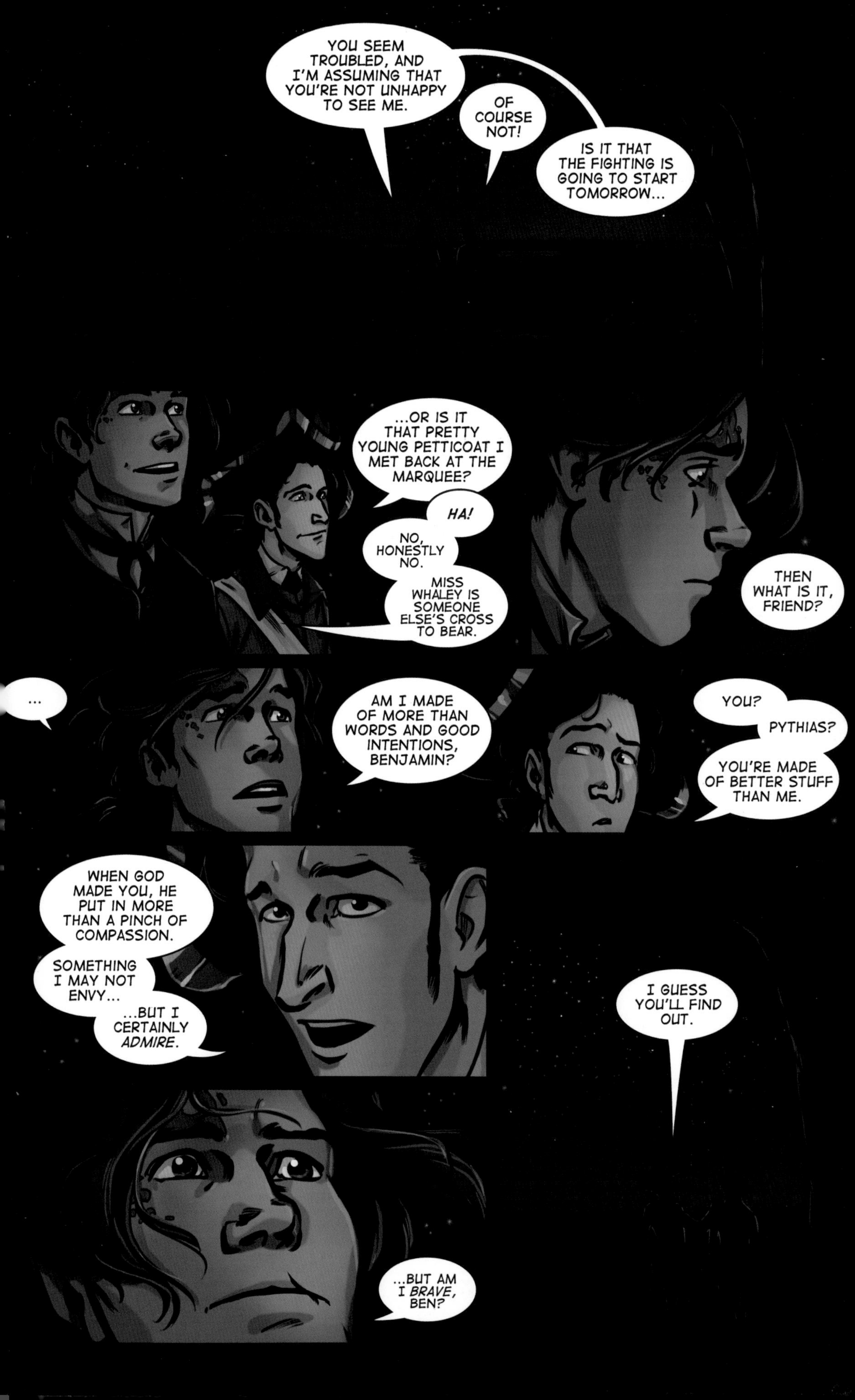
YOU SEEM TROUBLED, AND I'M ASSUMING THAT YOU'RE NOT UNHAPPY TO SEE ME.
OF COURSE NOT!
IS IT THAT THE FIGHTING IS GOING TO START TOMORROW...
...OR IS IT THAT PRETTY YOUNG PETTICOAT I MET BACK AT THE MARQUEE?
HA!
NO, HONESTLY NO.
MISS WHALEY IS SOMEONE ELSE'S CROSS TO BEAR.
THEN WHAT IS IT, FRIEND?
...
AM I MADE OF MORE THAN WORDS AND GOOD INTENTIONS, BENJAMIN?
YOU?
PYTHIAS?
YOU'RE MADE OF BETTER STUFF THAN ME.
WHEN GOD MADE YOU, HE PUT IN MORE THAN A PINCH OF COMPASSION.
SOMETHING I MAY NOT ENVY...
...BUT I CERTAINLY *ADMIRE*.
...BUT AM I *BRAVE*, BEN?
I GUESS YOU'LL FIND OUT.

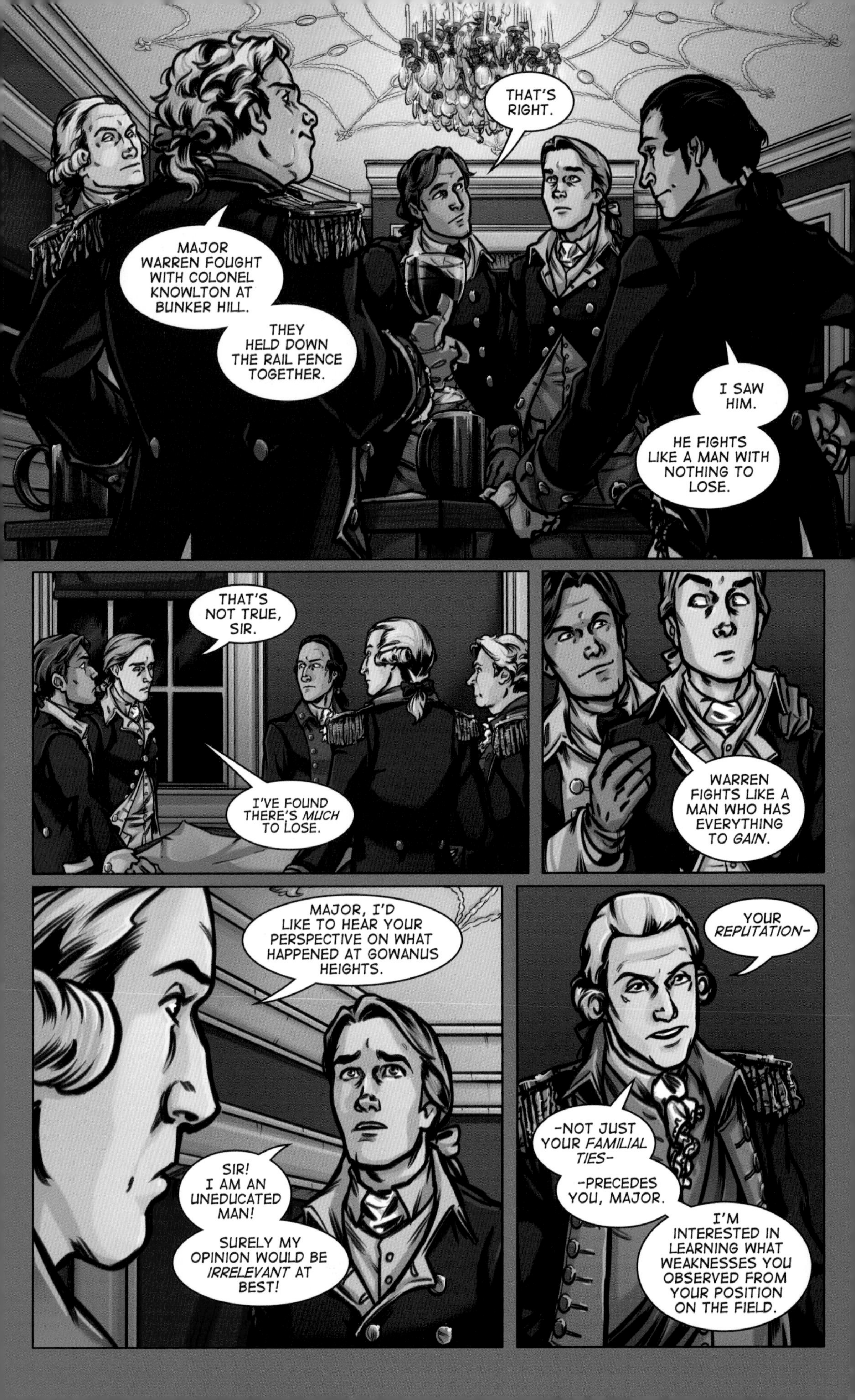
THAT'S RIGHT.
MAJOR WARREN FOUGHT WITH COLONEL KNOWLTON AT BUNKER HILL.
THEY HELD DOWN THE RAIL FENCE TOGETHER.
I SAW HIM.
HE FIGHTS LIKE A MAN WITH NOTHING TO LOSE.
THAT'S NOT TRUE, SIR.
I'VE FOUND THERE'S *MUCH* TO LOSE.
WARREN FIGHTS LIKE A MAN WHO HAS EVERYTHING TO *GAIN*.
MAJOR, I'D LIKE TO HEAR YOUR PERSPECTIVE ON WHAT HAPPENED AT GOWANUS HEIGHTS.
SIR! I AM AN UNEDUCATED MAN!
SURELY MY OPINION WOULD BE *IRRELEVANT* AT BEST!
YOUR *REPUTATION*-
-NOT JUST YOUR *FAMILIAL TIES*-
-PRECEDES YOU, MAJOR.
I'M INTERESTED IN LEARNING WHAT WEAKNESSES YOU OBSERVED FROM YOUR POSITION ON THE FIELD.

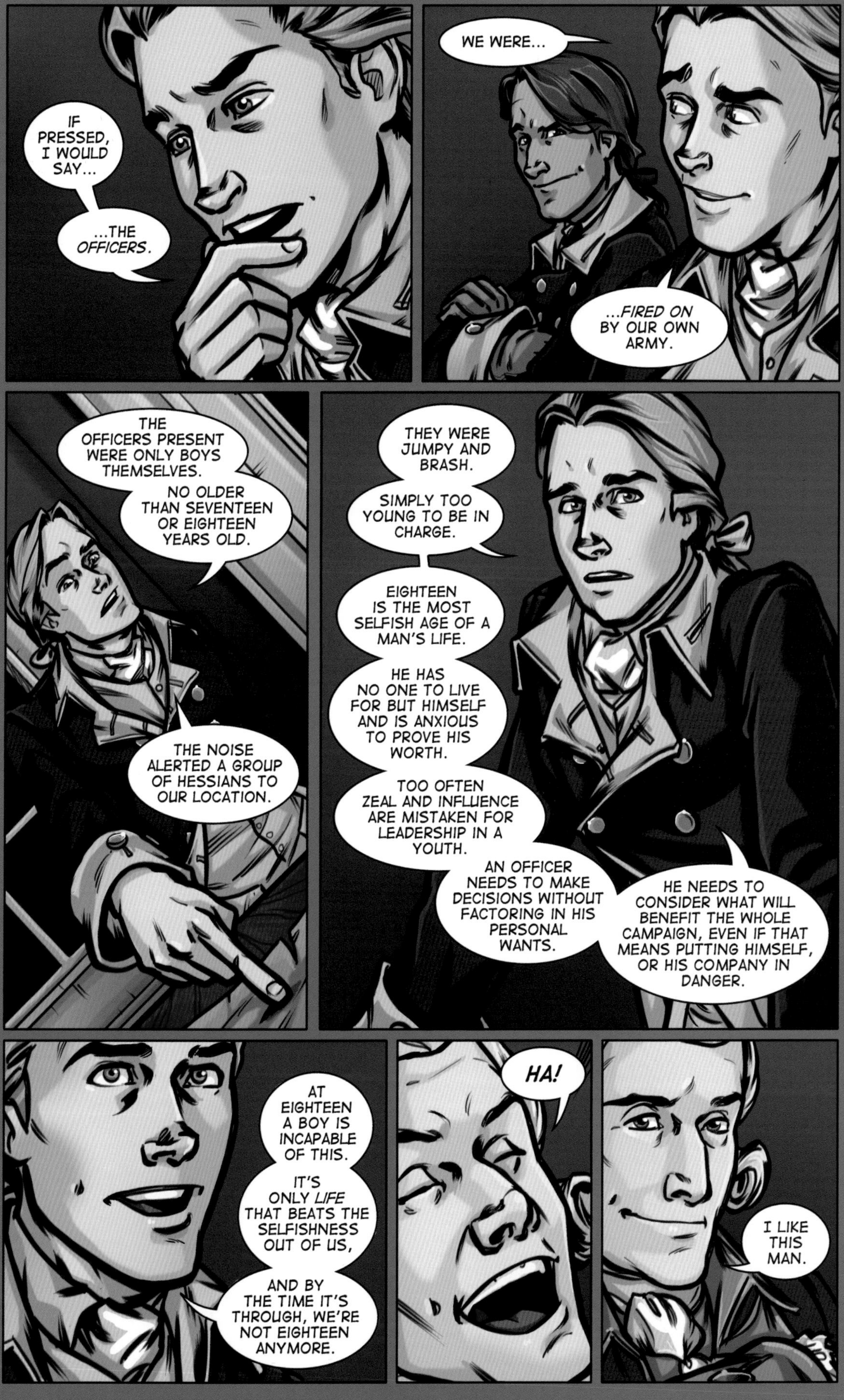
IF PRESSED, I WOULD SAY...
...THE *OFFICERS*.
WE WERE...
...*FIRED ON* BY OUR OWN ARMY.
THE OFFICERS PRESENT WERE ONLY BOYS THEMSELVES.
NO OLDER THAN SEVENTEEN OR EIGHTEEN YEARS OLD.
THE NOISE ALERTED A GROUP OF HESSIANS TO OUR LOCATION.
THEY WERE JUMPY AND BRASH.
SIMPLY TOO YOUNG TO BE IN CHARGE.
EIGHTEEN IS THE MOST SELFISH AGE OF A MAN'S LIFE.
HE HAS NO ONE TO LIVE FOR BUT HIMSELF AND IS ANXIOUS TO PROVE HIS WORTH.
TOO OFTEN ZEAL AND INFLUENCE ARE MISTAKEN FOR LEADERSHIP IN A YOUTH.
AN OFFICER NEEDS TO MAKE DECISIONS WITHOUT FACTORING IN HIS PERSONAL WANTS.
HE NEEDS TO CONSIDER WHAT WILL BENEFIT THE WHOLE CAMPAIGN, EVEN IF THAT MEANS PUTTING HIMSELF, OR HIS COMPANY IN DANGER.
AT EIGHTEEN A BOY IS INCAPABLE OF THIS.
IT'S ONLY *LIFE* THAT BEATS THE SELFISHNESS OUT OF US,
AND BY THE TIME IT'S THROUGH, WE'RE NOT EIGHTEEN ANYMORE.
HA!
I LIKE THIS MAN.

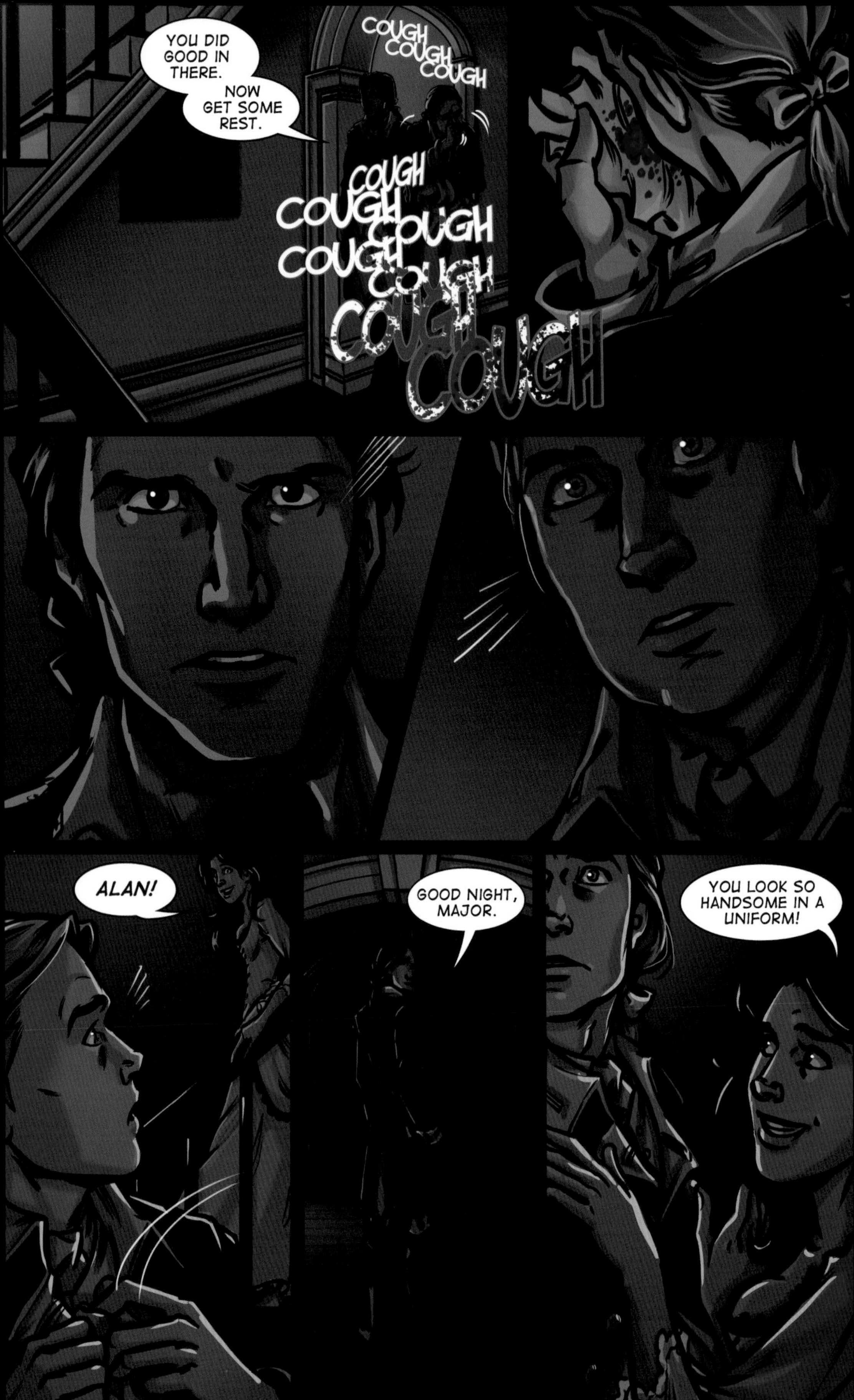
YOU DID GOOD IN THERE.
NOW GET SOME REST.
COUGH COUGH COUGH
COUGH COUGH COUGH COUGH COUGH COUGH COUGH
ALAN!
GOOD NIGHT, MAJOR.
YOU LOOK SO HANDSOME IN A UNIFORM!

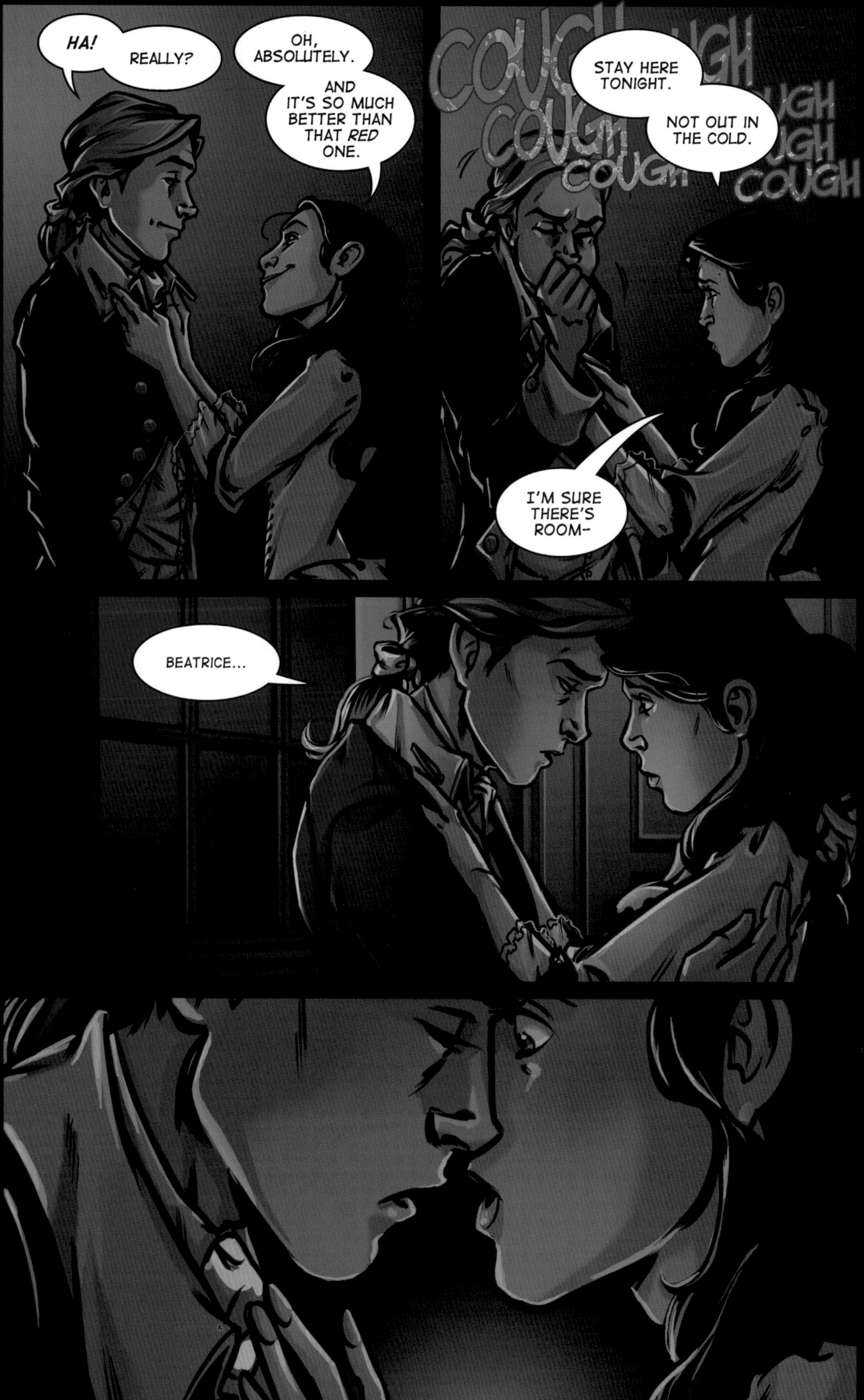
HA! REALLY?
OH, ABSOLUTELY.
AND IT'S SO MUCH BETTER THAN THAT *RED* ONE.
COUGH COUGH COUGH
STAY HERE TONIGHT.
NOT OUT IN THE COLD.
COUGH
I'M SURE THERE'S ROOM-
BEATRICE...

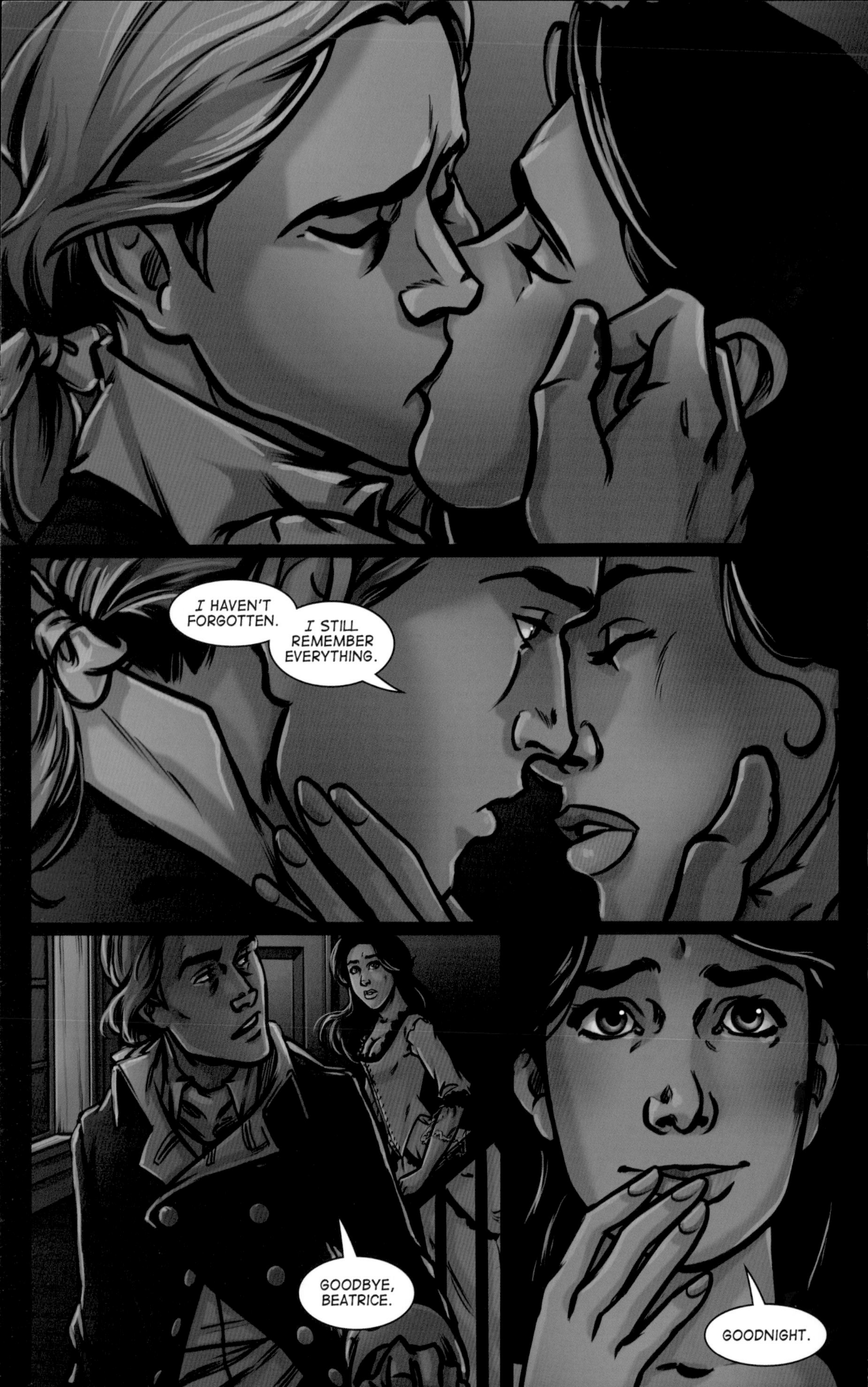
I HAVEN'T FORGOTTEN.
I STILL REMEMBER EVERYTHING.
GOODBYE, BEATRICE.
GOODNIGHT.

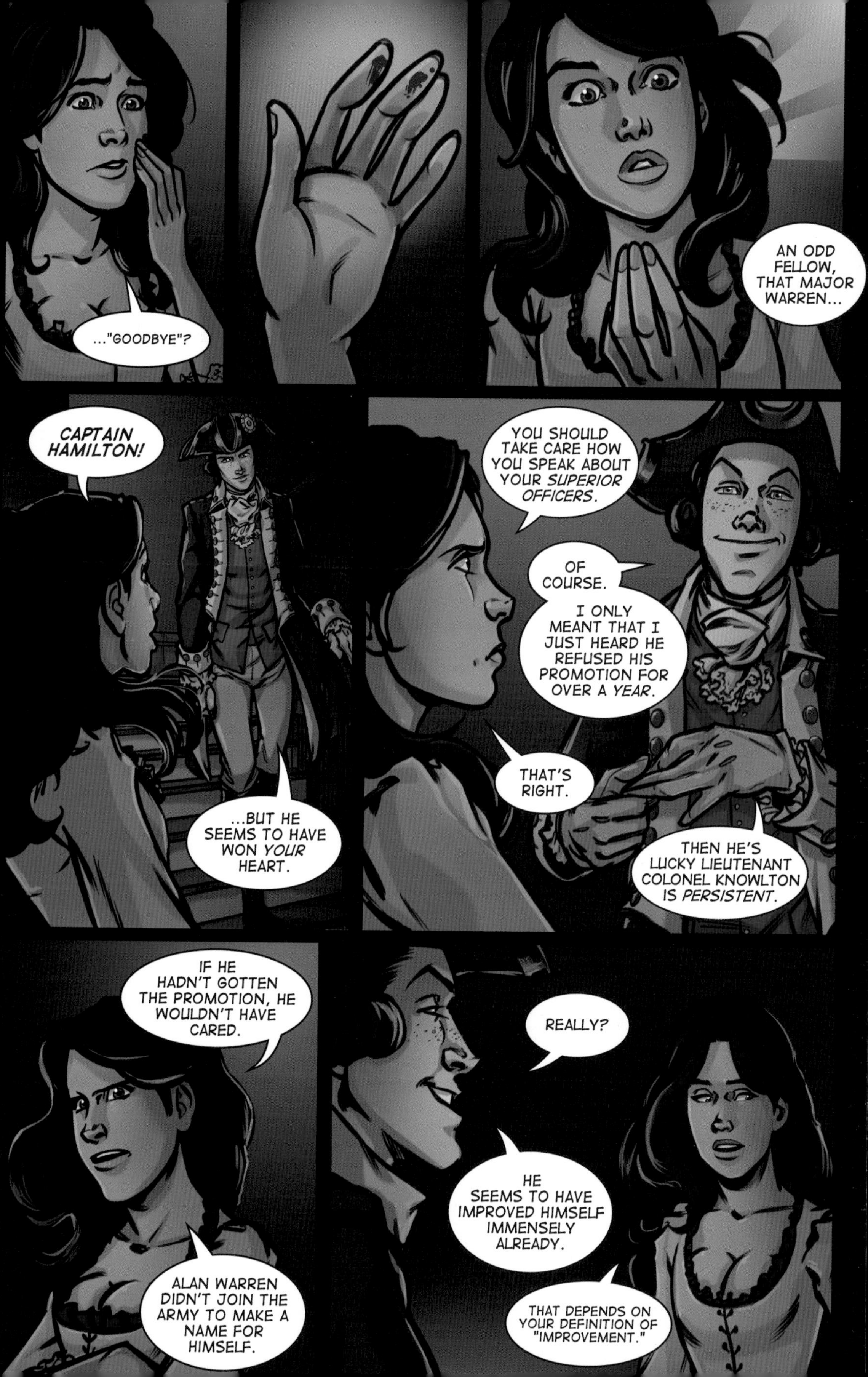
..."GOODBYE"?
AN ODD FELLOW, THAT MAJOR WARREN...
CAPTAIN HAMILTON!
...BUT HE SEEMS TO HAVE WON *YOUR* HEART.
YOU SHOULD TAKE CARE HOW YOU SPEAK ABOUT YOUR *SUPERIOR OFFICERS*.
OF COURSE.
I ONLY MEANT THAT I JUST HEARD HE REFUSED HIS PROMOTION FOR OVER A *YEAR*.
THAT'S RIGHT.
THEN HE'S LUCKY LIEUTENANT COLONEL KNOWLTON IS *PERSISTENT*.
IF HE HADN'T GOTTEN THE PROMOTION, HE WOULDN'T HAVE CARED.
ALAN WARREN DIDN'T JOIN THE ARMY TO MAKE A NAME FOR HIMSELF.
REALLY?
HE SEEMS TO HAVE IMPROVED HIMSELF IMMENSELY ALREADY.
THAT DEPENDS ON YOUR DEFINITION OF "IMPROVEMENT."

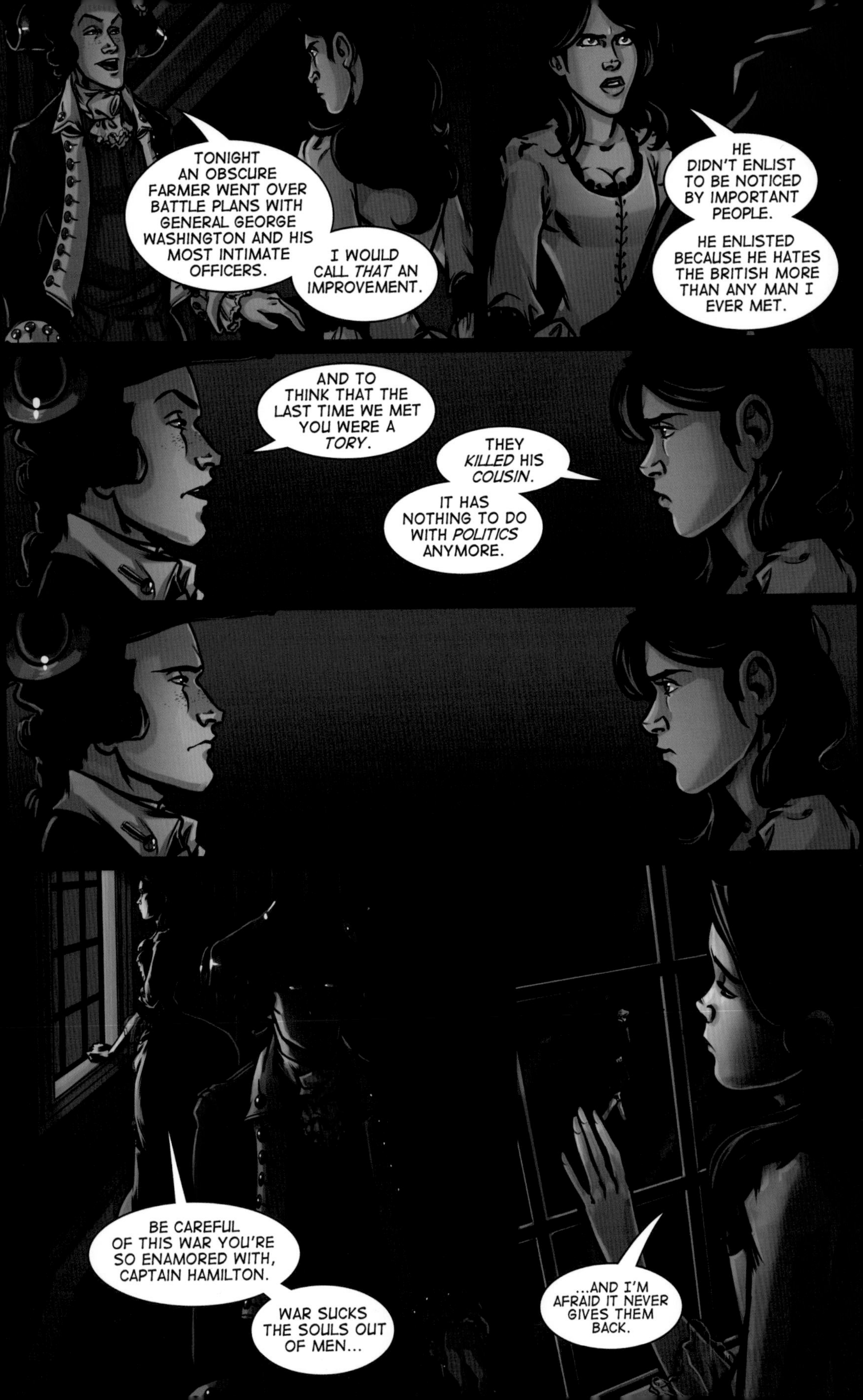
TONIGHT AN OBSCURE FARMER WENT OVER BATTLE PLANS WITH GENERAL GEORGE WASHINGTON AND HIS MOST INTIMATE OFFICERS.
I WOULD CALL *THAT* AN IMPROVEMENT.
HE DIDN'T ENLIST TO BE NOTICED BY IMPORTANT PEOPLE.
HE ENLISTED BECAUSE HE HATES THE BRITISH MORE THAN ANY MAN I EVER MET.
AND TO THINK THAT THE LAST TIME WE MET YOU WERE A *TORY*.
THEY *KILLED* HIS *COUSIN*.
IT HAS NOTHING TO DO WITH *POLITICS* ANYMORE.
BE CAREFUL OF THIS WAR YOU'RE SO ENAMORED WITH, CAPTAIN HAMILTON.
WAR SUCKS THE SOULS OUT OF MEN...
...AND I'M AFRAID IT NEVER GIVES THEM BACK.

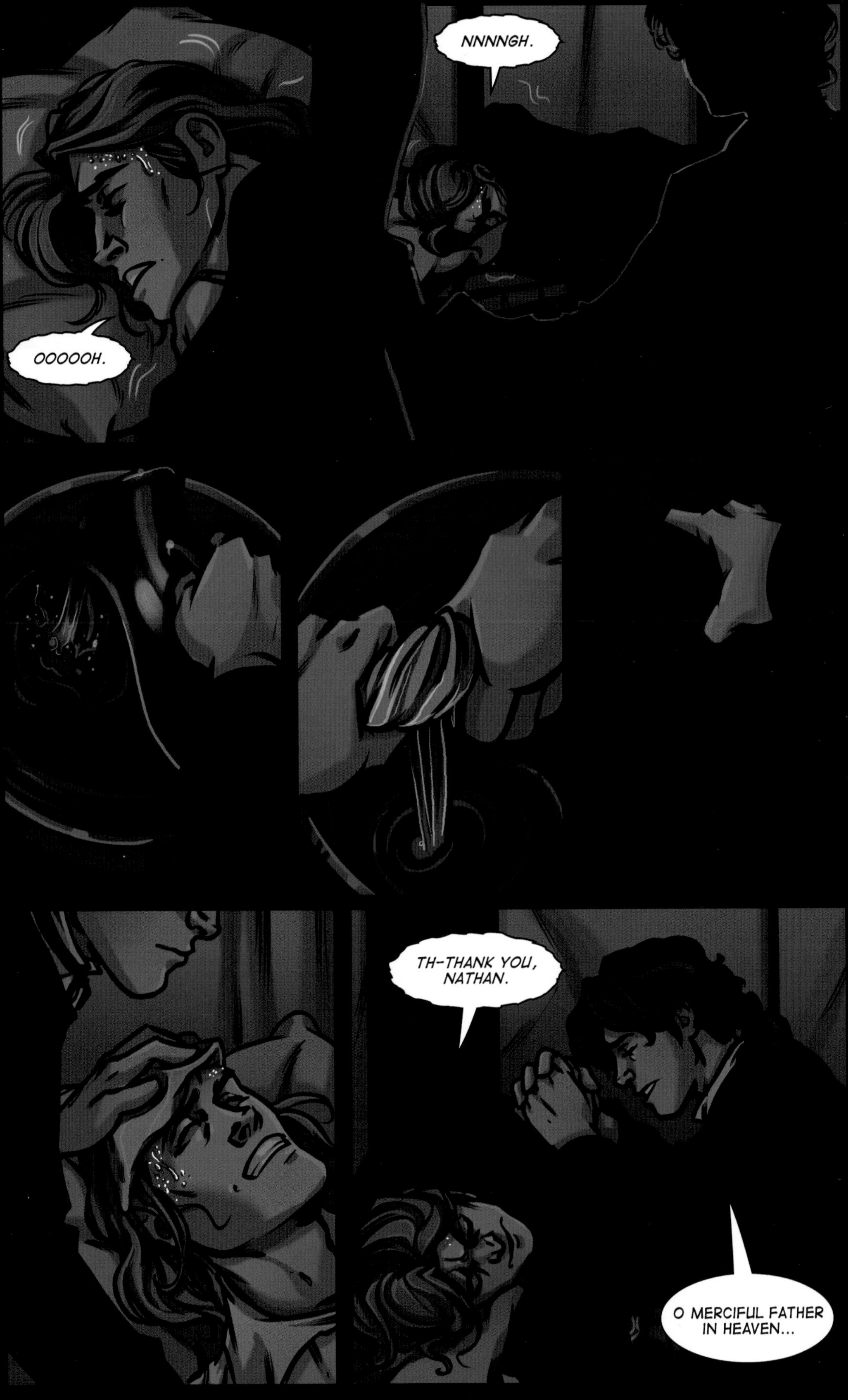
OOOOOH.
NNNNGH.
TH-THANK YOU, NATHAN.
O MERCIFUL FATHER IN HEAVEN...

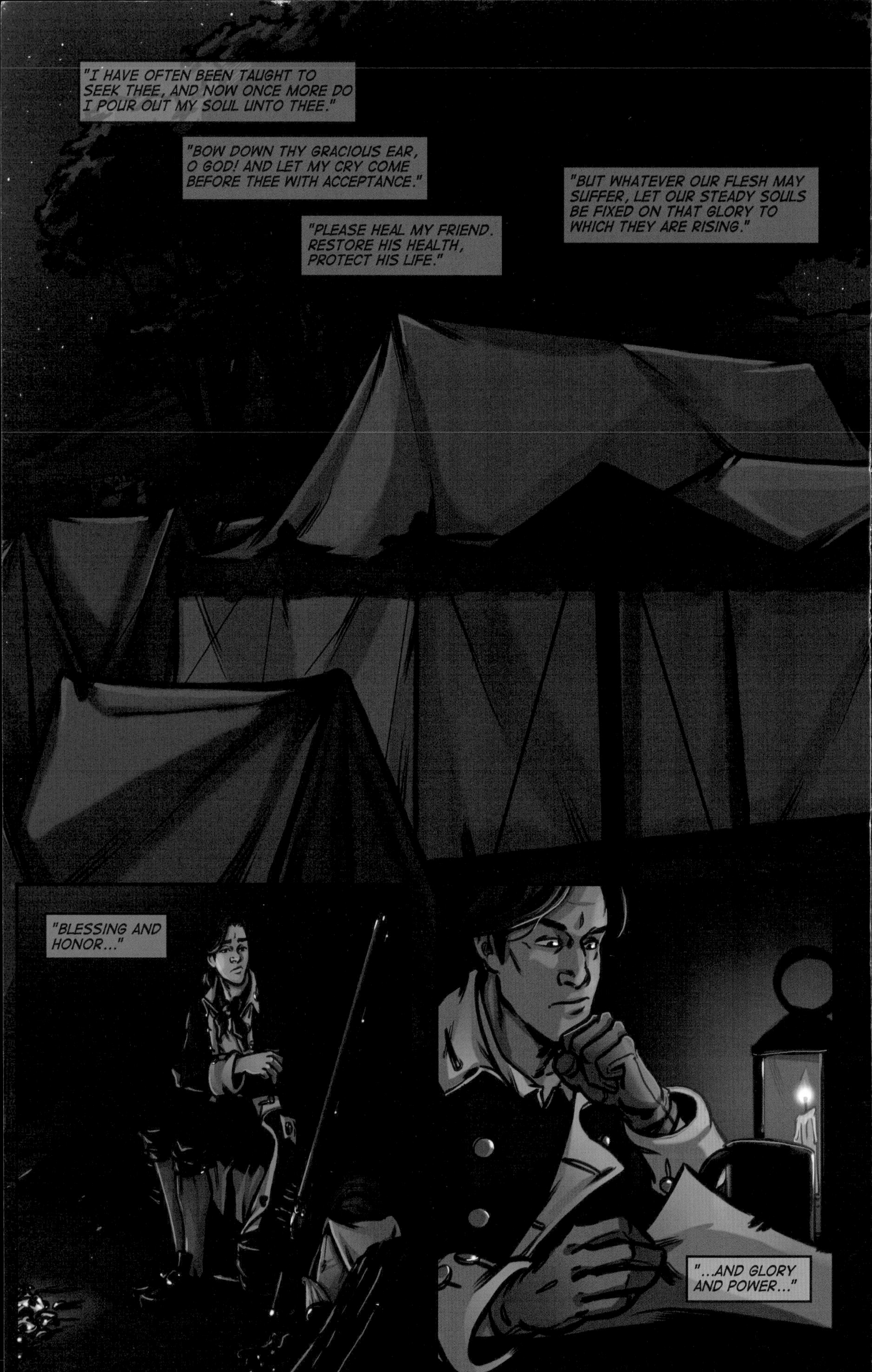
"I HAVE OFTEN BEEN TAUGHT TO SEEK THEE, AND NOW ONCE MORE DO I POUR OUT MY SOUL UNTO THEE."
"BOW DOWN THY GRACIOUS EAR, O GOD! AND LET MY CRY COME BEFORE THEE WITH ACCEPTANCE."
"PLEASE HEAL MY FRIEND. RESTORE HIS HEALTH, PROTECT HIS LIFE."
"BUT WHATEVER OUR FLESH MAY SUFFER, LET OUR STEADY SOULS BE FIXED ON THAT GLORY TO WHICH THEY ARE RISING."
"BLESSING AND HONOR..."
"...AND GLORY AND POWER..."

"LET OUR FAITH PERFORM ITS LAST OFFICE IN AN HONORABLE MANNER."

"LET OUR REMAINING MOMENTS ON EARTH BE SPENT FOR THY GLORY..."

"...AND SO LET US ASCEND WITH LOVE IN OUR HEARTS, AND PRAISE ON OUR FALTERING TONGUES..."

"...TO THE WORLD WHERE LOVE AND PRAISE SHALL BE COMPLETE."

"AND IF IT PLEASE YOU, O LORD, THE NEXT TIME MY DEAR FRIEND AND I MEET, WE ASK THAT WE WOULD FIND EACH OTHER WELL."

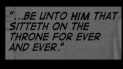

"...BE UNTO HIM THAT SITTETH ON THE THRONE FOR EVER AND EVER."

"AMEN."

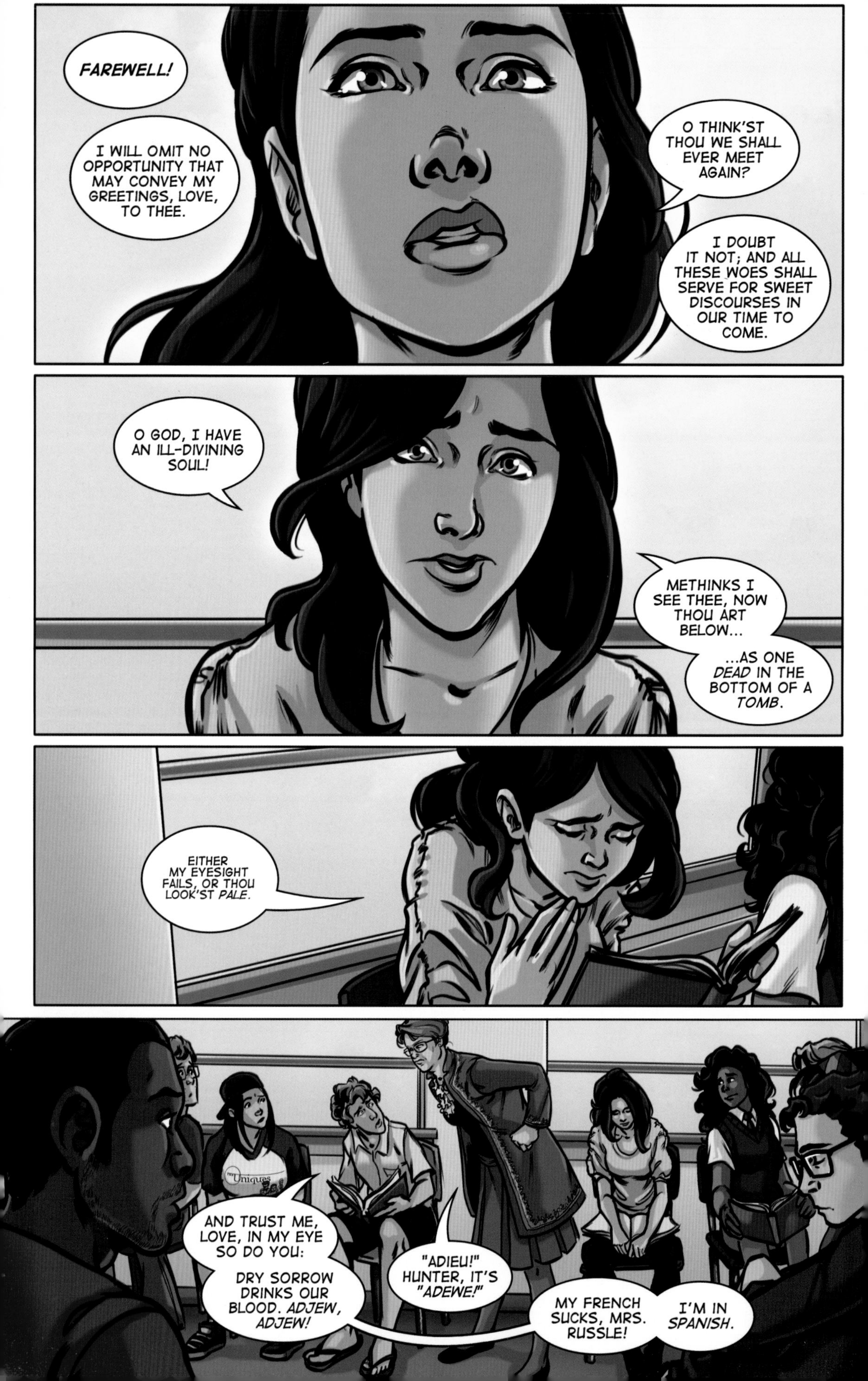
FAREWELL!
I WILL OMIT NO OPPORTUNITY THAT MAY CONVEY MY GREETINGS, LOVE, TO THEE.
O THINK'ST THOU WE SHALL EVER MEET AGAIN?
I DOUBT IT NOT; AND ALL THESE WOES SHALL SERVE FOR SWEET DISCOURSES IN OUR TIME TO COME.
O GOD, I HAVE AN ILL-DIVINING SOUL!
METHINKS I SEE THEE, NOW THOU ART BELOW...
...AS ONE DEAD IN THE BOTTOM OF A TOMB.
EITHER MY EYESIGHT FAILS, OR THOU LOOK'ST PALE.
AND TRUST ME, LOVE, IN MY EYE SO DO YOU:
DRY SORROW DRINKS OUR BLOOD. ADJEW, ADJEW!
"ADIEU!" HUNTER, IT'S "ADEWE!"
MY FRENCH SUCKS, MRS. RUSSLE!
I'M IN SPANISH.

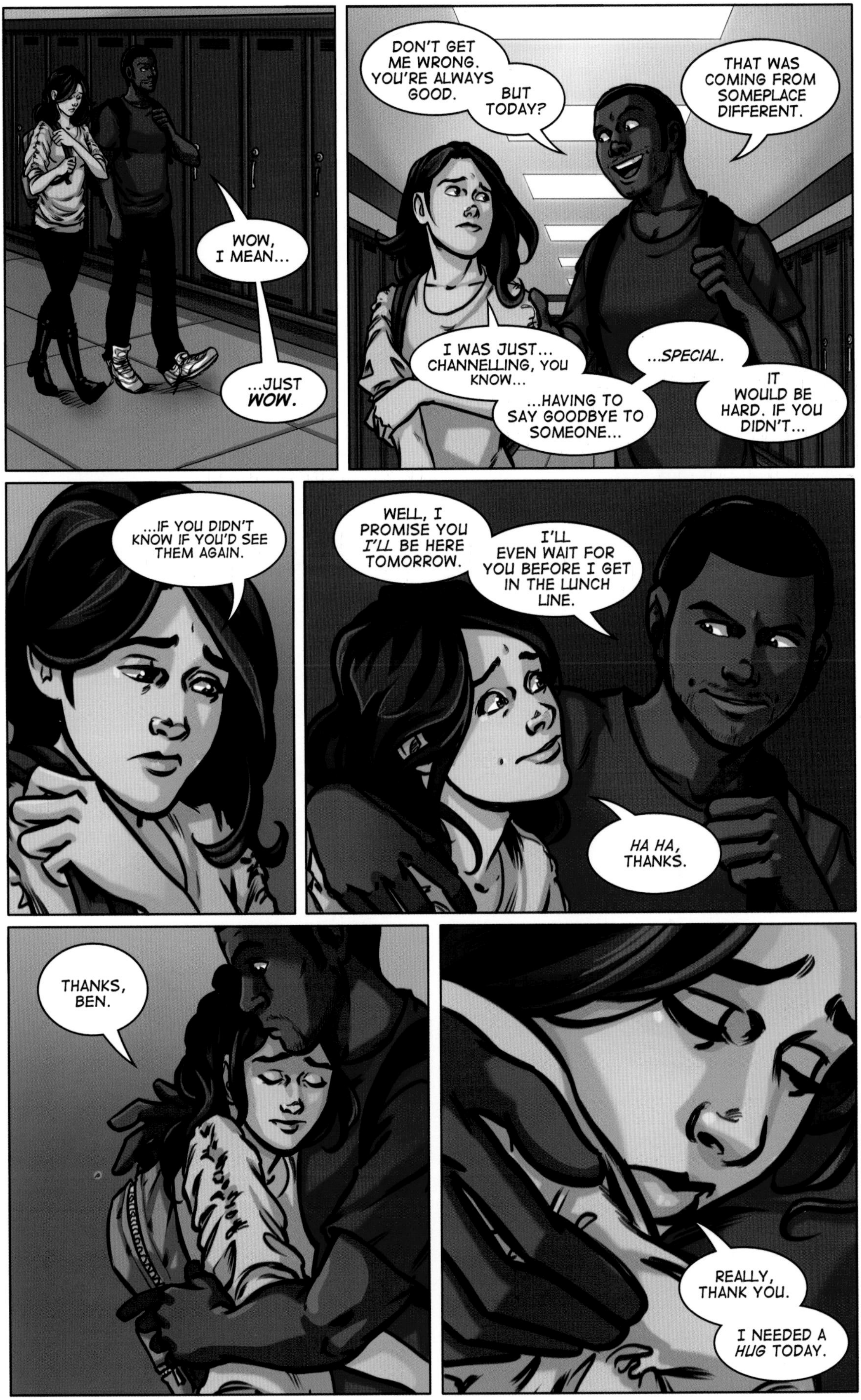
WOW, I MEAN...
...JUST *WOW.*
DON'T GET ME WRONG. YOU'RE ALWAYS GOOD.
BUT TODAY?
THAT WAS COMING FROM SOMEPLACE DIFFERENT.
I WAS JUST... CHANNELLING, YOU KNOW...
...HAVING TO SAY GOODBYE TO SOMEONE...
...*SPECIAL.*
IT WOULD BE HARD. IF YOU DIDN'T...
...IF YOU DIDN'T KNOW IF YOU'D SEE THEM AGAIN.
WELL, I PROMISE YOU *I'LL* BE HERE TOMORROW.
I'LL EVEN WAIT FOR YOU BEFORE I GET IN THE LUNCH LINE.
HA HA, THANKS.
THANKS, BEN.
REALLY, THANK YOU.
I NEEDED A *HUG* TODAY.

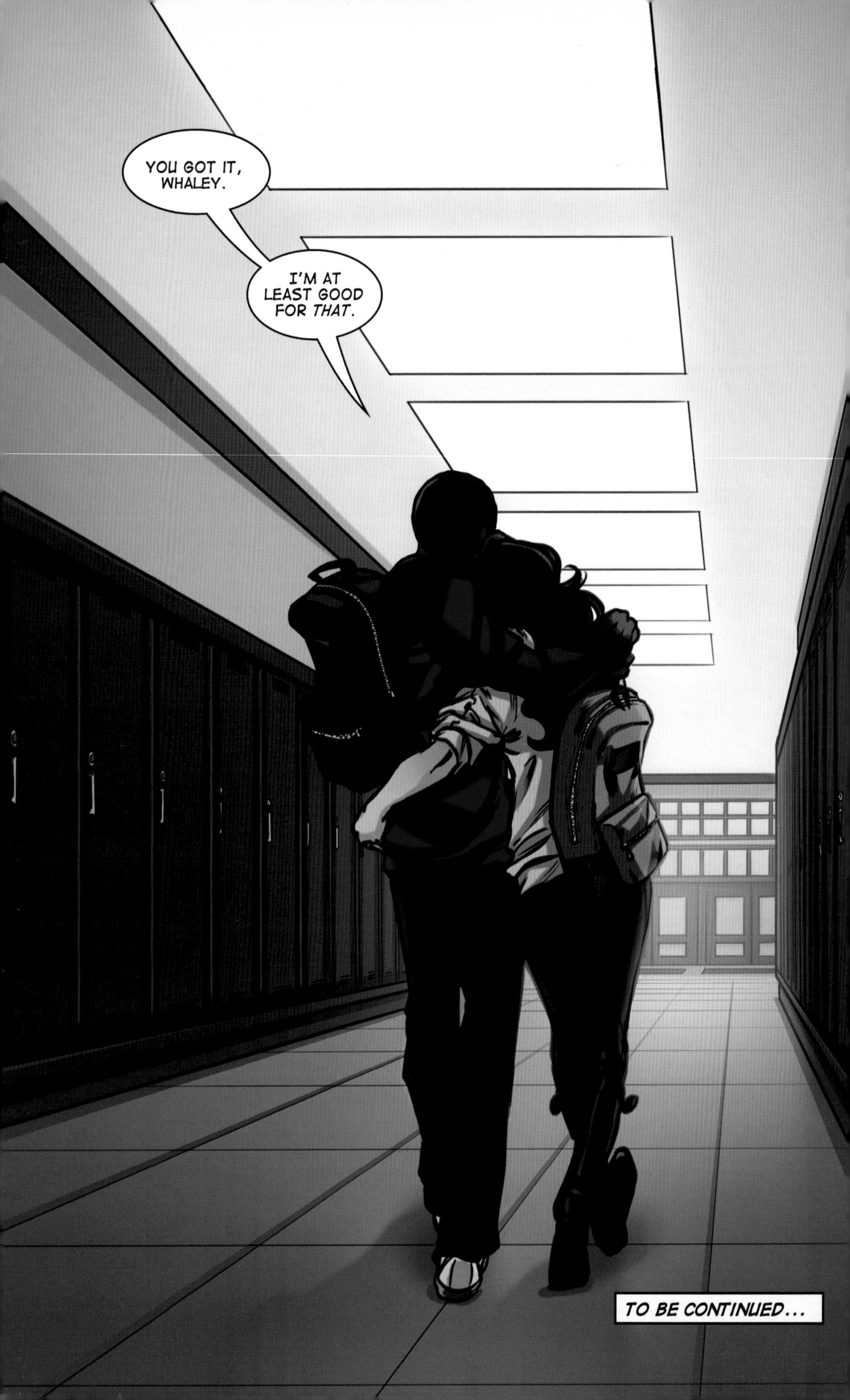
YOU GOT IT, WHALEY.
I'M AT LEAST GOOD FOR *THAT*.
TO BE CONTINUED...

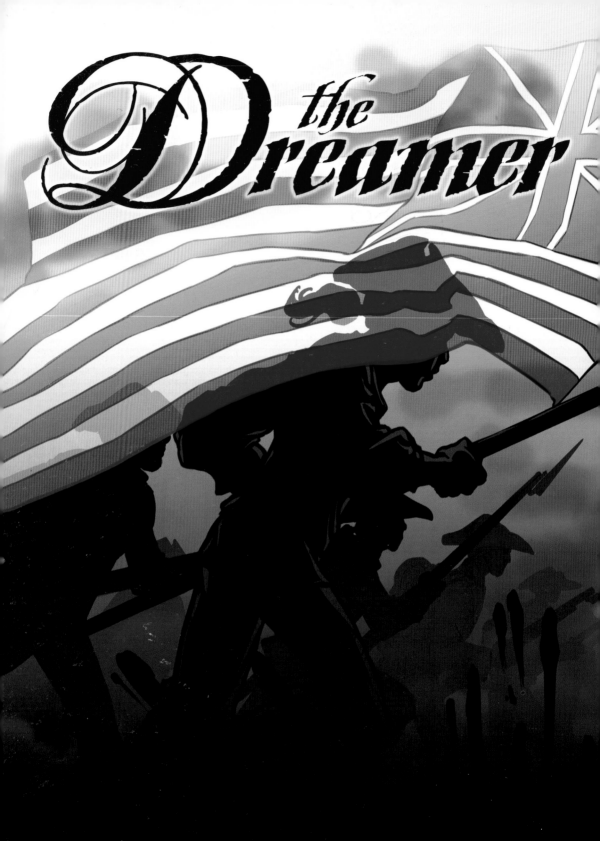

THE ADVENTURE CONTINUES ONLINE AT
WWW.THEDREAMERCOMIC.COM
WEEKLY UPDATES · EXCLUSIVE STORIES & MERCHANDISE!